THE SALVATION SCHEMA

THE SALVATION SCHEMA

By
M.B. ANDERSON

Published by
M.B. ANDERSON

THE SALVATION SCHEMA

Published by: M.B. Anderson
First Edition: 2025

ISBN (Hardback): 978-1-971-09100-6
ISBN (Paperback): 979-8-218-87691-3
ISBN (Ebook): 979-8-218-87693-7

Scripture quotations marked (KJV) are taken from the **Authorized (King James) Version**. This translation is in the public domain in the United States. Rights in the Authorized Version in the United Kingdom are vested in the Crown.

To my father and my sister, when we 'meet on that beautiful shore.'
To my ohana, the unshakeable foundation of grace.
And to my God, the author of true grace, beyond any schema.

"If you do not change direction, you may end up where you are heading."

Lao Tzu

TABLE OF CONTENTS

CHAPTER 1

UNDER THE FLUORESCENT SUN

Havenwood isn't just a town—it's a doctrine you breathe. My shoes always sounded too loud on those spotless sidewalks, as if the pavement itself kept score. The sunlight here isn't warm; it's a fluorescent glare that bounces off the picket fences, erasing any place to hide. I learned early that every street, every window, every gesture was a test. The neighbors are always watching. Even the air is sharp and clean to the point of hurting—like laundry soap, lye, and disinfectant. It's as if the whole town decided joy was a kind of dirt, and it had to be scrubbed away.

The spiritual vacuum in Havenwood was total. The First Baptist Church, with its massive white stone, towered over everything—both the landscape and our minds. Even from my bedroom window, I could see the sharp blue shadows it cast each evening, swallowing the last scraps of color from the world. Every Sunday, the heavy bells dragged us from bed and called us to obedience. The ancient doors smelled of varnish and cold marble. Inside, the air was dry, always tinged with dust and the thin, musty scent of hymn books— nothing comforting, nothing soft.

Life here wasn't measured by happiness—it was measured by performance. Nobody cared if you were joyful. They cared if you were correct, if your skirt was long enough, and if you showed up on time. Even the smallest joys—a shared joke, a bright scarf, a quick step—were dangerous. I learned to erase a smile before it formed, to lower my voice, to walk with careful, invisible steps. Your worth was determined by your last act of obedience, and the rumors about even the tiniest mistake lasted for weeks.

I used to wonder if anyone else noticed how silence collects in the corners. Sometimes, when the wind rattled the hedges, I'd imagine it was trying to sneak a laugh past the curtains. I never dared to join in.

The enforcers of order in Havenwood weren't just rules or vague threats—they were people, living and breathing, always watching. Sometimes I felt their gaze even when I was alone, as if every act of suppression had a pair of eyes attached. For me, the most relentless of them all was Deacon Robert—my father. He carried the town's doctrine like a badge and a weapon, never letting either rest for a moment.

Deacon Robert: The Burden of Perfection

My father deeply believed in his authority as the head of our household. His presence filled every room before he even entered—his footsteps were measured, deliberate, the soles of his shoes always clicking sharply on the polished wood. His faith was precise, sometimes frightening in its obsession. I remember him at the dinner table, reading scripture with his jaw clenched tight, his voice clipped and cold. There was never room for mercy—only right and wrong, and he never seemed to doubt himself for a second.

He was the head elder and chief accountant for the church—his days spent with ledgers; his fingers always stained with ink. Even at home, the smell of paper and ink seemed to follow him. He'd run a white-gloved finger along the mantle, searching for dust I couldn't even see, his eyes narrowing at the smallest flaw. Emotion was a mess to him—wasteful, even dangerous. He believed only discipline and order saved souls, and he wielded both like tools, convinced that love meant constant correction.

He saw his life as one long, necessary sacrifice. His job at the bank was demanding, but he said his real work started each night at home: patrolling the house, checking every lock, every curtain, searching for cracks that might let in sin. The outside world, to him, was a pit of chaos—every distant laugh or radio a potential threat. Our home was his lighthouse of obedience, and he kept it strict and uncompromising. My father always claimed his sternness was love, never hatred, but sometimes his voice shook with something that felt a lot like fear. He used to say he would drag me to heaven if he had to—bruised, resentful, stripped of everything but obedience. The cost, he told himself, was worth it.

His devotion made our house feel more like a clinic than a home. The air was always thin and cold, smelling of old paper and ammonia—never cookies or coffee. The kitchen was silent, the counters bare except for a single, perfectly folded towel. Duty replaced comfort. I could feel it in my chest every time I breathed—a pressure that never went away.

Sister Eleanor: The Cost of Compliance

My mother, Eleanor, was the silent engine of our home, her movements precise and nearly soundless—worn smooth by decades of submission. Once, she loved gardening and hymns—her hands were strong and sure in the Alabama soil, her voice bright in the kitchen. Now, longing flickered only for a moment—when she paused at a seed packet or caught herself humming. Her purpose was to maintain the silent, sterile environment my father demanded; she moved through the house like a shadow, her face set in a mask of faded caution.

Compliance was her survival. I watched her scan my father's face for any flicker of anger, moving through the house with the anxious energy of someone always bracing for a storm. She believed his approval kept us safe—any slip, a dusty shelf, a dish out of place, was enough to send a chill through her. She never defended me, not because she didn't care, but because standing up to him felt like challenging God Himself. She lived as if every day was spent on thin ice above freezing water.

Sometimes I saw guilt in her eyes when I flinched under my father's voice, but every time she tried to speak up, fear won. Silence was her shield.

Education and Isolation

School was just an extension of home—a place where silence and rules pressed in from every direction. The classrooms always smelled like chalk dust and disinfectant, the windows locked tight, trapping the heavy air. It wasn't about learning; it was about compliance. Friendships were discouraged, voices were kept low, and lessons were filtered and controlled. I learned early to keep my eyes down, to memorize the safe answers. Every day was just another rehearsal for obedience.

I attended Havenwood Christian Academy, the church's private school. Public schools were places of doubt and danger, according to my father. The Academy's curriculum was strict and censored: history was rewritten, and science was taught only if it aligned with church doctrine. I became an excellent student: quick, disciplined, focused—because there was no other option. My father watched every grade, every report card, like a spiritual ledger. Each perfect score wasn't a win; it was just proof I was toeing the line.

But success came at a price. Friendships were forbidden. My parents barred private conversations and unsupervised activities. My classmates were polite, but always at arm's length—never friends. After class, the cycle was always the same: a sterile home, a quiet church, and supervised bible study. Real conversation gave way to recitation. My adolescence drifted by, squeezed into the shape of other people's expectations, never my own.

One day, after the final bell, Rachel—a girl who always smiled at me in the hallway—waited by my desk. "Sarah, do you want to come over after school? My mom said—"

I cut her off quickly, glancing nervously at the classroom door, where Mrs. Simmons always seemed to linger. "No," I whispered, barely audible.

Rachel's smile faded. "Your dad never lets you go anywhere."

I shrugged, fiddling with my books. "He says it's safer if I stay home. He says the world's just waiting for me to mess up."

Rachel leaned in, her voice dropping. "You okay? You look exhausted."

At that moment, the classroom door opened and Mrs. Simmons entered, her gaze sweeping across the room. I tensed, watching her approach, heart pounding. She paused at the front, her eyes settling on me. "Sarah Thomas, you got something to say, or can we start today's lesson?"

"No, ma'am," I replied fast, slipping my polite mask back on.

Anxiety was my constant companion at the Academy. I was always being watched, even when no one seemed to be looking. Every perfect grade was an offering to my father's impossible standard. In the end, obedience was the only lesson I really learned at school.

CHAPTER 2

THE TIGHTENING NOOSE

Obligation ruled every inch of my life. Home was a silent, meticulously kept cage. Childhood meant negation: no laughter at the table, no colored dresses, no sugary treats. I learned to store up sensations—cut grass under my bare feet, the coppery taste when I bit my lip, the sun's warmth before the curtains closed. These memories became my secret stash. At night, I'd recall the sticky sweetness of a stolen peach, the rough bark of the trees, the velvet hush of a summer evening. In the sensory vacuum, I built a secret world inside myself— one where colors pulsed, and music played free from my father's rules. Outwardly, I was perfect. Inwardly, every forbidden pleasure took root and flourished.

No family photos or birthday reminders—only somber biblical verses in heavy Gothic frames. Every item declared joy forbidden and life serious.

Silence ruled our house. It felt more like a library where noise was a sin. Every footstep was measured and doors closed in whispers. Laughter was rationed, conversation carefully weighed before it was allowed to break the thick quiet. I learned to live like a ghost—so light on my feet, I barely stirred the air. Sometimes the silence pressed so hard on my ears that my own heartbeat sounded dangerously loud. It wasn't peace. It was the terror of stillness, a hush so complete that even the turn of a page seemed forbidden.

The world outside, with its chaotic, tempting noise of distant sirens and unbridled screams, pressed in against the windows, a constant source of dangerous, vibrant temptation. The most common, steady sound in the house was the rhythmic, relentless metronome of the grandfather clock, ticking away minutes that were never to be wasted.

In the Thomas home, the senses were intentionally starved, particularly those related to comfort and pleasure. Meals were simple, bland, and strictly functional—prepared solely for sustenance, never for pleasure or enjoyment. The food was consumed in silence, a necessary refueling rather than a social or joyful event. Flavors were deliberately minimized, almost erased, to avoid any suggestion of worldly indulgence or culinary delight. Spices and rich ingredients were viewed as frivolous temptations, reserved only for the wealthy and the sinful.

At dinner, the clink of forks against plates was the loudest sound in the room. My father didn't look up from his ledger when he said, "Sarah, hand me the salt."

I slid the salt across. My mother poured water, her hand shaking, and a little spilled. He still didn't look up. "Careful," he said—flat, but heavy as a stone dropped in water.

I hesitated, then tried, "I got a perfect score on my math test today."

He gave a tiny nod. "That's how it should be. God expects it."

The silence fell again, even heavier. I picked at my food, wishing someone would say something else, anything, to break the weight of it.

As a teenager, I felt the weight of this perfect, quiet world crushing my identity. The silence wasn't peace—it was a vacuum that sucked the air out of my lungs, draining away every bit of my real self. I became small, careful, invisible. I understood the theory: perfection brought you closer to God. But really, it just suffocated me. All I wanted was freedom, noise, a slip of laughter—anything that would prove I was still alive.

My rebellion was entirely internal—a silent, seething resentment locked behind a calm, controlled exterior. My real life existed only in my mind, a place where I critiqued sermons, imagined color, and let myself feel anger. I understood my parents: their actions weren't driven by cruelty, but by fear for my soul and unwavering devotion. They truly believed they were protecting me, not causing harm.

But understanding didn't make the constant judgment easier. I longed for connection but was forced into obedience; every word and gesture felt like a betrayal of my real self.

To survive the relentless scrutiny, I became a masterful actress. Every gesture was rehearsed, every glance controlled. I learned to speak in the formal, archaic language of the Church—spiritually safe, always calm and even. My face became a perfect, unreadable mask, hiding the desperate, rebellious thoughts that surged inside. In the mirror, I practiced holding a look of gentle obedience for hours, even as my mind raced with sarcasm and longing. My parents saw a dutiful, exemplary daughter—someone who had absorbed the lesson of quiet, pious womanhood. But I saw the truth: a deep, growing chasm between the flawless facade I presented and the vibrant, questioning spirit I knew myself to be. Every day, that gap widened—and I knew it was only a matter of time before I cracked, and the forbidden life inside me broke through.

The Catalyst of Freedom

What truly broke me wasn't a single event, but the chilling realization that my script was already mapped out, chapter and verse, by my father's uncompromising faith.

My academic record was flawless. I graduated at seventeen, with honors— just as my father demanded. But none of it felt like an achievement. Each accolade tightened the noose a little more. The diploma wasn't a key to escape; it was a certificate that I had played my part, never once stepping out of line.

I didn't face uncertainty—I faced a terrifying, absolute certainty. I was slated to attend the respectable (but intellectually dull) Christian college, where thought was discouraged, and compliance was rewarded. Immediately after, I'd be maneuvered into a marriage with a young deacon, carefully approved by my father for his spiritual rigor and sound financial prospects. After that, I would spend my life perpetually cleaning, perpetually serving, and raising children in the same sterile, silent cycle that had suffocated my mother. It wasn't just an unhappy future; it was a slow, complete erasure of my spirit—a beautiful, neat, respectable cage where my soul would simply wither into quiet obedience.

That thought was terror—a suffocating dread that seized my lungs and tightened my chest. I saw it as a life sentence of spiritual suffocation, enforced by the very people who claimed to love me most. I realized I had to choose between two terrifying outcomes: the danger of the unknown world, or the guaranteed death of my true self in Havenwood.

Driven by this overwhelming dread, I started taking long, secret walks on the desolate outskirts of town. I had to physically move to counteract the psychological stagnation. I was intensely drawn by the distant, intoxicating sound of highway traffic—not a pleasant noise, but a chaotic, uncontrolled roar that cut through the pious silence of Havenwood. That sound was freedom: the sound of people going places, making decisions, and breaking rules without consequence. That chaos, that danger, that raw possibility was infinitely preferable to the slow death of my soul in the quiet tyranny of Havenwood. It was a beacon calling to the desperate, hidden self I'd been forced to bury, urging me to trade certainty for the terrifying promise of the unknown. I didn't just hear the highway; I studied the state transportation maps at the public library—memorized the first morning bus route, departure time, even the cash fare. My escape wasn't an impulse; it was the outcome of a problem I had spent my adolescence solving.

The opportunity, when it came, was sudden, unexpected, and fleeting. I made my move just weeks after receiving it. My success bought me access: my father trusted me to help with church accounts. I studied his audit schedule, found the safe's secondary key, and tracked the mission cash. My perfect record became my cover. No one suspected a thing. Over four months, I quietly siphoned off small sums, building my secret escape fund.

The window of time was so small, so precarious, that it felt less like a choice and more like an absolute command from my deepest core. I knew I had to take the chance at the very first moment it appeared. It was a desperate, primal flight to save my own essence—a sudden, explosive break from years of controlled atrophy.

I pressed my palm against the cool glass and watched the sun set over Havenwood's empty streets. For a moment, I let myself imagine escaping—just stepping outside, breathing air that wasn't scrubbed clean. I didn't know then that everything was about to change. But now, looking back, I see the cracks were already there.

As the sun slipped below the horizon, the world of Havenwood—so rigid, so silent—seemed to hold its breath. What began as Sarah's story, told in her own voice, was only the beginning of the journey. From this point on, her choices, her struggle, and her quiet rebellion would be seen not just through her eyes, but as part of a larger world—a story in which she was both the center and one of many souls striving for freedom.

CHAPTER 3

THE SUNDAY ARMOR

The first time Sarah truly felt the weight of Havenwood's expectations was not during a sermon or a scolding, but in the thick, anxious silence of a Sunday morning. She stood at her bedroom window, watching the light struggle through stiff, starched curtains, her hands trembling as she buttoned the last pearl on her blue linen dress. Every movement was a performance—her mother's voice echoing, "Not too fast, not too slow, and always with grace." The smell of starch and perfume clung to her skin, a second, invisible costume that tightened with every breath. In those moments, Sarah was not a daughter, but an exhibit—on display for the town, for God, for the measuring eyes of her father.

The summer of 1972 baked Alabama's streets. Heat shimmered off the asphalt, and honeysuckle thickened the air. Sarah tugged on her white glove, scratched by her stiff Sunday dress, and caught her reflection in the car window, going through the motions.

Her outfit—the light blue linen dress, white gloves, and pillbox hat—was her Sunday Armor, designed to protect their reputation from the slings and arrows of local gossip. The linen felt scratchy and uncomfortable against the backs of her legs.

They were only four blocks from the First Baptist Church of Havenwood and from the inevitable public viewing. Havenwood wasn't a town where one could be unseen on a Sunday. Every polished fender, every starched collar, every respectful nod was part of a tightly choreographed, weekly performance. To fail to attend was to risk the slow, social death of exclusion.

Inside the car, the air was thick with the scent of her father's cologne, Old Spice, and her mother's silent, pervasive anxiety. The only sound was the low, solemn whir of the air conditioning struggling against the oppressive heat.

"Sit up straight, Sarah!" Her mother said, her voice low, eyes forward. "Mrs. Albright's nephew is playing the organ today. Supposed to be good. You remember what I said, right?"

Sarah knew the drill: smile politely, speak sparingly, ensure your responses are centered on the Lord, and present yourself as a girl ready for a godly future. She nodded, the tiny movement feeling significant in the constrained silence. Her eyes drifted to the untamed fields just outside the town limits—wild, overgrown with goldenrod and Queen Anne's Lace, and beautifully unkempt. The memory of bare feet in cool grass, the imagined feel of the wind tearing the pillbox hat from her head, filled her lungs with a quick, silent ache. She imagined stripping off the stifling dress, leaving the gloves behind, and running until she reached the interstate and the anonymity of the unknown world—the taste of freedom, sharp and sweet as the honeysuckle in June.

Her father gripped the steering wheel with the white-knuckled focus he usually reserved for reviewing the church's quarterly budget. He pulled the car into their reserved spot with precise, meticulous control.

"We're an example, Eleanor," Robert said, not looking at either of them. "People see us. The Lord's grace shows in how we live—how we look. Don't forget it."

"Yes, Robert," Eleanor said, almost by reflex.

Before opening his door, Robert inspected the spotless shine on his black leather shoe. He was the most respected deacon in the church, and his faith was as rigid as the spine of the King James Bible he carried. The family's perfection was his proudest accomplishment.

Before the heavy door's latch released, Sarah quickly smoothed the edge of her skirt. The fabric, positioned exactly two inches above her knee—the absolute limit of style—was her tiny, secret act of defiance. The linen's scratch against her leg felt like a welcome affirmation of rebellion. She took a deep breath, slipped on her mask of perfect obedience, and stepped out into the blinding sunlight to face the congregation.

The moment Robert, Eleanor, and Sarah stepped through the towering oak front doors of the First Baptist Church of Havenwood, the cool air of the sanctuary washed over them. The change in atmosphere was immediate: the stifling heat of the summer sun gave way to the cool, heavy blanket of expectation.

They walked the center aisle, their footsteps nearly silent on the thick, deep red runner. Sarah felt the usual phenomenon: the collective gaze. This wasn't a gaze of welcome; it was an inspection. As they moved, Sarah felt as if the entire walk was happening in slow motion. She met the eyes of old Mrs. Crenshaw, seated in the second row, whose lips were permanently pursed into an expression of patient, lifelong disappointment. Sarah understood the scrutiny was relentless; they were checking the perfection of the tie, the chignon, and most importantly, the exact position of Sarah's hemline.

Eleanor offered a thin, practiced smile to Mrs. Crenshaw, whose eyes immediately dropped to Sarah's knees before snapping back to Eleanor's face with a barely perceptible tightening of the lips. The subtle gesture proclaimed: *Two inches too high. Robert, you must control your daughter's vanity.*

Sarah felt the judgment like a physical sting, as if a wasp had landed on her bare skin. In that instant, it crystallized everything she loathed: her entire self— her thoughts, her wants, her hidden colors—reduced to a perfectly measured, yet still flawed, display of compliance. The two-inch rebellion at her hem was laughable, a ripple on the surface of a deep, churning sea. Her whole life script was written by others, and this moment was only the most recent scene. The scrutiny confirmed her choice. They would never stop measuring or correcting. If damnation was the consequence of wearing a slightly short hemline, she was ready for the fire of outright disobedience—she wanted to feel something real, even if it burned.

Sarah quickly dipped her head, avoiding eye contact, and slid into their usual spot in the third row. The polished wood of the pew felt cold and hard against her legs. As they settled, the service began. The organist, Mrs. Albright's talented nephew, opened the service with a flourish of chords, immediately filling the sanctuary with the resounding, familiar melody of "A Mighty Fortress Is Our God."

Sarah stood, hymnal in hand, the smell of old paper and mildew sharp in her nostrils. The words, once comforting felt cold and distant, echoing off the stone walls with a hollow resonance. She felt exposed and utterly alone, as if every voice but hers was singing from a place she would never reach again. The organ's vibration rattled her ribs, but it could not shake loose the numbness that had settled inside her.

The Sermon and The Spark

She tried to focus on the opening chorus, but the organ and choir only provided background noise for the real drama unfolding in her mind. The familiar shuffle of hymnals, the rustle of starched skirts, all faded as she watched a couple—the Taylors—two rows behind. Their daughter, Bethany, had been married last month in a lavish, church-sanctioned ceremony. Bethany's hair was perfectly smoothed, her smile a studied mask. Sarah wondered if Bethany ever felt the urge to bolt for the door, or if she had simply learned to hide the impulse better than Sarah had.

"Isn't that Bethany Taylor?" Robert whispered, leaning toward Eleanor with a flash of pride. "A beautiful testament to a Christian upbringing. A girl who knows her proper place."

Eleanor nodded, but her eyes flickered nervously to Sarah, a silent reprimand: *Why can't you be like Bethany?*

They sang a second hymn, the call to repentance and unwavering commitment: "Just As I Am, Without One Plea." For a few fleeting verses, the lyrics' unconditional nature offered a momentary reprieve, but the feeling was quickly snuffed out by the knowledge that the people singing these words judged her every move outside the sanctuary.

The hymns ended, and the entire congregation settled into a reverent hush. Reverend Smith ascended the steps to the mahogany pulpit, carrying his worn, oversized King James Bible. The sheer weight and archaic language perfectly matched the stern authority of the church.

"Brothers and Sisters," he began, his voice immediately booming and formal, reverberating through the heavy stained-glass windows, "We gather today to speak on righteousness and the final judgment."

Sarah slumped slightly in the pew, trying to disappear behind her mother's immaculate coiffure. This was the kind of sermon that made her stomach clench.

"There are those among us," the Preacher continued, sweeping his gaze across the third row, "who believe that grace is some kind of license for worldliness and disobedience! That the Lord's sacrifice means we can turn our backs on the Holy Law! Woe unto the self-deceived who trade their eternal soul for a moment of carnal pleasure!"

He lifted the Bible, holding it aloft like a weapon. "You are living in an era of moral pestilence! The streets outside are filled with the vanity of the age, the temptations of the eye, and the loud, mocking laughter of the ungodly! Do you think, for one moment, that the Lord's watchful eye does not see the pride in your dress, the lust in your glance, or the doubt hidden in your heart? The Word tells us that the day of reckoning is swiftly approaching, and there is no ledger for the soul save the one kept by God Himself!" He paused, allowing the silence to become a tangible weight. "The scripture is clear: 'Be not deceived; God is not mocked: for whatsoever a man soweth, that shall he also reap' (Galatians 6:7, KJV). Every frivolous skirt, every late night, every moment spent in the company of the ungodly is a seed sown—and we are told what the harvest shall be! Do not seek the approval of man, for man's judgment is fleeting, but the Lord's condemnation is eternal."

The organist punctuated the Pastor's crescendo with a low, ominous chord.

"You must not walk casually toward the abyss! The path to life is narrow, and the path to destruction is wide! And at the end of that wide, tempting path is the fire that consumes all doubt! This world is a testing ground, a momentary pause before the great, unforgiving division! You must repent of the smallest transgression, you must confess the slightest vanity, before the great doors of mercy are slammed shut!"

The Reverend slammed his fist down on the pulpit. "You must do the right thing! You must keep the law! For it is written: 'And if thy eye offend thee, pluck it out, and cast it from thee...' (Matthew 18:9, KJV). The line is drawn! You will obey, or you will immediately be sent into the eternal damnation awaiting those who choose the easy road!"

As Reverend Smith's voice thundered about hellfire, Sarah felt a sudden, sharp wave of nausea. The air, already thick with varnish and dust, momentarily seemed to carry a strange, metallic-clean, antiseptic smell, utterly foreign to the old church. She gripped the pew, feeling a disturbing sensation of being pinned down, utterly unable to move. She quickly blamed the heat and her own fear. That antiseptic smell was the distinct, sharp odor of the lye soap her mother used, intensified by the heat and the oppressive pressure. It was the smell of the constant erasure of life in their home, and now, it seemed to permeate the very air of the sanctuary. Her body was physically rebelling against the enforced sterility.

Inside her mind, a frantic, desperate argument began. She tried to conjure the soft, conditional promises she had memorized from a hidden children's book of parables—anything to counter the Old Testament terror. *He is slow to anger,* she thought desperately. *His mercy is new every morning.* But the booming voice crushed her meager defenses, leaving her exhausted.

She looked at the heavy stained-glass window depicting a rigid, stern-faced Christ and felt no comfort, only surveillance.

The service concluded with a final, somber hymn, and the true test began: the post-service social gauntlet.

"Sarah," Robert said, placing a heavy hand on her shoulder—a pressure that echoed the Pastor's judgment. "We will greet the Pastor, and then you will speak with the Deacons' wives. Do not wander. Our reputation must be maintained."

She nodded, her practiced smile barely concealing her exhaustion, and disappeared into the crowd. Near the water fountain, she saw him.

Jessie stood out immediately—waiting for someone, dressed in worn jeans and a frayed denim jacket, clutching a paperback. He was the outsider, the embodiment of the "worldly temptation" warned against from the pulpit.

Jessie wasn't looking at her hemline or her hat; he was looking directly into her eyes. There was no judgment, no piety—only a careless, easy smile that promised excitement and indifference to all the rules she was suffocating under. He saw her, not the Sunday Armor.

It was a small, quiet moment, maybe five seconds long, but it was enough. In his eyes, Sarah saw the open road, the wild fields, and the freedom she was desperate for. She saw her escape. She had just been told she was already headed for damnation; what did she have left to lose?

CHAPTER 4

FROM SANCTUARY TO SHADOW

She saw her opportunity as her mother stopped to exchange hushed pleasantries with Mrs. Albright, who was eager to resume her scrutiny of Sarah's ankles.

"Mother, I'm feeling a little dizzy. Would you mind if I get some water?" Sarah said, trying to sound casual.

Eleanor, barely glancing at her, waved her off. "Go on, but don't stop to chat. Just get your water."

Sarah didn't wait. She moved—not hurried, not slow—her dress shoes whispering over the linoleum. Each step felt like a silent act of rebellion. The hellfire still burned in her mind, but Jessie's scent—motor oil and cigarettes— was already overpowering it.

She stopped two feet from the water fountain, her back to the congregation.

Jessie gave her a lopsided grin. "You look like you're gonna bust out of here any second," he said, his voice low and rough, nothing like the church crowd.

Sarah turned, caught off guard by the directness and the eyes. "What?" she said, almost laughing at the absurdity of someone actually noticing her.

Jessie nodded at the Bible in her hand. "That book—you're holding it like it stole your lunch money."

Sarah hugged the King James tight. "It's just… It's the Bible," she said, feeling awkward.

Jessie shrugged. "If you say so. You just looked like you were on trial in there, not in church. That place is wound tighter than a snare drum."

Jessie didn't push. Instead, he pulled out a battered pack of cigarettes. "I'm actually leaving town tonight—got work down south. But I know a spot by the river where nobody cares who you are or what verse you got wrong. If you want to breathe a little, meet me there."

He scribbled an address on a greasy scrap of paper and handed it to her, his fingers brushing hers. "It's just an old bridge. Seven o'clock. If you show up, you show up."

Sarah stared at the paper—a direct invitation to defiance, to escape.

Sarah blinked. "Who even are you?"

Jessie grinned. "Jessie. I'm just passing through. You look like you're stuck here."

He turned and walked toward the side exit, leaving Sarah clutching the slip of paper. It smelled faintly of cigarettes and something powerfully alluring—anonymity.

The First Lie

A second later, Robert's voice cut through the air, sharp and demanding: "SARAH! Where have you been? Who was that young man?"

Sarah stuffed the paper in her pocket, pasted on a bright, innocent smile, and turned to her father. "Nobody, Father. Some guy just needed directions. I was getting water."

The lie caught in her throat, bitter as regret. But the damage was done. She could feel the slip of paper in her pocket—burning now, alive with possibility and fear.

Robert did not let up. His hand clamped down hard on her shoulder, steering her toward the knot of church leaders near the exit. "Don't you ever speak to such riff-raff again, Sarah. You have a position to uphold."

"He just needed directions, that's all," Sarah repeated, keeping her face as unreadable as possible.

They were now standing among the Deacons' wives, a cluster of women whose smiles were as starched as their Sunday dresses. Mrs. Albright, whose judgmental gaze had followed Sarah all morning, leaned in to Eleanor.

"That boy, Eleanor," Mrs. Albright muttered, her eyes still narrowed. "Never seen him before. You know how it is—you can't let just anyone talk to the kids."

Eleanor, cheeks burning, jumped in before anyone else could. "Just some out-of-towner, Mavis. Passing through. Sarah was just being polite." She squeezed Sarah's arm, a silent 'don't push it' warning.

The air was thick with the scent of stale coffee and cheap perfume—a nauseating blend. Every minute of forced small talk felt like another layer of "Sunday Armor" sealing her in. Their scrutiny was nearly unbearable.

Finally, after dissecting the merits of the sermon and the coming summer youth retreat, Robert released her. "To the car, Sarah. We have a great deal to discuss when we get home."

As she walked away, the image of Jessie's careless smile and the feeling of his fingers brushing hers was the only thing that kept her walking straight. Just as she passed the open sanctuary doors, a final, muffled sound reached her from within—a single, sustained, beautiful note from a hymn she couldn't quite place. For a dizzying second, that pure, clear sound wrapped around her, a gentle, powerful presence that cut through the fear and the lie. It was a moment of unearned peace, the comfort she had once felt before judgment clouded her faith.

But the moment was too gentle, too fleeting.

She reached the sedan, slipped into the passenger seat, and uncurled her fingers. The crumpled paper was damp with sweat, but the address—the promise—was still visible. She shoved it deep into the toe of her shoe, replacing the physical constraint of the armor with the secret, burning knowledge of her plan.

The ride home was silent, sterile. Her father didn't rage; his disappointment filled the car, heavier than any shout. Outside, the world blurred past in whites and greens; inside, time thickened, settling on Sarah's shoulders. She kept her eyes on the window, feeling the crumpled paper—the map to Jessie's bridge— dig into her foot. The silence pressed on her chest, each mile separating her from the freedom she'd tasted. Only the faint hum of the engine reminded her that the world was still moving.

The moment they arrived, Robert delivered his sentence, disguised as a schedule: "You will remain in your room, Sarah. There will be no phone calls. No reading."

He then retreated to his study, and the distinct click of the lock sealed him inside. That sound—the sharp, authoritative snap of the bolt—was the signal Sarah had been waiting for, the sound of her father retreating to his fortress of ledgers and scripture. It was the sound of her opportunity—her breath catching in her throat as she realized the window was open, if only for a moment.

As soon as she heard the study door lock, she shed her Sunday Armor. The white gloves, the tight dress, the slip—all of it was tossed onto the bed, a heap of discarded obedience that still held the faint scent of her mother's anxious perfume. She pulled on the oldest, softest pair of jeans she owned, a faded cotton shirt, and her worn sneakers.

Eleanor was already banging around in the kitchen, making Sunday dinner like nothing was wrong. The noise from the mixer and pans was the perfect cover for sneaking out.

At 6:45 PM, the setting sun cast long, anxious shadows across the lawn. Sarah eased her window open, pushing the sash up a fraction of an inch at a time until it was wide enough to open. The scent of honeysuckle and the distant hum of summer insects flooded the room—the sound of the world she yearned for.

She was terrified—her hands were slick with sweat—but the crushing fear of staying put under the perpetual judgment of Havenwood was finally greater than the fear of leaving.

She climbed onto the porch roof, the hot shingles rough and sticky against the soles of her sneakers. A bead of sweat traced down her spine as she crouched low, heart thudding in her ears. She dropped silently to the cool, evening grass below, her knees absorbing the shock, her breath tight and fast. For a split second, she hesitated in the shadow of the house, the familiar lines of her old life at her back and the wild expanse of the unknown before her. Then she ran—barely feeling the ground, following the vague directions Jessie had scribbled. Each stride shattered another layer of fear: the rustle of leaves, the slap of her shoes, the wild chorus of crickets and distant highway. Her heart pounded a desperate rhythm against her ribs, a drumbeat of self-will finally drowning out the hymns and the threats of hellfire. She didn't look back. The night was alive, and for the first time, so was she.

CHAPTER 5

THE PRICE OF DARING

Sarah ran until the manicured lawns of Havenwood gave way to cracked asphalt and then, finally, to dirt roads. She wasn't just running to something; she was fleeing the fear of Reverend Smith's hellfire and the suffocating silence of her father's disapproval.

The meeting spot was as Jessie promised: a rusted, abandoned railroad trestle over a slow tributary. The air here was different—a blend of damp earth, river mud, and forbidden freedom.

Jessie was waiting, perched on the rusted rail, denim jacket slouched around his shoulders, utterly indifferent to the clock. The sounds of the town had faded behind her, replaced by the whisper of water and the distant hum of insects. When he saw her emerge from the thicket of trees, his smile was genuine, wide, and entirely without expectation. He flicked a pebble into the water, the ripples catching the last gold of sunset, and nodded as if her arrival was the most natural thing in the world.

"Well, look at that," he said, rising slowly. "I figured you were too smart to show up."

"I'm not smart," Sarah managed, breathless and trembling slightly, leaning against the cold iron.

"No, you're not," he agreed, but his clear blue eyes held a warmth that made it sound like the highest compliment. "Smart girls don't sneak out of windows just to see what's outside. They just read about it in a book."

He set down a small, portable transistor radio that was quietly playing loud, bluesy rock music—a sound that would have instantly branded her a delinquent back in Havenwood. Jessie wasn't interested in her family's reputation; he was only interested in her frustrations.

They talked for a while, the conversation meandering through music, books, and what freedom might look like beyond Havenwood's fences. The easy rhythm made it possible for Sarah to say what she'd never said aloud.

"They talk about salvation like it's a report card," Sarah confessed, the words spilling out of her in a rush. "If you do the right things, you get the grade. If you don't, you burn. I just feel like I'm never going to earn it."

Jessie listened. "Sounds exhausting," he said simply. "It sounds like they don't trust you, and they don't trust their God either. If He's that easy to anger, what's the point?"

This simple validation—that her quiet frustrations with the church were real—was more potent than any sermon she'd ever heard.

He opened his pack. "You said you needed to breathe. This might help." He offered her a cheap cigarette and a bottle of warm beer. The bitter taste of the beer was sharp and chemical on her tongue. It wasn't pleasant, but it was an immediate, physical act of transgression. As the rock music played softly, they stood on the trestle. It was an experience she owned, unapproved and entirely her own. She was tasting sin and finding it to be liberating.

"You know, you're too pretty to look that worried all the time," Jessie said, turning to her. "And you're smart. You picked the fastest way out of that town, didn't you?"

"I don't know," Sarah whispered, tears welling in her eyes, not from sorrow, but from the shock of being seen.

"You do," he insisted gently. "You're beautiful, Sarah. And you are smart."

When he leaned in and kissed her, it wasn't the chaste peck of a courtship; it was a hungry, consuming affirmation that she was alive and wanted. It was the physical embodiment of the freedom he promised. The night deepened, the scent of damp earth, river, and his raw sweat overwhelming the memory of her father's Old Spice.

The single moment stretched into the whole night, a desperate, passionate act of rebellion against the conditional love of Havenwood. Sarah willingly traded the promise of a heaven she could never earn for the very real, immediate feeling of liberation in his arms.

The Discovery and The Verdict

Sarah didn't return until just before dawn. The sky was turning a sickly, pale gray as she crept back into the house, her body aching, her mind swimming in a dizzying mix of shame and lingering exhilaration. She was caught instantly. Her father was waiting in the hallway, a dark, rigid silhouette standing sentinel. He hadn't slept; his eyes were red-rimmed and terrifyingly still.

The air around Sarah was heavy with evidence: river mud on her sneakers, the stale scent of beer, and the lingering odor of cigarette smoke.

"You brought shame into this house," Robert said, his voice a low, flat whisper that carried more menace than a scream. "You have defiled the testimony of this family before God and man."

Sarah tried to apologize, but the words wouldn't come. "Silence!" he snapped. He finally moved, pointing to the small, muddy tracks her sneakers had left on the pristine rug. "That, Sarah, is the filth of the world. And you brought it in here. You chose the mud over the promise of salvation."

He marched to the phone and began dialing. As he did, Sarah felt unsettling dizzy. It was this feeling which confirmed that her transgression had been logged and processed. Her father glanced at her, and whispered, "the time for mediation is past. We must excise the rot before it contaminates the whole."

The Formal Inquest

Hours bled by in a suffocating silence that was far worse than any yelling. After Robert's initial, chilling whisper, he left Sarah standing in the hall, refusing to look at her. Eleanor moved through the house with a frantic energy, doing unnecessary cleaning, the clatter of her work serving as a furious, silent judgment.

Sarah was banished to her room to wait. She stared out the window at the familiar, sterile garden. She imagined her small bag, hidden beneath the floorboards, containing the cash and ledger sheets she had painstakingly prepared for her original escape. The emotional rebellion had been intoxicating, but now the cold, hard numbers—her true planned escape—were more necessary than ever. The clock on her nightstand seemed to stop; every minute stretched into an eternity. She walked to her dresser and touched the spine of a worn, forbidden copy of Jane Eyre hidden beneath a stack of hymnals. The simple feel of the binding—a connection to a world of defiant emotion and possibility—was a brief, aching solace before the inevitable confrontation.

Later that morning, Sarah stood shivering in the living room, dressed in an old, faded housedress Robert had ordered her to wear—a deliberate choice to strip away her vanity. The room was bathed in a merciless, spiritual floodlight, the sun streaming through the sheer curtains.

The doorbell chimed—a polite, unforgiving sound. Robert did not move toward the door. He stood by the mantelpiece, his back ramrod straight. "Remember this, Sarah," he said, his voice flat and hard, never turning around. "The love of God is for those who strive for righteousness... And you," he finally turned, his gaze cold, "have forfeited your claim."

The conversation with Reverend Smith and a leading Deacon was handled with terrifying surgical precision. It was not about her soul; it was about the family's standing.

"Sarah," Reverend Smith began, his face a mask of official, sorrowful condemnation. "Your actions are a scandal. You have been walking the wide road to destruction."

Robert stepped forward, taking control. "The family is ruined," Robert stated, his jaw locked. He looked directly at Sarah, but his words were addressed to the other men. "She has committed a personal betrayal. We will make immediate arrangements for her to be placed away from this town. Out of sight, out of mind. We will tell the congregation she has gone to attend to an ailing relative." He looked at her, his eyes burning with fear over the damage to his name, not with compassion. "You are a liability to the Lord's house."

Eleanor, meanwhile, remained seated, twisting her handkerchief. Her shame had fully internalized, leaving no room for maternal compassion.

The Church's Sentence: Reverend Smith closed his King James Bible with a decisive thud. "Sarah, until you can demonstrate absolute, unwavering obedience—and until the stain of this is forgotten—you are excluded from the fellowship of this church."

Her childhood home instantly became a place of crushing judgment and tension.

CHAPTER 6

THE UNDENIABLE CONSEQUENCE

Weeks dragged by after Sarah was cut off. The house, once spotless, now felt like a cage. Meals were quiet, broken only by Robert's hard stare or Eleanor's tired sighs. The punishment wasn't loud—it was simply being ignored. Every day felt heavier with the weight of what wasn't said.

People in town didn't just stop talking to Sarah—they acted like she didn't exist. At the grocery store, Mrs. Crenshaw stared at pickles for ten minutes just to avoid a hello. The way everyone pretended she was invisible was almost as bad as yelling at her. Hell wasn't fire; it was being cut off from everyone you knew.

Later that week, Sarah tried to call about a job at a shop out of town. Halfway through the call, the line just went dead. Maybe it was nothing, but she knew better. In Havenwood, even the phone could be used to shut you out.

Late one night, the house was wrenched awake by the sound of violent retching. Sarah, hunched over the toilet, was overtaken by wave after wave of sickness, her body crumpling until she collapsed on the cold tile. It wasn't a passing nausea—her skin was clammy, her vision tunneling, a primal terror clawing up her throat because she knew, in that moment, exactly what was happening to her.

Eleanor burst in, face ghost-pale, her hands fluttering uselessly at her sides. She didn't move to help or comfort; she simply stared, her mouth working but no sound coming out. It was the look of a woman who understood in one electric, horrifying instant: this was pregnancy. This was shame incarnate, and Eleanor—the lifelong enabler—was paralyzed by the knowledge of what it would mean for the family.

Sarah saw the shock pass over her mother's face, saw the calculation, the fear, and something like grief. But neither spoke. The silence was a scream.

This was no longer a youthful mistake that could be managed; this was a physical testament to sin, a living, permanent record of Robert's failure as a father and a deacon. Robert's cold fury intensified into a desperate, surgical need to eliminate the evidence. He saw the pregnancy not as a life, but as a stain—a permanent blight on his carefully constructed testimony.

The Calculus of Elimination

The next night, heavy drapes were drawn tight. Robert sat behind his desk, the brass lamp casting sharp shadows on the wall. Eleanor stood beside him, hands clasped, eyes red from silent tears—a mute witness in her husband's court.

"You've destroyed this family's name," Robert started, voice tight and angry. He had a notepad covered in phone numbers and travel plans, already halfway to solving the problem. He spoke to Sarah as if she were just another problem to be fixed, not his daughter. "You're not having this baby," Robert said flatly. "It's a stain we can't hide. We're going to fix it."

Sarah went cold all over. She tried, her voice shaking, "But you always said babies were a gift. The church says life is sacred. You said that, Dad."

Robert shoved the family Bible off his desk, sending it thudding to the floor. "The Bible's for the righteous, Sarah. You gave that up. The whole town already thinks the worst after Jessie. If you have this baby, we're ruined. For good!"

"The church won't know," Robert snapped, finally losing control. "We'll find a clinic—out of state. It'll be expensive, but we'll handle it. You'll stay with Aunt Martha, keep quiet, and when it's over, you'll come back like nothing happened."

He slammed his fist on the desk. "This is about survival, Sarah. If word gets out, everything I've built will be gone. My name is all you have, and you're throwing it away!"

A wave of cold nausea hit Sarah: the nausea of spiritual disgust.

Eleanor finally moved, placing a hesitant hand on Sarah's shoulder. "Honey, this is the only way," she whispered, voice trembling. "We just need to wipe the slate clean. Nobody has to know. Then we can start over."

Sarah's entire existence in Havenwood was conditional. Her parents were prepared to sacrifice her child and her soul just to silence the gossip. They were not seeking grace; they were seeking control.

They're willing to sacrifice a life just to save their own lie, Sarah realized, the thought landing hard. She stood up, not panicked but steady. Her parents weren't trying to protect her—they were protecting themselves.

That night, Sarah made up her mind. She wasn't going to a clinic, and she wasn't going to Aunt Martha's. She didn't know where she'd go—she just knew she had to get out. When the house finally went quiet, the only sound was the clock ticking. Every tick felt like a countdown to freedom.

She changed into old jeans and a loose denim shirt—clothes she'd worn to the bridge, clothes with no trace of her mother's perfume. As she dressed, a wave of weakness washed over her, leaving her legs feeling hollow. She stopped, dizzy and lightheaded. Just nerves, she told herself. Just the fear of what came next.

She dragged the dresser away from the wall, heart pounding. The floor creaked, but the house stayed quiet. With a hairpin, she popped up the loose floorboard. Underneath was her stash—a small bag of cash and the blue notebook where she'd kept every detail, $472.00. Every dollar she could scrape, every cent she'd risked taking from her father's accounts. She put it all in her old travel bag, slid the floorboard back, and shoved the dresser into place. One last quiet act of rebellion.

That careful, cold-blooded accounting of her freedom was the real measure of her courage. She walked to Robert's study, found a scrap of paper, and quickly wrote her terse note: "I am going where the judgment can't follow." She placed it squarely on Robert's pristine desk, weighting it down with a small, discarded hymnal.

The Unseen Compass

She paused at the window, the cold night air hitting her face. There was no plan, no map, only instinct. Yet, when she swung her leg over the sill, a strange, profound calm descended upon her. It was not courage, but a deep, unearned certainty of protection. As her feet touched the damp lawn, she felt a powerful, unseen force nudging her, guiding her steps away from the house and toward the road. It was a sense of quiet steering, of providence intervening in the final, desperate act of a terrified girl. Sarah did not look back. She slipped into the anonymity of the night, leaving behind the shame, the hypocrisy, and the cold, conditional love of Havenwood forever. She carried the secret life of her unborn child—the living, undeniable consequence of her brutal freedom. The true journey, she realized, had just begun.

She was no longer merely an absence in someone else's story. She was the author of her own.

CHAPTER 7

THE ROAD TO ANONYMITY

Leaving Havenwood wasn't a sudden break. It was a slow, bumpy ride on a rattling bus, every mile putting space between Sarah and her old life. The engine noise drowned out her father's voice. The press of strangers in the seats around her replaced the suffocating quiet of home. Every pothole and turn reminded her she was really leaving, piece by piece, starting over.

The battered Greyhound bus was her hiding place. Sarah rode in the last row, tucked in by the engine noise and the lingering haze of stale cigarettes. She kept her head down, hoping to blend into the anonymity of travel. The hum of the tires and the cold from the window kept her grounded. She was moving— finally away from the white walls and that silent house.

She kept her cash and blue spiral sub-ledger zipped deep in her bag, always within reach. The air was heavy—thick with smoke, wet wool, and the sharp tang of cheap air freshener. She had escaped her name and her past, but the terror lingered. Her father's condemnation and the threat of forced abortion kept her numb and alert, moving on instinct, always scanning the windows for dangers she couldn't yet name.

Despite the $472 she'd taken—a small portion of it had gone to the bus ticket out of Havenwood—Sarah refused to touch a cent unless she absolutely had to. That money was a last resort, her only chance at true escape if everything else failed. To spend it all now, while she still had her freedom, felt too risky—like erasing her only lifeline. Instead, she rationed crackers, made do with what she could find, and let hunger gnaw at her. It was better to be hungry than to be trapped again.

The journey was a blur of roadside diners, stale coffee, and the constant, dull ache of fear. She rode for nearly three days, the anonymous faces of fellow passengers passing like ghosts. Each time the bus hissed to a stop at a desolate terminal, she felt a spike of panic, convinced her father or a church elder would be waiting. She slept poorly, waking often to the memory of Robert's cold eyes and the imagined sound of Reverend Smith's voice thundering about unrepentant sin. Every mile was a victory, yet every rest stop felt like a chance for her past to catch up.

The discomfort was relentless. Her back ached from the hard seat; her stomach cramped with hunger. She rationed crackers and sipped lukewarm water, unwilling to spend another coin. The passing world—cornfields, gas stations, rusted towns—remained indifferent, a blur of lives that had nothing to do with hers.

At a grimy rest stop, Sarah splashed cold water on her face and studied her reflection—a stranger in denim. The vending machine glowed temptingly, offering candy and chips, but she chose another sleeve of saltines. The dry, floury taste was a comfort—punishing, plain, and safe. Even when she was free, her choices were still shaped by habit and fear.

At the city terminal, the engine's roar faded, giving way to the city's mechanical hum. Her first breath was a shock—diesel, frying oil, and cheap air freshener all mixing in the air. The low, electronic drone of the terminal felt as indifferent as the world outside. She realized the city's systems were just as total as Havenwood's, but here, anonymity was possible.

Brief Encounters on the Edge

Sarah kept to herself, barely speaking. She worried that any small talk might lead to questions she couldn't answer. The bus was full of strangers—an old man snoring with his head back, a teenager tapping out rhythms, a mom brushing crumbs off her kid's shirt. Sarah watched them, wishing she could feel that sure of her place. She leaned her head against the cold window, letting the rumble of the engine and the smell of diesel drown out the ache of being so alone.

Once, a friendly, overweight woman with a booming laugh sat next to her for a four-hour stretch.

"You look like you saw a ghost, sugar," the woman said, biting into a chicken drumstick.

Sarah managed a weak smile. "Just tired. Been on the road forever."

"Aren't we all? Where you off to?"

"Just... away," Sarah said softly.

The woman nodded, like she knew more than Sarah wanted to admit. "Sometimes just getting away is the best you can do. But you find your people—whether it's a church or a friend. World's rough, but not everything's sharp edges."

Sarah stared out the window, her reflection barely there. "I'll try."

The woman patted her arm, leaving a smudge of chicken grease. "You do that, sweetheart."

Sarah flinched and forced another tired grin. "Just moving to the city. Trying to find work," she said, giving the same vague answer she'd practiced for anyone who asked.

"Well, bless your heart. You can't live on crackers, darling. You need real food—especially for that little one." The woman pulled out a greasy bag of fried chicken. "Here, have a piece. What's your name?"

Sarah stared at the chicken, her mouth watering. It was more than hunger—it was the kindness that nearly undid her. But kindness came with questions, and she wasn't ready to let anyone in.

"No thanks, ma'am," Sarah said quickly. "My stomach's been off lately." When the woman asked her name, Sarah answered, "Rose." It tasted strange—like a stone in her mouth, but safe. The lie was a shield she needed.

The woman just shrugged and went back to her newspaper, letting Sarah sit in the smell of fried chicken and the sting of being alone. Hunger and loneliness felt safer than the questions she couldn't answer.

Sarah continued her vigil in the back seat, watching the road unwind, the roar of the bus engine a protective shield against the silence of her own guilt.

She arrived in the sprawling, indifferent city—a chaotic, relentless metropolis—late at night, her body aching and her nerves raw. The bus terminal was a cavern of echoing footsteps and flickering advertisements, the air pungent with exhaust and the sharp tang of bleach. In the depths of her first trimester, she stumbled into the city's indifference: the anonymity was both a balm and a terrifying void. In Havenwood, she was judged, but she was never hungry. Here, no one cared if she starved; she was just another shadow moving through the neon-lit corridors, another face in the endless tide.

She spent the first three weeks on the street, and the city quickly became a hostile entity. She slept sitting up on cold, splintered park benches, the wood biting into her back, or huddled deep in the overlit recesses of the bus terminal, where the perpetual hum of vending machines and distant shouts made sleep thin and useless. The asphalt burned her shoes during the day and bled cold air at night, soaking into her bones. The constant, low-grade fear of the streets—of footsteps behind her, of sharp voices in the dark—was compounded daily by the growing, cumbersome discomfort of her pregnancy. Every muscle ached; every morning felt like waking from a fight she barely survived.

One afternoon, sitting alone at a bus station terminal in a haze of exhaustion, she bowed her head, clutching the side of her growing belly. The cheap plastic chair squeaked beneath her, the linoleum sticky with spilled soda and old gum. The fluorescent lights buzzed overhead, casting pale shadows over her raw, bitten nails. The shame of her past choices and the intense physical hunger were a crushing weight she could barely lift, her stomach clenching at the smell of stale fries from a nearby trash container, her head throbbing with the effort of keeping herself invisible.

"Here, child. You look like you need this more than I do."

A rough, kind voice, unexpected and resonant, broke through her despair. Sarah's head snapped up. Standing over her was a man—older, with a deeply weathered face that spoke of years spent outdoors, and eyes that held an unexpected, deep, and gentle kindness.

He pressed a wadded ten-dollar bill into her cold, stiff hand. "Go get yourself something hot to eat," he insisted, his hand firm on her own. "Something warm, something real. And that little one, too."

Tears sprang to Sarah's eyes, the unexpected kindness a shock after weeks of crushing judgment and forced solitude. The warmth of his hand was the first genuine, unsolicited comfort she'd felt since leaving Havenwood.

"Thank you," she choked out, the single word feeling impossibly small against the size of the gesture. "Thank you, sir. God bless you."

The man merely smiled, a slight, peaceful upturn of the lips that seemed to hold no judgment at all.

Sarah blinked quickly, furiously wiping the hot tears from her eyes. She was determined to look at his face, to etch the features of this one pure act of charity into her memory. But when she looked back up, the man was gone. She scanned the crowded terminal. He was nowhere. The only sign he was ever there was the abrupt silence that followed his departure.

Sarah stared at the crisp bill, a clear, sudden act of unconditional grace, a moment of divine provision in her darkest hour. Yet her mind, scarred by years of religious conditioning, instantly rationalized the impossibility. *Luck. Not forgiveness.* She focused on the tangible money, not the impossible gesture, clutching the bill tightly. She had a life to protect, and the ten dollars was solid proof that she could continue her flight. She headed straight for the food counter, the survivor Rose now focused only on the tangible money, determined to survive.

CHAPTER 8

THE ILLUSORY STRENGTH

Sarah's isolation was total—she had fled her family, escaping their plan to send her away, while the church's condemnation left her spiritually and emotionally hollow. From childhood, safety had meant perfection: every rule followed, every smile measured, every answer rehearsed. But when she finally faltered, the fragile order of her world collapsed, and her sense of belonging vanished. Losing both family and church meant losing the only source of validation she had ever known. For years, she believed that doing everything right would keep her safe. But when she failed, the chaos that followed felt less like misfortune and more like a punishment she deserved.

She ended up at a worn-down boarding house, the only roof she could afford after weeks on the street. She carried nothing but a battered canvas bag and the clothes on her back. The hallway was dim, pungent with boiled cabbage, old carpet glue, and distant TV static. The boarding house shattered her escape fantasies. There was no fresh start here, and certainly no instant safety. This was Sarah's last resort—a room paid for by the week, not a place to rest, only to survive. As she stood there, uncertain, a door creaked open behind her.

A woman, voice rough from decades of cigarettes, looked her up and down. "You the new girl?"

Sarah nodded, pulling her coat tighter. "Yeah, just got here."

The woman kept her gaze steady. "So, you running from trouble or just starting over?"

Sarah gave a tired half-smile. "Does it matter?"

The woman grinned, lopsided. "Usually both, around here. I make coffee before work—just knock if you want some."

Sarah hesitated. "Thanks. Maybe I will."

"Suit yourself." The woman disappeared, leaving Sarah alone in the corridor, her battered canvas bag slung over her shoulder and her heart pounding in the unfamiliar quiet.

For a moment, Sarah lingered, absorbing this new reality. The floor creaked and trembled under every footstep from above. For the first time since leaving Havenwood, she realized there was no audience, no judge—just this narrow slice of anonymity, hers alone to claim or waste. She pressed a palm to the wall, steadying herself, and exhaled. This was not the freedom she'd longed for, but it was the first space that belonged entirely to her.

She found her room at the end of the hall—a cramped, yellow-lit box with a narrow bed and a single window half-fogged by age. She set down her bag and sat on the edge of the mattress, letting the silence settle around her. It was a mix of relief and terror. She was here, and she was utterly alone. She would have to decide what came next.

The days that followed blurred together, filled with small, necessary tasks— finding a grocery store, learning the sounds of the old pipes, and watching the shadows grow longer each evening. The loneliness was overwhelming, but it was in this raw, vulnerable state that Sarah first noticed Michael.

Michael entered her life at her lowest point. She met him in the first week after arriving in the boarding house. He was older and powerfully built, carrying himself with a quiet confidence that seemed unshakeable. His presence was undeniably intimidating, yet for the first time, Sarah felt protected rather than exposed. Michael didn't offer salvation or rescue. He offered strength, and in her state, that felt like safety.

Michael was different from anyone she'd known. When he looked at Sarah, he didn't see a lost, broken girl in need of rescue. Instead, he saw someone to claim, someone to possess—a relationship he believed cemented by the pregnancy she confirmed just weeks after moving in together.

The transition from her small, rented room to sharing Michael's space occurred over time, shaped more by necessity than choice. At first, Sarah tried to keep her distance, fiercely guarding what little independence she had salvaged. However, the reality of her new life—unpredictable landlords, dim hallways, and the mounting stress of her pregnancy—quickly eroded those boundaries.

Michael offered something rare in Sarah's world: stability. He gave her a place to sleep where she didn't have to fear eviction, a door she could lock, and meals—however simple—shared in quiet company instead of isolation. As her body changed and her resources dwindled, Sarah realized that living alone was no longer possible. The promise of safety, even if conditional, became too tempting to resist.

Sarah traded the illusion of autonomy for the concrete reality of shelter, hoping this new arrangement—however complicated—would give her the time and stability she needed.

"Forget all that God-fearing nonsense," he told her one night, waving away her past with a flick of his hand. "They cut you loose, Sarah. They proved they didn't want you. Now you belong to me. And I'm strong enough to hold onto you. You, and that child you're carrying."

It wasn't physical abuse that began the cycle; it was a slow, deliberate erosion of her emotional and spiritual autonomy. Michael started by critiquing her clothes, claiming he was "protecting her" from the glances of other men, and slowly forced her into drab, shapeless clothing. He discouraged her from keeping a steady job, insisting he needed her full attention—ensuring she had no independent income. The physical reality of her pregnancy became another tool for control. He policed her diet, not out of concern, but because, as he put it, "You're carrying my future asset. Don't ruin the merchandise with your weakness."

The Weapon of the Past

Soon after she moved into the cramped apartment with him, Michael, under the guise of "securing their future," inspected her worn travel bag. He found the blue spiral sub-ledger and the bulk of what was left of the $472.00 cash she had risked everything to steal. He didn't outright steal it; he co-opted it. He declared the money was now their "joint security fund," forcing her to open a new joint account, which he immediately controlled and quickly emptied for his own expenses. He would mock the ledger's contents, calling the meticulously coded entries a "child's game of lies," further breaking her spirit. In the end, nothing remained of her escape fund—Michael had taken it all.

This act—the neutralization of her only safety net—was the financial end of her autonomy. Every small triumph she achieved—a moment of laughter, a successful meal, a hopeful comment about the future—was met with a reminder of her past. "You think you know how to save money? And what did you get from wasting all that time with that boy, Jessie? Nothing. Look at yourself—without me, you'd be back on the street, desperate for scraps of forgiveness from all those hypocrites who never wanted you in the first place. You owe me, Sarah. You owe me everything." He expertly wielded her shame as a weapon, cementing her deepest conviction: she was unworthy and eternally lucky to have him. His control wasn't cruelty; it was the discipline she believed her sinful nature demanded.

He didn't need new ammunition; her past was a well-stocked arsenal. The growing life inside her became a physical testament to her confinement. Whenever Sarah showed signs of independence— a request to buy her own groceries, a suggestion that she might take a class, or even a moment of quiet he couldn't invade—he would unleash a calculated torrent of shame. He never let her forget the deacon's cold gaze or the weight of her father's disappointment. These weren't arguments; they were subtle spiritual bludgeons designed to reinforce the central lie: that she was inherently defective.

"You want to reach out to someone?" he'd challenge, his voice dangerously soft. "Who is it, Sarah? Who are you trying to run to? You think anyone from your past wants to hear from you now? They made it clear—you're not wanted. You're damaged. Only I want you. Only I will put up with this mess. No one else wants the pregnant disaster."

One afternoon, Sarah tried, carefully: "Maybe I could pick up some shifts at a local diner—just to save for a car or something."

Michael didn't even blink, but the air in the room went cold. "I already told you—no diner job, Sarah," he said flatly. "You don't need that pocket change, and I don't want you around a bunch of guys staring at you. I pay the bills here. Is that not enough?"

"I just want a little… I don't know, breathing room," Sarah said. "Maybe save up for something of my own."

Michael scoffed, standing to his full height. "Save what? You already blew your best shot with that Jessie kid. Do you know how to manage your finances? No, you handle me, I handle the money. That's how this works. Quit asking to screw up." He nodded at her belly. "You think those church folks would want you now? They'd just whisper and pity you. But I own this mess. You and the kid are mine."

When they left the apartment, his grip on her arm was non-negotiable, heavy, and proprietary. He insisted on driving everywhere, ensuring she never memorized bus routes or developed her own mental map of the city. He eliminated small, spontaneous pleasures, making her feel guilty for even wanting a coffee alone or a five-minute walk without his company. Every outside connection was severed, one by one, until Michael was the entire landscape of her world.

The Final Spiral

The cycle of abuse perfectly mirrored the striving for perfection she had done for her parents. After Michael's verbal attacks, which often left her weeping and curled on the floor, he would offer brief, intense moments of contrition and tenderness. He would hold her, whispering reassurances, showering her with temporary affection. Sarah clung to these brief respites like a desperate supplicant clinging to a temporary blessing, interpreting them as proof that if she could just be better, the abuse would stop.

But the spiritual numbness had become physical. Sarah was always tired, always ill, and constantly retreating into a blank space in her mind just to survive the hours. Michael saw her decline, not as a sign of his cruelty, but as confirmation of her inherent weakness, which only deepened his contempt. She was no longer a worthy possession; she was a drain on resources.

The realization that she must leave was not a flash of courage, but a cold, terrible assessment of inevitable death. One night, after a particularly vicious verbal attack, he watched her place a tired hand over her small, swollen abdomen. Michael didn't remark on her weight loss; he remarked on the life.

"If you ever think of running," he said, his voice deadly calm, "remember I know how to find you. And remember, that thing inside you? It's the only thing keeping you relevant. Don't risk it."

It was the threat to the innocent, the casual ownership of her future child, that shattered the final illusion of safety. He was no longer her protector; he was the slow, deliberate engine of her destruction. Remaining with Michael was merely a longer, more agonizing form of suicide. The alternative was the certain expiration of her unborn child's hope.

Every night, the urge to run grew sharper, pressing in on her like a hand at her back. Michael's control was suffocating, but beyond the apartment walls lurked a world that had already turned its back on her. Still, the thought of staying promised only slow ruin—a kind of vanishing Michael would never notice. The need to escape, fierce and primal, began to eclipse her fear. It was no longer just a wish; it was a pulse in her veins, insistent and wild, reminding her she was still alive.

Sarah waited. She didn't plan a confrontation or a dramatic exit. She simply waited for an afternoon when Michael was gone for an extended time—a specific, unplanned six-hour window that opened up only because his usual mechanic was suddenly unavailable. For hours, she rehearsed the route in her mind, the sequence of movements she would need to make her escape seamless. She gathered nothing—no clothes, no mementos, only the few crumpled dollars she had managed to find in a living room couch.

The moment finally arrived. Her body, fueled by pure adrenaline and the primal fear of him returning, moved with frantic silence. Her mind, usually a haze of confusion, achieved an uncanny, pinpoint clarity, as if every necessary step—the turn of the lock, the quiet slam of the exterior door—was being executed by a force outside herself. A final, shaky breath bridged the space between captivity and flight. She didn't look back at the apartment that had been her prison and her entire universe. She simply ran, heart hammering against her ribs, protecting the growing life within her, and leaving behind the shame, the conditional love, and the self-hatred that Michael had so expertly cultivated.

She traded the illusory strength of captivity for the terrifying vulnerability of anonymity, seeking escape not just from a man, but from the fatal pattern that dictated she deserved the pain. This devastating period of abuse and despair ended with a desperate flight, leaving her completely alone in an indifferent city, a spiritual shell awaiting the next profound loss.

CHAPTER 9

THE CALCULUS OF SURVIVAL

The frantic, hollow silence that followed Sarah's escape from Michael ended abruptly when her adrenaline finally gave out. Once again, she was back on the streets—alone, exposed, and with nowhere to go. The four claustrophobic walls of his control were replaced by the sprawling, indifferent concrete of the city. She had nothing but the vulnerable life in her belly and a handful of crumpled, cold dollars. There was no shelter waiting, no safety net, only the relentless reality of survival.

One sweltering afternoon, while Sarah waited for a bus transfer in the shadow of a decaying warehouse, she encountered a small, unexpected kindness. A young man named Leo, who often sat nearby conducting quick, quiet transactions out of a worn backpack, noticed her silent misery. He was not aggressive or pushy, and he never pressed her about his business. Instead, he simply walked over and placed a cold bottle of water and a slightly stale bagel gently beside her on the curb. He didn't ask for payment or conversation. His only words were a quiet, passing observation about how hard it was to find a decent meal in this part of town. It was a bizarre moment of grace from a man the world judged far more harshly than her. The small, quiet act of human recognition—a man seeing her need, not her condition—served as a strange, fleeting lifeline.

For the first three weeks, Sarah drifted from bus shelter to bus shelter, sometimes sleeping upright on splintered benches, sometimes huddled in the humid shadow of an industrial dumpster. She curled herself into corners of all-night diners or the overlit recesses of the city's busiest transit terminal, doing her best to stay invisible. The city's noise—a ceaseless, grinding soundtrack of air brakes, sirens, and shouted arguments—was both a balm against Michael's certain discovery and a terrifying reminder that she truly belonged nowhere. The air was a suffocating blend of diesel exhaust, hot asphalt, and the sharp, acrid stench of human poverty. Her body, burdened by the constant discomfort of her advanced pregnancy, protested every movement; each time she stood up, her strained back screamed in protest, a heavy reminder that she had no refuge, no comfort, and no idea where she might sleep the next night.

Finding work was an impossibility she faced daily. Employers took one look at her condition, her obvious homelessness, and her total lack of references, and turned her away with cold, practiced efficiency, their muttered "Liability" echoing her father's cruelest word. She was an invisible failure in a city that never stopped. Survival meant sacrificing pride, scraping for every cent. She took every odd job available—washing dishes for a few hours at a greasy spoon where the floor was perpetually sticky and the lighting was fluorescent yellow, or sweeping sidewalks for meager change. She kept her head down, never speaking more than necessary, a survival instinct honed by a lifetime of hiding. Her focus was absolute: breathe, hide, save. This intense, overriding directive gave her actions an unseen, guiding precision that helped her navigate the most dangerous areas of the city without incident, overriding her perpetual exhaustion.

Finally, driven by the absolute necessity of finding shelter before her child arrived, she made a difficult decision that required a deep betrayal of her own truth. She found a rundown motel on the city's outskirts, the kind of place that charged by the hour. When she applied for the cleaning job, she looked the manager—a thin, suspicious woman—directly in the eye and lied, claiming her condition was merely bloating from a chronic illness. The necessity of this deception left a wave of cold nausea in her gut, but the practiced smoothness of the lie belonged entirely to Rose, the new persona she had created. The meager pay, earned through relentless, filthy work scrubbing strangers' sins with industrial bleach, was enough to secure a tiny, mildew-streaked apartment three flights up. It was a miserable, hard-won haven with a stained mattress on the floor, a single working lamp, and, most importantly, a heavy, lockable door—a solid piece of metal that represented a stubborn, protective promise.

Every morning, before she left this sanctuary of mildew, Sarah performed the ritual of becoming Rose. It was an act of physical and mental separation. She scrubbed the chlorine from her hair, rubbed the persistent grime from under her fingernails, and applied a single, cheap, pale lipstick—a small act of secular defiance against the austerity of her past. This lipstick was Rose's fragile armor, projecting a necessary image of normalcy. As she stared at her reflection, she mentally recited the fictional history: divorced, here for work, no family.

The process was exhaustive, a fierce, protective discipline. Yet, sometimes, in the silence of the room, a brief, clear melody—a hymn tune she hadn't consciously thought of in weeks—would flicker through her mind, a gentle, uninvited presence suggesting the old life was not entirely extinguished.

The Anchor of the Heartbeat

Sarah's world shrank to a jagged, protective triangle: the apartment, the motel, and the free clinic. Her movements were governed by absolute paranoia. She never took a direct bus, preferring complex, indirect routes that required two or three transfers, a deliberate obfuscation she saw as an extra layer of security. Her eyes were constantly scanning. The sight of a man in a crisply starched white shirt or a woman carrying a large, leather-bound purse that hinted at a Bible triggered a spike of reflexive terror, forcing her to cross the street or duck into an alley. The ingrained fear of the church elder ran deeper than any rational thought could comprehend. The city had promised anonymity, but her past had instilled an enduring vigilance—a cold discipline that Sarah willingly obeyed.

With her first few paychecks, she found a government-run clinic for prenatal care. The waiting room was always crowded, hot, and smelled faintly of latex and stale cigarette smoke, filled with other tired, silent women clutching claim forms. These visits were a source of profound anxiety. Every time the nurse called out "Rose," Sarah felt a sharp spike of guilt at the lie, a small, immediate betrayal of the new life she was trying to build. The name was her most vital defense. She had meticulously constructed a concise, yet boring and plausible, backstory that provided a false sense of safety against the judgment she knew the truth would bring.

During her checkups, the overworked doctor would check the baby's steady heartbeat. The moment the cold gel hit her abdomen, Sarah would hold her breath, waiting. Then came the sound, magnified through the speaker, cutting through the anxiety and the hum of the clinic: the strong, quick *thump-thump-thump* of the tiny heart. The rhythm was a daily assurance, a physical manifestation of a covenant she had made, guided by an instinct deeper than fear. This was her only moment of true peace. Hearing that proof of life—the relentless, steady rhythm—was the one, undeniable thing she was fighting to protect, a small, physical miracle her parents could not abort and her father could not silence.

The cleaning work was brutal. The physical strain of hauling buckets and kneeling to scrub floors was intense, often leaving her breathless and doubled over in the stifling, bleach-scented air. During these moments of physical duress, she developed a silent, fierce communication with the child: *Hold on. I won't stop. I'll get us out of this.* She felt the baby's sharp, sudden kicks, which she interpreted not as discomfort, but as a will to thrive that mirrored her own desperate persistence. The baby was her living proof that she was not alone, a form of unconditional companionship.

The only person Sarah consistently spoke to at the motel was Marta, a middle-aged cleaning lady from Puerto Rico. Marta was loud and warm, with a heavy accent, and possessed a deep, practical wisdom forged in hardship. "You are too quiet, mija," Marta would say, pressing a plastic cup of overly-sweet instant coffee into her hand. "You carry too much sadness for one so young. You've got to talk, or the sadness will crack you like a dry dish." Marta's persistence was a steady, warm pressure that slowly wore down Sarah's fortress of silence. Sarah confessed to the anxiety of being entirely responsible for the life in her belly. Marta listened without flinching, becoming a fierce, protective force, showing Sarah that not all warmth came with a price.

The Final, Merciless Severing

The crushing weight of loneliness replaced the fear of hunger. She briefly sought companionship, attempting to anchor herself to the city's chaos through shallow, transactional relationships with men like Frank and Jonathan. They offered company; she offered silence about her past. Each time a man walked away, she felt the horrifying return of the terrifying emptiness of her exile, reinforcing her deep-seated fear of intimacy and her need for self-reliance. The city taught her that companionship was conditional on convenience.

One bitter, lonely night, months into her flight, Sarah reached her absolute nadir. Exhausted, ill, and utterly broken by the isolation, she desperately craved the lost familiarity of being cared for. Clutching a borrowed payphone receiver in the motel hallway, she dialed the familiar, seven-digit number for the Havenwood parsonage. The phone rang three times, each sound like an anvil dropping in the thick silence. The sound of her father's voice—sharp, formal, and utterly devoid of warmth—hit her like a physical blow.

"Father," she whispered, her voice thick with tears. "It's Sarah. I... I can't do this. I need help."

"Sarah," her father replied, his voice flat and perfectly controlled. "Your note indicated you were going where the judgment couldn't follow. That was your choice. We have protected the church. Your mother is currently hosting the Deacon's wives' tea. Do not call this number again. You will only jeopardize the fragile testimony we have managed to salvage."

The line went dead with a soft *click*. No questions about her safety, no mention of the child, and not a single word of regret or love. The conversation lasted less than sixty seconds, yet it destroyed the last vestige of her childhood hope. Her father's cold, final truth was absolute: her parents were more concerned with the fragile testimony of their social standing than the life or death of their own daughter. Robert's rejection was, in its profound cruelty, a merciful severing, cutting the final, illusory cord that tied her to her past and forcing her completely into her new, survivor self.

Later that night, sitting alone on her fire escape in total despair, a thought, clear and warm, pierced the haze: *You don't have to carry this alone. There is forgiveness.* It wasn't a voice; it was a sudden, absolute conviction, a flash of pure warmth that cut through the cold fear. Sarah immediately recoiled. *Forgiveness?* The word felt dangerous. She was certain it was a trick to make her drop her guard. "No," she whispered, clutching her stomach. "I earned this. I pay the price. Grace is a lie." As she shifted, a sudden, inexplicable coldness sank into the soles of her bare feet, utterly unsuited to the summer night. The cold was accompanied by a nearly imperceptible, deep vibration that seemed to travel up the metal of the fire escape. The physical distraction instantly grounded her, reinforcing the cold discipline of self-reliance just as she wavered toward spiritual vulnerability.

The finality of her father's rejection left Sarah hollow and cold, a deep numbness settling over her in the days that followed. She tried to bury the profound pain in the endless scrubbing of motel bathrooms, but the solitude only amplified her despair. It was during a brief, desperate respite, leaning against her cleaning cart, that Marta approached.

"There is an evangelistic seminar at the old Sanctuary Church downtown," Marta said, handing Sarah a well-worn flyer. The title promised: 'The Anchor of Hope: Unconditional Salvation.' "The preacher talks only about 'new beginnings' and 'unconditional love.' He says everyone gets a clean slate. You should come, mija. Before the baby comes, you should fill your cup."

Sarah stared at the flyer. The language—'new beginnings,' 'unconditional love,' 'salvation'—was exactly what she craved. But the image of the cross and the word 'Evangelistic' triggered a violent emotional spasm. She saw Reverend Smith's condemning face and felt the cold, hard certainty of her father's rules. *Unconditional love is a lie,* her internal fortress screamed. *It's bait.*

"No, thank you, Marta," Sarah said, handing the flyer back, her face suddenly hard, the muscle in her jaw tight. "I'm done with churches. I have all the new beginning I need right here." She patted her belly, reaffirming her choice. The flyer was a haunting, persistent reminder of a promise she couldn't trust. The survivor, Rose, instinctively rejected the lure, choosing the safety of self-reliance over the perceived vulnerability of faith.

CHAPTER 10

BUILDING SANCTUARY

Sarah met David six months into her tenure at the motel, still cleaning rooms. She was in the final weeks of her third trimester, a state that felt less like pregnancy and more like carrying a physical debt. She was enormous, moving with the slow, unsteady gait of someone constantly checking her center of gravity. The exhaustion was not just sleepiness, but a profound, chemical failure that left her muscles screaming. Her feet and ankles were permanently swollen—a tight, hot discomfort—and the baby pressed mercilessly on her diaphragm, making every flight of stairs an act of sheer will.

Her brief, transactional relationships with men in the city had only reinforced her belief that affection was always a temporary currency.

But David was different. He worked the graveyard shift at the nearby manufacturing plant, stopping at the motel coffee shop around dawn. He wore oil-stained coveralls and always smelled faintly of burnt metal and clean soap. Where her father demanded cold perfection and Michael had enforced claustrophobic control, David offered a gentle, steady presence that asked nothing of her but honesty. His peace was not the absence of conflict, but a quiet invitation to rest. With him, Sarah felt the first flicker of safety, as if she might finally be allowed to simply exist, unjudged and unburdened.

He was unassuming and non-demanding. His deep, steady brown eyes held simple concern, never judgment. Their conversations began with simple, unremarkable exchanges—a shared complaint about the stifling humidity, an observation about the motel's thin coffee. He didn't pry or ask her name beyond "Rose," content to exist in the silence alongside her. In Havenwood, words were weapons; with David, they were simply sounds used to mark time.

One particularly grueling morning, Sarah was leaning heavily on her cleaning cart, struggling to catch her breath. She had been on her feet for six hours, and the sciatica nerve in her right hip was singing a sharp, unbearable song. She was damp with sweat in the cool air, a symptom of her constantly overheating internal furnace. David watched her from his table, then rose slowly.

"You look like you need to sit down," David offered, his voice low and gentle. He didn't ask; he stated it, pushing a wobbly chair out for her without waiting for a reply. "You work too hard, Rose. That little one needs you to slow down."

Sarah gripped the handle of her cart, her knuckles white. "I'm fine, really. Just... catching my breath. I need to finish Room 204."

David didn't move the chair back, and his gaze was steady, calm, and utterly non-negotiable. "You're not fine," he said, his voice dropping slightly. "It's almost time for you to stop carrying the world by yourself. Just sit for five minutes."

Defeated by the truth in his observation, Sarah slowly sank onto the chair, massaging the throbbing ache in her ankles.

He placed his thermos on the table between them—a hot, heavy presence. He poured a cup of coffee and slid it toward her. This small, unsolicited act of provision—the immediate recognition of her fatigue and the life she carried without any hidden agenda—was the first truly unconditional observation she'd received since fleeing Havenwood. It wasn't pity, and it wasn't a demand; it was a simple, profound recognition of her humanity. For the first time in months, Sarah felt the fortress around her heart tremble.

The Foundation of Gentleness

David didn't try to save her or change her; he just made her life easier. His presence was as steady as the factory clock. He would leave her a large, hot thermos of black coffee on the counter before his shift ended, then wait.

He started walking her the four blocks back to her apartment every day. He didn't just match his stride to her slow, pregnant waddle; he would walk slightly behind her or just to the side, anticipating her frequent stops to shift the weight that was dragging down her spine. He instinctively knew when to offer his elbow when she navigated the uneven sidewalk, providing a steel anchor for her precarious balance. He would often carry the small handbag that felt like a ten-pound weight on her aching shoulder.

He noticed the subtle signs of a soul constantly on guard: the way she instinctively protected her belly with her hand, the quick flinch if a door slammed too loudly. David never commented on these tics; he just quietly moved closer to the curb when traffic was heavy, his silence a form of profound, unthreatening acceptance.

The trust he built led to the next step. One evening, he helped her carry a heavy bag of groceries up the three flights of rickety stairs. He took the stairs two at a time, protecting her from the inevitable, dizzying effort. As he stepped inside, the truth of her daily existence became plain: the air hung heavy and stale, the carpet was threadbare, and the corner "nursery" was a pathetic display—a pile of well-worn blankets next to a shaky, secondhand crib whose paint was peeling. It was a heartbreaking testament to her desperate, solitary hope.

Sarah braced herself for the inevitable question. But David didn't flinch. He didn't ask about the father, the past, or the lie of her name. His gaze was focused entirely on the crib.

Instead, he smiled, his eyes warm and accepting. He set the groceries down quietly. "We can do better than this, Rose," he said gently. "You and me and this little one. We deserve better."

Over the next several weeks, David's presence shifted from occasional visitor to something more permanent. His coat began to live on the back of her kitchen chair. One evening, David lingered at the sink, rolling up his sleeves to help with the dishes.

He glanced at Sarah, his voice tentative but earnest. "I know this is sudden, but… what if I stayed? For good. I could help more, and it's not like I've got anything better waiting at the plant dorms."

Sarah set down the dish she was drying, heart thudding. For a moment, the old fear of letting someone in flickered, but it was replaced by a deeper longing for the stability he brought. "I'd like that," she said, her voice soft. "It's not much, but it's ours."

David smiled, relief washing over his features. "Then let's make it a home."

That weekend, he moved in with a battered duffel and a secondhand toolbox. David's presence shifted from visitor to partner, not by accident, but with mutual consent and growing affection. He became her anchor, a daily participant in the work of building a home together.

The walls of their apartment were paper-thin, letting in the city's constant churn. The lack of privacy forced an intimacy between them. Late at night, when quiet finally settled, Sarah realized the noise was a kind of comfort. In Havenwood, silence was judgment. Here, thin walls were proof of life.

David's first job was making their space livable. He fixed the broken window pane, silencing the constant, chilling whistle of the outside wind. The stillness that followed was the first true quiet she had known in months, a peace that sank deep into her bones.

He expertly patched the crumbling plaster of the bedroom ceiling. He spent an entire evening taking apart and oiling the faulty pipes, finally silencing the incessant, maddening drip of the leaky kitchen faucet—a small victory against the chaos that had always defined her life. The apartment began to feel less like a temporary hiding spot and more like a potential home.

After finishing his repairs late one night, David paused in the doorway. "You know, Rose, you could paint the nursery corner any color you want. Doesn't have to be white or gray."

Sarah hesitated, surprised by the invitation. "I never thought I had a choice."

David grinned. "You do now."

A laugh escaped her, light and real as the promise in his voice.

His most profound act was transforming the corner nursery. He bought a bucket of cheap paint and painted the walls a soft, hopeful yellow, turning the shaky, secondhand crib from a grim symbol of fear into an object of hope. He did it all without once mentioning God, sin, or reputation—the three cornerstones of the prison she had fled. He was proving that love did not have to be conditional; it could simply be a matter of service.

One night, as they finished assembling a bookshelf, David set down his hammer and looked at her. "You know, Rose, you're the bravest person I've ever met."

Sarah met his gaze, surprised. "I don't feel brave. I just feel... awake."

David smiled. "Sometimes, that's enough."

David had done more than just fix the apartment; he had silently rebuilt Sarah's self-worth. In this atmosphere of simple, non-judgmental acceptance, Sarah slowly fell in love with him. He didn't ask her to be godly, beautiful, or obedient; he simply asked her to be safe. His presence—steady, strong, and entirely reliable—was the only thing that made the thought of the future not only bearable but possible. David was the proof that grace could exist outside the church walls, that unconditional love was not a trap, but a safe harbor.

A Vetting by Marta

One afternoon, before her pregnancy forced her to stop working entirely, Sarah was caught in a fierce summer deluge. She was forced to wait out the rainstorm with Marta in the motel's cramped storage closet. The rhythmic drumming of the rain on the roof and the constant, chemical scent of bleach and stale mop water made the small space feel strangely intimate.

Marta, who had keenly observed David's patient vigil over Sarah for weeks, didn't mince words. She leaned against a high stack of clean towels, her eyes following the streaks of rain on the tiny, high window.

"That man, David," Marta began, her voice a low, gravelly hum. "He is always here. Always waiting. I have seen men like Frank, always taking what they need. I have seen men like Jonathan, always looking for fun, like a dog chasing a shadow. But David, he is different."

Sarah looked away, defensive, her hand automatically resting on the curve of her belly. "He's just... a friend, Marta. He helps me with things. He fixed the faucet."

Marta chuckled, a warm, knowing sound that carried the weight of years. "He is not just helping you, Rose. He is building with you. He sees the life you are making. He is building the wall that keeps the bad men out, the bad memories out. He doesn't ask where you came from. He only asks if you ate today. That is the only question that matters."

"But why?" Sarah whispered, the raw question finally escaping her. "Why is he doing this? Nobody does something for nothing."

Marta looked Sarah in the eye, her gaze steady. "You're afraid of him because he's good, and you expect everything good to have a hidden cost—like the church or your parents' approval. You were taught that love is something that is earned, not given. That's the sickness you brought from home, *mija*."

She gently squeezed Sarah's arm. "But some people are simply decent. If you don't let him in, you'll float away. Choose the anchor he offers." The rain's drumming underscored Marta's warning.

The conversation was a mirror, reflecting Sarah's deepest fear: the fear that unconditional kindness was a trap. But Marta's pragmatic wisdom—that David was a stable, fixed point and not a judge—finally shattered the conditioning of Havenwood. It was the last bit of outside validation she would receive before committing fully to her new life. She realized her mother had failed her, her father had condemned her, but a cleaning lady in a supply closet was offering her the courage to accept grace from a factory worker.

CHAPTER 11

THE QUIET SHELTER

The small studio apartment, though cramped and carrying the faint scent of hydraulic fluid from David's clothes, was the first space Sarah had ever known that offered true amnesty. It was only one step above a flophouse, yet to Sarah, it felt like a sanctuary. The single window overlooked a brick fire escape and a brick wall, but the quiet she experienced there was the sound of grace.

She had spent the first several months in a state of hyper-vigilance. The ingrained Havenwood mandate—your worth is in your labor—was now dangerously intensified by the powerful, irrational nesting instinct of late pregnancy.

She scrubbed the already-clean linoleum floors and polished the few pieces of thrift-store furniture David had acquired, working constantly until her muscles ached. Every motion was a fight. The simple act of bending over was excruciating as the baby's weight pressed down on her pelvic girdle. She found herself scrubbing on her hands and knees because she couldn't stand the strain on her lower back, only to have the baby kick fiercely under her ribs, stealing her breath. Her hands were permanently swollen with carpal tunnel, making gripping the mop handle painful. The fear of being a "burden" or a "liability"—the greatest sin in her father's eyes—was a physical compulsion, making her feel unworthy of the shelter unless she was in constant motion.

David found her one afternoon, heavily pregnant and breathing shallowly after trying to lift a large, heavy bucket of mop water. He didn't rage, critique, or look disappointed. He just quietly took the mop, set the bucket down, and gently guided her to the dilapidated armchair.

"No, Rose. Stop," he said, his hands firm on her shoulders. "You don't need to earn your place here. You don't need to earn my help. Your job right now is simply to breathe. I want to do this. Your body is doing enough, growing that baby and resting."

His words struck her with the force of a physical blow. The absolute lack of condition in his voice was terrifying—it defied the very physics of her known universe. In Havenwood, rest was considered the devil's workshop. She stared at him, unable to comprehend a love that demanded nothing in return, only her presence.

The Grace of Stillness

The hardest adjustment wasn't the poverty or the city's noise; it was learning to be still. Even sitting was complicated. She had to constantly shift position because of numbness in her hips or the sharp, sudden pressure of the baby dropping. Lying down brought immediate, fiery heartburn that crept up her throat, forcing her to prop herself up with mismatched pillows.

Yet, she forced herself to sit on the small, warm vinyl cushion by the window, feeling the late-day sunlight, and simply exist. David brought home cheap, oversized library books—tales of adventure and faraway places—and she read them aloud to the bump of her growing child.

"It's not good for the baby to sit all day," she tried to argue one-night, folding David's work clothes with aggressive precision, trying to find a reason to keep moving. "I should be useful."

David just stopped her hands, holding the bundle of clothes. "You are useful, Rose, just by being here. You're safe. Right here. Let the world stand still for a minute. It won't fall apart if you do nothing."

The stillness itself was a quiet crucible. In the absence of endless tasks, the noise in her own mind became deafening, forcing her to confront the years of internalized shame she had carried. Her thoughts, previously muffled by nonstop labor, screamed at her that she was lazy, selfish, and a failure—the echoes of Robert's cold disapproval.

He taught her the grace of simple, unearned comfort. He would sit on the edge of the bed and patiently clean the grease from his hands, telling her about the broken-down bus motors, the complexity of gears and timing. He spoke of mechanics, not theology—of solving problems that were tangible and real. There was a cleansing beauty in his logic; every failed machine had a recognizable, physical fault, not a spiritual one.

One damp, chill afternoon, Marta appeared at the apartment door, carrying a brown paper sack filled with fresh oranges—a precious commodity in their neighborhood, a burst of sunshine against the gray city. Marta had tracked Sarah down, a feat of simple, protective determination, a silent promise that Sarah was still seen. David was out working, and Sarah let Marta in, feeling a mix of gratitude and the old, familiar shame of exposure.

Marta ignored the worn furniture and the thin carpet. Her gaze immediately settled on the corner David had transformed—the small crib painted soft yellow. She walked over, placing the sack of oranges next to it.

"This man, David," Marta said, turning to Sarah, her eyes dark and serious. "He is building a nest here, mija. He is not tearing you down to build himself up. He just keeps building the walls higher, keeping the cold out."

Sarah looked away, the question forming a familiar lump in her throat. "But why? I don't... I don't have anything to give him. He should be with someone better."

Marta chuckled, a warm, knowing sound. "You think you must pay for kindness, like a bill at the church door. But David, he is not from the church, no? He is from the world. In the world, sometimes kindness is just a gift." Marta pointed to the tiny, struggling houseplant Sarah was keeping alive on the windowsill. "You give that plant water, not because it works hard, but because it needs it to live. David is giving you water, Rose. You must drink."

The conversation was brief, but Marta's pragmatic, worldly wisdom cut through the theological fog of Sarah's upbringing. She confirmed what Sarah feared and desperately hoped: David was not a trap. He was a safe harbor. The kindness didn't stop there. Before she left, Marta pressed a small card into Sarah's hand—the address for the local WIC office, a federal program for Women, Infants, and Children, which provides nutritional assistance. Sarah felt a surge of the familiar shame at the idea of taking charity, but David saw it differently. "That's not charity, Rose. That's a social contract. You gave them your tax money, now they're giving you milk for the baby. It's just part of the world," he reasoned, successfully defusing her conditioned guilt. Marta had delivered her blessing and, without needing to be asked, left as quietly as she had come, leaving Sarah alone to face the undeniable truth. The apartment felt warmer after she left, heavier with the weight of recognized, honest love—a foundation that Havenwood had actively denied her.

In the hyper-present quiet of the final, agonizing days, the apartment became a pressurized cocoon of preparation. David now kept his hand constantly on her belly, waiting not just for a powerful kick, but for the first insistent sign of labor. The baby's movements were so forceful, they made Sarah gasp—a sudden, sharp jolt of pain right under her ribs—marking the raw intimacy of their shared anticipation.

One evening, staring out the window at the endless neon blur of the city, she finally broke. The emotional pressure of not having to perform—the relief that overwhelmed her—erupted in hot, heavy tears.

"David," she whispered, her voice barely audible, thick with shame. "I'm scared I'm going to ruin this. I don't know how to be a mother without... without rules. I don't know how to give love that isn't conditional."

David moved behind her, placing his hands on the curve of her belly, anchoring her to the present moment. "You already know how," he murmured against her hair. "You know what not to do. That's the best rule there is. We're going to make our own rules, Rose. And the first one is: Love first. Always."

In that tiny, shared space, the fear of Havenwood finally began to recede, replaced by the profound, quiet certainty of a shared future built on a foundation of grease, cheap linoleum, and unconditional love. The quiet shelter of Sarah's apartment, with its scent of old wood and paint, was preparing her for the greatest, most terrifying act of faith: becoming a mother. She was not learning how to give love; she was learning how to receive it.

CHAPTER 12

A NEW COVENANT

The labor was long, grinding, and brutal, the physical ordeal stretching Sarah's endurance to its absolute limit. It was thankfully conducted in the total anonymity of the city hospital's noisy general ward, a chaotic environment where the staff only cared about the precise metrics of the clock and the vital signs. Sarah used the name Rose for every form, sealing her separation from Havenwood—the simple lie felt like a necessary, protective shield. The room was bathed in harsh, relentless fluorescent light, and the air was thick with the chemical odor of antiseptic and the metallic tang of blood.

The physical pain was relentless, a wave of agony that stripped away everything but the immediate necessity of survival. Yet, the physical suffering was compounded by a far worse, internalized torment. During the worst of the contractions, old, toxic religious programming, honed by years of Reverend Smith's booming thunder, erupted in her mind: *This is punishment. You deserve this pain for your sins. You left the flock, and now you pay the price in the flesh.* The pain wasn't just physical; it felt like a moral validation of the cosmic debt she believed she owed. She gripped the cold, worn bed rails so hard her knuckles turned white, fighting not only the contractions but the crippling conviction that this suffering was merely the opening act of her eternal damnation.

But David, true to the quiet promise of his nature, stayed by her side. His presence was her only anchor in the relentless, isolating pain. The sterile room was loud with the doctor's clipped, professional demands, yet David remained a pocket of absolute, unmoving calm. He didn't quote scripture or demand fortitude, which would have felt like the cold judgment of her father. He simply held her hand, his own calloused palm warm and firm against her chilled, slick skin. His touch—practical, honest, and grounded—was a counter-sermon to the judgment in her mind.

He wiped the sweat from her brow with a soft, clean cloth, his movements gentle and patient, utterly focused. "Breathe, Rose. You're strong. Just breathe," he repeated, his voice low and steady, filtering out the surrounding noise.

Sarah choked out a word through gritted teeth. "I can't... I can't do this, David. It hurts too much."

His grip tightened, not out of command, but solidarity. "You are doing it. Look at me. Every time you breathe out, you are winning. Don't look at the light, look at me. Stay here with me. You are almost there."

His strength was a non-judgmental comfort. He didn't flinch from the reality of the blood and the sweat, treating the messy event with a quiet reverence Sarah had never known. His hand, worn and hardened from a life spent fixing things, was a physical testament to a grace that demanded nothing in return—only her focus and her will to survive. He was a silent, living proof that she was worthy of being cared for, even in her most vulnerable, desperate state.

When Sarah's daughter, Lily, was finally born, the event seemed to break the world open. The doctor's voice faded, the pain receded, and the baby's bright, immediate cry shattered the exhaustion and the silence of her trauma. In that sound, Sarah felt the shackles of her past fall away and shatter. It was the first moment in her entire life that felt entirely untainted by judgment, fear, or condition.

David was there, holding her hand, his face wet with tears of simple, unreserved love for both mother and child. He looked not at the nurses, or the doctor, or the world, but only at Sarah and the tiny, squalling life she had created.

As the doctor placed Lily in her arms—a small, warm, slick bundle of perfect humanity—Sarah felt a perfect, overwhelming sense of being anchored for the very first time.

David leaned in, his own breath ragged with emotion, and gently brushed his finger across Lily's miniature hand. "She's perfect, Rose. She has your spark," he whispered, his voice thick with wonder.

Sarah looked up at him, a slow, radiant smile transforming her face. "Her name is Lily," she confirmed, the sound quiet but firm. "It's a small, honest name. She doesn't need a congregation."

David simply nodded, his eyes mirroring her resolve. "Lily. Our new covenant." In that tiny, clean hospital room, surrounded by the reality of the city, they were a complete, untouchable family.

In the absolute quiet moments following the birth, Sarah's hyper-attuned senses, still ringing from the labor, focused on the sharp, chemical smell of antiseptic and the stark reality of the sterile room. But as she inhaled the clean, milky scent of Lily in her arms, it instantly replaced the fear-laced odors, becoming a potent, real-world antidote to the abstract dread that had governed her existence.

A Mother's Vow

The moment the doctor handed over her daughter, Sarah's brain was flooded with a tidal wave of oxytocin and endorphins. The intense hormonal surge acted like a profound, chemical exorcism, flushing out the remnants of fear and guilt. She didn't regard the child as a divine responsibility or as atonement for sin; she regarded her with a fierce, blinding, biological truth. Lily was not a theological debt to be paid, but a sovereign being to be protected.

Sarah's gaze locked onto her daughter's tiny, wrinkled face. This was the act of imprinting, and in that primal moment of skin-to-skin contact, the entire, rigid architecture of Havenwood's doctrine crumbled and disappeared. Lily's absolute, inherent worth—a gift simply for existing—became the only law Sarah needed. Lily was her new faith, her new focus, and her new moral compass. Her devotion was immediate, absolute, and unconditional, a sacred, secular promise whispered over the crib. This clean slate was not granted by any priest; it was fought for and earned with her own body.

The small, sterile hospital room quickly became Sarah's new sanctuary. David, radiating a quiet, profound pride that made him seem ten feet tall, was constantly in motion. He didn't have the money for traditional, frivolous flowers, but his determination to provide was expressed through practical, life-sustaining acts.

He brought her warm, nourishing broth from a nearby deli and meticulously cleaned the countertop. "You look tired, Rose," he'd whisper, gently rubbing her shoulder before checking on Lily. "Just tell me what you need. I'll get it. Don't worry about anything but resting."

The next day, Marta arrived, bypassing the formal welcome desk. She wore her work uniform and carried a small, hand-knitted baby sweater in a vibrant, hopeful cherry blossom.

"She is perfect, mija," Marta whispered, her huge, gaping smile lighting up her face. "So tiny. You did well, Rose. You fought for this life."

Marta stayed for a full, comforting hour, focusing entirely on the logistics of caring for a newborn. "You don't need to be quiet," Marta commanded. "You need to be effective. Sleep when the baby sleeps, and don't worry about the dishes." It was a final, essential lesson in unconditional acceptance, based on practical experience rather than abstract morality.

The sheer expense of the hospital stay—even at the city's cheapest clinic—made the reality of their new life stark and immediate. The thick, manila envelope of medical bills, delivered without ceremony, landed on the tiny kitchen counter with a cold thud.

Sarah stared at the column of astronomical numbers, the paper a physical representation of the massive financial debt they now carried. The paralyzing fear of her childhood resurfaced. *I wasn't earning my keep. I was a liability.* The terror of failing David and destroying his generosity was almost as intense as the pain of labor.

But when the thick envelope of bills arrived, David didn't hesitate. He made the commitment official, not with a wedding ring, but with a practical, permanent gesture. He quit his tiring, chaotic night shift and immediately secured a better-paying, steady day job doing heavy mechanical repairs for a city bus fleet.

He returned home every evening, his hands permanently stained with black grease and motor oil. This new routine ensured he was home every evening to share dinner, help rock Lily to sleep, and attend to Sarah. His consistent, unwavering presence was the true, deep security Sarah had always craved.

"You need to rest and be with Lily," he insisted one evening, pulling her close, the scent of motor oil and clean soap comforting her like a benediction. "This is your job now. We'll be fine. I'm strong enough for all three of us."

Sarah clung to him, the tears starting to fall again. "But the bills, David. The debt is so high. I have to find something, I can't just be... taken care of. I don't know how to be a liability."

He pulled back just enough to look her in the eye, wiping a tear streak with a greasy thumb. "Listen to me, Rose. You are not a liability. You are my family. You fought the world and brought Lily into it. That's worth more than any paycheck. The debt is ours, and I'll take care of it. I'm telling you this isn't a temporary fix. This is permanent. I'm not going anywhere."

"I believe you," she managed, resting her head back on his shoulder. "Thank you. For everything."

This quiet moment was a complete and staggering reversal of her entire childhood. She was safe, finally and absolutely. She rested her head on his shoulder, letting the decades-long fear drain away. The debt was paid, not with the currency of repentance or sacrifice, but with the simple, unconditional truth of his acceptance.

CHAPTER 13

A LIFE EARNED

The anxiety was silent. The long, cold night was over. Sarah's internal war had culminated in a deep, unshakeable conviction: the sanctuary was complete, and there was nothing left to earn. Months had passed, and the external reality began to match that conviction. David didn't propose marriage, nor did Sarah expect it. The formalities of the past—vows, public ceremony, and reputation—were utterly meaningless to her, reminders of a life built on rigid, enforced rules. He was simply her family; his commitment, a practical, non-negotiable reality built on the foundation of his new day shift.

He now worked heavy mechanical repairs for the city bus fleet, and that schedule was a quiet revolution. It ensured his presence was a daily, non-negotiable certainty. The rhythmic sound of his key turning in the lock every evening at 5:30 p.m. became the most comforting sound in her world, a constant, physical promise.

This consistent reliability—the man who came home—was the true, deep security Sarah had always craved. David was her anchor—solid, immovable, and entirely focused on their small, shared life. His constancy was the antidote to every unstable relationship and every conditional love she had ever known. His love was expressed entirely in actions, not words—a language Sarah finally understood and trusted after a lifetime of hollow sermons.

Sarah pressed her face into his shirt, but the words still caught in her throat. "But it feels... wrong," she admitted, her voice muffled. "I feel guilty just being here, like I should be out there, earning my keep. I don't know how to just be a liability."

David pulled back, placing his hands on her shoulders. His gaze was steady, cutting through her anxiety like a sharp tool. "Rose, listen to me. Being a liability is what your old life told you. You are my family, and that is a contribution. You brought Lily into the world. You manage this home. That's worth more than any paycheck I'll ever earn, and it's not conditional. Stop auditing your own worth. You are not a number on a ledger."

She swallowed, the fear receding a millimeter. "It's hard to stop. They taught me that if I stopped working, the love stopped, too."

"Then let me teach you something else," David said softly, pulling her in for a crushing hug. "Love is the anchor, not the boat's engine. It holds steady, no matter the storm."

This quiet, non-theological moment was a complete and staggering reversal of her entire childhood. In Havenwood, her worth was contingent upon unfailing labor and a meticulous public reputation. Now, her value was based on her simple being, on the core fact that she was the mother of the daughter he loved and the partner of his life.

The interior of their tiny apartment had undergone a profound sensory transformation, a change far more meaningful than any cosmetic repair. The oppressive atmosphere of Sarah's anxiety had been purged, replaced by the smells of creation and care: faint whiffs of clean linen and baby food, and the robust, warm yeast from David's homemade bread—a simple skill he practiced religiously every Sunday morning, filling the apartment with an edible promise of sustenance.

The thin tenement walls still let in the city's chaotic noise—shouts, bass music, distant traffic—but David had taught her to filter it. The city's noise was non-critical; it was indifferent. This indifference became a form of freedom, allowing Sarah to focus only on the safe, small sounds within their circle: the happy, rhythmic babbling of Lily, the comfortable whir of the old fan, and the low, steady sound of David's own breathing.

They created a simple, beautiful life amidst the chaotic, sprawling city—a life built on deliberate intention and quiet routine. The tiny apartment, though still showing its age with damp stains and creaking floorboards, became a sanctuary of domestic warmth. Every evening, the single bare lightbulb over the dinner table seemed to cast a soft, protective, golden glow over their small family.

On David's days off, they would undertake their weekly ritual: a trip to the small, neglected public park nearby. The park was crude—a meager square of cracked concrete, rusting metal playground equipment, and worn grass. Yet, for them, it was their sacred piece of the outdoors. David, ever the mechanic, had brought tools on his first visit to fix the two working bolts on the rusty swing set himself, ensuring Lily's safety with his own hands. This gesture—fixing the broken world for his family—was profound.

One Saturday, as they sat on the splintered bench, Sarah watched David hold Lily tight against his chest as he stood, slowly swaying with her in the low-hanging swing he had repaired.

"You know, I never thought I'd be grateful for a rusty swing set," she said, her voice filled with quiet joy.

David flashed a grin. "It's not the swing—it's who's flying."

Sarah laughed. "I think you're both flying."

Lily, held close to her father, let out a delighted, wordless squeal as the swing arced gently.

David winked at Sarah. "I'd better listen to the boss."

Sarah leaned back, the warmth of the late sun on her face, thinking that this was as close to paradise as she had ever come.

"I always thought beauty had to be clean," Sarah murmured, leaning back. "Like the church's polished wood and the white walls. But this place… It's broken, David. The grass is worn, the paint is peeling, and it's still the most peaceful place I've ever been."

David glanced over his shoulder, smiling the wide, unguarded smile she loved. "It's honest, Rose. It is what it is. No pretense. No one here cares if you stained your skirt or if the swing set is perfect. It's just sun and dirt and the sound of Lily laughing. That's good enough for me."

"It's good enough for me too," she whispered, feeling the perfect, unearned contentment wash over her.

The New Scripture: A Vow of Grace

Lily's growth set the precise, non-negotiable rhythm of their days. Sarah no longer operated by the arbitrary, fear-driven schedule of her past; she lived by the pure, honest demands of her daughter's needs—feeding, changing, and napping. This routine was a form of therapy, forcing her into the unthreatening present moment.

David was an attentive, dedicated father. He came home every evening exhausted from the heavy, bone-jarring labor, yet he always found the energy for their shared, vital rituals. He managed bath time every night, carefully supporting Lily's slippery, tiny body in the plastic wash basin. And he always delivered the bedtime story, his deep voice a comforting, low rumble.

One evening, Sarah paused in the doorway and watched David kneeling by the crib, his huge, grease-stained hand resting with exquisite gentleness on Lily's tiny, breathing back. He wasn't praying in the formal, condemnatory manner of her father; he was whispering a low, wordless lullaby—a pure transfer of protection and love.

David stood up, running a hand through his perpetually messy hair, and noticed Sarah in the doorway. He walked over, leaning against the doorframe next to her.

"She's asleep," he whispered.

"I know," Sarah replied, her voice low. "I was watching. That's what you call praying, isn't it? Just... being present."

He nodded, his arm wrapping around her shoulder. "I don't need a rule book to tell me how to love my two favorite people, Rose. I'm just telling her, 'I'm here. I'm going to keep you safe.' That's all the scripture I need now."

Sarah leaned into his solid, tired shoulder. "My father's prayers always felt like a threat. A demand for penance. Yours feels like a promise."

"It is a promise," David confirmed, kissing the top of her head. "No hidden clauses. No threats of withdrawal."

It was in these simple, quiet acts—the dependable routine, the constant tenderness— that Sarah discovered a sacredness she'd never known before. The simple, physical goodness of David—his capacity for patient, unconditional love—was her new scripture. His life was a daily sermon preached through labor and gentleness. Their home was consecrated not by a pastor's pronouncement, but by the tangible, daily proof that love was an action, a commitment, and a shield.

For months, the knowledge of the looming hospital debt hung like a phantom over Sarah, a symbol of moral and financial failure she felt she must repay. Though David had silently taken over the crushing burden, liquidating his modest life savings to make the payments, Sarah couldn't shake the anxiety until the final proof arrived.

One chilly Saturday morning, David came home from the post office. He held a thin, white envelope, but instead of the usual grim receipt, it contained a Statement of Zero Balance. He didn't wave it or celebrate; he simply handed it to Sarah as she fed Lily breakfast.

Sarah opened it, her hands trembling. The words, simple and blunt— "ACCOUNT PAID IN FULL. BALANCE DUE: $0.00"—hit her with the force of a revelation. This was the true, final act of their liberation.

She dropped the letter and buried her face against his chest, tears finally coming, not of guilt, but of profound, unearned relief. "It's finished," she choked out.

"It is finished, Rose," David confirmed, holding her tight. "No more debt. No more conditions."

The emotional pressure Sarah had been carrying since adolescence—the tight, constant coil of fear and performance anxiety—finally dissolved in the security of David's embrace. She was entirely absorbed, watching her daughter, feeling the perfect, heavy weight of contentment settle over her. *I earned this life through my sacrifice and my fight,* she thought with firm conviction. The anxiety was silent. The decades-long chase for worth was over. The sanctuary was complete, built on acceptance, not labor. There was nothing left to earn, only the simple, precious task of maintaining this perfect, peaceful, unconditional present.

CHAPTER 14

THE FULLNESS OF TIME

Their life transitioned seamlessly from the sweltering, anxious city heat of late summer into the crisp, gold-tinged air of autumn, and later, the quiet, bone-deep chill of early winter. The seasons changed, marking the steady passage of time not with upheaval, but with gentle inevitability. For the first time, Sarah felt herself settling into the rhythms of a life that was not dictated by crisis. This slow, predictable shift in the environment was a profound comfort. The passage of time was no longer a frantic countdown, but a quiet, joyful measure of Lily's rapid growth—the baby learning to hold her head up, then to roll, then to sit—and the steadfast certainty of David's love.

David's job repairing the city bus fleet—a noisy, grueling labor in the massive repair depot that Sarah never quite understood but fiercely respected—was the true, measurable foundation of their peace. He was a man of predictable routines and tangible output. Every afternoon, he would return home, smelling faintly of hot engine oil and metal dust, the grime deeply set in the calluses of his hands.

"How was the floor today?" Sarah would ask, taking his lunch pail, as he peeled off his work gloves.

"Sticky," he'd grunt, heading for the sink. "They're running the high-pressure hydraulics, so the air's thick with mist. Pay's good, though. Better than last month."

"Good pay means safety," Sarah would confirm, a financial fact that felt more concrete than any theological promise.

He would pause at the sink, rinsing the grit from his forearms. "It means we buy the expensive laundry detergent, Rose. And we pay the rent on time. It means we don't worry."

Sarah dried her hands on a towel, folding it neatly. "And because we don't worry, I can start planning. I was thinking... maybe a shift or two. Go back to cleaning at the motel."

David stopped scrubbing. "Cleaning? Why? We're fine, Rose."

"I know we are," she confirmed quickly, her gaze steady. "But I want to help build this safety net. Your pay is solid, but I want to contribute to our total. My own work, adding to what we have, for Lily. It's time we build our future together, not just rely on one income."

Unlike the clean, sterile, and performative virtue of her past, David's virtue was expressed in the dirt and the exhaustion he brought home. She trusted the weight of his tools and the honesty of his labor more than any scripture.

For Thanksgiving, a holiday Sarah had only ever associated with forced piety and excessive labor, David insisted on ownership of the day. He brought home a small, manageable turkey and, with the gentlest authority, commanded her to rest.

"I'm cooking," he announced, already tying an apron over his jeans. "No discussion, Rose. You're the guest."

The apartment, despite its tiny size, quickly filled with the rich, earthy, warm scent of roasting sage, melting butter, and slow-browning meat. Lily, safe and sound, was contentedly asleep in her carrier, tucked away near the warm radiator, oblivious to the culinary commotion. The air was thick with the honest smell of cooking, a visceral world away from the bland, duty-bound meals of her past.

Sarah leaned against the cool metal of the doorframe, sipping tea, unable to fully relax. "I feel completely useless just standing here," she confessed, watching him move with focused, proud energy. "My father would have me shucking corn and rolling out pastry dough simultaneously right now. It feels wrong to just... wait."

David stopped separating the meat, his knife resting on the cutting board. He looked at her, his expression warm but serious. "Rose, you've earned the right to feel wrong about something that felt right for them. You're doing the hard work of resting today. That's your job. What are you going to do—stand guard over the gravy?"

Sarah smiled slightly, a reluctant relaxation softening her shoulders. "It's just strange. I keep thinking I should be *earning* this comfort."

"You don't earn love, you receive it," he said simply, wiping his hands and taking her teacup to refill it with water. "That's the whole point of today. Now, sit down before I tie you to the radiator."

They soon sat at the tiny kitchen table, their plates laden with turkey, mashed potatoes, and roasted vegetables. David raised his glass of tap water, the surface shimmering in the golden light. He didn't offer a prayer, but a clear, grounded vow.

"To us," he said, his voice deep and steady. "To find the safe harbor when we thought we were lost."

"And to this food," Sarah added, her voice thick with relief. "It smells like it was cooked by someone who genuinely cares."

"It was," he confirmed, meeting her eyes. "No conditions on this plate, Rose. Just enjoy it."

The First Unassisted Steps

Their weekly ritual at the small public park, previously just a concrete patch of survival, became a sanctuary of sound and color during the autumn months. The air was now crisp and sharp, carrying the scent of damp earth and impending winter. The ground was transformed, no longer just cracked pavement, but covered in a thick, crunchy carpet of amber and crimson leaves. They walked slowly, their footsteps making a satisfying, resonant whisper.

"I love the sound of this," Sarah said, pausing to kick up a small spray of gold and crimson. "It drowns everything else out. It's like we're walking on a cloud of old time."

David nodded, adjusting Lily's scarf. "It's nature's honest rhythm. Just leaves and gravity. You know, I used to hate autumn in the city. It just meant cold work and long nights. Now... it means scarves and you bundling Lily up like a little bear."

"She does look like a bear," Sarah agreed, smiling. "But she smells like sunshine and baby powder. It's a vast improvement on a regular bear."

On one particularly memorable, wind-whipped day, Lily—now toddling confidently but still preferring to clutch a steady hand—took her first true, unassisted steps. She had been clinging tightly to the cold, rusty swing chain, determined to stand on her own but nervous about letting go.

"Lily-bug! Come to Papa!" David called, crouching low among the scattered leaves, his massive hands held open wide.

Lily looked from David to Sarah, her small brow furrowed in concentration. She let go of the chain. Just before her first impossible step, she issued a triumphant, gravelly sound, directed at the open arms waiting for her: "P-Pa."

For Sarah, the simple, honest syllable was a physical shock. It wasn't a demanding prayer or a theological mandate—it was a statement of trust, pure and without condition. It was the first pure word spoken in the new life they had built. A tear ran down her cheek, instantly cooled by the wind.

Lily took three wobbly steps across the leaf-strewn pavement, her tiny shoes shuffling through the dry, crackling leaves, pitching headfirst straight into David's massive, waiting embrace.

David roared with proud, deep laughter, holding her high. "She walked, Rose! And she said 'Papa'!"

Sarah moved quickly, but with a sudden, quiet reverence. "She did," she whispered, reaching out to stroke Lily's cheek. "She chose her word, and she walked right to the person who deserved it."

As David gently lowered Lily, Sarah slowly stepped back, absorbing the image. The sunlight caught the brilliant gold in the scattered autumn leaves and the powerful, proud relief on David's face. The scene was a perfect, crystalline image of protection and simple, uncomplicated love.

This is everything I built, she thought, the absolute conviction settling deep inside her like a warm, heavy stone. *Not God, not the church, not my father—me. With David.* The sanctuary was complete. The years of performance were over. She had earned her grace, and she would guard this unconditional present fiercely.

CHAPTER 15

A NECESSARY REBELLION

Sarah's hard-won peace in late autumn—a home shaped by David's steady labor and Lily's comforting routines—was about to be tested: Christmas was coming. For Sarah, the holiday brought a flood of old anxieties: memories of Havenwood's cold austerity, performative charity, and the forced gratitude she was expected to show. David understood the weight of these memories. Determined to rewrite them, he set out to make this Christmas different—a season of real warmth, not obligation. They couldn't afford a real pine tree, but David improvised. He found a string of colored lights—the slightly erratic kind that blinked out of sync—and spent an evening carefully winding them around the tall, battered mirror that stood against their living room wall. Lily was nearby, sitting contentedly and stacking bright plastic rings, as David transformed the mirror into the glowing heart of their celebration, reflecting and multiplying the small, bright defiance of their new tradition.

David stepped back, satisfied, and plugged the cord into the nearest wall socket. The room instantly sparked with color—ruby reds, emerald greens, and sapphire blues. The mirror's reflection multiplied every point of light into a shimmering, festive forest.

"It's a mirror-tree," he announced with a flourish. "It doubles the cheer and halves the pine needles, which is good for Lily and my cleaning time."

Sarah felt a surge of pure, uncomplicated joy. She hadn't felt this emotion without an accompanying pang of guilt since she was a small child. She laughed, a genuine, easy sound. "It's spectacular, David. It feels like we're finally making our own rules—like we're claiming a little bit of joy for ourselves, even when the world said we couldn't."

"A necessary one," he murmured, his gaze soft as the light played over his face. "Christmas should be nothing but joy. You don't have to report on it later. You just get to have it."

Later that evening, David presented a second gift: a small, secondhand train set—a tiny engine and three faded, chipped cars. It wasn't perfect, but when he finally got it running, it chugged with a high-pitched, insistent, rattling sound around the perimeter of Lily's crib. Lily, sitting up in her crib and clutching the worn wood of the rail, was utterly mesmerized by the hypnotic, clattering journey. The persistent, mechanical noise was a comforting, domestic racket, a clear sign that the simple magic of the season was alive and well within their four walls.

As Lily watched the train, David quietly came up behind Sarah, slipping his arm around her waist and pulling her close. His presence was an anchor.

"I know your Christmases weren't easy, Rose," he murmured, his voice low and solemn. "No joy, just expectation. Always having to earn the blessing. But this is ours now. No guilt. No performance. Just the light, and the two of you."

He reached out, his hand still bearing the faint, indelible mark of engine grease from his work, and gently traced the line of her jaw with his thumb. "I don't need a sermon or a stained-glass window to tell me what's holy," he stated with profound conviction. "This is quiet. This train. This small girl is sleeping safely. This is holy."

Sarah leaned her head heavily on David's strong shoulder. "It feels... blessed," she admitted, the word slipping out before she could stop it—a remnant of old conditioning.

She straightened slightly, correcting herself firmly. "No, not blessed," she insisted, her voice low and fiercely determined. "Not by anyone who demands payment. This isn't grace, this is real. You made it real. You built this joy with your hands and your sacrifice." She looked up at him, her eyes clear. "You are my proof, David. Not faith. You."

She kissed his cheek, a clear, intentional act of devotion. "Thank you. For giving me Christmas back."

"You never lost it," David smiled, kissing the top of her head. "You just had to find a quiet corner to open the package."

The Need for Severance

The security and unconditional light of their small, sparkling Christmas gave Sarah a surprising and powerful final wave of resolve. She felt a strong, undeniable urge to make a final statement to her past, not for reconciliation, but for absolute, permanent closure. It was the need for an official ending, a ceremony of severance.

She walked three blocks to the pharmacy, stepping deliberately through the crisp winter air, and bought the plainest Christmas card she could find—a generic watercolor landscape of snow and bare trees, utterly devoid of any religious imagery.

She sat at the kitchen table late that night, the only light coming from the gentle, cycling colors of the mirror-tree. David and Lily were asleep. She took the pen, her hand trembling slightly, tempted to write a manifesto of pain and justification. But she stopped. That was the old game.

She didn't sign her birth name, Sarah, nor her new name, Rose. She simply wrote three lines inside the card, choosing her words with meticulous, surgical care, cutting the past away with each stroke of the pen:

I am well. I am safe. I am loved.

She sealed the envelope with a faint, exhilarating sense of triumph and severance. Crucially, she wrote only her parents' address in Havenwood, leaving the return address entirely blank. This was a declaration of freedom, an irreversible act of psychological rebellion proving to herself that their judgment no longer held any power over her present.

She slipped out early the next morning, walking six blocks—far beyond her usual route—to the central post office. The air was sharp and cold. She held the card for a final moment, noting the clean line of the seal, before dropping it into the slot with a decisive clatter. As the card disappeared, she felt a profound, physical sense of cutting the final tether. She was not running from them anymore; she was simply and powerfully walking forward, into a life entirely her own.

Marta's invitation to a small New Year's Day gathering quietly expanded their circle of unconditional acceptance. Marta's apartment, just a few blocks away, was a sensory explosion the moment they stepped over the threshold: vibrant colors on the walls, woven blankets draped over battered furniture, and an intoxicating aroma—earthy chilies, fresh cilantro chopped in a wooden bowl, warm corn masa sizzling on a griddle, and the invigorating steam of strong, dark coffee. The air itself felt thicker, seasoned with generations of shared laughter, shouted stories, and the faint, comforting scent of old candles and spices lingering in every corner. The kitchen was alive with sizzling pans and Marta's booming voice, her hands moving with practiced speed as she fed everyone who entered.

Marta met them at the door, pulling Sarah into a tight, unsolicited hug. "Rose! David! You made it. Come in, come in! Leave your worries on the stoop. We only allow good energy inside today, you hear?"

Marta's daughters and several cousins instantly enveloped them. They didn't ask about David's job or Sarah's history; they just offered food and warmth. Lily was passed from warm hand to warm hand, giggling at the flurry of attention and the mix of Spanish and English chatter.

An older woman, Abuela, with kind, weary eyes, pressed a warm, damp tamale wrapped in a corn husk into her hand. "Eat, Rose! Too thin! You must eat. New Year, new strength!" the woman insisted.

"This is amazing," Sarah murmured to David, trying to process the absolute lack of conditions. "Their acceptance is genuine; there are no questions, no demands, only generosity."

David accepted a cup of coffee and wrapped his arm around her shoulders. "They just see you, Rose. They see you as you are—a good mother, a friend. This is what family does when it works right. They are just happy you showed up. Don't overthink the motive." Even as the room filled with laughter and clinking dishes, Sarah felt a wave of humility and belonging, her senses overwhelmed by the warmth and the honest chaos. For once, she let herself relax into the noise, the food, and the easy rhythm of Marta's world, absorbing the comfort as deeply as she could.

For the first time since leaving Havenwood, Sarah felt accepted, not just by David, but by a genuine, functional, and imperfect community. This noisy, spontaneous acceptance was built on shared human kindness that asked for nothing in return. She finally understood that belonging was not a conditional reward; it was simply a gift waiting to be received.

CHAPTER 16

THE UNEARNED YEARS

The fierce, deliberate act of establishing security that defined their first year gradually gave way to the quiet, unthinking rhythm of home. They had marked the final end of their flight with a small, joyous celebration for Lily's first birthday, an intimate ceremony that finally closed the door on their years of rootlessness and established their future. With the finality of that moment, their survival narrative faded, and the years began to blur into a single, cohesive stretch. Four years folded into the four hundred square feet of their tiny apartment. The calendar ceased to mark dramatic escapes or confrontations, and began simply to measure growth: Lily's height marked in pencil strokes on the bedroom doorframe, the slow accumulation of David's savings, and the softening of Sarah's perpetually guarded posture. She had shed the anxious stiffness of her past self; her face was less drawn, her eyes less prone to darting. She didn't look back anymore. She focused entirely on the small, manageable world she had built.

They had both aged, their youth giving way to the gentle weariness of constant, fulfilling work. David's smile lines deepened, his hands perpetually stained with oil and machine grit.

Their life was now set to a predictable soundtrack dictated by the building's thin walls. David often paused on his way to the kitchen, listening, a faint, amused smile on his face.

"Hear that?" he'd whisper, leaning close to Rose. "That's Mrs. Flores next door, singing her soap opera theme song again. Off-key, bless her heart."

Rose would smile, leaning into his warmth. "It's the sound of not being alone, but also not being watched. In Havenwood, quiet meant judgment. It meant they could hear everything you weren't saying."

"Here," David agreed, pulling her tighter, "noisy means life. It means we're just part of the symphony, not the soloists on trial."

The perpetually rattling radiator, the distinct smell of curry drifting up the stairwell on Tuesdays, and the distant, muffled arguments of neighbors were no longer intrusions. They were the gentle hum of a world moving on its own axis, a world that didn't care about Sarah's past, and a world where they were finally safe to exist openly.

Lily was the undisputed sovereign of this small world. At four years old, she was a fierce, small creature of profound curiosity and absolute trust. She had her father's dark, serious eyes, but her expression held her mother's hard-won joy. She was a master of routine. Every morning, she stood by the door, her cheek pressed to the cool wood, waiting for David to turn back for her specific, ritualistic good-bye.

"Papa's going to make the machines sing!" she'd announce, her voice a perfectly pitched echo of Rose's favorite phrase for David's work.

One rainy afternoon, Lily was building a complicated structure out of the brightly colored wooden blocks David had bought her. She paused, looking up from her creation—a perfectly symmetrical spire that seemed to defy gravity.

"Papa, why do the clouds leak?" she asked, looking out the steamed window.

David paused, mid-maintenance on a motorcycle part he'd brought home. "They leak because they get too full of water, kiddo. It's too heavy to hold."

Lily turned her serious, analytical gaze to Sarah, who was sitting at the table carefully stitching a tear in a dress that Lily insisted was her 'uniform.'

"Mommy, do people leak when they get too full of sad?"

Sarah's breath hitched, a faint, familiar pain tightening her throat. She knelt down, the needle still in her hand. "Sometimes, sweetie. When they're too full, the sad has to come out."

"But you don't leak," Lily stated, touching Sarah's cheek with a damp finger. "You're empty of sad now, right?"

Sarah swallowed, glancing quickly at David, who gave her a silent, steady nod. "I am empty of sad," she confirmed, the lie a necessary protection for the small, precious person in front of her. *I am never empty of the fear of it returning,* she thought, quickly refocusing on the present. "You keep me full of other things, sweetie. Things that don't leak."

Lily, satisfied, immediately returned to her blocks. Sarah looked down at the child's serious face, bent over her geometric task. "She is everything I ever wanted," she whispered to David. "She trusts the world."

David came over, resting a heavy hand on Rose's shoulder. "That's because you showed her it was trustworthy. You created this security, Rose. There's no performance for her. She just is. She's free."

Sarah felt a wave of deep, maternal satisfaction, but also a momentary, clinical chill—a brief, externalized sense of profound, heavy predictability, like a machine running perfectly toward a known end. She immediately dismissed it. *Anxiety. Pure anxiety. The old wiring.*

Their continued anchor to the outside world was Marta, who had become more of an elected aunt. Marta's presence was vital, offering not just acceptance, but the kind of robust, messy wisdom that Sarah found completely dependable.

Every Saturday morning, Sarah would meet Marta at the corner laundromat. Lily would sit happily in the rolling laundry cart, chattering away.

"You're too quiet, *mija*," Marta said one day, pulling a clean white sheet from the dryer with a sharp snap. "You hold your breath even when the air is clean."

"I don't hold my breath," Sarah responded defensively, stirring her coffee. "I just... I plan. I make sure everything is placed correctly so it won't break. I look ahead."

Marta set the sheet down and turned, her kind, weary eyes fixed on Sarah. "And what if something breaks? What then? You think your planning is stronger than life, Rose? Your fear of the future is stronger than this beautiful thing you have now?"

"My planning is why we're here," Sarah insisted, folding Lily's tiny socks with surgical precision. "My choices. Not luck. Not anything else."

"No, *something* made sure of that," Marta countered, her voice firm. "You fought for the path, but Rose, you didn't *create* the path. You just had the bravery to run down it when it appeared. You didn't know David would be there. You didn't know I lived two blocks away. You just ran."

Sarah hesitated. "That sounds like faith, Marta. I don't have that."

"It sounds like a grateful person noticing the lights stayed green when they needed them," Marta said, dismissing the theology with a wave of her hand. "You call it luck. I call it finding the grace that was already there, even if you don't call it by His name. You earned the life, but did you earn the chance to have it? That's the part that just shows up. Stop fighting the gift."

Sarah shook her head, focusing fiercely on the small, manageable laundry tasks. "The only certainty I trust is David's paycheck and the fact that Lily will need a bigger pair of shoes next month."

Marta just patted her hand, a gesture of warm, secular benediction. "That is good, Rose. Start there. Love the small certainties. And when the big uncertainties come, you will be strong enough to meet them."

The Fullness of the Present

Lily's voice filled the apartment now, a constant, cheerful noise, testing the volume levels of their security. She was learning to string words together, creating small, perfectly formed narrative universes. She loved to curl up in the evening while David read mechanical manuals, insisting on a story about 'Mommy, the great planner,' who always knew where the sunshine was hiding.

Sarah often watched David and Lily together—the great planner and the great builder—and felt the quiet triumph of having not just survived, but created. They had settled into a fullness that felt almost dangerously absolute. She was a mother, a partner, a friend. Her past was a dead letter sealed in a post office box six blocks away.

One snowy evening, as Lily slept soundly and David fixed a leaky faucet, Sarah stood at the window, watching the city lights blur behind the falling flakes.

"What are you thinking about, Rose?" David asked, tightening the wrench.

"Nothing important," Rose replied, but then admitted, "I was just wondering... if I can hold onto this. This quiet. This much... perfection. It feels like I'm waiting for the bill to arrive."

David put down the wrench, wiping his hands on a rag. He walked over and gently turned her from the window. "The bill was paid in Havenwood, Rose. Every tear, every sleepless night. We're in the clear now. The only thing you have to hold onto is Lily and me. And we're not going anywhere. We are your certainty." He looked at her, his eyes steady and unwavering. "This isn't a debt, Rose. It's a home. And we build our homes to last."

As winter deepened, covering the city in a brief, gritty layer of snow, Sarah's sense of security became absolute. The apartment was quiet and still, holding the hard-won warmth within. Lily was settled on the floor, entirely absorbed, playing with a single, small, oil-gleaming wooden block.

Lily kept dropping the block deliberately, waiting for the clatter before looking up.

Sarah smiled, picking up the block again. "You keep testing me, little one," she murmured. "Testing to see if the world will put things back, won't you?"

"She's checking for consistency," David said from the doorway, leaning against the frame, watching them. "It's the deepest trust there is: knowing the floor will always catch the block."

Sarah watched Lily, feeling the perfect, heavy weight of contentment settle over her. She knelt beside the blanket, placing the wooden block back precisely in Lily's reach, settling easily on the floor, no longer needing to stand guard.

It is finished, she thought, the absolute, unshakeable conviction settling over her heart like concrete. The anxiety was silent. The long, cold night was over. Her flight, her fear, her years of seeking acceptance—all of it culminated here. *The sanctuary was complete. There was nothing left to earn, nothing left to fear, only the simple, precious task of maintaining this perfect, peaceful, unconditional present.* She listened to the fading sound of Lily's laughter, the quiet hum of the heater, and the distant city noise beyond the window. In this cocoon of warmth and routine, the world finally felt possible.

CHAPTER 17

THE CONTINGENCY PLAN

Six months later, their fifth-floor walk-up was bathed in the thin, hopeful light of an early spring morning. The window was open just an inch, letting in the faint, distant sounds of the city waking up—the clatter of a truck, the distant siren—sounds that Sarah no longer registered as threats, but as the steady, reliable hum of their new life. Lily was five, a whirlwind of boundless energy and precise, precocious questions, and her current fixation was kindergarten.

David and Sarah sat at the chipped kitchen table, a battlefield of coffee mugs, half-eaten toast, and glossy, brightly colored school brochures.

"Okay, let's look at the numbers again, Auditor," David teased, running a hand through his perpetually messy hair. He tapped the Riverside Prep brochure. "The tuition is steep, yes. But with the promotion and the overtime I'm putting in, we can manage it comfortably. It has the strongest science track, and it's only five blocks from the shop. I could pick her up every day."

Sarah didn't look up from her notes, which were filled with meticulous columns comparing bus routes, accreditation scores, and playground square footage. Sarah loved the structure of the data; it was controllable.

"Proximity to your work is convenient, David, but Green Meadow Co-Op is five blocks from our apartment," she countered, pushing the competing brochure across the table. "And convenience is secondary to efficiency. Riverside Prep is almost entirely a passive learning environment. Green Meadow uses a parent involvement model—you and I are in the loop. We know the teachers, we know the curriculum, we know the security measures. It keeps the world transparent."

"It keeps the world audited," David corrected, a genuine smile in his voice. He reached across the table, covering her hand with his large, warm one. "Rose, darling, the world doesn't need to be perfectly linear anymore. Lily needs to learn that life has surprises.

She is proof that surprises can be good." "She is proof that planning and dedication yield positive results," Sarah murmured, but she interlaced her fingers with his. She hated the word 'surprise.' Surprises were accidents, and accidents led to chaos. Yet, the deep satisfaction of this moment—planning their daughter's future, together, openly—was undeniable.

David had gotten his lead mechanic job two years prior under circumstances that were, in Sarah's relentless analysis, an extreme statistical anomaly. The previous candidate had suffered a minor injury and withdrew the day before starting. To David, it was a "miracle." To Sarah, it was simply the universe adjusting itself to allow her superior qualifications to prevail.

It was not luck, Sarah argued internally, watching David's happy, confident face. It was simply the failure of someone else's plan, creating an opening for mine. She quickly suppressed the lingering, unsettling thought that a benign, invisible force might actually be clearing their path. That sounded too much like the faith she had fled.

Lily suddenly emerged from under the table, disrupting the quiet tension. She stood between them, holding the small, familiar, oil-stained wooden block—the same one David had carved and given her years ago. "Mama! Papa! This block is the most important part of the spaceship," she announced, holding it up like a trophy. "It's the engine, and it makes us go straight to the new school!"

Sarah laughed, pulling Lily into a hug that smelled of morning breath, sugary cereal, and the faint, comforting trace of fabric softener from her pajamas. "That's wonderful, sweetheart. We're building your future, piece by piece, just like you build your towers." The warmth of Lily's small arms around her was grounding, a reminder that even the most uncertain days could begin with a simple, joyful embrace. "We're building our future," David echoed, his eyes meeting Sarah's over Lily's head. "Go show Marta your engine, kiddo. I think she just came up."

The Sudden Silence

The atmosphere in the room shifted instantly. Marta stood in the apartment doorway, her canvas tote slung low, but her presence was unnaturally subdued. Her usual greeting—a loud, exuberant Spanish phrase—was replaced by a forced, fragile smile. Her vibrant red blouse, typically a defiant splash of color against the city's gray, seemed jarringly out of place, almost like a warning flag.

"Marta! Come in, you look like you've been standing in the rain, and it's a beautiful day," David said, moving immediately to the small coffeemaker.

"Lily, mi vida," Marta said, her voice thin and strangely formal. She hugged Lily tightly, the embrace lingering a moment too long, a desperate clutch. "That is the best spaceship I have ever seen. You will fly to the moon and back."

Sarah felt a cold, professional stab of alarm. Marta kept pressing the back of her hand to her cheek, a nervous tic Sarah had never once witnessed in the fiercely grounded woman. She immediately slipped into crisis-management mode.

"What is it, Marta?" Sarah asked, her voice clipped, demanding facts. "Is it Miguel? Your sheets are still in the dryer at the laundromat. What's the problem?"

Marta took the coffee, but left the mug untouched. She looked from David's concerned face to Sarah's tightly controlled expression, and a flicker of profound sadness crossed her eyes. "I... I can't stay long, *mija*," she finally managed, her voice barely above a whisper.

"Why?" David asked, his posture tense.

Marta took a deep, ragged breath. "I went to the doctor last week. The lump... It's breast cancer, Rose. They say it is aggressive."

The glossy school brochures on the table suddenly looked like meaningless scraps of paper. Sarah felt the world fracture again. *The plan is compromised. The anchor is sinking.*

"Marta, no," Sarah whispered, the words catching in her throat. The words caught in her throat. She tried to lift her arm to reach across the table, but the shock was so profound it felt like a brief, internal seizure—a sudden, absolute refusal of her brain to accept the data. She forced the gesture, her hand finally meeting Marta's.

Marta grasped her hand, her skin unnaturally cold. "It's okay. We caught it early. But it is a fight. And my sons and daughter... they are waiting for me back in San Juan. They have the time and the space for the chemo. They want me home, Rose."

"Puerto Rico? You're leaving?" David's voice was hollow. "But... we need you here."

"You don't need me, David," Marta said, a tear finally escaping. "You have each other. My cousin, Hector, is taking over my apartment and my motel route. He's quiet, a good man. I'm leaving next week. This is the hardest part, Rose. Leaving you, who I watched finally, finally learn to breathe clean air."

Sarah buried her face in Marta's shoulder, the tears coming, hot and unexpected. "You always told me to trust the grace that appears, Marta. To trust the path. Why now, when everything is perfect, does this happen?"

Marta rubbed Sarah's back, her grip strong. "The path doesn't promise perfection, *mija*. It promises exactly what you need. And maybe," she pulled back, her eyes sharp and clear, "what you need now is to learn that your house stands even when a wall comes down. You built this life yourself. Not me. Not David. You. And now you are strong enough to stand alone."

The next week passed in a blur of hastily organized boxes, the shriek of packing tape, and tearful goodbyes. David and Sarah drove Marta to the bus station, Lily clutching the small, ceramic owl Marta had given her. The terminal was crowded and bright, filled with the smell of diesel and coffee, the floor sticky underfoot. Marta hugged them all tightly, her perfume a swirl of flowers and spice, her laugh trembling just beneath the surface as she fought back tears.

"We will write, Rose," Marta promised, pulling her into a final, crushing embrace. "You are my family now. You are not alone."

"Be safe," Sarah managed. The security of their world had just lost its loudest, most colorful pillar.

Driving home, the silence in the car was crushing.

"She'll be okay," David said finally, his voice thick.

"She was my contingency," Sarah whispered, staring out the window. *Sarah* felt a deep-seated, familiar panic—the fear of being exposed, of being the sole, visible target.

She glanced down at her hands resting in her lap. The panic was a physical, internal tremor, the familiar rush of blood chilling her extremities. *It must be the stress,* Sarah told herself, flexing her hands sharply until the feeling receded.

When they walked back into the apartment, Sarah looked around the small living room. The afternoon sun filtered through the window, but instead of warmth, it illuminated dust motes dancing in the air, making the room seem not cozy, but unnervingly sterile. The familiar rattling of the old radiator sounded less like the engine of life and more like the rhythmic, automated hiss of a machine sustaining existence.

It's still home, Sarah asserted fiercely, pulling Lily close. *We are here. We are safe. And we will simply adjust the plan. The plan is not broken; it just has fewer moving parts.* But this time, the conviction felt brittle, a sheer act of will against the chaos of reality.

CHAPTER 18

THE UNCONDITIONAL COVENANT

Three weeks after Marta's tearful, unsettling departure, the apartment felt like a boat that had suddenly lost its ballast. The physical structure remained—the chipped kitchen table, David's organized toolbox, Lily's bright, mismatched blocks—but the quiet, confident stability Marta's presence had always provided was gone. Now, every sound outside the window, every unexpected phone ring, sent a tremor of the old, familiar terror through Sarah's core. Marta's parting words—"what you need now is to learn that your house stands even when a wall comes down"—felt less like comfort and more like a cruel, immediate challenge. The wall had fallen, and Sarah was sure her house, built on a five-year lie, was about to follow.

David was on the floor, doing what he called "engine maintenance" on Lily's favorite wooden block—the one she insisted was the key component to her spaceship. He rubbed the block with a rag, the faint scent of machine oil mixing with the sweet, powdery smell of Lily's crayons. Lily, a whirlwind of five-year-old energy, sat opposite him on the stained rug, her face scrunched up in serious concentration as she watched him polish the oil-stained wood. The air was heavy, quiet, and deceptively peaceful, broken only by the gentle scrape of wood against cloth and the occasional giggle as Lily narrated a space adventure under her breath.

"Papa, why does Mommy not have any baby pictures of herself?" Lily asked suddenly, her voice cutting through the silence of the room like a tiny, perfectly tuned knife.

The question was so precise, so completely outside the perimeter of their carefully structured life, that Sarah froze. David didn't even flinch. He just kept rubbing the block with a cloth.

"Everyone has baby pictures, Lils," David replied easily, not looking up.

"But Mama says hers got wet when the pipes broke in her old apartment," Lily insisted, her small brow furrowing with suspicion. "And her old apartment was where her father lived, but she says she doesn't have a father. So which one is the true story, Papa?"

The air left Sarah's lungs. It was an impossible riddle solved by a five-year-old who simply sought linear truth. Her lie, once a solid fortress, had crumbled under the relentless logic of a child.

A sudden, cold wave of exhaustion passed over Sarah, not normal fatigue, but a dizzying sense of dislocation. Her body felt strangely fragile and impossibly thin, as if the physical space around her had expanded to vast and sterile proportions. The feeling was fleeting, leaving behind the faint, metallic taste of antiseptic and an intense, shivering vulnerability. (She dismissed the physical sensation: Just the pressure, gripping the edge of the chair until her knuckles were white.) But the urgent clarity of Lily's question made the truth an absolute necessity. She could not build her daughter's future on this cracked foundation.

The days after Marta's departure blurred into a haze of unease, each new question from Lily or gentle gesture from David gnawing at the secret Sarah had carried for so long. The house, which had grown so stable, now felt suspended in a fragile equilibrium, the truth straining just beneath the surface.

One evening, as twilight bled into the corners of their apartment, Lily's innocent questions grew persistent, and Sarah felt the mounting weight of her own unfinished story.

"David. It's time," Sarah said, the name 'Rose' already feeling like a costume she was shedding.

He immediately understood. He picked up Lily, kissed the top of her head, and said, "Sweetheart, why don't you go tell Marta's owl how important that engine block is? Mommy and Papa need a grown-up talk."

Lily, sensing the unusual gravity, nodded quietly and carried her block to her room.

David moved slowly to the couch next to Rose. He didn't touch her, but his steady, oil-stained hands rested on his knees, a picture of unflappable readiness. He simply waited.

"My name isn't Rose. It's Sarah," she began, the real name feeling sharp and unfamiliar on her tongue. "Sarah of Havenwood. My father, Robert, is a deacon. A powerful man built on nothing but *testimony*—on public appearance."

She paused, gathering the strength to recount years of stored shame. "When I got pregnant, it wasn't a mistake they could hide. It was a physical stain. They were going to ship me away to my aunt's house and pay for an... an elimination. They called her a stain. They called it fixing the mistake."

Her voice broke. "My father told me his reputation was my only inheritance, and I had forfeited my right to grace. He chose his pride over my life, over *her* life. I ran from all of it—the rules, the shame, the conditional love. I took the name Rose because I needed to be someone they couldn't find, someone who had no past."

Tears finally breached the fortress she had maintained for years. "I lied to you, David. About everything. For years, I have been waiting for you to find out and judge me. I am damaged goods. I am a catastrophe they had to get rid of. I risked this entire life we built... and I risked *you*."

The Unearned Covenant

David reached up and gently wiped a tear from her cheek. He didn't look shocked or betrayed. His expression was one of simple, resolute clarity.

"I knew," he said, his voice a low, steady rumble.

Sarah stared at him, bewildered. "You... what?"

"I knew Rose wasn't your whole story," he clarified, his eyes unwavering. "The way you still flinch when the apartment door slams, the way you scrub everything with too much bleach—that doesn't come from a simple divorce. That comes from running from a monster. That comes from a fear that is deep and cold."

He took her trembling hand and held it. "Rose built the fence, but Sarah built the house. The woman who works two jobs, who protects our little Lily with a fierce, quiet devotion. The woman who got up every single morning when the world told her to lie down and die, and learned to manage the fear. That's who I met. That's who I've been planning kindergarten with."

He paused, glancing toward Lily's closed door. "I don't care about a deacon's testimony, Sarah. I care about *yours*. Your truth is right here, in the next room, five years old, asking too many questions, and demanding to be loved, no conditions attached. That little girl is the absolute proof that you chose the right thing."

He looked at her, and the gentle kindness in his eyes was the grace she had craved her whole life. "Havenwood is gone, Sarah. It's just us now. And Lily."

As he spoke, a profound, unearthly peace descended upon the room. The silence wasn't the heavy, suffocating silence of Havenwood; it was a vast, settled stillness. It felt like an immense, unseen hand had gently released the years' pressure on her heart, confirming that she had finally chosen the right path — the true anchor Marta had spoken of. It wasn't luck, and it wasn't a transaction. It was the simple, bewildering reality of unconditional love.

"Thank you," she whispered, the single word carrying the weight of years of shame and newfound freedom.

He sealed their covenant not with a prayer or a rule, but with a kiss of quiet, absolute acceptance on her forehead, a promise that the house would stand.

They sat in comfortable silence for a long time, the only sound the faint, happy murmur of Lily talking to Marta's ceramic owl in the next room. The apartment was filled with the gentle clatter of cups and the soft ticking of the wall clock—a rhythm that, for once, brought comfort rather than anxiety. Sarah was still trembling, but the tremor was now external, not internal—the residual shaking of a collapsing structure. David finally shifted, pulling her against his shoulder. His shirt smelled of machine oil and honest sweat, a scent that had become the signature of her safety. She closed her eyes, breathing in the warm, familiar smell, feeling her heartbeat slow in time with his.

"Sarah," he tested the name, the consonants round and solid. "It fits you better. Like a strong spine."

She leaned her head back against his collarbone, tears having dried into cool streaks on her cheeks. "Rose was easier to protect. Sarah... Sarah is the one they wanted to get rid of."

"Then Rose gets to retire," David murmured, his voice rumbling softly in his chest. "You earned this, Sarah. This quiet. This boring, messy apartment life. You ran five years straight for this." He kissed the top of her head. "No more looking over your shoulder. That part of the story is closed. We'll tell Lily the truth when she's ready. A simple, easy truth."

"I never thought I'd hear someone say 'you earned this' without a list of conditions attached," she confessed, her voice thick. "They always followed grace with a tax. You had to prove you were worthy of the blessing."

He squeezed her shoulder. "That's not how love works, baby. That's how contracts work. We don't have a contract; we have a covenant. Unconditional. You don't have to keep earning your place here."

A smile, genuine and utterly relaxed, finally touched her lips. "I think I like the sound of that. Covenant. The one that doesn't break."

The lightness that settled over her was profound. It wasn't just the absence of fear, but the presence of an absolute, unassailable security. She looked around the apartment, which just an hour ago had felt brittle under the shadow of Marta's departure. Now, the chipped paint seemed unimportant. The dust motes dancing in the afternoon sun were just light, not illuminated flaws.

Marta's words echoed back to her: *Your house stands even when a wall comes down.* Rose had feared the collapse of the wall (the lie), but David's acceptance had proven that the house—their life together—was built not on the wall, but on the foundation they had poured together. She realized that the gentle intervention she had always felt—the serendipitous meeting with David, Lily's perfectly timed, innocent question—had all been converging on this single, safe moment. She had traded her father's conditional testimony for David's unconditional truth, and in doing so, had finally claimed the real, unearned grace she'd been promised long ago. David wasn't just her protection; he was the confirmation that her escape was sanctioned.

CHAPTER 19

IRREVOCABLE SAFETY

The first, almost involuntary act of her newfound freedom was the removal of the silver ring. For years, it had been a heavy, cold guarantee of her vigilance, symbolizing the brittle, defensive life of 'Rose.' Now, it felt like a pointless weight. Sarah walked to her bedroom closet, opened the mahogany jewelry box, and tucked the ring deep into a velvet-lined compartment, burying it beneath a tangle of bright, colorful scarves she hadn't dared to wear. The simple click of the box closing was the sound of a chapter ending, definitive and final.

In the weeks that followed, Sarah and David settled into a rhythm of gentle rediscovery. The old anxieties—echoes of Havenwood, the weight of exile, the ghost of conditional love—no longer ruled the air. Instead, their home was filled with small, vital rituals: the clatter of Lily's crayons at the kitchen table, Sarah's laughter echoing down the hallway, David's steady presence in the evenings as he fixed a loose cabinet hinge or read quietly beside her on the couch.

They began to reclaim the ordinary. Sarah started a small herb garden on the windowsill, her hands in real soil—a sensation she'd been denied for years. She taught Lily how to pinch fresh basil, the scent of green filling the apartment and mingling with the rich aroma of baking bread. David, for the first time in years, lingered over breakfast, his laughter low and easy, his hand always finding Sarah's as they planned their days.

One rainy Saturday, as thunder rolled in the distance, Sarah and David built a fort out of blankets in the living room. Lily shrieked with delight as they curled up together, reading old library books by flashlight. Sarah, her hair falling loose over her shoulders, felt a fierce gratitude for the safety of the moment—

and for the permission, finally, to let herself rest. The world outside might still be uncertain, but here, inside these walls, their family was whole.

There were moments of old fear—when a phone rang unexpectedly, when a letter from Havenwood arrived in the mail. However, these moments no longer dictated the household's mood. David would simply hold Sarah's hand, anchoring her with a steady look, reminding her that this new life was built on truth, not performance.

That evening, they hosted David's colleague, Kyle, a man whose only real interests were data architecture and his cat, ensuring the conversation remained pleasantly mundane. Sarah had only met him briefly before, always tense and watchful as 'Rose.' Tonight, David's unburdened smile was contagious.

As they sat down to a perfectly roasted chicken, the scent of rosemary and lemon filled the small dining room, and mingling with the faint aroma of baking bread, Kyle turned to David. "I must say, David, I feel like I only ever got fleeting glimpses of your wife before. She always seemed… on her way out the door." The meal was warm and rich, the candlelight flickering on the plates, laughter echoing off the old, painted walls—a stark contrast to the cold, silent meals of the past.

David reached out and placed his hand on the back of Sarah's neck. "Kyle, this is Sarah."

Sarah met Kyle's gaze easily. "It's lovely to properly meet you, Kyle."

The name—Sarah—left her mouth as easily as breathing. It was solid, owned. It wasn't the alias of a fugitive; it was the name of a wife, a mother, and a host. The truth hadn't fractured their world; it had finally cemented it. The dinner was a series of perfect, mundane moments: Lily drawing a purple octopus at the kitchen counter, Kyle accidentally spilling a drop of Cabernet, which Sarah simply wiped up without a second thought, and David laughing—a deep, full-throated sound she'd always craved.

Later, after Kyle had left, David found Sarah in the laundry nook, folding Lily's small dinosaur-print pajamas, still radiating warmth from the dryer.

"I called the realtor, just like we planned," David said, wrapping his arms around her waist. The smell of detergent and the faint, clean scent of her shampoo lingered between them. "The bungalow on Hawthorne is showing tomorrow morning. We're locked in for a viewing."

"I've been planning the garden," Sarah confessed, leaning back into him. "It faces south. We can grow proper climbing roses and maybe even a small herb patch for the kitchen. Imagine: fresh basil for pasta, right outside the window."

They spent the next hour side by side on the living room rug, actively designing their new life. They debated how many coats of sage green would be needed for the wide porch, sketched out where Lily's swing set would sit, and agreed on a layout for David's new den.

A Promise of Celebration

David pointed to the tablet screen, where a lush, sun-drenched photo of the backyard was displayed. "And once the house is closed, and we're settled, we need to celebrate. Really celebrate. Not just a housewarming. A life-warming."

Sarah laughed, "A weekend road trip up the coast? Maybe rent a tiny cabin in the mountains?"

"No," David said, his voice dropping to a serious, beautiful pitch. He paused, turning his body to face hers fully. "I mean Maui. Two weeks. We take Lily to see the turtles, we hike up to the waterfall, and we just exist for a while, surrounded by blue water and nothing else."

Sarah's eyes filled instantly. The sheer audacity of the plan—the vulnerability, the expense, the absolute commitment it implied—was overwhelming. "Maui. That's... that's immense, David."

"The risk is gone, Sarah. We don't have to be small anymore. We can be immense," he insisted, pulling her closer. "We can build the life we deferred."

As Sarah began excitedly listing what she'd pack for Lily, David rested his chin on her head, gazing over her into the dim living room. He kept his thoughts entirely to himself, a private oath. He had already purchased the ring—a new one, made of platinum and cut with a stone that caught the light like fire. He had kept it in a secure location for months, waiting for the moment he could finally give it to *Sarah*, not Rose.

We're buying the house first, he thought. *That's the foundation. And then, on that beach in Maui, I'll ask her to marry me. No secrets, no fear. Just a vow.*

He smiled, filled with the joy of a man whose future was not only certain but actively under construction. The life they were building wasn't temporary, conditional, or subject to recall. It was earned.

"I know what I want to cook for dinner Sunday night in the new house," Sarah whispered, her voice thick with emotion. "A huge lasagna, with enough leftovers for a week. A meal that says, 'We are never moving again.'"

David only tightened his embrace, secure in the knowledge that this house, this trip, and his hidden promise would forever cement their happiness. He had finally made it home. They were irrevocably safe.

CHAPTER 20

THE ELEVENTH-HOUR JUDGMENT

The brief, precious months following the confession were filled with a dazzling, ordinary peace. Sarah felt completely transformed, existing simply as *Sarah*—no longer a ghost or a fugitive, but a woman finally free to breathe the same air as her future husband and daughter without that crushing, internal guilt. The heavy fear that had been her constant companion for years had finally lifted, replaced by a simple, profound security. The relief was almost physical, like shedding a coat of lead.

"I still think a pirate theme is best," David murmured, leaning over the kitchen counter the night before, tracing patterns on the back of her hand.

Sarah had smiled, resting her head against his shoulder. "A pirate theme is fantastic, but she's turning six. We should at least *discuss* the Princess option. I found a cake that looks like a castle." Just talking about Lily's sixth birthday party, planning for a future that stretched out stable and visible, was an act of profound, forward-looking faith she had never dared before. Their home felt fully cemented, their family whole, finally resting in the unassailable certainty of unconditional love.

The week passed in a gentle rhythm, each day reinforcing the sense that their troubles—at least for now—were behind them. Saturday arrived with the kind of bright, ordinary promise that made the city's hum feel like music. David, Sarah, and Lily were headed to the public library—a rare, full family outing where David insisted on pushing the cart around.

"Mommy, can we get that one about the giraffe who learns ballet?" Lily chirped from the back seat, her voice tiny and sweet, punctuated by the *click-clack* of her two favorite toy bracelets.

Sarah turned slightly in the passenger seat, her heart swelling at the sight of Lily strapped safely into her car seat. "We can look, sweetie. But you have to promise to check out at least one book about space. Remember how we talked about astronauts?"

"Astronaut giraffe?" Lily asked, giggling.

David chuckled, reaching over to give Sarah's knee a gentle squeeze. "Astronaut giraffe it is. She's got you wrapped around her little finger, Sarah. And me too, honestly."

He was humming along softly to an old nineties song on the radio, his left hand resting easily on Sarah's knee, his right on the steering wheel. She leaned her head back against the headrest, a smile fixed on her face, just drinking in the sight of her daughter's boundless, uncomplicated joy in the rear-view mirror. The sun poured through the windshield, warming her face. *This is it*, she thought. *This is everything. This is what safety feels like.*

Then, a sudden, searing flash of white light from the left. The screech of tires. The impossible, deafening roar of metal twisting and tearing.

Sarah's world became a kaleidoscope of shattering glass and crushing force. The seatbelt locked, biting into her shoulder. Her head snapped back, then forward, impacting something soft and yielding. The air was ripped from her lungs, replaced by the acrid stench of burning rubber and gasoline. Then, a profound, ringing silence, broken only by a high-pitched whine in her ears.

She forced her eyes open, vision clearing slowly as dizziness ebbed. A pounding headache throbbed in her skull. She tasted copper—blood from the hot, sticky dampness on her forehead. *Just a fender bender,* she thought, her brain grasping for order. *We're okay. We're all okay.*

David was slumped against the steering wheel, a dark bruise blooming on his temple. His breathing was shallow and ragged, but he was struggling to move.

"D-David?" Sarah croaked, her voice weak.

"Sarah? My head," he groaned, pushing himself upright, wincing in agony. He immediately looked back. "Lily! Is Lily okay? What happened?" He fumbled at his own seatbelt release with a trembling hand, trying to turn around.

Sarah didn't answer him. Her focus was a singular, desperate tunnel directed backward. The rear of the car was a crumpled, unrecognizable mass of metal. Lily's car seat was still there, but horribly askew, trapped amidst the wreckage.

"Lily?" Sarah called, her voice raw and desperate. "Lily, baby girl? Say something! Mommy's here!"

There was no sound. Only the unnatural silence from the back seat was more terrifying than any scream. No sound. No click-clack of toy bracelets. The silence was absolute.

She clawed at the seatbelt release, a simple button that had become an immovable block of granite. Her fingers, slick with her own blood, fumbled uselessly. Her left arm felt useless, the shoulder searing with agony with every tug. She pushed, she hammered, she pulled the heavy nylon strap, screaming now, not for Lily, but in pure, trapped frustration. "Help! Somebody help! Please! David, get it off me!"

David, still pinned by his own locked belt, stretched his hand toward her. "I can't reach, honey, push the button! Harder! I'm trying—I'm pinned!"

She ripped at the belt with her good arm, the nylon strap burning her palm, until finally, with a sharp, grating *click*, the buckle gave way.

She scrambled over the center console, ignoring the screaming pain in her shoulder and the sharp spike in her ribs. The air was thick with the stench of coolant and burnt metal. Every movement was a struggle against the collapsed plastic and upholstery. Her only need was to breach the impossible physical barrier to her child. She had to touch Lily to find the warmth. As she reached the rear, she spared a dizzy, peripheral glance out the passenger window—a faint image of twisted metal and a blurred shadow of a figure stumbling away—but the sight registered only as noise.

Her gaze fixed on Lily: through the twisted metal, a dark, spreading stain on the white dress. She noted the small, perfect shoe that was still on, but the headrest was bent, and Lily's neck was resting at a tilt that defied physics, defying the laws of life itself. A sickening, impossible angle to her small head. The air in Sarah's lungs felt like ash.

"Lily? Lily, wake up! Please, baby, wake up!" Sarah choked out, her voice dissolving into a whimper as she shook the child's tiny, still shoulders. The lack of response, the chilling unnatural stiffness, was the brutal hammer blow that shattered her final defense. She pressed her ear to Lily's chest, searching for the slightest flutter, hearing only the roar of her own blood and the distant siren beginning to approach.

The colossal wave of agony in her head and body, suppressed by pure adrenaline, rushed back in a consuming, crashing tide. Her vision tunneled to a pinprick of blackness. Her knees buckled over the transmission hump, and before she could hear David's terrified, heartbreaking cry of her name, Sarah's world went silent. She collapsed back onto the ruined upholstery, her body giving in completely to shock.

Hospital and The Truth

Sarah woke to the blinding, sterile white of a hospital ceiling. She blinked, once, twice, the throbbing behind her eyes so immense it felt like her skull was cracking. A soft, continuous beep filled the silence, a rhythmic intrusion of life. She was strapped down, her left arm bandaged and secured, an IV drip needling into her right hand. The bed felt hard and restrictive, like a cage that prioritized function over comfort, leaving her body oddly stiff and unfamiliar.

She tried to move, a jolt of pain seizing her left side. Immediately, a shadow moved near the door.

A nurse, a young woman with dark hair pulled into a tight bun, hurried over. "Oh, good, you're awake. Welcome back, dear. I'm going to page Dr. Evans, okay? Just relax for me." The nurse's voice was high and nervous.

A moment later, a man in scrubs—the doctor—stood over her, holding a chart. He spoke in a low, practiced tone, the one people use when delivering news they've delivered too many times before.

"Rose? You're in the emergency trauma ward. My name is Dr. Evans. You suffered a fractured clavicle and three cracked ribs, but nothing life-threatening. We've stabilized you. Your husband, David, is in recovery from his shoulder surgery. He's stable, too."

Sarah tried to speak, but the rising panic for Lily immediately overshadowed the physical pain. The knowledge of her own injuries was a dull, distant hum, muted by an intense, singular focus on her child. She managed a rasping, "Lily. My daughter. Where's Lily? Is she with David?"

Dr. Evans sighed, the subtle change in his posture shattering the last of her self-deception. His eyes—tired, empathetic—fixed on hers. He placed the chart gently on the foot of the bed.

"Rose," he began, his voice dropping to a near-whisper. "I am deeply, deeply sorry. We did everything we could. But the impact... your daughter, Lily, passed away instantly at the scene."

The words didn't register as fact. They were just sounds in a language she didn't speak. Her mind immediately rejected the phrase.

"No," Sarah said, the denial absolute, a cold, hard shield in her mind. Her voice was flat, empty. "No, that's wrong. She's fine. She was just talking about the astronaut giraffe book. She's probably sleeping, she gets carsick sometimes, and she just needs her blanket. You need to check the records again. She was turning six. You have the wrong room." She tried to point, but her fractured arm rebelled with blinding agony.

The doctor sat on the edge of the bed. His mouth moved, forming shapes. *Grief counseling... a wonderful chaplain on staff... support groups for parents... the process…* The syllables were thick, meaningless cotton wool in the silence of her mind, a well-meaning blur of administrative tragedy she couldn't process. She heard only one word clearly, repeated in the agonizing loop of her own heartbeat: *Instantly. Instantly. Instantly.*

After the doctor left, a police officer entered, a woman with tired but kind eyes and the distinct posture of a detective. The starch in her uniform was faded, the silver badge scuffed at the edges. She pulled up a chair a respectful distance from the bed. The faint scent of rain clung to her coat, and her hands were steady as she opened her notepad, her gaze gentle but unflinching.

"Rose, I'm Detective Miller," she said softly, her voice low and even. "I want to offer my deepest condolences for your loss. We won't keep you long; your health is our top priority. Right now, I just need to establish that you are stable and explain the nature of the crash."

Sarah simply stared, the weight of the universe pressing on her chest, waiting not for questions, but for the answer to the unspoken *why*.

The detective leaned forward slightly, her gaze steady. "We have secured the scene and detained the other driver. He fled, but we apprehended him. Rose, the driver, was heavily impaired. His blood alcohol level was three times the legal limit. He was drunk. Completely out of it. We are preparing to file charges of vehicular manslaughter."

The word—drunk—snapped the fractured pieces of Sarah's mind into horrific alignment. It was an obscene intrusion. Not sick. Not fate. It was a careless, malicious human choice. A deliberate, delivered strike, executed by a mundane monster. This was not the elegant justice of a vengeful God; this was the chaotic, brutal unfairness of the world reaching in to take what was hers. The careless hand of another had reached out and taken her most precious thing.

Her mind fractured instantly, dissociating from the pain. She was no longer thinking in terms of logic or theology; she was experiencing pure, agonizing sensory overload. The rhythmic beep… beep… beep… of the heart monitor was now a screaming, relentless metronome counting down the seconds since Lily's last breath. The white sheets were too bright, the air too cold, the plastic IV tube in her hand an alien, unbearable trespass. She could feel the dull, metallic taste of hospital air coating her tongue.

He was drunk. The phrase triggered a lightning-fast, chaotic sequence of images: The tiny, still shoulders. Lily's bright pink bicycle helmet, perfectly fine, was sitting by the front door yesterday. The unseen hand of God—was that what they called it? No, no, it was not sickness, not fate. It was simply a violation, a debt collector arriving at the worst possible moment.

She felt utterly disconnected from her own body, watching herself on the bed, a heavily bandaged doll named 'Rose' who had just been told the worst thing in the world. The hospital bed, the very cage that promised healing, now felt like the final, most contaminated space on Earth, holding the proof of her failure.

The cold certainty of her curse rushed in, a necessary anchor in the chaos. Everything good—David, the brief safety, Lily's life—had been borrowed, and the interest payment was now due. Lily was the payment. To stay now meant to inflict the crushing, perpetual weight of her contaminated existence onto David. *I ruined him.*

Sarah lay staring at the ceiling tiles, her vision blurring at the edges where the clinical white met the sickly beige paint. The doctor's words—"brief," "sudden," "unrecoverable"—were meaningless echoes in the sterile space. Her body was a collection of minor aches, but the true pain was in the catastrophic, spiritual collapse unfolding in her mind.

She had spent years running from the judgmental God of her youth, the God who punished transgression. When she found David and then Lily, she had convinced herself she was safe. Unconditional love had become her shield; her life was proof that the chain had been broken.

But now, lying in this unforgiving room, the old, dark theology returned with the force of a tidal wave. The death of her child was not a random tragedy. It was a verdict. It was the final, undeniable proof that the curse was real, that her past debt hadn't been erased—it had just been transferred to the purest thing she had ever touched.

God didn't take the tax, she thought, the realization cold and absolute. *God took the offering.*

She remembered the preacher who had warned her as a girl: *You can outrun the police, but you cannot outrun the shadow of your sin.* Lily was the price, the payment for Jessie, for Michael, for leaving the fold. This was not grief; it was cosmic despair. She was an infection that brought ruin to everything she loved, and she now understood: she was unforgivable.

The oxygen monitor beeped steadily, an indifferent rhythm marking the seconds of her damnation. She closed her eyes, clutching the sterile sheet, wishing the injuries had been worse, wishing she could simply disappear into the anesthesia, because she now understood: she was unforgivable.

What had she done to the world to make this tragedy happen? The answer was horrifyingly simple: she had existed. She had dared to ask for happiness she hadn't earned.

CHAPTER 21

THE WEIGHT OF SORROW

The room was a harsh landscape of sterile white and beige. The only sounds were the hollow hum of the HVAC and the relentless beep of the oxygen monitor. Sarah lay beneath a thin sheet, more object than woman, her mind an open wound: she was the curse, Lily the price.

The shuffling sound of worn leather shoes paused outside the door. David didn't knock. He simply leaned his head in, his face a hollow mask carved out of unshaven, two-day-old grief. He looked older, grayer, and dangerously lost. His clothes—the same rumpled shirt and dark jeans from the afternoon they were supposed to be going to the library—were wrinkled and spotted with the invisible dust of a road accident, a pathetic badge of their shared, catastrophic trauma. His eyes were red, not from tears, but from a dry, relentless shock that locked his emotions in a permanent state of denial. He was operating purely on the adrenaline of logistics, yet to allow himself to truly feel the pain.

He entered silently and sat on the uncomfortable plastic chair beside the bed, the plastic sighing softly under his weight.

"The doctor... they let me see her," David whispered, the simple statement hitting the air like shattered porcelain.

At the mention of Lily, Sarah's quiet facade shattered. A strangled, animal sound tore from her throat. Her shoulders began to tremble violently, and the first wave of hot, unstoppable tears spilled down her temples, soaking into the pillowcase. She didn't try to wipe them away; they were the physical manifestation of the rupture inside her soul.

"I called Father Thomas," he continued, desperately clinging to the practicalities. "He's making the arrangements. We... we have to talk about what she would have wanted." He swallowed hard, his throat tight. "Lily always hated that yellow dress, remember? She wanted the blue one for Christmas photos. I need to make sure we pick the right one for..."

His voice broke, and Sarah's breathing became ragged, choking on the sheer impossibility of the moment. She curled her hands into fists against the sheet, fighting for air.

"She wanted to wake up," Sarah said, the words barely audible, broken by a harsh, tearing sob that convulsed her whole body. It was the first thing she'd said aloud, a single, agonizing plea to a universe that had already judged them.

David recoiled, his face stricken. He reached forward to touch her, then stopped, his hand hovering uselessly. He saw the physical pain of her weeping, but couldn't reach the source of her self-condemnation. He needed her to be his partner in grief; instead, he found a person drowning in solitary, catastrophic guilt.

"I tried to stop them from taking the car," he said, the urgency in his voice rising. "They said the other driver was drunk. That's what matters, Sarah. We didn't do this."

Sarah slowly turned her head, her face wet, her eyes bloodshot and swollen, the expression one of absolute, terrifying certainty. The words were difficult, forced out between shuddering breaths.

"It doesn't matter," she wept, the tears flowing faster now. "The report is finished."

"What do you mean, 'finished'?" he demanded, seeing only hysteria. "We haven't signed anything. We have a right to sue them—"

"No, David. The report on *me* is finished. The verdict is in." Her conviction was absolute, terrifying in its certainty, delivered through the painful, rhythmic heaving of her chest. "I lost her. And now you've lost me. You should go. There is nothing left here but the debt."

David stared at her, seeing the woman he loved consumed by a guilt he couldn't penetrate, her face streaked with tears that were not just for Lily, but for the life she believed she had ruined.

The Unbearable Weight of Normalcy

A different nurse, younger and brisk, arrived moments later, interrupting the silence with an impersonal cheerfulness. She carried a massive arrangement of white lilies and purple irises, cheap and cloying, clearly from a business acquaintance. Sarah could smell the sickly sweet scent of the lilies, a smell Lily had hated. The fragrance mixed with the salt of her tears, creating a nauseating, physical oppression.

"From a Mr. Peterson," the nurse announced, placing the bouquet on the small dresser opposite the bed.

Sarah closed her eyes, trying to block out the sight of the perfect, fragrant blooms that seemed to mock her. *Difficult time.* The phrase was a lie. This was an ending.

A low, muffled chorus of shrieks and laughter drifted in from the street below. With slow, deliberate effort, Sarah rolled her head on the pillow toward the window. It was a beautiful, clear autumn day.

Below, in the patch of lawn across the parking lot, two children were playing tag, their bright coats miniature streaks of color against the faded green grass. A girl, perhaps six, Lily's age, stopped, threw her head back, and laughed, a sound so rich with life it pierced the sterile air of the room. The sheer, terrifying normalcy of life continuing—the sun shining, the laughter, the innocent motion of tiny legs—crushed her, triggering a deeper, more agonizing breakdown.

She turned her face back into the pillow, her body racked by silent, brutal weeping. She bit down hard on her lip until she tasted blood, trying to stifle the sobs so they wouldn't scare David, but her shoulders convulsed. The movement sent a stab of pain through her bruised ribs, a pain she welcomed as penance.

That should be my laughter, she thought, the realization of her failure hitting her with the force of a tidal wave. *It was my job to protect that sound, and I failed. I lost the world's most precious thing in a collision of steel and poor judgment. She was six. She was going to the library. Outside, the sun painted stripes across the hospital floor, indifferent to her pain.* Every image of Lily—the missing tooth, the purple backpack, the way she tucked her chin when she was concentrating—was a fresh, excoriating stab. The room itself felt haunted, every surface echoing with the absence of Lily's voice.

The grief stopped being a sensation and became an ideology of self-hate.

The Finality of Condemnation

She felt the cold, familiar presence of the shadow she had been running from since childhood—the curse she foolishly believed she had escaped. The shadow hadn't just caught up; it had claimed the collateral.

You don't get to be happy. You don't get to have light. You don't get to keep the prize.

David watched her weep, paralyzed, unable to bridge the gap between his manageable grief and her devastating, self-inflicted judgment. He saw the cold isolation, the rejection of his love, and his own anger began to turn to bewildered, agonizing pain. He had come for shared comfort; he had only found condemnation.

He stood up, his legs stiff. He reached into his coat pocket and pulled out a small, glass vial of pain pills the hospital had given him for his bruised ribs. They were still mostly full. He stared at them—tiny, white promises of temporary peace—then dropped them onto the bedside table. It was a silent, desperate offering, a physical surrender to the idea that pain should be chemically numbed. Sarah's eyes, though swollen shut, registered the sound. She knew what he had left.

He didn't touch her. He didn't say goodbye. He merely noted the precise, mechanical *beep-beep-beep* of the oxygen machine, a sound that would forever anchor her to this bed, this moment of catastrophic loss.

He only paused at the door, turning back once to look at the profile of the woman he loved, whose shoulders continued to shake violently with desperate, choked sobs—a woman already slipping away from him.

"I'll be home," he said, his voice husky with unshed tears of his own. "Call me when they let you out. We'll talk about the funeral then."

The door clicked shut. The click of the latch was the sound of a prison door closing, leaving Sarah in the absolute, crushing silence of her own weeping. She slowly turned her head, looking at the vial of pills on the table, their white promise a cold, indifferent invitation. The profound, heartbreaking loneliness of realizing her sorrow was now a wall, not a bridge, cemented her descent.

She was alone. Utterly, terribly alone, in a silence only broken by the terrifying roar of divine judgment inside her head. Her path to destitution had begun.

CHAPTER 22

THE HOUSE OF GHOSTS

Sarah's stay at the hospital lasted exactly forty-eight hours. Victims of car accidents who sustain minor physical trauma—bruised ribs, superficial lacerations, and the crippling shock of the event—are often held for observation to ensure there are no delayed internal complications. But for Sarah, the clock was less a measure of medical safety and more a ticking countdown to her condemnation. When the hospital staff finally signed her release forms, they handed her a small plastic bag containing her meager personal belongings and a booklet on grief counseling, a pamphlet she immediately crumpled into her coat pocket like offensive material.

David was there, waiting in the harsh fluorescent glare of the discharge lounge, looking exactly as he had two days prior: rumpled, haunted, and strangely focused on the mechanics of living. He didn't embrace her. He took her elbow, the touch purely functional, and guided her to the car.

The drive home was silent. Each passing intersection was a knife twist, the familiar streets now distorted and corrupted. She registered the blue awning of the ice cream parlor where Lily had thrown a spectacular tantrum over sprinkles, the flash of the school crossing guard's neon vest, and the yellow swing set in the public park. Each sight was a perfectly preserved memory, now violently sealed behind glass, untouchable and agonizingly precious. Sarah stared out the window, tears already tracking fresh, wet paths through the dried salt on her cheeks.

The apartment itself was the final, devastating witness. It looked too bright, too normal, settled beneath the benevolent, innocent light of the afternoon sun. As David fumbled with the key, Sarah felt a physical tremor of dread. Entering the house meant confronting the silent, tangible ghost of the life they had just destroyed.

Inside, the air was still, thick with the scent of unlit vanilla candles and the faint, sweet trace of Lily's bubblegum toothpaste. David moved immediately to the living room, gathering stray mail and tossing it onto the credenza, trying to impose order on a universe that had just demonstrated its utter chaos.

Sarah stopped in the hallway. Hanging from the wooden coat rack, right beside David's work satchel, was Lily's bright pink raincoat.

She reached out slowly, tentatively, as if the waterproof fabric might scald her. Her fingers brushed the cool plastic of the sleeve, and the sheer, violent reality of the loss exploded through her. Lily had worn this two days ago. She had been *real*.

A broken cry escaped Sarah, louder and more desperate than any sound she'd made in the hospital. She pressed her face into the damp sleeve, inhaling deeply, searching for the faint, elusive scent of child, playground dirt, and sunshine. There was nothing. Just plastic and the smell of the dusty hallway.

She collapsed right there, sinking to her knees beside the coat rack, her body wracked with shattering sobs. She didn't weep; she wailed, the sound ugly, involuntary, and primal.

David dropped the mail with a thud. He rushed over, pulling her up into his arms, but she was rigid, pushing against him. Her tears were not just sorrow; they were a form of self-flagellation.

"I didn't kiss her goodbye, David," she choked out, the words a confession and a plea for punishment. "I rushed her. I told her we were running late. I didn't kiss her goodbye!"

"Sarah, stop. You have to stop," David whispered, tears welling in his own eyes as he felt her splintering away from him. He couldn't handle her grief on top of his own. He was the one managing the utilities, calling the insurance company, and ordering the flowers. He needed her to be the mourner; she was instead the executioner.

When she thrashed, the pain in her bruised ribs flared—a white-hot bolt of lightning. She didn't flinch away; she pressed into it, craving the physical penance of the injury. She deserved every sharp gasp it cost her. He helped her to the bedroom, closing the door on the perfect, pink coat hanging in the hall.

The next two days blurred into an agonizing fugue state. Sarah could not sleep. Even in the dead of night, when the house finally settled into its deepest silence, her mind betrayed her. She would lie on her side of the bed, staring at the ceiling, where Lily had painstakingly applied glow-in-the-dark stars six months prior. They weren't visible now, but Sarah knew where every tiny, plastic point of light was. She saw them anyway—a pale, imaginary galaxy of promises that would never be kept.

She would roll over, pressing her face into the pillow, trying to silence the memories, only to be ambushed by the phantom sensation of a small, warm foot kicking her back in the middle of the night. Her pillow became perpetually damp, saturated with silent, desperate weeping that lasted until the brutal, uncompromising dawn.

On the third day, David insisted they had to finalize the funeral details. They sat at the kitchen table, which was now dominated by folders of pamphlets from the funeral home.

"The priest suggests Saturday," David said, pushing a brochure across the table. "We have to decide between cremation and burial. I… I don't know. Lily loved the garden."

Sarah looked at the brochure, her eyes skimming the text about caskets and urns. It was nauseatingly surreal.

"The blue dress," she said, her voice thin and flat, interrupting his logistics.

"What?"

"The blue dress. She wanted the blue one. The velvet one from Christmas."

"Right. The blue one," David confirmed, relief in his voice that she had offered an actionable detail. "And the music? They need music."

Sarah shook her head slowly, tears beginning to well up again, but this time they were silent and deep, streaming steadily down her cheeks onto the wooden table. "No music. David, she's too little for silence. It should be noise. It should be chaos. It should be me screaming. Anything but silence."

"We can't scream, Sarah," he said, rubbing his eyes, his patience fraying. "I need you to be strong. If we both break, there's nothing left. I need one foot on the ground."

"There is no strength left," she whispered, leaning forward, the tears dripping steadily. "I used it all up. I used it to kill her. Just pick the place, David. Just pick the place where I have to say goodbye."

He looked at her, then down at the table, seeing only his own profound loneliness mirrored in her self-destruction. He picked up the phone.

The Blue Dress and the White Casket

The day of the funeral was a blur of black cloth, hushed voices, and the crushing, cloying scent of lilies—the same scent from the hospital, now inescapable.

Sarah allowed herself to be dressed and led through the motions by David's sister, whose face was a mask of pity. The church felt vast and cold, its heavy oak doors and stained-glass windows mocking the smallness of their tragedy.

The moment Sarah walked into the sanctuary, the air was knocked out of her lungs.

At the front, resting beneath a towering spray of flowers, was the casket. It was not the adult-sized mahogany box she'd vaguely pictured, but a horrifyingly *small*, perfectly rendered box of white wood. The paint gleamed in the dim light, too bright against the somber pews. It was the size of Lily's favorite treasure chest, only made of death. It was small enough to be a toy chest. It was small enough to fit a six-year-old child. The sight of it stole the air from Sarah's lungs, the world narrowing to that one, impossible box.

Sarah stopped dead in the aisle. The elegant control she had maintained through the last few days evaporated in a single, visceral shock. Seeing the size of the box, the ultimate, undeniable evidence of Lily's small, finished life, broke her entirely.

She couldn't breathe. She swayed, and David, who had been supporting her, felt her weight abruptly shift. She wasn't weeping now; she was shattering. A ragged, choking sound tore from her throat, and she collapsed, pitching forward onto the deep red carpet.

David's face crumpled. He grabbed her, pulling her up against him, but she was hysterical, thrashing against his hold, screaming soundlessly into his coat.

"No! No, no, no, no, no!" she managed to gasp, the words swallowed by massive, gulping sobs. "She's too small! It's too small, David! She doesn't fit!"

He held her tightly, shielding her from the dozens of faces turned toward them, his own body shaking with the enormous, silent effort of holding them both together.

She was vaguely aware of her cheek pressing against the rough wool of his suit jacket, aware of the heavy, flowery sweetness of the air, and the terrifying, empty weight of her arms.

The small, white casket sat waiting, and Sarah, trapped in David's rigid embrace, felt the profound, total realization of her guilt and her loss. The judgment was complete. She had lost the prize, and now the world was forcing her to look at the empty space she had left behind.

She was dragged, not walked, to the front pew, where she sat staring at the box, her face wet, her throat raw, her weeping a desperate, desolate sound that filled the heavy silence of the church. The sight of that small white box was the final, devastating payment for a life she believed she never should have had. The judgment was complete. The world had forced her to look at the empty space she had left behind.

The graveside service was brief, a cold wind whipping the priest's words away from the huddled group of mourners. The raw earth beside the small plot looked black and hungry.

When the moment came for them to lower the casket, Sarah reached out, her hand flying out instinctively to stop the descent. She felt the heavy, unforgiving silence of the assembled people, but she didn't care.

"No," she pleaded, stumbling forward, her black coat flying around her. "It's cold! It's dark down there! Lily hates the dark! David, tell them to stop! Tell them she needs her nightlight!"

She was pulled back, gently but firmly, by David and his brother. In that instant, David wasn't just exhausted; he was terrified. This wasn't grief; this was lunacy, a complete unraveling he couldn't anchor. She watched the little white box disappear, and when the first spade of dirt hit the polished lid with a hollow, sickening *thud*, Sarah screamed. It wasn't a cry of grief; it was a shriek of physical agony. The sound seemed to tear her vocal cords, and she sank, finally, completely, into the ground, her knees giving out.

David caught her, his face a mask of exhaustion and defeat. He helped her stand, and she stood there, swaying, watching the shovel fill the hole, burying not just Lily, but the last vestige of Sarah's connection to the living world. The debt was paid, and the receipt was the small mound of fresh earth.

The funeral ended, but for Sarah, the mourning had just begun. The tears had run dry, leaving behind a hard, crystalline shell of absolute emptiness.

CHAPTER 23

SILENCE

A week after the funeral, their small apartment had become a painful cage. The unit was compact and poorly constructed, its main feature the unforgiving way it failed to muffle the sounds of the outside world. There was no buffer, no shield. The apartment had once been comfortably full of the bright, insistent noise of a six-year-old—a little girl who was supposed to be celebrating her sixth birthday and starting first grade in the fall. Now, every creak and every sigh was loud, but it was the subtle sound of the next-door neighbors—a low, distant drone of a television or the faint, sharp ring of a phone—that truly emphasized their isolation. Silence wasn't the absence of sound; it was the suffocating density of their mutual, trapped awareness, constantly juxtaposed against the indifferent beat of normal life.

Just down the short hall, Sarah existed solely in Lily's small bedroom.

She hadn't moved her own clothes; she simply inhabited the space. The air here was heavy and sweet, still carrying the ghost-scent of child sweat, strawberry toothpaste, and the dusty vanilla of Lily's beloved, threadbare stuffed rabbit. The room itself was a riot of color, a grotesque contrast to Sarah's grief: amateur pencil drawings covered the door, and the floor held a stack of kindergarten school projects still waiting to be filed. On the bedside table, a small pink piggy bank sat, meticulously organized with five crisp dollar bills Lily had been saving for a trip to the zoo.

Sarah slept curled up in the narrow twin bed beneath the thick, bright rainbow quilt. The full-sized bed she had shared with David in the adjacent room was a terrifying, cold landscape of shared failure. But here, confined by Lily's small, familiar walls, her crushing guilt felt appropriate.

When she woke, she would stare at the posters of neon-colored unicorns until her eyes blurred. Sometimes, as she stared, a sudden, intrusive sensation would break the silence—not a sound, but a fleeting feeling of cold, metallic pressure against her temple, accompanied by a faint, antiseptic smell of clean air that instantly vanished, leaving only the scent of dust and her daughter's room. She felt a profound, physical revulsion toward resting, an immense, unbidden instinct to move, to stop lying still and submit to oblivion. This driving force, this painful refusal to fully submit to despair, was the unseen current that subtly steered her away from the final, irreversible collapse. Sarah, however, experienced it only as the malicious insistence of her guilt, forcing her to endure the shrine of her own failure.

She kept the door locked, the cheap brass plate offering meager security. She did not eat; the very thought of food felt like a betrayal.

The Acoustic Pressure

In the small living room, David fought the silence with logistics and labor. His grief was a vast, frozen thing, manageable only by focusing on the reliable metrics of the physical world. He was a man drowning, clinging fiercely to the life raft of procedure. He spent hours on the phone with the insurance adjuster, speaking in a low, measured monotone. Every word was easily audible to Sarah just down the hall, registering as cold, bureaucratic efficiency.

He compulsively cleaned. The chemical smell of Pine-Sol and bleach now dominated the stale scent of the old carpet. He scrubbed the kitchen grout and mopped the dining space—anything to replace the emptiness with the scent of work and normalcy. All the while, the apartment itself offered no shield: a faint, muffled sitcom laugh would occasionally filter in from the neighbor's wall, or the clank of distant plumbing, reminding David that the world hadn't stopped spinning for them.

He made several hesitant attempts to breach the barrier.

Tap. Tap. "Sarah? It's chicken broth. Just a tiny mug. You need protein." He waited, his ear pressed to the jamb. He could hear the low, dry, rasping cadence of her weeping—a mechanical sound, like sand sifting. He stood there so long his knees began to ache before finally shuffling away in defeat. *Silence.*

Tap. Tap. "Sarah, the insurance needs the car title. It should be in the lockbox. Can you just… text me where it is?" He heard the distinct *thump* of her turning over in the small bed, and the heavy rustling of the quilt. Then, the silence resumed, heavier than before.

He realized the lack of privacy was their shared punishment. Sarah knew he could hear her pain, and she offered it to him as both a sign of her suffering and a weapon of rejection. By locking him out of Lily's room, she signaled that his pain, focused on logistics and survival, was secondary and unforgivable.

The Chasm

The inevitable eruption came on a Tuesday afternoon. David, exhausted by the relentless quiet, decided to box up some of the artifacts of Lily's presence. He walked into the tiny living room, drawn to the small shelf where Lily's school portrait sat next to a ceramic bowl she had painted at a summer day camp.

He picked up the small, brightly glazed bowl. It was slightly lopsided, painted with crude blue and green streaks that Lily had proudly labeled "Abstract Seaweed." He intended to place it in a plastic bin for safekeeping.

Sarah appeared silently in the doorway.

"What are you doing?" she asked, her voice a low, dry rasp that immediately filled the small space.

"I'm just protecting it," David said, his heart pounding. "We can't have this out right now, Sarah. It hurts too much."

"Protecting it? You're erasing her. You're putting her *away*," Sarah spat, her hands trembling.

"I'm trying to hold onto my sanity! We can't live in a museum of pain forever!" David's voice was sharp with desperation, instantly loud in the small room. "I'm trying to make sure we don't trip over her memory every two seconds!"

"You want to forget her!" Sarah shrieked, the sound instantly painful and confined. "You only care about clean surfaces and insurance forms!" This rage was a raw, primal energy, another wave of that fierce, unbidden force that compelled her action.

David's stoicism was finally shattered. "This isn't just about *your* guilt, Sarah! I lost my daughter, too! But you've locked yourself away, punishing me for surviving! You've made this tragedy all about *your* failure, and you've left me with nothing but phone calls and cold dinners! You have weaponized your suffering to destroy the only thing we have left: our partnership!"

His words—*destroy our partnership*—stripped away the last veil of their fragile arrangement. She lunged, grabbed the ceramic bowl, and hurled it with frenzied, unexpected strength at the exposed brick of the faux fireplace.

The bowl struck the rough brick with a sound like a small, confined explosion, shattering into countless glittering, brittle shards. The abstract seaweed, the crude blue streaks, and all the fragile, tangible evidence of Lily's existence were instantly reduced to dust and sharp, scattered pieces.

David stared at the debris, his face pale, as he breathed in the dust and the metallic scent of destruction.

No further word was exchanged. David watched Sarah retreat down the short hall, her back rigid. He heard the distinct, final *click* of the lock on Lily's bedroom door. He did not follow. He did not clean up the mess.

That night, David lay in the full-sized bed, listening to the thin separation between their world and the next. The faint, steady thump of the neighbor's bass from their stereo continued, utterly meaningless and yet overwhelmingly present. Sarah lay just feet away in the twin bed. They were separated by a single sheet of drywall, yet the silence between them was deeper and colder than any ocean. The accident had not brought them together; it had merely excavated the irreparable chasm between the two people who were now tragically, intimately trapped together. David stared at the ceiling, thinking not of Lily, but of the sharp ceramic dust still littering the floor of the adjacent room, a physical manifestation of the shattered marriage he could no longer bear to touch.

CHAPTER 24

A QUIET EXTINGUISHING

Several months after the accident, the violent chasm that had opened between them following the funeral had deepened into total, unmoving estrangement. The silence in the apartment was no longer the shocked quiet of fresh grief; it was the stale, suffocating quiet of a sealed tomb. Every surface was coated in a thin, grey film—the dust of untouched memories, the residue of a life they no longer knew how to clean. The bright, hopeful colors Lily had brought into their home had faded to muted pastels under the oppressive atmosphere. David existed only in the periphery, a ghost who ate silently at the counter and slept with his back turned. They were two planets orbiting a dead sun, their gravity gone, merely drifting in parallel.

A week prior, in a rare, desperate burst of hope, Sarah had written to Marta. It was a physical letter, detailing the paralyzing grief, the chilling silence, and the guilt that felt like concrete shoes. Marta, hundreds of miles away in San Juan and fighting the relentless tide of breast cancer, was the only person left Sarah felt she could truly talk to. Mailing that letter had felt like throwing a final, fragile bottle into a turbulent sea. For several days, Sarah had clung to the hope of a reply—a single paragraph of Marta's unwavering, unconditional warmth— as the only thing keeping her tethered to the world.

Now, Sarah sat at the kitchen table, her elbows propped on the cool Formica. Her usual ritual—coffee so black it tasted like ash, followed by the day's first calculated wave of numbness—was interrupted by the thump of mail hitting the floor by the front door.

Tucked between a mundane gas bill and a brightly colored advertisement for car insurance was a small, sturdy envelope of cream-colored paper. The paper felt thick and expensive. The stamp was warm, bearing the bright, unfamiliar seal of Puerto Rico. But it was the address—her name scrawled in a rounded, hesitant script, utterly foreign and heavy—that made her breath seize in her chest.

She tore it open, the sound unnaturally loud in the kitchen's silence. Her eyes blurred over the Spanish words until they landed on the English signature: Isabella, Marta's eldest daughter. The words that followed were a cold hammer blow against her last, fragile column of hope.

Dear Mrs. Sarah, I am writing to you because Mama always said you were her sister of the heart. Mama passed away three days ago. She was tired, yet peaceful. We held her hand and played your silly 80s songs. She told me to tell you, 'Your house stands even when a wall comes down.' I hope you find peace.

The paper slid from Sarah's fingers, fluttering to the floor like a dying moth. Marta, the only person who had ever offered unconditional warmth, was gone.

The shock, combined with months of isolation, dissolved Sarah's last shred of self-control. Operating purely on the instinct of a terrified child who only knew one place to run, she reached for the phone. Her hand shook violently as she punched the old landline number—the sequence once as familiar as her own name.

It rang only three times before her father, Robert, answered. His voice was not warm, nor even guarded; it was clipped, precise, and immediately conveying the message that she was an interruption to his perfectly scheduled life.

"Yes? What is it?"

"Dad? It's Sarah." Her voice cracked, a tiny sound of pure distress.

"I recognize your voice. Your mother and I were in the middle of reviewing the vestry committee notes for the fall fundraiser. What do you need? I told you not to call."

"Dad, I... I just got a letter. Marta passed away, my friend from Puerto Rico. And I can't. I just can't breathe. Lily. It was Lily's accident. I can't do this anymore."

The Final Severance

A silence stretched, colder and longer than before.

"Marta? I don't believe we know a Marta," Robert finally said, the name sounding foreign and insignificant on his tongue. His voice sharpened with forced control. "Lily? Sarah, what are you talking about? Who is this Lily? And what is this 'accident' that involves you and this person? We have been quite clear."

"Lily was my daughter," Sarah managed, the confession scraping against her throat like broken glass. "She was turning six. She died in a car accident months ago. I lost her, Dad. I lost my baby."

The silence on the line turned absolute, thick with horror and surgical condemnation. The casual dismissal of her profound grief felt like a surgical act of denial, compounding the trauma of Lily's death with a fresh, shattering sense of shame—the knowledge that her agony was not just inconvenient, but fundamentally wrong and deserving of isolation.

"I'm not calling about appearances, Dad. I'm calling because I'm losing it. I need... I need you to be my father right now. I need help."

"Robert is absolutely right, dear," her mother, Eleanor, suddenly cut in, her voice sounding near the receiver, sharp and clear. "This is an unacceptable lapse in composure. You must be strong. We are. We expect you to manage this misfortune without further scandal. You simply must find a way to cope."

"So that's it?" Sarah whispered, tears finally, uselessly, stinging her eyes. "My daughter is gone, my closest friend is dead, and you just want me to cope?"

"We want you to be productive," Robert interjected, settling the issue with brutal finality. "Grief must be channeled, Sarah, not wallowed in. You have made your choices, and we must maintain our distance. We cannot permit any further communication that jeopardizes the fragile reputation we have salvaged."

The line clicked dead. The sound was not a dial tone, but the seal of a coffin closing. Her parents had weaponized their distance, confirming the worst lie the trauma had already told her: that she was defective and unworthy of comfort.

The receiver landed with a muffled clack against the linoleum, a sound far less impactful than the silence that followed. Marta's loss had taken the last vestige of unconditional love from her life. Her parents' words, however, did something worse: they stripped away the final, desperate hope for human connection, classifying her daughter's death as a mere misfortune that threatened their social standing.

Sarah remained suspended over the silence, her body strangely light. The tears that had sprung from the initial desperation dried instantly, leaving a residue of salt and an absolute sense of alienation. The grief did not multiply; it transformed into secondary trauma—the crushing realization that her survival was solely her burden. Her guilt at failing Lily now fused with the shame of her parents' rejection, making her feel radioactive—too dangerous for anyone to touch.

The apartment no longer had a wall down; the entire foundation had crumbled. The void she had been struggling against for days finally opened up completely, silent and welcoming beneath her feet. There was nothing left to lose, nowhere left to fall. Just the slow, cold slide into the void she had been fighting for months.

CHAPTER 25

FADING GHOSTS

It had been too many months to count. The calendar on the kitchen wall, still stuck on the month of the accident, felt like a deliberate insult. Time wasn't a river anymore; it was a stagnant, oily puddle reflecting the ceiling lamp.

Sarah caught her reflection in the darkened microwave door—a gaunt stranger with sharp, unfamiliar angles. Her clothes hung loose, tenting over ribs that were too visible. Insomnia had eroded the cushioning beneath her skin, leaving her eyes shadowed, hollowed-out sockets. She survived on the ragged edges of sleep, held together by coffee and the bitter, metallic burn of the fentanyl.

She no longer called it *medication* or *escape*. It was an accountant of pain. It came in, balanced the books, and for a few precious hours, left her debt-free. The downside was the cost: not just money, but memory. Lily's memory.

Four months ago—at the four-month mark of their grief—the prosecutor had called. The man who had been behind the wheel, the drunk driver who had turned the light into darkness, had checked out. A suicide note left behind, a final, spiteful theft of their last shred of justice. There would be no trial, no sentence, no public reckoning. David had screamed, throwing a chair through the living room window—the only time he had shown pure, unfiltered emotion since the accident. But Sarah felt only a deeper cold. The man who caused her pain had taken even the right to hate him, leaving her guilt with no external target, forcing it inward. It was a hole that even the fentanyl couldn't fill; it was a permanent, aching vacuum where revenge and closure were supposed to be.

She stood in the center of the living room, feeling the dizzying weight of the silence. David's duffel bag, fat and defiant, lay near the front door. The apartment was a monument to their failure to pack away the grief. On the corner table, beneath a haphazard pile of unpaid bills and empty takeout containers, a sliver of shocking pink remained: the tattered corner of a paper napkin featuring a faded fairy tale castle. This, along with a slightly crumpled pirate eye-patch found underneath a magazine, was a relic of Lily's sixth birthday. The pirate or princess theme promotional materials were still spread across the table. Sarah had been too numb, too paralyzed, to even sweep up these planning remnants, leaving the abandoned promise of joy to decay beneath the evidence of sorrow.

She closed her eyes, trying to conjure Lily's face. She pictured Lily's laugh—a small, high, hiccuping sound. But when she focused, the image wasn't warm and blurry like an old photograph; it was stark, bright, and unnervingly pristine, like a high-resolution display. It made her chest seize with a cold fear that had nothing to do with grief. *Why does her hair look so precisely rendered?* she thought, rubbing the spot above her ear where she sometimes felt that fleeting, clinical pressure. *It's too perfect. I can't feel the real texture of it anymore.* It was as if her mind was retrieving a file, not experiencing a true memory. That sense of *perfection* made the loss ache even more deeply than the simple fading. The ghost was being polished away.

The air in the apartment tasted of stale nicotine and desperation. David emerged from the bedroom, looking equally ravaged but functional. His face was lined, his hands yellowed from chain-smoking cheap cigarettes, and the tremors in his right hand—which he now steadied with a cheap bottle of bourbon he kept in his jacket pocket—were constant. He wore a jacket heavy enough to conceal the slight bulk of his new habit, the needles and powders that kept his own overwhelming grief at bay. They were two separate chemical reactions, both reaching critical mass.

He didn't look at her; he looked at the floor.

"I called the landlord," David said, his voice flat, gravelly from neglect. "I told him I'm moving out. The lease is up in several weeks. You can take over the lease, month-to-month."

Sarah didn't move. The fentanyl had muted the shock, leaving her only with a curious, detached interest in the shape of his words.

"Month-to-month?" she repeated, her voice sounding thin.

"Yeah. That way, you're not locked in. And I'm not locked in." He picked up a box labeled 'Taxes and Documents' and set it down heavily by the door.

The Price of Silence

He reached into the deep pocket of his worn denim jacket and pulled out a wad of folded cash, crumpled and disorganized. He dropped the bills on the kitchen counter next to Sarah's abandoned coffee cup. "For the month-to-month rent," he murmured, avoiding her eyes. "There's about eight hundred here. It's... what was left over." Sarah looked at the money, then lifted her gaze to his face, her brow furrowed in thought. "Where did you get this?" she asked. The money was unexpected. David was broke. He finally met her eyes, and the sheer emptiness in them made her recoil. "It's the last asset," he said, his voice flat, devoid of emotion. "The final, stupid investment we never got to make." The coldness of his statement—the liquidation of some unnamed, hopeful future to pay for a month of oblivion—was stunning. It wasn't just a physical separation; it was the liquidation of their entire history.

"And where exactly is 'not locked in' taking you, David?"

He finally lifted his head, and the anger was a cold, pure sheet of ice. "Anywhere that doesn't smell like this. Anywhere that isn't a tomb where the only activity is you waiting for your next fix, and me waiting for you to stop punishing me for being the one who drove the car that day."

Sarah flinched, a sharp, involuntary tremor that was the first true emotion she'd felt all morning. "I don't punish you, David. I just can't look at you. You walk around with that martyr face, scrubbing floors, calling insurance, like you're cleaning up *my* mess."

"Maybe I am!" David exploded, his voice raw. "What else is left? The man responsible took the easy way out and stole our trial. He stole our right to see justice done, Sarah. So all that rage, all that guilt, it had nowhere to go but right here, at the two of us! You retreated into that room, and I retreated into..." He trailed off, gesturing vaguely toward the hidden pockets of his jacket. "...into everything else." His words were heavy, laying bare the true consequence of the driver's final act: the complete internalization of their shared trauma. "You checked out the moment Lily closed her eyes. You decided that room—that little twin bed—was your new coffin, and you've been laying waste to everything outside of it ever since."

"I need more than several weeks," she whispered, the numbness beginning to crack. "I have medical bills. And I have... expenses."

His gaze finally dropped to her arm, then back to her face. He didn't need to ask. The track marks were impossible to hide, even under the long sleeves she wore religiously. He saw the skeletal frame beneath the fabric. He saw his own reflection in her desperation.

"You have a job at the motel," he stated, devoid of emotion. "You'll have to take the night shifts. All of them. Just don't let it kill you before you figure out what you're actually mourning."

He pulled the apartment door open. The sound of the outside world—a car horn, distant laughter, the ordinary, indifferent rhythm of life—flooded the space. It was too loud.

"David," Sarah said, the name a plea for salvation.

He hesitated, his back to her, silhouetted in the brutal afternoon light. "Goodbye, Sarah. Maybe one of us can stop hurting someday."

He stepped across the threshold, and the door closed with a soft, definitive *thud*.

The silence that followed was different. It wasn't the shared, suffocating silence of two people trapped together; it was the vast, echoing silence of utter abandonment.

Sarah walked to the kitchen, found the liquor bottle David had left behind on the counter, and poured the remaining contents down the drain. She needed clarity now, or at least, a functional kind of fog.

Motel shifts. Lily's first-grade teacher had told her she had such a keen attention to detail. Sarah remembered that little boast, and for a terrifying second, the memory felt *more real* than the kitchen she was standing in.

She went to the payphone in the apartment lobby, dialed the manager's number from memory, and left a message: *I need all the hours you have. Nights, weekends. I can start tonight.*

The medical bills, the crushing rent in this place that held her pain, the desperate, escalating need for the numbing agent—it was a new arithmetic of survival. She was trading her remaining time, her sleep, and her body just to afford the ability to forget, piece by calculated piece, the memory that was already starting to feel so strangely, chillingly *rendered*. She was sacrificing her life to pay for a ghost.

CHAPTER 26

THE FIRST FOG

Three nights after David closed the door, the apartment was no longer a shared tomb; it was just a husk. Sarah's life had narrowed to a single, agonizing equation: work to afford the numbing agent, and the numbing agent to survive the work.

Her state was not grief; it was a functional shutdown. The shattering, intense pain that had broken the ceramic bowl was gone, replaced by a vast, cold detachment. This wasn't a choice; it was a psychological defense mechanism, a self-induced anesthesia against the traumatic reality. Her connection to her own body felt tenuous and unreliable, leaving her in a constant state of mild depersonalization. She moved and spoke in mechanical motions, watching her hands punch key codes and swipe credit cards as though the actions belonged to a character in a movie she had only mild interest in. The world felt too bright, too loud, too *real*, while she herself felt porous and distant, like an echo of a person. The fentanyl hadn't just dulled the pain; it had created a necessary barrier.

Before every shift, Sarah performed the same ritual—the Litany of Neutrality. She did not seek euphoria; that was a complication, a peak that would inevitably be followed by a crippling trough. Her goal was simply to reach zero, a flatline of emotion where consciousness existed purely to monitor basic functions.

She sat in the cramped cab of her rusted car, parked three spaces away from the Seabreeze Inn's dead neon sign. Her hands, steady and surgical, retrieved the small foil square and the rolled currency. There was no pleasure in the preparation, only clinical necessity. The cold metal of the key she used to manage the powder felt alien against her skin.

When the small, precisely measured line disappeared, there was the familiar, quiet rush—not of joy, but of a vast, spreading silence. It began behind her eyes and flowed down into her limbs, canceling the static of anxiety and the agonizing frequency of memory. It was the sound of a thousand screaming questions suddenly being muted. When she finally locked the car, she was a professional automaton, ready for eight hours of non-existence.

The motel was perfectly suited to her functional state because it also existed outside of time. It was twenty miles from the nearest ocean, but it smelled perpetually of stale tobacco, institutional cleaner, and the sickly-sweet decay of forgotten things.

Sarah was the graveyard shift sentinel, from 11 PM to 7 AM, the hours when the town slept. The toxic, pulsing green glow from the neon sign cast an unnatural hue across the plastic-laminate counter. Her world was a small rectangle dominated by a dusty rack of travel brochures and a quiet, persistent hum from the aging ventilation system.

Her duties—check in the late arrivals, answer the dead-quiet phone, clean, and perform the nightly "lock-down"—were simple enough, but the calculus of need constantly ran beneath the surface of her mind. She glanced at the ancient cash register, where the day manager kept a small float. Her stash of fentanyl was running desperately low, and every dose, every breath of manufactured silence, cost money. She was less than fifty dollars away from complete withdrawal, and the register was a foot away. The temptation wasn't about wanting more; it was about the primal, animal need to avoid the inevitable, crushing return of everything she had muted.

In the Deep Corners

Tonight, the lockdown duty required her to clean the tiny staff area tucked behind the back office. This was where the air was thickest, laced with residual odors of maintenance supplies, stale fast food, and desperation. The space held a microwave, a single water-stained armchair, and three rusted metal lockers belonging to the maintenance crew.

Sarah attacked the small space with an industrial-strength degreaser. It was a cleansing ritual, a desperate need to scrub away failure that had driven David to clean the grout months before. Now, it was her own failure she was trying to eradicate. She didn't feel rage or sadness, only an immense, blank necessity to wipe away the grime of existence.

She knelt by the bottom of the middle locker, scrubbing away a stubborn, dark, sticky patch near the baseplate. As she dragged the rag across the floor, it caught on something wedged between the locker's base and the wall. She reached blindly, pulling out a handful of dust, three expired tokens for a local arcade, and a piece of paper.

It was a flyer.

The paper was thick, glossy, and impossibly colored, a stark contrast to the mold and beige decay of the room. It showed a simple, stark cross under a bold, impossible headline: *The Anchor of Hope: Unconditional Salvation. A Seven-Day Evangelistic Seminar*

Below the title, in smaller print, were the seminar dates—long past, from the time when she still believed in promises—and a contact number. Sarah stared at it, the name Marta flashing briefly in the barren landscape of her mind. This was it—the flyer Marta had pressed into her hand what felt like a lifetime ago, urging her to seek a clean slate during her pregnancy. It was a relic, a forgotten promise, an impossible lifeline thrown from an era that no longer felt like her own history.

The sight of it brought a momentary, raw intrusion of reality—a spike of sharp, immediate pain that the fentanyl had struggled to prevent. *Marta is gone. This is irrelevant.*

She crumpled the glossy paper, the sound sharp and grating in the silence. Her conscious, numb mind decided instantly: Rejection. She stood up, intending to drop the wad of paper into the nearby trash bin by the counter. But as she moved, her hand dipped instinctively into the back pocket of her jeans.

The flyer, still crumpled but strangely intact, now rested against the small of her back. She didn't register the action; it was a reflex, a tiny, unbidden, animal refusal to discard the last tangible piece of connection to unconditional love. The act went unnoticed, swallowed by the functional fog that had become her only defense.

She worked through the night, selling four hours of sleep to a traveling businessman and renting a room to a pair of weary, arguing students. Each transaction was a small, quiet act of self-immolation. She was the sentinel of emptiness, the ghost guarding a non-existent sea, trading her time for the illusion of peace, never realizing that the memory of hope—the unwanted, discarded flyer—had just secured a place closest to her spine.

CHAPTER 27

THE NEW ARITHMETIC

The silence that had settled over the apartment was no longer the silence of shock; it was the heavy, pressurized silence of an airless tomb. After David left, the space didn't just feel empty—it felt hollowed out. This profound vacuum amplified every external sound into an excruciating intrusion. Sarah's days were spent in a chemical haze, but her nights at the Seabreeze Inn had become a brutal exercise in mechanical functionality.

The Seabreeze Inn night shift was a graveyard of low-stakes despair: the scent of stale chlorine and industrial air freshener, the hiss of the vending machine, and the sight of dead-eyed travelers checking in late. Sarah moved through the hours like a machine, her face a mask of exhausted politeness, her mind focused on a singular, urgent countdown.

Her entire existence was now dedicated to a litany of neutrality. She knew the precise moment her last dose would start to fail—usually around 7:30 AM, just after her shift ended. If she drove home without immediately addressing the impending crash, the anxiety would surge first, an electrical current running through her veins, followed by the first cold wave of withdrawal: clammy skin, a relentless drip from her nose, and myalgia—the deep, aching muscle pain that felt as though her bones were being stretched. The drug wasn't about the high; it was about holding the line, ensuring her body remained on a flat, gray, functional plateau where the sharp peaks of memory and the deep troughs of physical agony could not reach her. The only way to survive was to constantly outrun the sickness.

On Wednesday morning, standing over a cup of instant coffee, she did the new arithmetic. David's last wad of cash was gone. The rent was due in several days, and she had zero savings. The math was impossible—a chasm that cash from her paycheck alone couldn't possibly cross. The only remaining assets were the physical remnants of the life she had just lost. The drug had demanded everything else; now it was coming for the memories.

The withdrawal tightened its grip, turning her stomach into a knot of electric tension. She drove to a pawn shop three towns away, choosing anonymity over convenience.

After she sold several items from her home, she drove toward the discreet, familiar alley behind the laundromat where she made her daily transaction. The immediate goal was accomplished, but the money in her hand was tainted. As the familiar warmth of the chemical washed over her, dulling the edges of her racing mind and easing the cramps in her gut, she felt the first, sharp pang of regret. This money bought her three more days of sanity.

The Agony of Ordinary Joy

The week dissolved into the routine of dosing and working. By the morning, Sarah was deep into a post-shift crash, her reserves entirely depleted. She lay in bed, blankets pulled up, trying to cling to the last vestiges of chemically-induced sleep. Her body was a battlefield.

The piloerection—the medical term for goosebumps—was constant, giving her skin the texture of refrigerated chicken. Her legs felt possessed by a frantic, internal vibration, the agonizing onset of restless leg syndrome that urged her to thrash or walk, yet rendered her too exhausted to move. Every bone ached, and her gut was roiling.

Then, the sound started.

It was impossibly faint, a quiet, acoustic guitar and a man's low singing voice, muffled but distinct, leaking through the shared wall from the next-door unit. It wasn't loud enough to violate any rule; it was just a soft, gentle hum of communal life. The man was singing a simple, earnest hymn about grace and comfort.

Sarah hissed through clenched teeth. That quiet, gentle sound of undisturbed, simple faith was an agony she could not tolerate. It was a sound that belonged to a world she was permanently locked out of.

She snatched the nearest pillow and smashed it over her head, pressing it down hard enough that the rush of blood in her ears became a dull roar. The lyrics were still there, somehow, slipping past the thick barrier: "The Lord is my Shepherd... I shall not want..."

I shall not want, she thought bitterly, fighting the urge to claw at the plaster wall. I want one single hour without this sickness. I want my daughter. I want my life back.

She twisted onto her stomach, shoving the corner of the heavy duvet into her other ear, trying to burrow away from the sound. Her mind, already frantic from withdrawal, began a torturous internal argument. She counted the uneven ceiling tiles, counted the threads in the blanket, trying to find a pattern, a focus, anything to drown out the low, steady rhythm of the hymn. The noise of their happiness—the faint, high note of the wife joining the chorus, the tiny, muffled pop of a child's laughter that followed—was a physical irritant, sharp and clean, a constant reminder of the chaos of her own body and the devastation of her soul.

The singing finally stopped near noon, replaced by the mundane sounds of a vacuum cleaner starting up. The quiet left behind was oppressive. Sarah was shaking, sweat beading on her forehead, utterly defeated by the combination of physical withdrawal and psychological distress.

CHAPTER 28

PAWNED PIECES OF A LIFE

The withdrawal was a monster Sarah couldn't outrun—a living thing that hunted her every hour, every cell of her body. Her skin crawled with a sensation so raw and electric it felt as if her nerves had been stripped bare, a torment called the 'shivers of the soul' in the darkest corners of the opiate world. She was hot and cold at once; sweat prickled along her scalp while shivers rattled her spine, her teeth chattering with a violence she couldn't control. Every breath tasted of panic and failure. Just hold on. Just get through this one. She needed a dose—not for pleasure, but for a fleeting return to that gray, functional plateau where pain became background noise and memory lost its edge. I just want a few hours of normal.

She could barely remember the drive—only the way her hands trembled on the wheel, knuckles bone-white as she gripped it tight enough to hurt. The streets blurred past, indifferent to her agony, until she reached the small, independent pawn shop she'd come to rely on. It was the kind of place that never asked questions, where desperation was the universal language and dignity just another item to be traded away. I shouldn't be here again. I have nothing left to give.

Inside, the air was heavy with the scent of old metal and regret. Sarah laid out the remnants of her life on the counter: a faded plastic tiara, a chipped ceramic mug painted with childish hearts, a storybook with dog-eared corners— little things that had once belonged to Lily, each one a memory she was now forced to ransom. Her hands shook as she arranged them, trying not to look at the dealer, fearing that a single glance would shatter her thin composure. She could hear her own voice, harsh and accusing, echoing in her mind: What kind of mother sells her daughter's treasures for a fix?

"It's sentimental value," she mumbled, her voice barely audible, bracing for the insult she knew was coming. Maybe she'll see the truth of it. Maybe she'll offer more. Please, just this once.

The dealer, a woman with kind eyes that seemed to carry the weight of a thousand similar exchanges, didn't bother to haggle. She saw the desperation, not the items, and slid forty-five dollars across the counter. It was a paltry sum—an insult to Lily's memory, a mockery of everything these objects had once meant—but it was enough for the next fix. Forty-five. That's all your daughter is worth today. Sarah nodded, blinking back tears that burned not with grief but with the brutal relief of survival. You're pathetic. But you're alive, and that's all that matters right now.

She stumbled out into the daylight, clutching the bills so tightly they wrinkled beneath her fingers. The world outside was bright and indifferent, the sun glaring down with the same relentless clarity as her own self-loathing. I said I'd never do this. I said I'd keep at least one thing. Twenty minutes later, when the familiar chemical calm finally dulled the agony in her muscles and quieted the storm in her mind, she didn't feel relief. Instead, a fresh wave of sickness washed over her—a nauseating, hollow ache of self-hatred. You traded your child for peace you don't even deserve. You haven't just sold a handful of objects. You've sold the last physical evidence of your daughter's existence, and with it, another piece of your own soul.

As the physical objects vanished, the apartment grew perceptibly colder and emptier. The wood floor, once covered by rugs and furniture, now echoed her footsteps. The emptiness was a physical presence, a hostile entity that swallowed light and sound. The air in the living room began to smell faintly of dust and neglect, mixed with the acrid, stale scent of her own unwashed clothes.

Every evening, when she returned home from the Seabreeze Inn, she would stand in the increasingly barren living room, and the silence would roar in her ears. She felt like a ghost haunting her own grave, observing the slow, methodical stripping away of her identity.

The Absolute Final Strip

She had exactly zero dollars left in the bank, and her next paycheck was a week away. The landlady's note appeared on her door at 9:00 AM sharp: a friendly reminder that rent was due.

The last month of grinding, selling, and medicating had accomplished nothing but delaying the inevitable. She had spent the relics of her life just to survive each day, and now she faced eviction.

That morning's physical withdrawal was the worst yet. It was no longer just restless legs and sweating—it was full-body, mind-numbing agony. Her body was wracked with dry heaves, her stomach spasming violently over the toilet. The muscle cramps were so intense that she couldn't fully straighten her fingers. She lay curled on the floor, weeping—not from sadness, but from pure, biological misery.

She knew what she had to do. There were only two objects left of significant value that could possibly cover the gap and buy her one more month: her car and, as a final, cruel comfort, her mattress.

Two men arrived in a beat-up pickup truck to collect the mattress. They haggled aggressively, offering seventy dollars. She accepted, unable to sustain the conversation, and watched them scrape the mattress over the threshold. She was now sleeping on the bare box spring.

The car was next. A buyer paid her seven hundred and twenty dollars in cash—an amount that, for the first time in a month, felt like a lifeline. She didn't look back as he drove away. The loss felt like a physical amputation; she had sacrificed her independence, her escape route, and the last shred of mobility that connected her to a normal life.

She paid the landlady in the main office, the act feeling less like stability and more like postponing an execution. She was left with *ten dollars*, which she placed in her *back pocket*.

Her new reality began the next night, as she prepared for her 11 PM shift. The Seabreeze Inn was four miles away, a daunting, dead stretch of suburban road.

At 10:30 PM, Sarah put on her threadbare windbreaker. The air was cold, damp, and thick with the scent of night-blooming jasmine and exhaust. As she started walking, her shoes felt heavy on the pavement. The streetlights cast long, lonely shadows that stretched and shrank with every labored step.

She thought about Lily, who used to beg for rides in the car, pretending the backseat was a rocket ship. She thought about David, who used to drive her home after the night shift, sharing the quiet darkness. Now, there was no sound but the scuff of her own worn-out sneakers and the frantic, shallow rhythm of her breath.

Four miles felt like a thousand. By the time she reached the glowing, toxic green sign of the Seabreeze Inn, her legs were burning, her lungs ached, and her back was screaming from the cumulative withdrawal damage. She was sweating, cold, and utterly alone, a pedestrian in a world built for cars. She was entirely dependent on her own two exhausted legs, which were entirely dependent on the chemical she was desperately trying to afford.

She had hit rock bottom. And the only sound was the cold, hollow echo in the empty apartment she would return to at dawn.

The Catastrophe

It was 3:45 AM. Sarah had just completed her nightly cleaning routine and found five dollars in a lobby couch. The lobby was silent, the quiet amplified by the throbbing in Sarah's temples. The air conditioner felt like it was blowing ice directly onto her spine. A guest, an older man in a pristine silk robe, approached the desk with a room service receipt in hand.

"Excuse me," he said, his voice loud in the quiet space. "This charge for the imported water is incorrect. I specifically asked for tap. I need it adjusted now."

Sarah stared at the receipt, willing the numbers on the thermal paper to stop vibrating. Her brain felt slow, thick, and resistant to processing even simple arithmetic. She fumbled with the keyboard, her fingers mistyping the adjustment code three times. Then, the involuntary symptoms started: her leg suddenly kicked out—a powerful, deep spasm that shook her whole body. She grabbed the edge of the desk to steady herself.

The guest watched, his annoyance turning to disgust. "What in the hell is wrong with you?"

Mr. Henderson appeared from the back office, having heard the commotion. He didn't need to ask. The evidence was overwhelming: the profuse sweat in the air conditioning, the uncontrolled leg kicks, the inability to speak, and the vacant, unfocused terror in her wide-pupilled eyes.

He stepped around the counter, addressing the guest first. "Sir, I apologize. Your bill will be adjusted immediately. I will handle this." The finality in his voice brooked no argument.

He waited until the guest walked away, then turned to Sarah. His face wasn't angry; it was tired, utterly defeated.

"Sarah. Look at me." His voice was a low, devastating rumble. "We both know what this is. You're shaking so bad you can't hold a pen. I've watched you deteriorate. I am done covering for you. You're a liability, and I can't risk this floor anymore."

She shook her head violently, the movement making her dizzy. "Please, Mr. Henderson," she pleaded, the words wet and desperate. "I just need one more day. I just need to catch up. I'll go to the clinic. I promise, I can clean up. I can't lose this job, it's all I have left."

"There's no cleaning up here, Sarah," he said, his eyes reflecting a deep disappointment. "The job is over. I watched you walk in this week, and you looked closer to death than to the counter. I'm doing you a favor, sending you home before you collapse here." He reached behind the desk and picked up a brown paper bag. "I printed your final HR documents. They're processing the partial deposit. Clock out. Leave your badge. Don't come back."

Sarah stood frozen, watching him input the termination into the computer. She was dismissed, abandoned, and utterly cut adrift. She was a liability, not an employee. She was nothing. She numbly took off her cheap polyester jacket, placed her badge on the counter, and started the four-mile walk home.

CHAPTER 29

END OF THE LEDGER

The four-mile walk began with the knowledge that only a single five-dollar bill remained—a useless, folded piece of paper. It was the last ghost of solvency, a token of a life that no longer existed, which was spent on a dry tuna sandwich at a small convenience store next to the motel.

She managed only two painful bites before the withdrawal nausea turned the food into a brick in her throat. She found herself standing over a dumpster, the open brown bag still in her hand. This food was the final physical buffer between her and complete collapse, yet her body rejected it instantly.

It was then she saw him. Tucked against the cold, grease-stained concrete sat a dog, gaunt and skeletal. Its ribs were stark monuments beneath a matted coat, and its eyes, large and dark, held the defeated exhaustion of an animal that had long since stopped fighting the cold hunger. It didn't whine or beg; it simply waited for the end.

The dog was a mirror.

Sarah stopped. She looked at the remaining sandwich. She knew she desperately needed every calorie for the agonizing walk ahead, but the realization was cold and clear: She was already dead; the dog was merely starving. Her own survival instinct had been fatally compromised.

Ignoring the violent tremors in her hands and the screaming protest of her knees, she lowered herself to the ground. She pulled the remaining tuna filling from the stale bread and placed the moist, cold pile directly onto the pavement. The dog's head lifted slowly, hesitantly, then lunged, devouring the food in two frantic, grateful gulps.

Sarah remained kneeling, watching this final, small act of nourishment. The last of her physical hope was gone, freely given. A single, hot tear—the final one—traced a line through the grime on her cheek. She didn't speak, didn't touch the dog. She simply stood, leaving the empty paper bag and her last piece of strength behind. The dog's quick gratitude was the final, devastating punctuation mark on her act of ruin.

From that moment, the walk was a forced march through a living nightmare. Her body executed its complete betrayal. The chemical agony—the deep, marrow-searing cold and the electrical tremors—intensified with the speed of an avalanche.

She stumbled past the Old Library Cafe, and the memory of David, his smile slow, his hands reaching for hers across the chipped wooden table, was an electric shock of grief. She had thrown away the certainty of his love for this shivering, absolute void.

She dragged herself past the Community Center. She saw Lily in her favorite bright yellow "sunshine coat," clutching a bouquet of daffodils, her pure eyes looking up. The memory stole her breath, forcing a painful, dry heave from her chest. She had destroyed her daughter's sunshine. Every step was an accusation.

She was navigating the final, residential blocks when she heard a low, raspy voice.

"Hey, can you spare anything? Anything at all, please."

She didn't stop. She didn't look up properly. The figure was simply a dark, ragged blur slumped against a brick pillar—another ghost in her crumbling world, indistinguishable from the thousand others she had avoided. But this time, she didn't avoid him. She was moving in a trance, numbly past the point of self-preservation.

Her fingers felt around her pockets and, reaching into her *back pocket*, she pulled out the crisp, singular bill. *The ten dollars.* Her final link to the world of buying and selling, of paying utility deposits, of having a future.

Sarah knew this money was meaningless. It wouldn't buy her salvation, it wouldn't pay her rent, and it wouldn't bring David and Lily back. It was only an anchor, binding her to the crushing obligation of trying to survive. She felt a profound, cold liberation in letting it go.

Without breaking her stride, without a word, without even making eye contact, she simply extended her shaking hand and dropped the $10 bill into the blurred figure's waiting, cupped palm.

The figure mumbled something—"Bless you," maybe, or "Thank you"— but Sarah was already gone, moving into the deeper dark. She had given away her last meal, and now, she had given away her last dime. She had surrendered the final, fragile scrap of her ability to fight.

She reached the complex, a skeletal silhouette collapsing against the final guardrail. The key fell from her hand, rattling on the asphalt, but she didn't care. It took three agonizing tries before she got the key into the lock.

Inside the barren, unheated apartment, she didn't even try to stand. She crawled the last few feet across the raw wood floor to the box spring. Her breathing was shallow, ragged, and wet. She collapsed onto the thin blankets.

There was no money left to hide, no treasure to protect, no illusion of a buffer.

She reached her empty hand under the box spring, the gesture an automatic reflex of habit. Her fingers met only dust and the bare wood frame. The absence was absolute.

Sarah lay back, staring into the dark ceiling. She was truly empty now—of calories, of funds, of hope, and finally, of the will to mourn. She had made it home. And home was absolute zero.

CHAPTER 30

THE COLD DESCENT

Sarah didn't wake; she was jolted into a hyper-conscious state of pure, chemical misery. The effect of the final dose was gone, leaving only the raw, screaming nerve endings of her body. She was submerged in a deep crash, an experience far worse than anything before because there was no future reprieve, no dose waiting at the end of the night shift.

Her entire body was a generator of relentless, violent movement. She thrashed helplessly on the thin blankets atop the box spring, her arms and legs cycling in painful, involuntary spasms—the terrible, private dance of the "kicking disease." Her muscles felt as if they were being simultaneously stretched and torn apart, making the simple act of lying still an absolute impossibility. The mattress had been her sanctuary; the box spring was a cage.

The silence of the apartment, once so loud, was now replaced by a deafening, constant internal static. A high-pitched, metallic hiss filled her ears, drowning out all thought, a soundtrack to the chaos in her mind. Every external sound—a distant dog bark, the scrape of a passing car—was amplified into a shattering trauma.

She was wracked by dry heaves, her stomach convulsing so violently that her ribs ached. There was nothing left to expel, only bile and the sour taste of self-loathing. The effort of these spasms was exhausting her last reserves of physical strength.

The apartment was stripped bare, a mausoleum for everything she'd lost. The kitchen counter was empty, the floor icy under her skin, the windows smeared with a film of neglect. Even the faded stains on the wall seemed to have retreated, as if the apartment itself was recoiling from what she had become. Shadows hung heavy in every corner, the air dense with the residue of old meals, old arguments, and old hope—now replaced by a relentless, gnawing emptiness.

Sarah's search was desperate and animal. On hands and knees, she scraped her raw fingers along the wooden planks, her cheek pressed flat to the splinters as she peered under cabinets and behind pipes. Every inch of her body ached from the effort, but the need was greater than the pain. She overturned a cracked mug, pried at the floorboards, even sniffed at the faintest white dust, hoping it was something more than just plaster. The ghosts of habit screamed at her to keep looking, but all she found was the cold, unyielding confirmation that her stash was truly gone. There would be no reprieve, no magic rescue, not even a stray pill to stretch her collapse another hour.

With her energy spent, she slumped onto the floor, her breath clouding in the morning light that slanted through the blinds. The dust motes spun in the air, catching sunbeams in a cruel parody of beauty. Her body was a mass of pain, her skin slick with sweat and cold, her muscles twitching uncontrollably. Her mind was a riot of regret, every failure replaying on a loop: the faces she'd disappointed, the money she'd stolen, Lily's laughter and Lily's absence—each memory sharper than the last. The high-pitched whine in her ears grew louder, drowning out even her own sobs, until she was left with nothing but the numbness of loss and the certainty that survival had finally abandoned her. Alone in the center of her ruined world, Sarah faced the full, haunting weight of what she could never get back.

The World Closes In

The morning stretched into a fevered blur, Sarah drifting in and out of consciousness, the high-pitched ringing in her skull now joined by the relentless ache of her body. She could barely distinguish between the real and the imagined: the weightless sense of falling, the phantom pressure of hands on her shoulders, the imagined sound of Lily's voice calling her name. But all of it was drowned out by the oppressive silence of the apartment—until, suddenly, that silence was annihilated by a pounding so loud it rattled the glass in the windows.

BAM. BAM. BAM.

The sound was not just a knock; it was an assault—a physical demand that shattered the fragile barrier between Sarah and the world outside. Her heart tripped into a wild, juddering panic. Each blow on the door seemed to reverberate through her bones, spiking her withdrawal into a fresh, agonizing terror. The tremors in her limbs became violent, her breath coming in short, desperate gasps. She pressed herself against the floor, trying to disappear, but there was nowhere left to hide.

A pause. Then the soft, sinister scrape of paper—an unhurried, almost contemptuous gesture—as something was shoved beneath the door. The footsteps receded. The silence that followed was even worse than the pounding, thick and punitive.

Moving took everything Sarah had. But the drive to know—the raw instinct to survive, not hope—pushed her body forward. She crawled, her elbows and knees scraping painfully over the bare wood. Each movement was a test of endurance, her muscles burning, her mind clouded by dread. When she finally reached the threshold, she lifted her head just enough to see a single white sheet of paper resting on the floor: a formal, legalistic Notice to Vacate, its language cold and final. The landlady had made it official—her last tenuous link to safety was severed.

For a long moment, Sarah could only stare at the paper, her body shuddering with exhaustion. The notice seemed impossibly far away, even as it lay inches from her. Finally, with effort that made her whole body tremble, she forced her aching arm forward and closed her fingers around the page.

Sarah's fingers trembled as she picked up the notice. In the harsh light, the words seemed to mock her. Her home, her only sanctuary, was now just a condemned shell—a place where every sacrifice, every desperate act, had been rendered meaningless by a single sheet of paper. She let it fall from her hand, the rectangle glowing in the morning sun, and lay back, stunned by the absolute certainty of her ruin. The world had closed in, and there was nowhere left to run.

The Last Refuge

The crawl to the bathroom felt endless, the apartment behind her blurring into a tunnel of pain and shame. The tile beneath her hands was cold, almost biting, and the fluorescent light overhead cast a jaundiced, clinical glare on the walls. She barely registered the cracked grout or the faint, mildew-soured smell that lingered in the corners. All that mattered was enclosure—a place small enough to contain her collapse.

She slumped against the bathtub, her cheek pressed to the icy porcelain. For a long moment, she just breathed, listening to the harsh, uneven sound of air scraping through her throat. It was the opposite of comfort: the tub was hard, the air stale, the silence brutal. Yet, it was the only place left where she could fall apart without witnesses.

With the last dregs of energy, Sarah climbed into the tub, her movements clumsy and desperate. The porcelain was shockingly cold against her skin. She curled up, knees to her chest, arms wrapped tight, making herself as small as possible. The tub was streaked with mildew and empty—a blank canvas for oblivion.

For a time, she simply existed in the harsh overhead light, letting it bleach her thoughts to static. Her mind was a blur of physical sensation: the ache in her bones, the burning in her gut, the relentless hum of withdrawal. She felt the fight drain from her body, replaced by a numb, mechanical breathing that grew shallower by the minute. The static in her head—once a shrill background noise—now rose up, drowning out everything but the bare fact of survival. She reached for the faucet, her hand trembling so violently she could barely grip the handle. When she managed to turn it, a rush of cold water poured in, hammering her legs, filling the basin with a merciless, rising chill.

She lay there, shivering, as the cold crept up her body, numbing her skin and dulling even the sharpest pain. She watched the water climb, inch by inch, up her thighs, her hips. The sensation was surreal, both a punishment and a perverse comfort—a surrender to the inevitable.

As the water rose, the static in her mind finally fractured, and memory poured in with a savage, unfiltered violence. Lily. Not her face, not her voice, but the shocking, physical absence. The memory was not gentle; it was a blade, an accusation. She saw Lily's hand, not reaching for comfort, but pointing—at the mess, at Sarah's failures, at the sum of everything she had lost.

Images came in a torrent: the sticky-sweet smell of cotton candy at the fair, Lily's small hand gripping hers, the blue ribbon from the science fair, a heavy apartment key, the taste of the first forbidden dose. Each fragment cut deeper, a montage of love and ruin. The static tried to reassert control, but the memories were too fast, too sharp. One image rose above the rest: Lily, laughing, alive on a bright, impossibly clean beach. That laughter was the last thing Sarah could hold onto—a fragile, radiant thread in the dark.

The water kept climbing. The cold was now absolute. The pressure of the noise and the weight of memory converged into a single, unbearable moment. Her body curled tighter in the bottom of the tub, every muscle trembling. There was nothing left but surrender: to the cold, to the silence, to the truth of everything lost.

But as her body began to give out, as numbness pulled her toward unconsciousness, Lily's laughter echoed through her mind—a single, unreachable note of light in the mounting dark. Even as her consciousness slipped away, Sarah clung to that sound. It was the only warmth left in the world, and she held it, fierce and desperate, as the water and the static finally threatened to pull her under.

CHAPTER 31

THE PARENT WHO SURVIVED

The moment of ultimate surrender was not peaceful; it was a state of agonizing apathy. Sarah lay curled on her side in the porcelain basin, her spine pressed against the cold, sterile curve of the tub. The withdrawal spasms—the relentless kicking, the cramping in her jaw, the involuntary clenching of her fists—still assaulted her, but she had stopped fighting them. They were merely the final, irrelevant tremors of a machine shutting down.

The running water, already past her hips and thighs, slowly crept toward her stomach and chest. It was lethally cold—a chill that had pierced the thin blanket of her skin and was now sinking into her bone marrow. The pressure was heavy and suffocating, yet strangely clean. The constant, high-pitched chemical buzz that had defined the last day of her life roared in her inner ear, but its meaning was gone. It was just white noise now, the sound of an empty broadcast. She had nothing left to protect, nothing to achieve, and nothing to lose. This was the dark peace she had sought.

It was through this deafening void, through the drumming cascade of the faucet, that a sound pierced the silence: laughter.

It was not the jarring, amplified noise that usually tormented her, but a delicate, bright melody. It sounded exactly like Lily's laugh—a joyous, unrestrained chime that had once made her own shoulders shake. Sarah's eyes, dull and unfocused, blinked slowly. The vision of Lily on the beach, radiant in the sunlight, flashed behind her eyelids. It's finally happening, she thought, her lips too dry and stiff to form the words. My mind is giving me the gentle exit. The phantom laughter was a comfort, a cruel, beautiful hallucination beckoning her away from the pain. She held onto the sound, letting it wash over her like a final, soothing wave of warmth.

The sound, however, lingered just a moment too long, developing a rough edge, a tinny distortion. As it began to resolve into the mundane sound of a family's television next door, the illusory comfort vanished, leaving her stranded once more in the escalating cold of the tub.

Then, the background noise resolved itself into a specific, deliberate voice. It was a man, his tone deep and gentle, almost conversational, yet his words carried an unnatural, unnerving clarity through the water-logged tiles and the cheap drywall. It was the soft, insistent voice of an evening evangelical speaker, the sound slightly muffled but every syllable clear.

"...to anyone hearing these words, if you are broken, there is a God that loves you. That is calling you away from the suicidal situation you are in."

Sarah's breath hitched—a sharp, ragged intake of air that hurt her dry throat. The coincidence was impossible, terrifyingly precise. The buzzing in her head, challenged by the specificity of the message, momentarily broke. The rush of the faucet, which had seemed so loud, suddenly felt distant, secondary.

The voice continued, planting a seed of foreign thought: "For God so loved the world that he gave his only begotten Son, that whosoever believeth in Him should not perish, but have everlasting life" (John 3:16 KJV).

The familiar scripture did not register as dogma or religious platitude; it struck her as a brutal, agonizing truth. His only begotten Son.

She lay trembling in the icy water, the final, desperate surrender giving way to a white-hot realization that cut through her despair. He wasn't a distant judge or a cosmic manager of fate. He was a parent who had lost His child. A Father who had watched his Son die. That made Him a survivor. The Ultimate Survivor.

The knowledge was electrifying. All these years, she had felt utterly alone in her grief, her pain too immense for any other human being to truly comprehend. Yet, the voice in the wall was suggesting kinship with the divine. This massive, eternal entity was also wounded. He carried the same unhealed scar.

How did He survive?

The question was not theological; it was existential. It was the only question that mattered to the broken, childless mother in the bathtub, her damp hair plastered to her cheeks, her breath fogging the air as the cold water crept higher. It gave her one thing the drugs had never offered, one thing the abyss could not take: a reason to learn. The ache in her bones sharpened into a thread of purpose, cutting through the numbness.

With a desperate, animal grunt, Sarah forced her left arm to move. The effort was astronomical. The muscles in her arm were weak, shaky, and cold, protesting the command with severe spasms. It felt like trying to lift a boulder through wet cement. Her knuckles scraped the porcelain as she hunted for the cold, chrome faucet handle.

The urge to collapse, to let the water reach her upper chest and neck, was overwhelming, but the single thought—*How did He survive?*—was a filament of pure steel holding her will intact.

Her frozen fingers finally curled around the pitted metal. She squeezed, grinding her teeth as she twisted the handle with every ounce of physical and psychological strength she possessed.

Creeeak.

The sound was a raw, metallic scream that echoed in the tiled room. The running water stopped. The resulting silence was instant, thick, and deafening. Sarah lay still, utterly spent, shivering violently in the now-still, mounting cold. But her eyes were open, fixed on the dirty ceiling, and the thought persisted. She needed to know the secret of the surviving parent.

CHAPTER 32

BETWEEN TWO WORLDS

The silence was louder than the water had been. Sarah lay motionless in the stopped, freezing water, her heart pounding a sick, irregular rhythm against her ribs. The chemical ringing in her ears screamed again, trying to regain dominance, but the question—*How did He survive?*—had cauterized a tiny, clean space in her mind. It was a purpose—the first in years—and it didn't involve a needle or a bag of powder.

But that new purpose required action, and action required a body that obeyed.

For several agonizing seconds, Sarah simply listened to the faint drip of water echoing in the bathroom. The world outside the tub felt impossibly far, but the memory of the voice—its warmth and clarity—called her back. She gathered her remaining strength, focusing on the promise of something beyond pain. Crawling out of the bathtub was a process of sheer, grunting will. Her muscles were locked in painful rigor, and the withdrawal tremors racked her from scalp to heel. Every fraction of movement sent bolts of fire through her joints. She managed to flop herself over the edge of the tub and onto the tiled floor, where she lay for a full minute, her cheek pressed to the cold tile, gathering the energy to move again.

She had to get out. She had to find the source of that voice.

Her movement was less a crawl than a wounded, dragging motion through the bathroom doorway. The cold, raw wood of the living room floor was a map of her collapse. She bypassed the Notice to Vacate—it was just paper now, irrelevant—and followed the sound's ghost, tracing the shared wall that separated her empty shell from the lives next door.

She reached the living room wall, rising onto a wobbly elbow, her ear pressed to the paint. She could hear the faint, comforting murmur of life: the low drone of the television, the clink of dishes, and the soft, steady voice of a woman speaking. It was a symphony of simple domesticity.

The family was named The Millers; Sarah knew this only through the occasional pieces of misdelivered junk mail she would toss back onto their mat. They were a quiet, small family—a husband, a wife, and the small child whose laughter had provided the fleeting, phantom welcome in the tub.

As Sarah listened, she heard the woman's voice, which was quiet and kind: "...just the one car, dear. We need to leave soon if we want good seats at the seminar. We are already late."

The seminar. The event. The source of the secret.

It was her only way out. She could not walk four miles in this condition. She had to beg a ride. This was the final, most humiliating confrontation of her ruin.

She dragged herself to the Miller's front door. She stood, leaning heavily, her body shuddering so violently she risked falling. She was a sight of total degradation: pale, sweating, hair matted to her temples, wearing only the thin, filthy blankets that had been her prison sheets.

With a trembling hand, she raised her knuckle and managed a pathetic, barely audible tap-tap against the wood of her neighbor's door. A moment of silence stretched taut. Then, the sound of a bolt sliding back.

The door opened to reveal Maria Miller, a small, gentle woman in her early forties with kind, wide-set eyes and a simple, braided hairstyle. She was dressed in a neat, conservative skirt and sweater—the picture of quiet domesticity. The sight of Sarah, a skeletal wreck covered in grime and reeking of fear, barely standing, made Maria freeze. Her hand flew to her mouth, and she gasped softly.

"Oh my God. What... what happened?"

Sarah couldn't manage a full sentence. Her tongue was too thick, her voice a raw whisper shredded by dry heaves. The effort to form the words was more painful than the cold in the tub.

"Seminar," Sarah rasped, pointing a skeletal, shaking finger toward the sound of the TV. "Church. The... the grieving. Can I... come with you? Please."

Maria's face was a study in shock, pity, and immediate revulsion. She looked back over her shoulder into her warm, brightly lit apartment, then back to the apparition in her doorway.

"We are going to the old church just down the road. We're leaving now," Maria said, her voice tight but not unkind. She closed the door halfway, the latch clicking but not fully engaging.

A minute later, the door reopened a crack. Maria didn't step out, but she quickly pushed a small pile of items through the gap: a dark bath towel, a plastic cup of water, and a bundle of faded, oversized sweatpants and a pullover. "Take this. Please," Maria instructed. "You need to clean up and get dressed. You can ride with us, but we have to go now."

She shut the door, the noise of the sliding bolt confirming the barrier between their two worlds. Sarah didn't care. She drank the water in painful gulps and managed to pull on the clothes, the clean fabric offering a small, unfamiliar comfort. The journey was not over, but the direction had finally changed.

CHAPTER 33

WHEN CERTAINTY BREAKS THE STORM

The ride with Maria and Mark Miller was steeped in silent, thick tension. Sarah, now marginally covered in the Millers' borrowed, oversized clothing, endured the journey in a fog of shame, nausea, and grinding anxiety. The Millers kept their windows down a crack, letting the cool night air into the car. Their daughter, tucked in her car seat, occasionally stared without comprehension at the trembling woman with the dead eyes. The car smelled of fresh laundry and faint vanilla—a scent of intense normalcy that felt like a mocking reflection of the life Sarah had lost.

The church was an old, humble brick building, slightly set back from a main street. It lacked the grand steeple or stained glass of larger denominations. Inside, the space felt lived-in, layered with years of service and community. The air was heavy, smelling less of sterile air conditioning and more of old wood, dust, and a persistent, faint aroma of aged paper and leather-bound Bibles, mixed with the residual scent of strong, recently-brewed coffee—hints of its identity as an old, bilingual ethnic church that regularly hosted outside events and fellowship meals.

Just inside the door, a very elderly woman with kind, deeply-lined eyes greeted them. She paused, her smile momentarily wavering when she saw Sarah's distressed state, then quickly recovered, offering a gentle, nonjudgmental nod. "Welcome back!" she whispered to Maria and Mark, her focus briefly settling on Sarah. "And welcome to you! We're happy to have you with us." Her voice was sweet and caring. She handed Sarah a thick study bible and a cheap, thin English-language study guide titled "Hope for the Future." Sarah gripped the paper, focusing on the simple shapes of the letters to ground herself as her body fought the drug's absence.

Maria quickly steered them toward a back pew, strategically leaving a decisive space between her family and Sarah.

A moment later, the pastor stepped onto the low, wooden stage. His presence brought a sense of calm. He radiated a quiet, steady authority that transcended the humble setting. Wearing silver-rimmed glasses and a dark suit, he carried himself with the approachable confidence of a mentor rather than the bombast of a revivalist. He leaned into the mic, his voice deep, warm, and measured—delivering each word with sincerity and gravity, never showmanship.

"Good evening, everyone. My name is Pastor Anderson," he said. After a few brief announcements that Sarah barely registered, he shifted his focus.

He paused, then began to pray, his tone gentle and familiar. "Lord, we just pray now for guidance, Your Holy Spirit, as we talk about one of the most misunderstood questions on the planet: what happens at death. Lord, the only way we can really know is to go to Scripture and see what You said happens. We pray for Your guidance, Your Holy Spirit, in Jesus' name we pray." The pastor's language was never formal or rehearsed; he spoke as if God were a friend in the room, welcoming all into the conversation, and Sarah found comfort in the absence of religious performance.

After the prayer, his tone shifted, his eyes looking out over the room with a focused intensity that seemed to bypass the crowd and land directly on her.

"Tonight," he continued, holding up the study guide, "we talk about the end of things. However, we begin by discussing the start. The biggest question is not, '*What is my future in Heaven?*' The biggest question is: *How do I live when the storm is still raging?*"

He then shared his story, his voice dropping to a low, powerful register. "A few years ago, I didn't know the answer to that. I was in the hospital, sick, completely isolated. I saw death. I stood at the threshold, and I understood, intimately, the fear that comes when everything you trust—your breath, your strength, your future—is taken away. I was face-to-face with the end of my story."

His experience—the personal, brutal confrontation with mortality—was precisely the secret Sarah sought. He spoke with the hard-won authority of a man who knew what it felt like to be abandoned to the void.

"The greatest fear," he said softly, "is not the grave. It is walking alone before the grave. My point is this: you can't answer the question of death until you understand how to accept life."

Pastor Anderson moved away from the stage and walked among the first few rows, his voice gaining a new urgency. He began to contextualize human suffering, lifting it out of the realm of random tragedy and into a cosmic war.

"Why do good people suffer? Why do children die? Why does a loving God permit this pain?" he asked. "The Bible calls this the Great Controversy. The suffering you feel isn't random; it is the fallout of an ancient, cosmic conflict between Christ and a powerful enemy—an enemy who works tirelessly to destroy hope and life."

He paused, looking directly at the rows near the back. "Don't ever believe that your pain is solely your fault. There is a spiritual battle raging, and you, my friend, are caught in the middle. We are warned of this adversary: 'Be sober, be vigilant; because your adversary the devil, as a roaring lion, walketh about, seeking whom he may devour:' (1 Peter 5:8, KJV). The storm is not God's punishment; it is the enemy's assault."

The Unchanging Character of Love

He returned to the pulpit, his tone shifting from one of warning to one of profound assurance. "But the enemy's power is limited by the unchanging character of God. We must understand the kind of being who promises us hope. The Bible tells us something foundational about Him that we can hold onto when the world is chaos: 'He that loveth not knoweth not God; for God is love' (1 John 4:8, KJV).

"God is love. His law, the Ten Commandments, isn't a list of arbitrary rules; it's a mirror reflecting His loving character. We are dying, not because God is mean, but because sin—the transgression of that loving law—brings death. 'For the wages of sin is death; but the gift of God is eternal life through Jesus Christ our Lord' (Romans 6:23, KJV). God's solution isn't to change the law; His solution is to change *us* by giving us Jesus."

Pastor Anderson addressed the core of true hope: assurance. "How do we know this isn't just a nice story? How do we know that Christ will actually return and end this controversy? Because God doesn't just promise—He proves it. He gave us prophecy."

He emphasized that God's plan for the future, laid out thousands of years ago in books like Daniel and Revelation, is history written in advance. "Prophecy is the anchor in the storm. It removes doubt and fear by showing you the roadmap. When you see history aligning perfectly with ancient Scripture, you realize the promise of hope is not wishful thinking—it is a certainty you can stake your life on."

He lifted his Bible high. "We don't need to guess about tomorrow; we have a God who revealed it all. 'We have also a more sure word of prophecy; whereunto ye do well that ye take heed, as unto a light that shineth in a dark place, until the day dawn, and the day star arise in your hearts:'" (2 Peter 1:19, KJV).

As Pastor Anderson spoke these final words, something shifted inside Sarah's mind. It was a dizzying, terrifying release. She realized that everything she had been taught—the rigid, unforgiving gospel preached by Reverend Smith in Havenwood—was nothing more than a legalistic torture.

Reverend Smith, with his booming voice and furious fist slamming the mahogany pulpit, had focused the entire weight of eternity on Sarah's outward conformity: on her hemline, her vanity, and her fear. His message was purely conditional: *obey the law perfectly, or face eternal damnation.* Smith saw her pain as proof of her deserved fate, demanding she pluck out her eye of offense. He had used the Bible as a weapon of scrutiny to keep the congregation in line, turning the love of God into a constant threat. In Smith's church, God was the ultimate Auditor, and she was always failing the inspection.

Pastor Anderson, in stark contrast, didn't mention her clothing or her past. He didn't focus on *her* sin as the primary issue, but on the cause of all suffering. He reframed her anguish, calling it not God's punishment but the "enemy's assault," the inevitable fallout of the Great Controversy. He used Scripture not to condemn her but to give her context, painting God as the ultimate Rescuer, whose character is purely Love. Anderson's calm, measured voice offered a certainty based not on her ability to perform, but on God's proven ability to keep promises laid out in prophecy.

Smith had demanded a spotless life Sarah couldn't deliver, driving her straight into a death wish. Anderson was offering an *instruction manual for re-entry,* grounding her survival not in her own strength, but in an external, unshakable reality based on grace. The intense shivering in her hands finally began to subside.

As Pastor Anderson moved among the congregation, a hand rose in the back—hesitant, trembling. It was not Sarah's, but the question was hers: "Pastor, God gave His only Son. How did He survive that loss?"

He paused, letting the sanctuary grow utterly still. He opened his Bible and read with deliberate gravity, "And, behold, the veil of the temple was rent in twain from the top to the bottom; and the earth did quake, and the rocks rent" (Matthew 27:51 KJV).

He looked up, his voice tender. "When Jesus died, the earth itself trembled, the rocks split, and the great veil in the temple was torn from top to bottom. The Scriptures show us that all creation felt the agony of the Father's loss.

God's heart was not untouched—He suffered with His Son. But the Father also knew the resurrection was coming. He knew that love would have the last word, that death would be defeated, and that His Son would rise again. That same hope—the assurance of resurrection, of reunion—is what He offers to every parent, every child, every person who has tasted grief. God survives not by ignoring pain, but by sharing the victory to come. He draws near to every grieving soul and says, 'Your story doesn't end in the grave. My Son's resurrection is the promise of yours, too.'"

He lifted his Bible again and concluded with one more verse, his voice resonant with hope: "For he hath made him to be sin for us, who knew no sin; that we might be made the righteousness of God in him" (2 Corinthians 5:21 KJV). "God gave everything—His Son became what we are, so that we could go where He is. That is the hope that carries us through every storm, and the certainty that breaks it."

The Pastor closed the session with a simple, "Good night, everyone, and God bless," then stepped down to greet those in the front. Sarah opened the study guide, looking at the first topic in bold letters. She decided she was staying.

CHAPTER 34

REST FOR THE WEARY

The Millers' car waited quietly at the curb outside the old church. The small, humble building, lit by a single wrought-iron lamp, stood as a stark contrast to the surrounding night's darkness.

As they left the sanctuary, the elderly attendant with kind eyes who had greeted them upon arrival stood by the double doors. She smiled warmly at Sarah, "Have a good night, dear," the attendant said softly.

She didn't look up, only managing a whispered, "Thanks."

Mark buckled their daughter in the child seat, and Sarah sat next to her. Maria started the car, pulling quietly into the dark street.

Maria broke the silence softly, her voice low. "How are you holding up, Sarah? That was... a lot of information to process all at once."

Sarah's throat was tight, and the motion of the car felt dizzying. She stared out the window, focusing on the rhythmic blur of the streetlights. "Fine."

Mark, catching her reflection in the rearview mirror, didn't press. "She's right, it's okay if you aren't. It takes time for the mind to catch up to the soul. Just tell us if you need us to pull over."

"No," Sarah managed, the single word sharp.

Mark let out a quiet, understanding sigh. "Try to let it settle tonight. Lean on the study bible and study guide they gave you. Let the promise of rest be your anchor."

"Okay."

Despite her minimal responses, the frantic, self-destructive tension that had consumed her for months was not gone—the physical withdrawal was a cold, familiar knot in her gut—but it was eclipsed by a single, revolutionary idea: context.

She was no longer just Sarah, the ruined mother heading toward a desolate end. She was a combatant thrust into the "Great Controversy," and her failure was irrelevant to the objective truth offered by God. Her subjective pain was not the final word.

The thought, *I must stay alive to hear the rest of the plan*, had replaced the thought, *I must end this*. This shift, from suicide to survival, was the most important decision she had ever made. She fought back the surging, terrifying hope with fierce internal resistance, biting her cheek to anchor herself in the pain, needing control before she completely shattered.

The Gospel of Rest

Alone in the small, temporary apartment, the humming of the refrigerator became the sound of absolute silence. Sarah opened the study guide, her hands trembling as she sought the section that promised the impossible: what happens at death.

She didn't find descriptions of fire, judgment, or ghosts wandering in limbo. She found a single, revolutionary word that slammed into her like a physical blow: sleep. The notes described death not as a destination, but as an unconscious state, an absolute void of thought, pain, and time, reserved only until the resurrection.

Unconscious. The word resonated with the deepest hope she had dared not articulate. It meant Lily wasn't alone. Lily wasn't confused. Lily wasn't experiencing the cold, crushing isolation that Sarah had imagined for years. The horror of her guilt—that Lily was suffering *because* of her—began to loosen its grip.

Sarah had to validate it. She hunted for the supporting verse, her vision blurring until she found the heavy, black print. The ancient text confirmed that the theological foundation of this rest was absolute: "For the living know that they shall die: but the dead know not any thing, neither have they any more a reward; for the memory of them is forgotten" (Ecclesiastes 9:5, KJV). The words were plain. The words were a lifeline.

This concept, the notes explained, was confirmed repeatedly by Jesus' own words. She turned the page and found the familiar story of Lazarus, where Jesus first equated death with slumber. The notes detailed the disciples' confusion when Jesus said, "Our friend Lazarus sleepeth; but I go, that I may awake him out of sleep" (John 11:11, KJV). When the disciples failed to understand, thinking He meant natural rest, the text noted that "Jesus spake of his death: but they thought that he had spoken of taking of rest in sleep. Then said Jesus unto them plainly, Lazarus is dead" (John 11:13-14, KJV). Jesus used the word "sleep" to describe death, clarifying it only when the disciples' confusion demanded it. For the divine, death was a temporary, peaceful pause—a sleep from which He had the power to awaken anyone.

It was the next reference, however, that struck Sarah with the force of a personal message. The notes immediately brought up the story of Jairus's daughter, a twelve-year-old girl—a child. When Jesus entered the house filled with professional mourners, He commanded them to stop their frantic activity, saying: "Weep not; she is not dead, but sleepeth" (Luke 8:52, KJV). Jesus used the exact same gentle language for a child that He used for His adult friend. Sarah read the passage repeatedly, the black ink blurring with her tears. *Lily was a damsel. Lily was a small girl, precious and innocent, and Jesus saw her not as a corpse or a tormented soul, but as one who was merely resting, awaiting the simple command: Talitha cumi—Little girl, arise.*

Lily was not suffering, confused, or alone in some cold abyss. She was simply resting, suspended in painless slumber, waiting for the trumpet call. The image of her daughter was no longer one of agonizing loss but of absolute peace.

The agony was mine alone, Sarah realized, leaning her head against the cool wall, tears finally flowing —not of despair, but of raw, seismic relief. *But she is already at peace.*

The notes went on to explain that because time does not exist for the sleeping dead, the moment of Lily's death and the moment of her resurrection would feel like the very same instant. The promise was simple, concrete, and world-shattering: *stay alive, cling to this hope, and you will be present when Lily wakes up.* Her purpose solidified instantly: *to survive long enough for reunion.*

The Pillars of Endurance

With the "why" answered, Sarah turned to the practical "how" of survival, reading through the notes on endurance that Pastor Anderson had stressed for troubled times. This wasn't just doctrine; it was a battle plan against the anxiety and temptation that had haunted her for months.

The first pillar was simple: *Reject Fear, Find Strength.* The notes emphasized that worry is futile, as no person can 'add a single hour to your life' by being anxious. She had spent a year consumed by fear, but the counsel was to shift her reliance entirely to the Divine presence. The message repeated the core assurance: "Fear not: for I have redeemed thee, I have called thee by thy name; thou art mine" (Isaiah 43:1, KJV). This God was not a God of the past or the future, but the "I AM"—present with her right now, in this painful, dark room. She internalized the promise: if you pass through the waters of overwhelming grief or walk through the fires of tribulation, God will be there. He would not leave her on her own. He would be her stronghold (Psalm 27:1-3) against the overwhelming tide of her addiction and despair.

The second pillar encouraged her to embrace power, love, and self-discipline. The notes presented this as the counter-spirit to her fear and lack of control: "God did not give us a spirit of fear, but a spirit of power, of love, and of self-discipline" (2 Timothy 1:7). *Power* was the strength to choose survival over collapse. *Love* was the command to stop hating herself, recognizing that she was called by name. *Self-discipline* was the key to managing the agony of her withdrawal and the chaos in her mind. This was the common sense, the deliberate act of choosing life and health over self-pity and addiction. Sarah realized she was not expected to fight this spiritual war with her own limited, failing willpower. The strength, the power, was a gift, a promise of protection that meant her feet were now on solid ground, safe under "the shelter of the Most High" (Psalm 91:1-2).

She closed the notes. The decision was final. She was no longer running *from* her life; she was fighting *for* her life, and for her future reunion. She lay down on the unfamiliar bed, the silence no longer oppressive but protective, and for the first time in over a year, she found *rest*. The battle would begin anew with the light, but Day 1 had concluded in victory.

CHAPTER 35

A PLACE AT THE TABLE

The thin light of the morning was a cruelty, not a comfort. Sarah awoke to an internal earthquake. Withdrawal was no longer a dull ache; it was a full-body seizure of cold sweat, muscle tremors that rattled her teeth, and a knot of nausea that promised violence. This physical agony was a grinding, present reality that threatened to consume the delicate, theological truce she had established the night before.

She did not venture out. She did not open the curtains. The apartment was a tiny, dim fortress where she waged war against herself. The only weapons she possessed were the words scrawled on the seminar study guide, now crumpled and damp in her shaking hands. She was not clinging to paper; she was fighting to breathe, anchoring her sanity to the promises of sleep and endurance written on the page. Every pulse of fear—the certainty that Lily was gone, that she had forfeited her right to try—was countered by the silent, repeated assertion that Lily was merely resting, not suffering.

She had survived the first night, a victory won solely in the dark. But now the sun was rising, and the anxiety was compounding, threatening to shatter her resolve before she even took a step. To go back to the seminar was to re-enter the light, to face the truth, and to commit to the brutal, necessary war she had just declared on her own life. This was Day 2, and the ground was burning.

A Place at the Millers' Table

The silence of Sarah's dim fortress was shattered by the bright intrusion of life next door. She could distinctly hear the low, comforting murmur of Maria and Mark's voices—an anchor of domestic normalcy—interrupted by the bright, clear laughter of their daughter. Then, an olfactory assault: the rich, deep scent of chili and cooking spices, so potent and real that it scraped across the barren landscape of her hunger.

Then came a sound she didn't recognize: a soft, hesitant knock on her door, unlike the vicious, demanding raps of debt collectors or her own panic. It sounded delicate, almost like a secret.

Sarah dragged herself to the door and peered through the peephole. Standing there were Maria and a little girl, seven years old, clutching a favorite stuffed animal.

Maria smiled, her expression a careful balance of warmth and understanding. "Hello, dear. This is our daughter, Leah. She just turned seven."

Sarah turned the lock. The brass cylinder screamed a protest, loud and scraping in the silence of her withdrawal. Her hand trembled violently, and she had to lean her weight against the frame just to gain enough purchase to slide the deadbolt free. She did not want to open it. To open the door was to invite the light in, to reveal the *truth* of her existence.

She pulled the door inward slowly, grudgingly, creating only a narrow, vertical sliver of an opening, like a fearful eye squinting at the world.

The motion felt like tearing herself in half. As the door finally gave way, the contrast was immediate and painful. Maria and Leah were framed in the brightly lit doorway of *their* home next door, radiating a golden, uncomplicated warmth. This glow was a stark, warm counterpoint to the deep shadow Sarah inhabited. Maria and Leah got a clear, instant view into the cave Sarah had made: the single, unmade mattress on the floor, the blackout curtains sealed tight, the total, empty stillness. It was cold, dark, and profoundly desolate. Sarah braced, waiting for the pity, the judgment, or the recoil.

But Maria's smile didn't waver; her focus remained entirely on Sarah, extending grace without judgment of the barren environment. Leah, however, didn't seem to notice the emptiness at all. Her wide, innocent eyes were fixed solely on the invitation.

Leah peered up, a streak of flour visible on her cheek. Her voice was a sweet, unaffected chime. "Mommy made chili and cornbread," Leah whispered, holding up a small hand. "It's really yummy. Would you please come eat dinner with us?"

The request, delivered with such open-hearted simplicity by a child, broke through Sarah's shame like nothing else could have. She wanted to refuse fiercely; sitting at a clean table felt like a public judgment, like walking onto a stage where her failure was the only visible character. But the reality of the food was too immediate, and the hollow ache of hunger—real, physiological hunger—outweighed the reflexive self-loathing.

Maria stepped forward and, without hesitation, took Sarah's shaking arm. Sarah instinctively reached back and pulled the door shut, the heavy click of the lock feeling like a desperate act of self-preservation.

"We don't stand on ceremony," Maria said gently, her eyes meeting Sarah's with absolute sincerity. "Our daughter is just finishing up her homework in the living room, so just ignore the chaos. We're just going to eat. And you need fuel for the fight."

Maria led her into the home. The difference was stunning. Sarah's apartment was a cold box, silent and still; the Millers' was a vibrant, lived-in space. Leah sat cross-legged on the rug, crayon in hand, a few toys scattered around her in a state of benign, domestic chaos. The air was thick with comfort.

In the kitchen, an island of comforting order, Mark stood by the stove, a simple apron tied over his shirt, exuding an air of competence and calm. The warmth radiating from the oven and stove was a physical balm. Mark turned, saw Sarah, and gave her a slight nod of acknowledgment, no pity in his expression, only welcome. He didn't ask; he simply pushed a sturdy wooden chair out from the table for her.

Sarah sat down, the simple chair feeling solid beneath her. Before Mark served her, Maria reached over and gently wrapped her fingers around Sarah's left hand, while Mark did the same for her right. Sarah froze, utterly unaccustomed to this level of casual, unearned physical contact. Her hands were still trembling, and she felt exposed.

Mark bowed his head slightly, his voice deep and warm. "Our Father which art in Heaven, Lord, thank you for the food which you have given to us and for the new friend we made. Protect us each day and provide for us. In the name of Jesus, we ask all these things. Amen."

The prayer, simple and direct, felt like a powerful shield. It acknowledged her presence—a "new friend"—without demanding anything in return. Mark immediately handed her a large, steaming bowl of chili and a thick slice of cornbread. The chili was deep red, thick with beans and meat, topped with melted cheese that hadn't quite cooled. It was perfectly seasoned, spiced just enough to wake up her deadened taste buds without overwhelming her still-sensitive system.

She ate slowly, deliberately. The first spoonful was a revelation—the rich, salty, deep flavor tasted like life itself. The physical nourishment was instant, silencing the hollow, echoing hunger that had plagued her for days. The Millers didn't demand conversation; they simply talked amongst themselves about Leah's day at school, Mark's work, and the recipe for the cornbread. Sarah was permitted to be silent, to simply be fed. Maria kept her glass refilled with clean, cold water, a small act of unconditional care that brought a sharp, unexpected sting of tears to Sarah's eyes.

For the first time in over a year, Sarah was in a safe space, consuming food that was meant to nourish, not just quiet the demons. The small act was a radical act of grace, a profound, unearned fortune that affirmed her right to exist in the world again.

Exposure in the Sanctuary

With full stomachs and a sliver of time remaining, they quickly gathered their things. Mark tossed Maria the car keys, and the four of them—Mark, Maria, Leah, and Sarah—left the apartment building. The drive across town was short, mostly silent, and felt like traveling light-years. The physical nourishment had provided a strong anchor, but the emotional exhaustion of sitting at a 'normal' table quickly pulled her back toward isolation.

They found a parking spot near the back entrance. As they entered the church sanctuary, Maria said warmly, "We'll save you a seat up front, dear."

"I think… I'm just going to sit back here," Sarah managed, her voice barely a whisper, needing the deep shadows of the last row to hide the tremors in her hands and the shame in her eyes.

Maria and Mark exchanged a brief, quiet look. They settled into their seats two rows from the front, allowing Sarah to think she had won the concession.

But as Pastor Anderson approached the pulpit and the small crowd quieted, Leah, who was already seated, fidgeted and then glanced over her shoulder. Her eyes, innocent and utterly devoid of judgment, found Sarah immediately in the deep shadows of the last row. To Leah, this was not a place of refuge; it was simply a person sitting alone.

Without a moment of hesitation or permission, the little girl slipped out of her seat and ran softly down the aisle toward the back. Maria and Mark reacted quickly, too late to stop her, but ready to intervene if needed.

Leah reached the back row, her small face earnest. She reached up, gently took Sarah's shaking hand in her own, and, with the soft, determined pull of a child, she tugged on her arm.

"You can't sit back here," Leah whispered, her voice a pure, sweet chime. "We saved you a spot. Come sit with us."

Sarah felt a rush of mortification and a profound, strange surrender. She was being invited forward not by duty, but by a genuine, unforced act of affection. The kindness was too pure to resist. She collected her belongings and let Leah lead her forward. Maria quickly intercepted them, guiding Sarah into the family's row. Sarah found herself exposed to the light, flanked by Mark and Maria, with Leah seated safely nearby, and terrified of this sudden, bright visibility.

The Relentless Pursuit

Pastor Anderson stepped up to the pulpit, paused, and cleared his throat. "I have to admit," he started, his voice honest and quiet, "I had an entirely different sermon prepared—something about the final days, actually. But late last night, I felt a deep, undeniable compulsion to throw away every note. Tonight, I want to talk about something more immediate: the universal human feeling of being unwanted."

He began by speaking about that feeling, the experience of being lost. "Have you ever felt like you were standing in a great crowd, yet felt completely invisible? Have you ever looked at your own past, your own mistakes, and concluded that you are, to put it plainly, scrap metal? Discarded, worthless, fit only for the heap?"

He paused, letting the silence settle over the quiet room, making space for every person's private shame. "The core truth of our faith is this: God's love is not a passive thing that waits for you to become worthy. It is a relentless force that actively pursues the unworthy. It is the love of the Shepherd who leaves the ninety-nine sheep safe in the fold just to climb the cold mountains for the one lost, bruised, and terrified lamb. As Christ said, 'What man of you, having an hundred sheep, if he lose one of them, doth not leave the ninety and nine in the wilderness, and go after that which is lost, until he find it?' (Luke 15:4, KJV). It is the love of the Father who doesn't just wait on the porch for his prodigal son; he *runs* to him, showering him with unconditional honor: '...But when he was yet a great way off, his father saw him, and had compassion, and ran, and fell on his neck, and kissed him'" (Luke 15:20, KJV).

He leaned into the microphone. "This relentless love is best shown in a man named Zacchaeus."

The Sycamore Tree

"Zacchaeus was the chief tax collector—a wealthy, powerful man, but he was also a thief, a collaborator with Rome, and a profound social outcast. He climbed the ladder of success only to find himself completely alone at the top. When he heard Jesus was passing through, he wanted a look. But he was too short to see over the crowd, and he was too ashamed to face the people he'd wronged. So, he did the only thing he could: he ran ahead and climbed a sycamore fig tree."

Pastor Anderson's voice grew passionate. "We are all in a sycamore tree right now. Our tree might be a demanding career, an addiction, a habit of hiding our true selves, or simply the isolating fear of being judged. We climb high, hoping to catch a glimpse of God, but remaining safely on the periphery. We think, 'If Jesus saw *me*, truly saw my dark thoughts, my secret habits—He would certainly pass me by.'"

"But the most beautiful part of this story is that Jesus didn't just walk past the tree; He stopped beneath it. He looked up, right through the dense leaves and the thick branches of Zacchaeus's self-protective hiding place, and He called him by his name. Jesus didn't say, 'Zacchaeus, if you promise to fix your life, I'll consider visiting.' He issued an immediate, personal command of grace: 'Zacchaeus, make haste, and come down; for to day I must abide at thy house'" (Luke 19:5, KJV).

"The truth is, Jesus's love doesn't wait for us to clean up our act; it steps into our chaos. It is a love that actively claims you, regardless of your past. He sees you, He knows your name, and He will climb any obstacle you build just to tell you: 'For the Son of man is come to seek and to save that which was lost' (Luke 19:10, KJV). You are not scrap metal; you are a prized possession he has relentlessly sought."

Sarah felt the sermon hit her with a seismic shock. *The tree.* It wasn't just Zacchaeus's tree; it was hers. For years, her sycamore had been the cynical walls she built around herself, the anonymous hiding places in the city, the calculated distance she kept from anyone who could possibly know the truth. She had lived her whole adult life as a fugitive running from an inevitable judgment, convinced that if God saw her, He would only see the *damage* she had caused.

But the Pastor's words reversed the entire orientation of her world. If God is the Shepherd, then her being lost was merely the *trigger* for His search, not the reason for her condemnation. When he spoke of Jesus looking up through the branches, Sarah's breath hitched. She hadn't run far enough. He had found her. He had seen past the crowd of her failures and called her by the name she hadn't even realized she was waiting to hear. She was not running *from* judgment; she was being pursued by love. The idea that she was a 'prized possession' and not 'scrap metal' felt less like comfort and more like a massive, undeserved weight of worth suddenly placed upon her soul.

Sarah sat wedged between Maria and Mark, feeling their steady, protective warmth. She had just heard the message of the Invisible, Divine Presence who seeks the lost, and she was physically anchored by the real, tangible presence of the friends who had made space for her to receive that truth. Day 2 ended not in isolation, but in the certainty that she was claimed, sought, and finally safe.

CHAPTER 36

PROVISION IN THE WILDERNESS

The sun rose, fierce and yellow, flooding the apartment with a gold that felt less like judgment and more like a fragile promise. Sarah blinked into the light, her mind slow to adjust. For the first time in weeks, she didn't feel crushed by dread as she woke. The memory of yesterday—of sitting in a church pew, of being seen and fed by strangers—settled around her not as a revelation but as an anchor. She was still here. Her heart was still beating. Her story, impossibly, was not over.

She pushed herself upright, every bone in her back protesting. The bedroom was heavy with the scent of old sweat and hopelessness. She refused to linger there. Stumbling into the kitchen, she reached for the eviction notice taped to the counter. The due date glared at her, red and final: one week left. She stared at the numbers until they blurred, then forced herself to focus. She would not surrender to panic. This was no longer about defeat—this was a campaign.

Eviction: Problem A.

Solution: She needed money, which meant a job.

Job: Problem B.

Her stomach twisted, a cold, hollow ache gnawing at her resolve. She opened the cupboard—empty, except for a single cracked mug. The hunger hit her with a wave of nausea so strong she had to clutch the counter, fighting the urge to sob. If she didn't eat soon, she'd spiral. She could feel it.

Then, a sound—a faint, almost apologetic knock—broke through the silence. Sarah froze, heart pounding, and peered through the peephole. The hall was empty. She opened the door anyway and looked down.

A small cardboard box sat against the wall. No note, no name—just a box, with a dishcloth draped over the top. Inside: a bag of rice, a package of pasta, a jar of sauce, two cans of chili, and a box of granola bars. Her throat closed up. She touched the dishcloth and knew instantly—Maria's lavender detergent. The Millers. They had seen her, really seen her, and answered before she could even ask.

Tears burned her eyes, but she refused to let herself collapse. She ripped open a granola bar, forcing herself to eat slowly, chewing each bite with the deliberate focus of someone making a vow. This wasn't a meal for comfort or escape. This was fuel. She would use it.

When the last crumbs were gone, Sarah wiped her mouth and squared her shoulders. She needed a job, not a miracle. The old methods—endless scrolling, phone interviews—were lost to her. She had nothing but her two feet, her hands, and the borrowed clothes Maria had given her. Her fingers trembled as she tied her hair back. The sweatpants and pullover were clean, but screamed "desperate." Still, better desperate than defeated.

She stepped out into the morning, the air sharp and cold, the streets almost painfully bright. Each footstep echoed her determination. She walked past the dry cleaner, the hardware store, the vacant storefronts—her hope flickering with every "Help Wanted" sign that wasn't there. By the time she reached The Daily Grind, her legs ached, and her faith wavered.

But there it was: a handwritten sign taped to the glass. HELP WANTED – IMMEDIATE OPENING. Inquire Inside.

Her hands shook. She caught her reflection in the dusty shop window next door—gaunt face, wild hair, borrowed clothes. Not impressive. But her eyes were steady, and her jaw was set. This was it.

She closed her eyes, whispering, "Dear Lord, I don't know if you're listening, but thank you for the box. Just let me get through this next part. Amen." She took a breath, straightened her spine, and stepped inside.

The coffee shop was a rush of sound and warmth. Beans grinding, milk steaming, a woman with a mane of wild red hair shouting orders. Alex, her name tag read. Sarah waited, almost invisible, until Alex finally looked her way.

"Can I help you?" Alex barked, barely pausing.

Sarah's voice was stronger than she felt. "I saw your sign. I need work. I'm a fast learner. I'll start today."

Alex sized her up with a skeptical stare, taking in the sweatpants, the wary eyes. "Waitress. Early mornings, on your feet, minimum wage plus tips. You up for it?"

"I am," Sarah said, her voice unwavering. "I need the money, and I'll work as hard as you need."

Alex's mouth twitched in what might have been the beginning of a smile. "Tell me about the worst customer you ever had."

Sarah took a breath, dredging up a memory from the motel: a drunk guest at 2 a.m., a screaming match, a night that ended with her calling the police and cleaning up smashed glass. She told the story simply, focusing on the solution, not the drama. Alex listened, nodded, and thrust a form across the counter.

"Start at six tomorrow. Bring ID. Don't be late."

Sarah barely made it out the door before a laugh, wild and incredulous, burst out of her. She had a job. She had a way out—however small. It wasn't glory. It was survival. But it was hers.

She walked home, clutching the granola bar wrapper like a talisman. She was still broke, still on the edge, but now there was a thread of hope pulling her forward.

The Trial and the Double Blessing

That night, Sarah sat wedged between Mark and Maria in the third row of the sanctuary, the light from the pulpit a warm halo in the gathering dusk. Leah colored quietly beside her, the child's presence a silent comfort. But Sarah's mind was racing, nerves jangling with the knowledge that tomorrow, everything would change again.

Pastor Anderson took the stage with the energy of a man on a mission. "Pharaoh was driven by fear," he thundered. "A fear of a threat that wasn't real. He created his own terror—he saw God's people and imagined only crisis. He tried to oppress them, but God had other plans."

Sarah listened, every word striking her like a bell. "The lie is that God will spare you from the fire," Pastor Anderson said, leaning over the pulpit. "The truth is, God will preserve you through it. Your shame, your debt, your hunger—these are the trials. But the blessing is coming. You are not suffering for nothing. God multiplies your pain into future strength."

He spoke of Jochebed, Moses' mother, who set her son afloat on a river of fear and death—and who, by faith, received him back from the enemy. "You have to let go to be blessed," he said, his voice ringing. "You have to step into the river before you see the rescue."

Sarah felt a tear slip down her cheek. Her mind went to Lily, to every lost thing, to the desperate prayers she'd thought no one heard. But the promise was this: God heard. Even when she couldn't speak, even when her voice was gone, her child's cry—and her own—had reached heaven.

The sermon ended in a swirl of music and murmured prayers. As people filed out, Sarah found herself drawn forward, compelled by something bigger than fear. She waited as Pastor Anderson greeted others, then, when it was her turn, she stood before him, her hands shaking.

"My name is Sarah," she managed. "Tomorrow is my first day at a new job. It's just a waitress job. It feels… small, after everything."

Pastor Anderson's eyes softened, and he placed a steady hand on her shoulder. "That job is your ark, Sarah. Your first step out of the storm. Every act of faithfulness is sacred. You walk into that place tomorrow, and you claim the double blessing. God multiplies what you surrender. You survived the night. You found your manna. Now you start again."

Sarah nodded, clutching the study Bible to her chest. The waitressing job was no longer a humiliation. It was a beginning—a fragile, determined hope, burning like a candle at dawn.

CHAPTER 37

THE ARK AND THE APRON

The dawn was still hours away, but Sarah was already awake, her heart pounding a frantic rhythm against her ribs. She was no longer a woman who slept easily. Instead of falling back into the fitful darkness, she reached for her study Bible, making a new, conscious decision that morning. This was to be her first intentional daily devotional—a quiet ritual to anchor her shaky life to a promise. The Bible felt solid in her hands, a literal lifeline she was choosing to hold on to.

She flipped past the sermon notes she'd scribbled—*Trial, not punishment. Double blessing*—and landed on a highlighted passage in the book of Psalms. It was her new morning ritual: reading until the fear subsided, trading her panic for a single, actionable thought. She read from Psalm 55:22 (KJV): *'Cast thy burden upon the LORD, and he shall sustain thee: he shall never suffer the righteous to be moved.'*

The words were not a magical disappearance of her problems, but a refocusing of her thoughts. She was still jobless and facing eviction, but today she had a task, and that task was her immediate form of righteousness. She had promised herself she would live for the double blessing, and today, that meant successfully enduring her first shift at The Daily Grind. Survival was the first act of faith.

Sarah moved to the bathroom mirror in her tiny, sparsely furnished apartment next door to the Millers. The uniform she had been told to wear—a plain white t-shirt and dark pants—was simple enough, but the anxiety was a knot of iron in her gut.

The rent. That was the immediate, unyielding enemy. She was already days past the due date, and a formal eviction notice was the terrifying consequence hanging over her. Her pockets were empty; she had no savings whatsoever, and her entire meager future rested on what she earned today. The total amount felt like a mountain built of fear and shame. The old Sarah would have succumbed to the paralyzing panic. The new Sarah recited Philippians 4:13 (KJV) like a battle chant: *'I can do all things through Christ which strengtheneth me.'*

Maria came over just as Sarah was locking her door, a small, paper-wrapped cinnamon roll warm in her hand, along with a mug of coffee.

"Good morning, Sarah. You need something solid in your stomach. First days are tough," Maria said, gently passing the mug to Sarah.

Sarah took a bite of the pastry, the sugar and spice a welcome comfort. "Thank you, Maria. I feel like I'm going to forget everything. This is so far from... anything I've ever done. I'm honestly terrified of messing up the orders."

Maria gave her a quick hug, her eyes warm and practical. "Everyone messes up. It's a coffee shop, not a courtroom. The secret is to keep moving and never take a plate back to the kitchen without it being empty. That's what an old friend taught me when I worked retail years ago. You'll be fine. Just focus on the basics, keep your head down, and remember you're doing what you have to do to rebuild. It's a stepping stone, Sarah. I'll be praying for that rush hour crowd to be gentle."

Sarah walked the short distance to The Daily Grind, a small, brightly lit local coffee shop. The dense, intoxicating aroma of dark-roast coffee and sugary pastries was a welcome assault on her senses. Inside, Alex greeted her with a brusque nod.

"Morning, Sarah. Grab this," Alex said, tossing a stiff, faded yellow apron across the counter. It was a manager's hand-me-down from a previous employee. It felt heavy—a tangible symbol of her fall, but also, as Pastor Anderson had implied, her ark—the vessel of her preservation.

"Today's your trial by fire. It's Friday. We get the end-of-week lunch rush starting around eleven. You're covering Section 5—it's the seating area right by the windows, a good mix of families and singles. You'll be serving the breakfast sandwiches and baked goods, running coffee, and clearing tables. Don't worry about the espresso machine today; stick to refills and orders. Just smile, keep the coffee flowing, and for God's sake, write everything down!" Alex instructed, her voice quick and efficient.

The Trial by Fire: The Miracle of Endurance

The first hour was a deceptively gentle introduction, a slow trickle of regulars ordering simple black coffees and taking up corner booths. Sarah managed the routine of fetching fresh pots and wiping down counters, the physical movement a relief from the internal churning.

Then, exactly at 11:30 AM, the side door flew open, and a deluge of people—office workers, travelers, and early weekenders—flooded the shop. The coffee shop became a roaring symphony of steam wands, clattering spoons, and urgent calls for refills. The air thickened with the smell of roasting beans and a frantic energy. The Rush had hit.

Sarah's brief training dissolved instantly. She was supposed to manage five tables in her section, but the flow was relentless. She made her first mistake at Table 2, forgetting to check if the patron wanted milk and having to walk back to the counter, feeling the hot flush of embarrassment. By the time she reached Table 3, Table 5 was already flagging her down for napkins and a sugar refill. She accidentally mixed up two table numbers on the order pad and dropped a pastry napkin, watching it float under a crowded booth—a small, but visible, failure.

The pressure mounted not only from customers but also from within. The old voice of Deacon Robert, cold and judgmental, whispered: *You are incompetent. You fail at everything you touch. You will never earn that rent.*

She finally reached the service window to place an order for a new group at Table 12—a large, multi-generational family—and realized she had not only forgotten to write down the complex details but was also blocking the other servers. Her mind, usually razor-sharp, was a blank slate. Her hands shook as she held a tray of steaming mugs, ready to run a delivery. This was a full-blown crisis of confidence disguised as customer service.

She froze. The panic seized her throat, turning her legs to lead. She saw Alex's intense red hair turn toward her, a clear sign of impending criticism. The old Sarah would have collapsed here, surrendering to the shame.

Suddenly, a quiet, insistent thought cut through the screaming noise—a thought that didn't even feel like her own. It was the residue of the quiet discipline she'd started that morning. She remembered her new devotional, and the steady strength of the promise she'd tried to plant in her heart: something from Psalms, maybe—"Cast your burden on the Lord, and He'll carry you; He won't let the righteous fall"—or however it went. The words were a quiet, powerful interruption to the screaming panic, a reminder that the devotional had been a moment of spiritual preservation that extended into her workday, proving she was not alone, even in this small, humiliating moment.

She took a deep breath, centered herself, and rushed back to the order screen, intercepting Alex before she could speak.

"Table 12 is two sausage, egg, and cheese on croissants, one bagel with cream cheese and salmon, a fruit cup with no melon, plus a triple-shot latte with oat milk, extra hot," Sarah recited the complex, easily forgotten order perfectly. She hadn't written it down, but the information was suddenly, flawlessly available to her. It was a small, immediate miracle—a tiny reprieve of memory in the face of chaos, a small piece of the promised preservation, allowing her to keep moving.

The Double Blessing: Evidence of the Covenant

The remainder of the shift was a relentless, grueling dance. Sarah moved with a driven purpose, managing to turn her anxiety into focused action. She kept her eyes on the floor, her feet burning with every frantic trip back and forth. She made small mistakes, but she apologized quickly and pressed forward. The shame she expected to feel never materialized because she was too busy working actively fighting for her next day.

It was Table 9, a large group of young professionals in nice clothes, who provided the test of her endurance and her reward. They had been especially challenging: one woman requested her latte be remade three times—"It's not foamy enough. No, now it's too foamy." Another required separate water glasses, both with and without ice, and their order included all customized cold brews and three gluten-free muffins, which required separate plates. Sarah managed to handle their requests with a calm, almost serene patience that surprised even Alex, who watched from the counter. She never let her smile drop.

When they finally stood to leave, Sarah approached the table to clear the mountain of empty cups and scattered sugar packets.

Under the saucer of the last empty coffee mug lay a single, crisp, $100 bill, weighted down by a neatly folded napkin. Sarah picked it up, confused, thinking it was a mistake. She checked the itemized receipt: the total bill was $68. She looked for the customers, but they were already out the door, laughing as they walked down the street. It was an astonishing, deliberate overpayment.

Maria had told her that a good day for tips might push $80, but this single tip was over 140% of the bill. She checked the $100 bill; it was unmistakably real.

A wave of pure, unfiltered faith washed over her. This wasn't just luck or some random act of kindness—it was too specific, too generous, too perfectly timed, arriving right as her fear of eviction and empty bank account reached its peak. It made her think of that verse in Deuteronomy—something like, "The Lord will open up His good treasure and bless the work of your hands."

She finished her shift, her body aching but her spirit alight, and tallied her receipts in the back office. The day's total in cash tips alone—$175—was more than double the daily minimum wage for the 8 hours she worked. The $100 tip was the tipping point. Coupled with the absence of any other funds, she realized she had earned enough in that single, grueling day to cover the immediate financial crisis and buy precious time to secure the full rent.

It was the double blessing Pastor Anderson had promised. Her failure and shame were the trial, the stained apron the cross, and the unexpected provision was the reward. She hadn't just survived her first day; she had been given a tangible sign that her trials had indeed been working for her a far more exceeding weight of glory. She walked out of The Daily Grind—the scent of coffee clinging to her uniform—not as a woman hiding in shame, but as one who had successfully navigated her first act of preservation and claimed the double blessing promised.

CHAPTER 38

WHEN FIRE MEANS FREEDOM

Sarah finished her grueling Friday shift, her body running on pure adrenaline and the shock of success. After tallying the tips—the astonishing $175 windfall—she was riding a wave of spiritual and physical relief. She hadn't just survived; she had been gifted a double blessing, which bought her precious time against the specter of eviction.

She hung her faded yellow apron by the back sink and turned to face Alex, who was cleaning the espresso machine with the focused intensity of a surgeon. Alex didn't offer praise lightly.

"You didn't fold," Alex said, her voice gruff, not looking up. "You dropped an order pad, and you almost put the oat latte in the regular milk pitcher. But… you kept moving. You didn't cry, you didn't freeze, and you never stopped smiling, even when Table 9 was having a meltdown. I've seen seasoned pros crack under a Friday rush like that." Alex finally looked up, wiping her hands on a cloth. "You're off tomorrow. Saturday is your reward and your chance to recover. Please arrive here by Sunday evening at 6 PM sharp. Now go."

Sarah's spirit soared. The manager's grudging approval and the gift of the day off were exactly what she needed. She clocked out, the scent of coffee and yeast clinging to her uniform, and started the short walk back to her apartment. The journey was a slow, deliberate march of victory, but she had little time to savor it.

The Quick Turnaround

The Evangelistic Seminar began at 7:00 PM, and Sarah was cutting it close. She arrived at her apartment, moving with the rapid, efficient pace she had learned in the diner. She focused on the spiritual exercise she had started that morning: moving with purpose, concentrating on the necessity of action. A quick shower washed away the coffee residue and the Friday rush tension. She changed into the simple, modest dress Maria had helped her select, her hands moving instinctively to smooth the fabric, a gesture of settling into her new life.

When the light knock came, she was composed and ready. Maria, Mark, and Leah stood waiting, their faces reflecting the quiet sense of commitment to their faith. Leah held a new coloring book, her smile wide.

"Ready for tonight?" Mark asked, offering her a steady hand as they started toward the car to drive to the church.

"Ready," Sarah replied, her voice firm. This time, she wasn't just observing; she was reporting for duty.

Pastor Anderson stood on the main stage. Behind him, the massive screen displayed an image of a stylized abyss, deep red and unsettling, with smoke curling upward. He wore a dark suit with a calming, deep blue tie, signifying truth and reflection. His demeanor was earnest and deeply focused, presenting himself not as a judge, but as a fellow traveler deeply burdened by the prophetic truths he was about to share.

Pastor Anderson began with a low, intense voice, immediately gripping the room.

"Tonight, we turn the page past the gentle words of blessing and preservation," he announced, his gaze sweeping the audience. "We look tonight at the Revelation of Jesus Christ, and we must face the final reckoning. This is the crucial turning point. We are preparing to discuss the prophecies of the beast, the mark, and the signs of the times, but before we do, we must ask: What is the end of the wicked? What is the *final* answer to sin? It is found in Revelation 20:14 (KJV): 'And death and hell were cast into the lake of fire. This is the second death.'"

He gestured to the image of the inferno on the screen, but his expression was one of profound sadness, not triumph. "My brothers and sisters, we must humbly accept that God does this work of destruction, but the prophet Isaiah calls it His 'strange act' (Isaiah 28:21, KJV). It is alien to His nature! His nature is to create, to heal, to restore. This final act of eradication is a painful necessity, like a surgeon removing a cancer that, if left, would destroy the entire body."

"But I know what many of you are thinking," he continued, walking closer to the edge of the stage. "You've been taught, perhaps your whole life, about an endlessly burning hell, about eternal, conscious torment. You read in Revelation about the wicked being tormented 'for ever and ever' and it sounds like a torture chamber with no end. This is the greatest deception, as it paints our loving Father as a vindictive monster."

He held up his hand. "This is where we must humbly let the Bible define its own terms. The Greek word aion and the Hebrew olam, often translated as 'forever,' do not always mean endless. They simply mean 'as long as the subject lasts,' or 'to the end of the age.' The Bible itself gives us the key. Look at Jude 1:7 (KJV) It says Sodom and Gomorrah are set forth as an example, suffering the vengeance of... what? 'Eternal fire.' Are those cities still burning today? No. The fire was eternal in its results. It burned until there was nothing left to burn. Or in Exodus 21, a servant who loves his master stays 'for ever'—meaning, for the rest of his life. The duration is defined by the subject."

"So, when Malachi 4:1 (KJV) says the wicked shall be stubble, and the day 'shall burn them up... [and] leave them neither root nor branch,' it means exactly that. It is a complete, total, and final destruction. The wages of sin is DEATH (Romans 6:23, KJV), not unending torment! If sin earned you eternal life—even a tormented one—the devil would have won a perverse, eternal victory! But Christ's victory is decisive!"

He pointed back to the screen. "The Lake of Fire is not a torture chamber designed to extend suffering; it is the ultimate act of mercy, where God wipes away the scars of sin forever. This, friends, is the Second Death. The first death—the one your loved ones may have experienced—is a sleep. The Second Death is the final eradication from which there is no resurrection. It is the end of the sin problem."

Sarah listened, rapt. The fear of an eternal, burning hell—a terror instilled by her father, Deacon Robert, as a constant threat—had been a dominant spiritual anxiety her entire life. This pastor was dismantling that fear with Scripture, re-framing judgment as an act of merciful finality. The logic was crushing, liberating. Her past mistakes, the life she had destroyed—they would be burned up and forgotten, not held over her head for eternity. It meant her daughter, Lily, who was now sleeping, would be waking up and stepping into the promised new heaven and new earth, where the possibility of pain, shame, and sin would be permanently removed.

As the Pastor spoke, a deep, profound contrast emerged, contrasting her entire religious upbringing with this new, overwhelming truth. Her mind involuntarily flashed back to the stifling air of the First Baptist Church of Havenwood and the voice of Reverend Smith, allowing her to analyze the old terror against the new clarity.

The Contrast of Truth

Reverend Smith, in the flashback of Sarah's mind, had always used the threat of eternal damnation as a tool of control, demanding perfection in micro-morality—every skirt, every glance—to escape a torturous fate. That fire was endless, punitive, and the terror of it had always made her body physically revolt. His sermons focused solely on Sarah's failings and the need to earn her way out of an infinite ledger of sin. The pressure had always been crushing: *You must obey, or you will immediately be sent into eternal damnation.* Sarah now recognized that this focus on self-preservation and performance was the very definition of using the Lord's name in vain, as all sought their own, not the things which are Jesus Christ's (Philippians 2:21, KJV).

Pastor Anderson, however, presented the Lake of Fire as God's decisive act of sanitation. The fire was not eternal punishment, but final eradication. It wasn't about the *earning* of grace; it was about the immediate, decisive action of accepting the promised victory. The focus had shifted from her past mistakes to her future preparedness. Instead of being pinned down by the terror of conditional obedience, she was liberated by the call to active surrender. The fear of perpetual torment was replaced by the clarity of a ticking clock demanding that she enter the "ark" and "keep moving."

Pastor Anderson then brought the sermon to a point of intense application, referencing his earlier pragmatic instruction. "This is why your life must not be stagnant!" he urged, his voice rising with conviction. "I told you: you must not be the mouse that waits for the cheese to return! You must have your spiritual go bag ready! Every decision you make this week—at your business, in your home, at your job—must be made through the lens of: Is this preparing me for the Second Coming, or is this anchoring me to a world destined for the Lake of Fire? You must be moving, searching, growing! The end is near! You are called not to escape, but to act!"

He then spoke directly about the global mission, showing pictures on the screen of people meeting secretly on rooftops. "We are seeing people in Bangladesh, in Guam, in nations where the government forbids the gospel, making a choice for Christ! They are reading the Word, often on solar-powered radios, meeting in secret, facing real persecution! If they can make a decisive choice in the face of imminent danger, what is your excuse for complacency right here, tonight?"

The weight of the message settled upon Sarah. Her tip money had been a comfort, but it was just a temporary fix. Her waitressing job was her immediate focus, but it was only a small part of the larger, urgent mandate. Her newfound routine of a Friday-morning devotional and her new commitment to live suddenly felt less about personal healing and more about a global, ticking clock.

She thought of the chaos of her Friday shift, the moment she had almost froze, and the way the verse from Psalms had anchored her, allowing her to recite the complicated order perfectly. That was the preservation he preached, the ability to act righteously—*to keep moving*—even when surrounded by the fire of fear.

Pastor Anderson finished, his voice dropping to a powerful, earnest whisper. "If you are ready to stop being stagnant, if you are ready to prepare your spiritual go bag, if you are ready to accept God's judgment as a merciful and utter destruction of sin, and the beginning of your new life as a total, humble surrender—then make your commitment now. The invitation is open. Get in the ark. Let your final words be: I surrender all!"

Sarah closed her eyes, the bright red image of the Lake of Fire seared into her mind, no longer an instrument of fear but a necessary, cleansing truth. She needed to do more than just survive her week; she needed to act. Her past was gone, her future was imminent, and the time for half-measures was over.

Pastor Anderson stepped back from the pulpit, his intense focus softening into a pastoral warmth. He bowed his head, and the sanctuary fell into a profound, shared silence.

"Our loving Father," he prayed, his voice humble and clear, "seal these truths upon our hearts. Give us the courage to act, to leave the world destined for fire, and to step fully into the safety of Your ark. Give us a spirit of preservation, not of fear. And as we part tonight, fill us with the peace that You give only to Your children. Bring us all together again in that great resurrection morning, when sin and death will be no more. We ask this in the precious name of Jesus. Amen."

He looked up, a genuine smile reaching his eyes. "Thank you all for coming. The sun has set, and the holy hours are upon us. I wish you all a peaceful and very Happy Sabbath."

Sarah, Mark, Maria, and Leah shuffled out of the pew and into the aisle with the rest of the dispersing crowd. The words echoed in Sarah's ears, creating an immediate, jarring dissonance. *Happy Sabbath?*

She was quiet as they walked through the cool night air to the car, the single phrase turning over and over in her mind. In Deacon Robert's church, the "Sabbath" was just an archaic word for Sunday, a day of stiff clothes and cold judgment. But Pastor Anderson's greeting, delivered on a Friday night, felt specific, intentional, and entirely new.

Once they were in the car, with Mark driving and Maria in the passenger seat, Sarah finally leaned forward from the back, where she sat beside a sleepy Leah.

"Maria," she whispered, trying to keep the confusion from her voice. "I must have misunderstood something. Why did Pastor Anderson say 'Happy Sabbath'? It's Friday."

Maria turned in her seat, her expression one of gentle realization, as if remembering this was foreign territory for Sarah. "Oh, dear, you didn't misunderstand at all. He said it because it *is* the Sabbath. The Sabbath isn't Sunday."

Sarah felt a cold prickle of disorientation. "But… all my life, I was taught… Sunday is the Lord's Day. That's when we rest."

Mark caught her eye in the rearview mirror, his voice steady and calm. "That's what most of the Christian world believes, Sarah. But the Bible is very specific. The Sabbath is the *seventh* day of the week, not the first. God blessed it at the very foundation of the world, in Genesis. It's a memorial of His creation. It begins at sundown on Friday and goes until sundown on Saturday."

Sarah sat back, the information settling on her like a heavy blanket. Another pillar of her Havenwood upbringing had just crumbled. First, the truth about hell, and now, the very day of worship. She thought of the Fourth Commandment she had memorized as a child: *Remember the sabbath day, to keep it holy... The seventh day is the Sabbath of the Lord thy God: in it thou shalt not do any work...* (Exodus 20:8, 10 KJV). She had always mentally substituted "Sunday" for "seventh day." Now, she saw the chillingly precise language.

Then, a stunning realization: Alex had given her Saturday off. Her "reward" day, her "chance to recover," was the *entirety* of this Biblical Sabbath. It wasn't a coincidence. It was providence. She had been given this day, a day she had just learned was holy, completely free of the obligation to work.

They arrived at her apartment building, and the Millers walked her to her door, a small, protective ritual they had adopted.

"So… tomorrow… Saturday… that's your day of worship?" Sarah asked, the concept still feeling alien.

Maria smiled warmly. "It is. It's not a day of rules and 'thou shalt nots' like you might be thinking, Sarah. It's a gift. A whole day to rest from our jobs, to unplug from the chaos, and just... be. We rest, we eat together, and yes, we go to church in the morning to study and worship as a community."

Maria paused, her gaze kind. "Since Alex gave you the day off... it feels like a small miracle, doesn't it? We would be so honored if you would join us. Church starts at 10 AM. There's no pressure at all. It's just a quiet day, a gift of time. You could bring your study Bible."

Sarah looked down at the heavy Bible in her hand, the one she had already begun to mark up. She had a whole day free from the diner, a day to investigate this new, monumental truth. A day to *rest*—a concept her body and soul craved almost as much as food.

"I… I need to read about it first," Sarah said, her voice firm with a new, scholarly purpose. "I need to see it for myself in the scriptures."

Mark nodded, his expression full of respect. "That's the best way. As the Bible says, be like the noble Bereans and 'search the scriptures daily, whether those things were so' (Acts 17:11, KJV). We'll see you in the morning, if you feel led. Good night, Sarah. And truly, Happy Sabbath."

Sarah locked her apartment door; the sound of the bolt sliding home felt different tonight. It wasn't locking the world out; it was sealing her in with a new, urgent purpose. The apartment was cold, but she barely noticed. She sat at her small table, laid the study Bible open, and turned not to the prophecies of Revelation, but straight to the beginning.

Her eyes scanned the words in Genesis 2:2-3 (KJV): *And on the seventh day God ended his work which he had made; and he rested on the seventh day from all his work which he had made. And God blessed the seventh day, and sanctified it...*

Blessed and *sanctified*. From the very beginning.

She then turned to Exodus 20, reading the Fourth Commandment with fresh eyes, the words leaping off the page as if she had never truly seen them before. The chapter ended with her realization that her day of rest tomorrow was not just a reward from her boss; it was a direct, divine invitation.

CHAPTER 39

TRUTH WRITTEN IN STONE

Sarah woke on Saturday morning not to an alarm, but to the sharp, protesting ache of her own body. The eight-hour shift at The Daily Grind had been a trial by fire, and every muscle in her legs and back screamed in rebellion. She sat up slowly, the box spring on her apartment floor offering little comfort. For a moment, the old, familiar dread washed over her—the anxiety of the coming rent, the fear of failure, the crushing weight of her past.

Then she remembered: it was Saturday. She had no work. Alex had given her the day off.

The second, more profound realization followed immediately: *Happy Sabbath.*

This was the day Pastor Anderson had spoken of. This was the holy time, the 'Sabbath rest.' It was her first full day off since before the addiction, and a day that, according to her new, fragile understanding, was a divine gift.

For a moment, she simply lay still, listening to the quiet. The unfamiliar peace in the room was thicker than the silence had ever been—a pause not of emptiness, but of invitation.

This was only her second morning attempting a daily devotional, but it was her first with such a specific, world-altering question. Her entire life, "Sabbath" was Sunday, a day of performance and dread. Pastor Anderson and the Millers claimed it was Saturday, a day of rest and memorial. The contradiction was staggering.

Driven by the same desperate need for truth that had led her to the seminar, she opened her study Bible. The pages felt cool, the scent of old paper a comfort in the cold room. She turned not to the prophecies, but to the law.

Her eyes scanned the familiar words of the Fourth Commandment, but she read them as if for the first time, the language suddenly sharp and specific:

Remember the sabbath day, to keep it holy. Six days shalt thou labour, and do all thy work: But the seventh day is the sabbath of the Lord thy God: in it thou shalt not do any work... For in six days the Lord made heaven and earth, the sea, and all that in them is, and rested the seventh day: wherefore the Lord blessed the sabbath day, and hallowed it (Exodus 20:8-11, KJV).

The seventh day. Not the first. And the reason wasn't arbitrary; it was a *memorial.* It pointed back to Creation, to the very beginning. Sarah felt a prickle of disorientation. Deacon Robert had preached the commandments, but he had never once explained *why* they observed Sunday in light of this text.

But what about Jesus? This was the critical point. Havenwood's entire theology rested on the idea that Christ's resurrection had changed the day. Sarah's hands, still sore from carrying coffee trays, flipped through the New Testament, searching for the proof.

She found Luke 4:16 (KJV) first: *And he came to Nazareth, where he had been brought up: and, as his custom was, he went into the synagogue on the sabbath day, and stood up for to read.*

As his custom was. It wasn't a one-time event. It was His habit. His way of life.

She kept searching, her heart pounding. What about after His death? Surely the disciples changed it. She landed in the book of Acts, following the travels of Paul: *And Paul, as his manner was, went in unto them, and three sabbath days reasoned with them out of the scriptures... (Acts 17:2, KJV).*

As his manner was.

She sat back, the Bible open on her lap. The evidence was overwhelming, written in the plain, unambiguous language she had been taught to trust but never truly allowed to read. This wasn't a minor discrepancy. This was foundational. The Sabbath was a direct, weekly, 24-hour appointment with the God of Creation, an appointment Jesus Himself kept, and an appointment her entire religious upbringing had ignored.

The realization was both liberating and terrifying. It was liberating because her body *craved* this rest, and now she had a divine command to take it. It was terrifying because it meant the entire structure of her father's faith was built on a foundation of human tradition, not scripture. The "double blessing" from yesterday—the miraculous tips, the unexpected day off—now felt inextricably linked. Alex hadn't just given her a day to recover; she had been the unwitting instrument of providence, clearing Sarah's schedule for her first, true Sabbath.

She knew she had to go to church with the Millers. Her study had answered the "what"; she desperately needed to see "how."

But as she stood up, a new, sharp wave of shame hit her. She looked down at the clothes she wore—the same thin, worn pants and t-shirt she had slept in. They were all she had besides the faded yellow work uniform, now crumpled in a corner and smelling of coffee and sweat.

She couldn't go. The barrier wasn't spiritual; it was material. The old Sarah would have retreated, locking the door and letting the shame win. The new Sarah, emboldened by her devotion and the call to *act*, knew this was another test of humility. *Active surrender.*

At 9:30 AM, she knocked on the Millers' apartment door. Maria opened it, her face breaking into a wide, warm smile. "Sarah! Happy Sabbath. We're almost..." She trailed off, instantly reading the distress and shame on Sarah's face.

"Maria," Sarah began, her voice cracking, her eyes fixed on the floor. "I... I want to go. But I can't." She gestured helplessly to her own worn-out clothes. "I have nothing to wear. Nothing clean. Nothing... appropriate."

Maria's smile didn't falter. Her expression was filled with a deep, practical kindness. "Oh, honey, that's not a problem. Not for one second. You wait right there."

She disappeared for a moment, and Sarah could hear her rummaging in the next room. Maria returned holding a simple, dark blue skirt and a clean, white blouse on a hanger. She also held a steaming to-go cup and a small paper bag.

"These were mine from a few years ago, before Leah kept me running so much," Maria said with a gentle laugh, handing over the clothes. "They should fit. They're just clean clothes, Sarah. Nothing fancy. Just a way to be comfortable."

Then she pressed the cup and bag into Sarah's other hand. "And this is for you. Hot coffee, black, just how you like it, and a banana nut muffin. You can't worship on an empty stomach. Go get changed. We'll wait."

Sarah took them, the soft, ironed fabric and the warmth of the coffee, feeling like a profound, multi-layered gift. "Thank you," she whispered, the simple words carrying the weight of her gratitude.

Sarah rushed back to her own apartment. As she pulled on the borrowed clothes, she thought of the "Sunday Armor" of her youth—the stiff linen, the white gloves, the pillbox hat. That was a costume of *inspection*, designed to prove her worth and repel judgment. This borrowed skirt and blouse felt different. They were a uniform of *belonging*, given freely, asking nothing of her but her presence. It wasn't armor against scrutiny; it was a blanket of grace.

When she returned, sipping the life-giving coffee, Mark, dressed in a simple button-down shirt, was on the floor with Leah. He looked up and smiled. "Good morning, Sarah. You look ready."

"We get to have haystacks for lunch after church!" Leah announced, abandoning her book to hug Sarah's legs. "It's my favorite."

Sarah had no idea what haystacks were, but Leah's uncomplicated joy was infectious. She was being welcomed not as a project or a convert, but as a friend.

A Gathering Without Judgment

They drove to the church. In the daylight, the 'old brick building' looked even more humble. It was clean, functional, and utterly lacking the imposing, judgmental architecture of Havenwood.

The real difference was the people.

As they walked in, Sarah instinctively tensed, bracing for the 'pre-service gauntlet' of scrutiny, whispers, and judgment she had endured her entire life. But it never came.

The lobby was full of people talking, laughing quietly, and hugging. Children ran past, holding small lesson papers. A group of teenagers was clustered around a table, animatedly discussing something. The attire was varied: some men wore full suits, while others wore simple slacks and sweaters; women wore dresses, while others wore skirts. It wasn't a display of wealth or piety; it was a gathering.

An elderly woman handed Sarah a small booklet. "Welcome, dear. This is the Sabbath School quarterly. Happy Sabbath."

"Sabbath School?" Sarah whispered to Maria as they were led into the main sanctuary.

"It's the first part of the service," Maria explained. "We break into small groups and study the lesson for the week. It's like a Bible study before the sermon."

They didn't sit in the main pews. Instead, Mark led them to a corner of the sanctuary where several chairs were arranged in a small circle. About ten other people were there, Bibles open. Sarah found herself in a small, intimate classroom.

Maria introduced her to the group leader, a kind-faced man named James. "James, this is our friend, Sarah. It's her first Sabbath with us."

The group welcomed her with genuine smiles. What happened next stunned Sarah. The leader read a passage, and then he asked for questions.

A woman in the group raised her hand. "I was reading in Daniel eight this week, and I'm still confused about the 2,300-day prophecy. It says, 'unto two thousand and three hundred days; then shall the sanctuary be cleansed.' I just don't understand how that applies to us."

In Havenwood, such a complex, public question would have been seen as a challenge to authority. Deacon Robert would have silenced it instantly.

Here, James smiled. "That is an excellent, deep question. Let's open our Bibles and look at the cross-references together..."

For the next forty-five minutes, Sarah watched in silence as the group *discussed, debated,* and *searched* the scriptures. They were not being told what to believe; they were *discovering* it together. It was a faith of active, rigorous study, not of passive, fearful recitation. It validated her own desperate need to "search the scriptures" for herself.

Finally, a bell chimed softly. The small groups began to merge, finding seats in the main pews for the worship service. The atmosphere shifted from an academic study to one of quiet reverence. Sarah sat with the Millers, her heart pounding with a strange, new anticipation.

Pastor Anderson, looking less like the urgent prophet of the seminar and more like a shepherd, stepped up to the pulpit.

The Sabbath Sermon

Pastor Anderson looked out over the congregation, his expression warm and pastoral. His sermon this morning was not the fiery, prophetic warning he had delivered the night before. His tone was that of a teacher, a historian, and a concerned shepherd.

"Good morning, church, and Happy Sabbath," he began, his voice calm and inviting. "This morning, I want to talk about a subject that is very close to all of our hearts. It is the 'why' behind our worship. For those who are new to this message, you may have found yourself in the same position I was in many years ago: looking at the Bible with your own eyes, seeing the clarity of the Fourth Commandment, and then looking at the rest of the world and asking a simple, profound question: If the Bible is so clear, why do billions of sincere, God-loving Christians worship on Sunday?"

Sarah leaned forward, her breath catching in her throat. This was the exact question that had been burning in her mind all morning.

"First," the pastor said, "let us be clear. Our Christian friends who worship on Sunday are not pagans. They are our brothers and sisters. They love Jesus, believe in the resurrection, and follow what they have been taught. Our discussion today is not an attack; it is an investigation. It is a humble attempt to answer the question, 'What happened?'"

He opened his Bible. "Let's begin by confirming our foundation. Did Jesus change the day? We know from Luke chapter four verse sixteen that it was His custom to keep the Sabbath. Did the disciples change it? We know from Luke 23:56 (KJV) that even after He died, they... 'rested the sabbath day according to the commandment.' Even His death didn't change the commandment for them."

"But, Pastor," he said, adopting the voice of a questioner, "what about the resurrection? Didn't they worship on Sunday to honor the resurrection?" He shook his head. "Find me one verse. Just one. Show me one text in the Bible that says, 'The Sabbath is now Sunday because I rose from the dead.' It's not there. In fact, the disciples didn't even believe He had risen on that Sunday morning. They were hiding, heartbroken, and afraid."

"What about 'breaking bread' in Acts 20:7? That was on the first day of the week!" He smiled gently. "My friends, if we are to change a commandment of God, we'd better have more than that. The Bible says in Acts 2:46 that they were 'breaking bread from house to house daily.' It was a common meal, not a new holy day. What about the collection in 1 Corinthians 16:2? Paul asks them to 'lay by him in store' on the first day of the week. This was not a church offering. It was a financial calculation, a setting aside of funds at home after the work week, to prepare for a special famine relief project. He was telling them to do their accounting on Sunday, not hold a worship service."

"So," he said, his voice becoming more serious, "if the Bible doesn't command it... where did Sunday come from? The Bible prophesied this would happen. It warned us of a 'falling away.' The prophet Daniel, in Daniel 7:25 (KJV), saw a power that would arise and 'think to change times and laws.' Not just any laws, but God's laws. And not just any time, but God's time."

He then transitioned from his Bible to history. "Friends, this change did not happen during the time of the apostles. It was a slow, gradual creep, like a shadow falling over the church in the centuries that followed the writing of the Bible. In the 2nd and 3rd centuries, we see a rise in anti-Semitism. Some Christians wanted to distance themselves from the Jews, who were hated in the Roman Empire. Resting on Saturday was seen as 'Judaizing.' So, they began to worship on both days, and gradually, Sunday became more prominent."

"But the true catalyst," he said, his voice dropping, "was politics. In the 4th century, a Roman Emperor named Constantine was a pagan—a worshiper of the sun god, Sol Invictus. His empire was falling apart, and he saw a new, rising religion—Christianity—as a way to unify it. And he saw a day that both groups could almost agree on."

"On March 7, 321 AD, Constantine passed the very first national Sunday law. Not a Christian law, a civil one. It was designed to honor the 'Venerable

Day of the Sun.' It was a political merger. Pagans could honor their sun god, and Christians could honor the Son of God. It was a compromise, and that compromise became tradition."

"A few decades later," Pastor Anderson continued, "the church council solidified this. The Council of Laodicea, in 364 AD, passed a law that forbade Christians from observing the Sabbath on Saturday. It said they were not to 'Judaize' and that they should honor the new day. Suddenly, keeping the Bible Sabbath was grounds for persecution, not by pagans, but by the church itself."

Sarah's mind reeled. *A political merger. A tradition.* This explained her father. *Deacon Robert wasn't following the Bible; he was following the tradition passed down from this council, a tradition so old it felt like scripture.*

"But here is the final, most crucial point," the pastor said, holding up a small black book. "We don't have to guess. The very power that Daniel seven predicted tells us it made the change. I am reading from The Convert's Catechism of Catholic Doctrine."

Sarah felt a hush fall over the congregation.

"The catechism asks: 'Which is the Sabbath day?' The answer: 'Saturday is the Sabbath day.' It then asks: 'Why do we observe Sunday instead of Saturday?' The answer: 'We observe Sunday instead of Saturday because the Catholic Church, in the Council of Laodicea, transferred the solemnity from Saturday to Sunday.' The Bible is clear: the commandment is for Saturday. The tradition of man is for Sunday."

He closed the book. "My friends, this isn't about attacking another faith. It is a humble acknowledgment of what history reveals. This is about who we will obey. Do we follow the commandments of God, written in stone by His own finger? Or do we follow the traditions of men, established for political convenience? The Sabbath is not a burden; it's an invitation. It's a sign that we belong to the Creator, not to the empire. It is the great seal of God, a memorial of His power, and a shelter in the coming storm."

He looked directly at Sarah, or so it felt. "Today, if you are resting in this truth for the first time... welcome home."

Sarah looked down at the borrowed skirt, her eyes blurred with tears. It wasn't just a day. It was a *choice.* It was the first, and most profound, act of separation from Havenwood and everything it stood for. It was her first step into the ark.

CHAPTER 40

FROM LAW TO LIBERTY

The sanctuary erupted in a soft, reverent murmur as Pastor Anderson finished his sermon. Sarah felt paralyzed, rooted to the pew, the entire framework of her religious understanding having been systematically dismantled and replaced in the space of forty minutes.

The commandment wasn't changed by Christ; it was changed by Constantine. It was a political compromise, not a divine command.

The truth was a scalpel, painful but cleansing. It meant the crushing legalism of Havenwood—the arbitrary rules, the endless fear—had been focused on the wrong day, worshiping a tradition built on human authority rather than God's clear word. The shame she felt was not for the Pastor or the message, but for the blindness of her past.

Mark gently placed a hand on her shoulder. "He's always available after the service. Do you have questions you want to ask him directly?"

Sarah nodded, clutching her Bible as if it were the only solid object left in the world. She needed to ask the hard questions, the ones that every doubt-filled reader of the Bible would ask, the verses used for decades to justify the change.

The Hard Questions: The Law and the Cross

Sarah waited until the flow of well-wishers had subsided, feeling the quiet support of Mark and Maria standing a respectful distance behind her.

Pastor Anderson saw her approach, his smile deepening as he recognized her from the seminar. "Sister Sarah," he greeted her warmly. "Welcome to your first Sabbath with us. How are you?"

"Pastor, that sermon was… everything I needed to hear, but it creates a deep fear," she admitted, her voice low and tight. "My father, Deacon Robert, always used the Apostle Paul's words to dismiss the commandments. He used Colossians 2:14 to say that Christ nailed the entire Law, including the Sabbath, to the cross. He said we are under grace, not law."

Pastor Anderson nodded slowly, recognizing the depth of her struggle. "That is the most common and most powerful objection, Sarah. And it is because the church has blurred the essential distinction between the two systems of law in the Bible. You must understand: there are two laws."

The Two Laws: Moral vs. Ceremonial

"Think of it this way," he instructed, turning his Bible to show her the passages. "God gave two sets of laws. One set—the Ten Commandments, the Moral Law—was written on stone by God's own finger (Exodus 31:18, KJV). It deals with sin: murder, theft, and dishonoring God. These ten commands are eternal because they are a reflection of God's unchanging character of love. Did Jesus abolish the command, 'Thou shalt not kill'?"

"No," Sarah whispered.

"Exactly. And the Sabbath is the only one of those ten commandments that starts with 'Remember.' It is the seal of the Moral Law. If the Sabbath were abolished, then the command against taking God's name in vain, or the one against adultery, would be abolished too, because they all stand on the same foundation—the Ten Commandments. The New Testament confirms the Moral Law; Paul himself says, 'Do we then make void the law through faith? God forbid: yea, we establish the law'" (Romans 3:31, KJV).

He continued, "The second set was the Ceremonial Law. These laws—sacrifices, feasts, new moons, burnt offerings—were written in a book by Moses's hand and placed beside the ark (Deuteronomy 31:26, KJV). These were the rituals, the handwriting of ordinances mentioned in Colossians 2:14. What did they do? They pointed forward to the Messiah! The lamb pointed to Christ. The temple pointed to Christ. The daily ritual said: 'We need a Savior.'"

He stressed, "When Jesus died, He fulfilled those ceremonial laws. You don't need to sacrifice a lamb anymore, because the Lamb of God has come! That is the law that was nailed to the cross (Colossians 2:14). But the Moral Law, the Ten Commandments, the rule against lying—that still stands. And the

Sabbath is part of the Ten. Paul in Colossians instructs us to stop observing the ceremonial sabbaths, such as the feast days, because Christ has come. He is not telling us to break the command written in stone."

Sarah felt the last brick of her father's legalism fall away. The logic was irrefutable. The Sabbath was about Creation, not the Temple ritual.

The Signs of Sanctification and Authority

"Okay, Pastor, I see the two laws," Sarah said, her voice stronger now. "But what about the argument that Christians are supposed to be free from the law? My father said the law is a curse. He said, 'Christ is the end of the law for righteousness' (Romans 10:4, KJV). If the law is ended, why keep the Sabbath?"

Pastor Anderson smiled. "That is a beautiful verse, Sarah, and absolutely true. Christ is the end of the law for righteousness, because we cannot earn righteousness by keeping the law. Only Christ's grace can give us that. But if you turn your mind to Psalm 119:172 (KJV), what does the Bible say about the law? 'My tongue shall speak of thy word: for all thy commandments are righteousness.'"

"The law is not a curse; it is a mirror showing us where we fall short. Grace saves us, but grace does not give us permission to sin! If the law is done away with, then sin is done away with, because 'sin is the transgression of the law' (1 John 3:4, KJV). Grace and Law are a team: Grace forgives the past; the Law guides the future."

Sarah hesitated. "And what about the Lord's Day? Many churches say the Bible calls Sunday the 'Lord's Day' in Revelation 1:10."

Pastor Anderson gently shook his head. "They do, but let's be honest about the context. The phrase 'Lord's Day' is used only once in the entire Bible. We must let Scripture interpret Scripture. Which day did God, the Lord, claim, bless, and call His own in the Ten Commandments? He called the Sabbath, the seventh day, 'the sabbath of the Lord thy God.' (Exodus 20:10) The Sabbath, which Christ kept, is the day the Bible defines as belonging to the Lord. Any other interpretation forces an external tradition onto that one ambiguous verse in Revelation."

"And to your question of why it must be Saturday," he continued, his eyes intense. "That is the question of authority and covenant. The Sabbath is a sign. The Bible is clear in its message. Turn to Ezekiel 20:12 (KJV): 'Moreover also I gave them my sabbaths, to be a sign between me and them, that they might know that I am the Lord that doth sanctify them.'"

He tapped the verse emphatically. "The Sabbath is the sign that God is the one who sanctifies you—who makes you holy (Ezekiel 20:12). If you choose a different day, you are choosing your own sign of holiness, or you are agreeing with the earthly power that changed the day. The Sabbath is God's signature on the Moral Law. If a King makes a decree and seals it with his royal signet ring, and you replace that ring with a counterfeit seal, you are rejecting the King's authority. The Sabbath is that signet ring. It demands our complete obedience, not our convenience. It is the difference between accepting God's appointed time and substituting man's preferred time."

"I understand," Sarah murmured. The Sabbath was an active sign of surrender, a weekly acknowledgment of who held the authority in her life.

The Ark of Community: Haystacks and Hospitality

After a brief, powerful prayer with Pastor Anderson, Sarah joined Mark and Maria. Maria immediately guided her out of the sanctuary and down to the church hall, which had been transformed into a space for the weekly potluck lunch.

The hall was loud with happy chatter, the sound of spoons scraping plates, and the joyous confusion of children. There were no cell phones on the tables, no news blaring from a corner television. It was pure, unadulterated human connection.

"This is where we live out the rest of the Sabbath gift," Maria explained, loading two plates from a vast spread of food. "No cooking, no shopping, just fellowship and good food. Everything here was cooked yesterday, before the Sabbath began, or is a cold, simple dish."

Sarah looked at her plate, which was a colorful, delicious mess of flavors she'd never expected to find in a church basement.

"The basics are chili beans, cheese, lettuce, tomatoes, and corn chips," Maria said. "No cooking required on Sabbath! It's a simple, deconstructed meal where everyone builds their own."

"What… what are these?" Sarah asked, pointing to the mixed pile.

Leah, who had been waiting for the signal to dig in, beamed, jumping up and down. "They're haystacks!"

Leah grabbed a spoon and demonstrated on her own plate. "First, you take the corn chips, and that's the hay! They are the foundation, holding all the goodness! Then you put the chili beans all over the chips—that's the mud and the warmth! Then you put the cheese, lettuce, and tomatoes on top—that's the sunshine and the happy farm field! You mix it all up, and it tastes like a fun party!"

Sarah watched, tears pricking her eyes. The haystack—a simple, playful, communal meal—was the perfect emblem of this new faith. It wasn't about rigid tradition; it was about taking simple, God-given things and mixing them together with joy and fellowship, resulting in something profoundly satisfying. It was the antithesis of the stiff, joyless formal meals of her youth.

The Call to Live It Out

As they ate, a woman named Sandy, who had been in Sarah's Sabbath School group, came over. She carried a plate piled high with her own messy haystack.

"Sarah, I'm glad you asked the pastor about Colossians. That verse tripped me up for years," Sandy said, sitting down heavily. "I finally realized that the law shows me I'm a sinner, and grace saves me from my sin. The Sabbath is a part of the law that God gives me to help me stop sinning and start remembering who He is. It's a date night with the Creator."

Maria added, "Think about your job, Sarah. You told us you only had the uniform and your body aches. The Sabbath is the weekly physical reminder that you are not a slave to your job. You are not defined by the coffee machine or your constant financial pressure. God literally commanded that for 24 hours every week, you must stop worrying about survival and remember that He is your source. That's freedom. It's His way of telling us, 'I take care of you, not your hustle.'"

Sarah looked at the haystack on her plate, then at the happy, resting faces around her. Her old life had been a frantic Tuesday, a life of endless labor and debt. Her father's faith had been a rigid, demanding Sunday, a day of earning a merit she could never achieve.

The Sabbath was a Saturday. It was a borrowed skirt, a shared meal, a rigorous study, and a command to rest that somehow demanded the most complete surrender of all.

She finished her food, the warmth of the coffee and the kindness of the Millers settling deep into her soul. She was ready. Ready to leave the world of fear and performative religion behind. She was ready to begin Chapter 40 in her own life, a life built not on tradition, but on truth, grace, and obedience.

"How do you manage the work part?" Sarah finally asked Maria. "I have to work Sunday evening, and I have to work Monday. How can I observe the Sabbath without compromising my job? It feels like I have to choose between God and eating."

There was a moment of thoughtful silence as the table absorbed the weight of the question. The conversation around them faded, replaced by the sound of children laughing and forks scraping plates—a gentle reminder of the ordinary miracles in their midst.

Maria squeezed her hand. "We have a prayer for that, Sarah. And we have a loving God who works miracles. We'll figure it out, together. The God who gave you this day off is the same God who will make a way for you to keep it."

CHAPTER 41

DRAWING THE LINE IN FAITH

The late afternoon sun of Sarah's first Sabbath filled the Miller's small living room, casting long, golden stripes across the worn but comfortable rug. After the joyous chaos of the potluck, Leah was finally asleep, and a quiet, profound peace settled over the apartment. Sarah, Mark, and Maria sat in the soft silence, nursing cups of herbal tea, the remnants of fellowship—a half-finished Bible lesson, a stray corn chip—scattered nearby.

Maria broke the silence first, her voice gentle but purposeful. "You asked about managing work, Sarah. That's the rubber-meets-the-road part of the truth, isn't it?"

Sarah nodded, twisting the handle of her mug. The earlier fear of her schedule had been temporarily drowned out by the flood of new doctrine and the warmth of the community. Now, the fear resurfaced, cold and sharp.

"It is," Sarah admitted, keeping her eyes on the swirling steam. "I have tomorrow evening, Sunday, and then my full shift on Monday. I know I have to ask Alex for Saturdays off, but it feels like professional suicide. This is the only job I have. If I refuse a shift… she could just let me go."

Maria reached out and placed a hand over Sarah's. "That is the moment where faith becomes sight, sweetie. You've found the truth, and now you have to choose to stand on it. God never commands us to obey and then leaves us to starve. We have to give Him a chance to show up."

Mark leaned forward, placing his elbow on his knee. His approach was always more analytical, grounding the faith with practical steps. "We need a plan. When you go in tomorrow, you can't just say, 'I can't work Saturdays.'

You need to frame it professionally, firmly, and with grace. Remember what Pastor Anderson said: obedience isn't burdensome; it's an act of worship."

Internally, Sarah's anxiety spiked. She swallowed past the lump in her throat, reminding herself that the Millers didn't know the full desperation of her financial situation. For them, losing the job meant a tight month; for Sarah, it meant a swift descent into the worst kind of poverty. The stakes were impossibly high, but she had to trust that the God who commanded the rest would provide for the need.

"Okay," Sarah said, taking a deep breath. "What's the script? How do I make this sound less like a demand and more like a necessary boundary?"

Maria instantly slipped into character. She straightened her back, adopted a slightly impatient, businesslike expression, and cleared her throat.

"Alright, I'm Alex," Maria said, her voice dry and quick. "Sarah, I need to talk about next week's roster. You need to pull a double Saturday, we're short-staffed."

Sarah stammered, caught off guard by the immediate pressure. "Oh, um… Alex, I… I can't work Saturdays anymore."

Maria-as-Alex frowned. "'Can't?' What do you mean, 'can't,' Sarah? You signed on for open availability. Is there another job? I need reliability, not excuses."

Mark intervened gently. "See, Sarah? You let the fear creep in. You gave an excuse, not a statement of fact. You are a valuable employee; please remember that. This is not about being unreliable; it's about a new, non-negotiable commitment."

He gave Sarah the lines. "Try this: 'Alex, I need to inform you of a permanent schedule adjustment. Going forward, I will be unavailable from Friday sunset to Saturday sunset due to a religious commitment. I am available any other time, and I am willing to take extra shifts during the week to make up the hours.'"

Sarah repeated the sentence in her mind, feeling the power of the word 'permanent.' It closed the door on negotiation.

She tried again. Maria-as-Alex was now even tougher.

"'Look, Sarah, I like you, but Saturdays are mandatory for everyone here. If you can't work Saturdays, I won't be able to keep you on. It's non-negotiable for the business.' What do you say?" Maria challenged.

This time, Sarah felt the new strength of her conviction rise up. She wasn't asking permission; she was stating the truth of her life.

"Alex," Sarah said, meeting Maria's eyes firmly. "I understand the business needs. My availability for all other shifts—Sunday evening through Friday evening—is completely open. However, my availability permanently excludes the hours between Friday sunset and Saturday sunset. I sincerely hope this can be accommodated, but my commitment to the Sabbath is non-negotiable."

Mark gave a satisfied clap. "That's it, Sarah. You didn't argue, you didn't preach, and you didn't beg. You presented a fact. The ball is now in Alex's court, and you can trust God to influence her decision, whatever it may be."

Maria's face softened, dropping the role. "And if she says no, then you will know with complete certainty that God has something better for you. That fear you feel? The fear of the unknown? That's where Jesus wants you to lean on Him."

The Sunset of Rest

As the conversation drew to a close, Mark checked his phone for the exact time. "Sabbath is almost over, Sarah. The sun is just about to dip."

They walked out onto the small, shared balcony behind the apartment building. The western sky was a spectacular canvas of fiery orange, deep rose, and fading violet. The low rumble of traffic sounded far away, muted by the hush of the holy hours.

Maria began to softly sing a simple hymn about the close of the day. Sarah stood between the Millers, feeling the last vestiges of the Sabbath peace settle over her heart. For twenty-four hours, she hadn't touched a dirty dish, worried about money, or run from her problems. She had simply *rested* as God commanded. And she had found profound truth in that rest.

This is worth fighting for, she thought, watching the last sliver of sun disappear below the horizon. *This feeling of peace is more valuable than any paycheck could ever be.*

As the light faded, Sarah closed her eyes and offered a silent, private prayer that was both a plea and a vow. She surrendered the fate of her job, her rent, and her fragile new life into the hands of the Creator. *You are my source, not The Daily Grind. If you want me to keep this Sabbath, you have to provide the means.*

The next evening, Sunday, felt like a return to the noise. Sarah dressed in her faded uniform, the borrowed skirt and blouse folded neatly on her bed. She walked the few blocks to The Daily Grind, the rehearsed script running on a loop in her head.

Alex was behind the counter, wrestling with a massive delivery of coffee beans. She looked tired and irritable.

"You're late," Alex barked, not looking up. "The delivery guys are backed up, and the espresso machine is jamming. Get the beans sorted first, then start pulling shots. I need you on the machine tonight."

Sarah paused, taking a deliberate moment to center herself. This was not the time to be meek.

"Alex, before I start my shift, I need a quick word with you about my permanent schedule," Sarah said, making sure her voice was clear and even.

Alex dropped a heavy sack of beans with a grunt, finally looking up. Her eyes were hard and tired. "Make it fast, Sarah. This is Sunday rush."

Sarah stood her ground, remembering Mark's instruction to be firm. "Alex, I need to inform you of a permanent schedule adjustment. Going forward, I will not be available for work between Friday sunset and Saturday sunset due to a religious commitment. I am available any other time, and I am willing to take extra shifts during the week to make up the hours."

"Religious commitment," Alex repeated flatly. She leaned against the counter, folding her arms. "You know Saturday availability was the one condition of hiring you last week, right, Sarah? The difference between profit and loss is often that Saturday. Why the sudden, uh... commitment?"

Sarah knew she couldn't retreat now. "I am sorry for the inconvenience, Alex, but this is a change I must make. I am committed to this job and will ensure all my other shifts are covered and performed well. But Saturday is non-negotiable."

Alex stared at her for another agonizing moment, analyzing the new determination in Sarah's posture. She reached for the roster, pulled out a pen, and drew a thick, slow line through Sarah's upcoming Saturday shifts.

"I see," Alex finally said, her voice dropping to a low, cold register. She snapped the pen shut, her eyes fixed entirely on Sarah. "I'll accommodate your... commitment for now. But if your attendance drops, or if you cause me any issue, you are gone."

CHAPTER 42

UNSHAKEN BY TRIAL

On Monday morning, Sarah stepped into The Daily Grind, her body weary but her spirit fortified by Sabbath peace. The weekend's calm—Saturday's rest and the Sunday seminar—was already fading, replaced by the tension of ordinary routine. Today would be the first real test of Alex's uneasy truce.

She found out quickly what Alex's condition—*But if your attendance drops, or if you cause me any issue, you are gone*—truly meant.

Alex didn't fire her, but she did far worse: she made Sarah's job miserable.

"Morning, Sarah," Alex said, her tone devoid of warmth. She slammed a mop and bucket onto the counter. "Since you have this... commitment that limits your weekend hours, we need to ensure you're maximizing your productivity during the week. You're on deep cleaning today."

Deep cleaning meant the jobs everyone else avoided. Sarah spent the first two hours on her hands and knees scrubbing the sticky grout lines around the base of the counter—a task usually reserved for the night crew. She was then assigned to meticulously inventory the dozens of specialty syrups in the cramped, hot storage room, double-checking every expiry date, while Alex hovered nearby, finding tiny, insignificant flaws in the arrangement.

"That 'Salted Caramel' is leaning, Sarah. Fix it," Alex snapped, standing with her arms crossed. "If we lose even one bottle due to carelessness, it comes out of your tips."

Sarah didn't argue. She knew Alex was looking for a reaction, a crack in her composure that would justify firing her. However, the memory of the Sabbath rest proved to be a surprising shield. The frantic, terrified Sarah of a few weeks ago would have crumpled, cried, or shouted back. This Sarah, however, had the sermon's words echoing in her mind: obedience isn't burdensome; it's an act of worship. She was enduring this not for Alex, but to protect the sacred time she had claimed for herself.

She worked flawlessly, diligently, and silently. She fixed the leaning syrup, wiped down the sticky baseboards, and kept her smile pasted on, even when she had to wipe up a spilled pitcher of iced tea from the floor. By midday, her back ached more intensely than it had after the Friday rush, but she had survived the morning.

During her short lunch break, Sarah huddled in the small, staff-only nook behind the kitchen. Her meager savings, combined with the tip windfall, gave her less than a week until the eviction deadline she had been desperately hiding.

Her heart dropped further when she saw a generic flyer advertising a competing coffee shop, offering a $500 sign-on bonus for full-time, open-availability staff.

The timing felt like a direct taunt. God had commanded her to close the door to work on Saturday, and immediately, the crushing reality of the market offered her an easy escape—a job with double the hours and a bonus, provided she sacrifice her commitment.

It's either the Sabbath or the roof, Sarah thought, the pressure so intense it felt like a physical crushing in her chest. The flyer mocked her conviction: $500 for one Saturday morning of work. The cost of her peace was exactly the price of her housing. She needed to ask for help, but how could she admit to Mark and Maria that she was just days away from sleeping next to a dumpster? They had given her so much already—food, clothes, and her spiritual awakening. To confess her destitution now felt like a betrayal, a request for a debt that could never be repaid.

At 5:45 PM, Sarah gratefully clocked out, the scent of industrial cleaner mixed with stale coffee clinging to her hair. She walked the few blocks back to her apartment, quickly changing out of her uniform and splashing cold water on her face. Her exhaustion was profound, a total depletion not just of energy, but of emotional reserve.

When she knocked on the Millers' door at 6:30 PM, Maria opened it instantly, her cheerful expression fading slightly as she took in Sarah's tired eyes.

"Rough day at the Grind, honey?" Maria asked, handing Sarah a bottle of cold water.

"Alex is running me ragged," Sarah admitted, forcing a small smile. "She's trying to find a reason, I think. But I'm holding my ground." She consciously avoided mentioning the Final Notice, burning a hole in her pocket.

"Good for you," Mark said, appearing from the kitchen with Leah, who was already dressed for the outing. "The fight isn't against Alex; it's for your soul's rest. Let her run you ragged; God sees your faithfulness. Now, let's go. Pastor Anderson is scheduled to speak about the two witnesses tonight. That's always a powerful, heavy topic."

Sarah followed them to the car, sinking into the passenger seat. She had spent the entire day fighting a boss who hated her new boundary and staring at a financial deadline that threatened to destroy her. She was empty. As Mark pulled away from the curb and they drove toward the quiet, humble church, Sarah realized she wasn't just going to a seminar. She was running toward the only place where she felt safe—the ark of community and truth. She desperately needed to hear Pastor Anderson's voice, to be reminded that the chaos of her life was temporary and that God's promises are permanent.

The Two Witnesses

When they finally arrived at the church, Sarah took her seat, her Bible open to the book of Revelation, exhausted from the day's trials. Pastor Anderson stood before them, his blue tie catching the light. Tonight, the screen behind him displayed an image of two ancient, fiery torches held high against a pitch-black sky. He wore the same sincere, burdened demeanor, emphasizing that the truth was not designed to entertain, but to solidify faith.

"Last week," he began, his voice low and intense, "we discussed the final reckoning—the promise of eternal rest from sin and struggle. But how do we know these things are true? How can we be certain that this plan is secure? Because God preserved the message! Tonight, we dive into Revelation chapter 11, where Jesus Christ guarantees the life of His message, a prophecy that touches the very pages of the Book you hold in your hands. We are going to meet the Two Witnesses."

Pastor Anderson moved to the screen, which now displayed Revelation 11:4 (KJV).

"The Bible identifies these witnesses with glorious, powerful symbols: 'These are the two olive trees, and the two candlesticks standing before the God of the earth.'"

"A candlestick, or a lampstand, provides Light! Psalm 119:105 tells us the Word is a lamp to our feet! The first witness, the Old Testament, illuminated the path to the Messiah. The second witness, the New Testament, illuminates the Messiah who came! They provide the complete truth to a world staggering in darkness.

"And they are the two Olive Trees. In prophecy, the olive oil fuels the light, symbolizing the Holy Spirit. The Bible is not just literature; it is a Spirit-filled book. It possesses the divine power to convict, to change a life, and to lead the soul to Christ. This Light and this Power—the Old and New Testaments—were given a great commission: to bear testimony through the ages, no matter the opposition."

The Pastor then outlined the duration of their suppressed ministry.

"This commission was tied to a massive period of prophetic time, the one thousand two hundred and sixty days—or 1,260 years—of spiritual supremacy. And during this dark age, the Witnesses prophesied in sackcloth—the garments of mourning and obscurity.

"From A.D. 538 to 1798, the glorious light of God's Word was systematically muzzled. It was locked away in dead languages, chained to altars, and kept from the grasp of ordinary people, replaced by human traditions and doctrines. They were grieving, they were hidden, but they were never silent.

"The Witnesses were still dangerous! They brought plagues and judgment—the spiritual fire of the truth itself—against the institutions that opposed them. God protected them, keeping the flame of truth alive through faithful believers who suffered and died to preserve the Scriptures, a testament to the fact that God's Word cannot be defeated by decrees or dungeons."

The image on the screen changed to show books being cast into flames, framed by the chaos of a revolution. Sarah leaned forward, gripped by the historical fulfillment of this dark prophecy.

"When their 1,260-year testimony was fulfilled, the prophecy declared that a terrible power, the beast rising out of the bottomless pit—the symbolic power of atheism and rebellion—would make a final war against them, overcome them, and kill them.

"This climactic moment found its stage in the late 18th century, in the nation of France. Spiritually called 'Sodom and Egypt' because of its atheism and moral collapse, the French Revolution formally abolished the Bible, outlawed Christianity, and installed the 'Goddess of Reason.' Copies of the Scriptures were publicly dragged and burned. For three and a half literal years, the Word of God was dead in the street, and the world rejoiced, believing they had finally silenced God.

"But the Word of God is not mere ink and paper! At the precise end of that three-and-a-half-year period, in 1797, France rescinded its anti-religious laws. And what happened next was the most spectacular resurrection in modern history: 'After the three and a half days the breath of life from God entered into them, and they stood on their feet, and great fear fell on those who saw them.'"

Pastor Anderson's voice rose, filled with triumph. "Immediately, the Great Bible Societies were born! They began translating the Scriptures into every language, printing them at a low cost, and distributing them to every corner of the globe. The light that had been suppressed for a millennium burst forth, standing upon its feet with unprecedented power. The Witnesses were vindicated, ascending to a place of global influence. They testified then, and they testify now, that God's message is indestructible!"

A Call to Surrender

Sarah felt a surge of energy, a powerful conviction that this Book she held was not just a relic, but a living, dangerous weapon of light. It was the absolute guarantee that the salvation promised to her—the destruction of her past and the hope of her future—was completely secure. Her eviction notice and Alex's tyranny suddenly seemed fragile compared to the history laid out before her.

Pastor Anderson brought the sermon to a close with its final appeal, returning to the themes of urgency and action. "My brothers and sisters, the two Witnesses have proven their identity. They have survived every empire and every philosophical assault. They are alive! The light is shining, and the power is flowing. Your job is not to protect the Bible; your job is to allow the Bible to protect you!

"I asked you last week: Do you have your spiritual go bag ready? That bag must contain the Word of God! If the world could not kill this message, what are you waiting for? Stop being stagnant! Every decision must be measured against this resurrected Word! If you are ready to finally accept the complete, living authority of the Old and New Testaments as the ultimate truth for your life—if you are ready to surrender completely to the message that cannot be killed—then let your decision be known. Let's finish this race together!"

Sarah looked down at the pages of Revelation 11, tracing the words. The history was undeniable. Her fears were gone, replaced by the sheer clarity and power of God's promise. She didn't just need the Bible to survive; she needed to become a living, acting witness to its truth. The time for observation was over.

CHAPTER 43

SAFE IN THE HANDS OF GOD

The spiritual energy from the Monday seminar, which had felt like a surge of pure light, began to feel like a distant hum by Tuesday morning. Sarah walked into The Daily Grind to find Alex's harassment had become more strategic. The physical labor of deep cleaning was gone, replaced by calculated psychological pressure.

Alex had moved Sarah from the counter to the drive-thru window, the busiest and most chaotic station.

"Today you're responsible for the order queue," Alex announced, tapping the digital screen. "I expect zero errors and a service time under sixty seconds per vehicle. If a car waits longer than ninety seconds, it counts as an incident."

It was a setup. The drive-thru was a tiny box of anxiety, prone to miscommunications, complicated custom orders, and the incessant timer ticking on the screen like a countdown bomb. Alex sat in the office, watching the camera feed, ready to pounce.

Sarah, now mentally prepared for the persecution, focused solely on the resurrected Word she had heard the night before. *God's message is indestructible.* She took the crushing pressure of the sixty-second rule and turned it into a meditative focus. *Keep moving. Act with purpose.*

When the line backed up due to a customer ordering eight separate, complex iced drinks, Sarah didn't panic. She politely asked the customer to pull forward and wait, managing the flow smoothly while maintaining a genuine smile. When Alex came out, ready to deliver a reprimand, she found no fault. Sarah's speed and perfect order-taking were frustratingly efficient.

By lunchtime, Sarah felt a profound exhaustion settle in her bones, a different kind of weariness than the day before. This was the exhaustion of constant vigilance, of fighting an invisible battle against discouragement and stress. The financial deadline loomed large; Friday was only seventy-two hours away.

During her lunch break, Sarah didn't look at the eviction notice, but she deliberately pulled out the flyer for the competing coffee shop. The offer of a $500 bonus for sacrificing Saturday morning felt incredibly merciful, yet equally demonic.

Just one Saturday, the thought whispered. *Pay the rent, get stable, then recommit. Survival first.*

When she arrived at the Millers' home that evening, Sarah was quiet, her usual attempts at cheerful composure having failed her. Mark noticed immediately.

"You look like you carried the whole coffee shop home," he said gently. "Don't worry, we're going to the seminar tonight. Let the Word carry you for a change."

They drove to the church, and Sarah felt the familiar comfort of the small congregation.

Pastor Anderson stood on the stage, the screen behind him now displaying two peaceful hands folded in prayer, emphasizing the contrast with the candlesticks the night before. Sarah's mind still swam with the questions of her peers—questions about the twenty-four Elders and the struggle of keeping new commandments—showing that everyone was wrestling with this new truth.

"Earlier in this series, we saw the final reckoning—the merciful, decisive destruction of sin in the Lake of Fire," Pastor Anderson began, his voice calm, like a pilot addressing passengers through turbulence. "That truth gives us certainty. Tonight, we turn our attention to the period before that final judgment. We talk about the great mystery that faces every human being: What happens when you die?"

The Pastor paused, letting the silence settle.

"If the wicked are not tortured forever—if the final fate is a merciful, everlasting destruction—then what is death itself? The world tells you that the moment you die, you are instantly transported to heaven, or instantly dropped into hell, or that you become a floating spirit, aware of everything you left behind. But is that what the Bible—the resurrected, indestructible Word—says?"

He directed them to the Old Testament, a book, he reminded them, that God Himself called a Witness to the truth.

"The Bible defines death in one clear, consistent, comforting way. It is a sleep! Look at Ecclesiastes 9:5 (KJV): 'For the living know that they shall die: but the dead know not any thing, neither have they any more a reward; for the memory of them is forgotten.' Death is an unconscious rest until the resurrection. It is a profound, total silence. If you suffer from shame, if you struggle with chronic pain, if you are harassed by a tyrant—the moment you close your eyes in death, you are at perfect rest. You have no consciousness, no awareness of time, no knowledge of the past, until the Lord calls you forth at the Second Coming.

"This doctrine is the ultimate promise of grace. Why? Because the dead cannot hear or answer the devil. They cannot worry about their bills. They cannot be persecuted by a cruel employer. They are simply resting in the sure hands of their Creator, waiting for the trumpet sound of resurrection."

"Now, someone always asks, 'Pastor, if the dead are unconscious, what about the verse that says the spirit goes back to God?' That is a crucial question, and the Word has a clear answer. Turn to Ecclesiastes 12:7 (KJV): 'Then shall the dust return to the earth as it was: and the spirit shall return unto God who gave it.'"

"This is not confusing at all! The 'spirit' here is the Hebrew word 'ruach,' which simply means the breath of life or the spark of vitality—the electricity that makes the machine run. The Bible tells us that when God first created Adam, He combined two elements: the dust of the ground (the body) and the breath of life (ruach). When we die, those two components reverse the process: the dust returns to the ground, and the ruach—that impersonal life spark— returns to God, who is the source of all life. It is not the conscious, thinking soul that returns; it is the power source shutting down. The person, the individual, is in a profound, dreamless sleep."

The Unspoken Truth

Sarah listened, and the word *Lily* echoed like a bell inside her heart. The terror she had carried—the crushing guilt that her daughter's death had been a judgment—was suddenly confronted by the Word of God.

Pastor Anderson then shared a profound truth, a truth that seemed to speak directly to Sarah's heart.

"But what about our loved ones taken too soon?" he asked the congregation, his voice softening with deep empathy. "Why would God take a righteous person or a child away from us? Some believe it's a punishment, but the Bible gives us an answer of divine mercy. Turn to Isaiah 57:1-2 (KJV)."

The verse filled the screen: 'The righteous perisheth, and merciful men are taken away, none considering that the righteous is taken away from the evil to come. He shall enter into peace: they shall rest in their beds…'

"Here is the profound comfort, beloved," the Pastor emphasized, his eyes scanning the room. "When God takes the righteous to their rest, it is often an act of protection. They are not taken in anger, but in mercy—they are taken away from the evil to come. Your loved one is not missing out on a glorious life; they are spared the sorrow, the suffering, and the great final tests that are approaching this world. They are already in their bed of peace. They are resting. They are secure."

Sarah made a small, suffocated sound, a sound she hadn't realized she was making until Mark's hand gently settled on her shoulder. Tears, hot and heavy, streamed down her cheeks, not tears of despair, but of profound, aching relief. Lily was not haunting the earth; she was not in torment. She was safe. Lily was resting, protected, sleeping in the certain hope of resurrection. The decade-long spiritual terror dissipated like smoke. Her immediate, temporary troubles with Alex and the landlord, the 'evil' of her current circumstance, suddenly seemed small and fleeting compared to the sheer, merciful truth of her child's eternal safety.

The sermon concluded: "The Word testifies that there is no eternal hell for the lost and no immediate, conscious reward for the saved. There is only rest in Christ, guaranteed by the Word, until the great morning. This is the true peace that guards the heart of every believer."

Maria and Mark watched Sarah closely as they stood to leave. Sarah's eyes were swollen, and the fragile peace she had achieved in the auditorium was now battling the emotional exhaustion of her release. Maria rubbed her back gently as they walked to the car.

"That was... deeply affecting, Sarah," Mark murmured, his voice laced with concern, walking toward the car. "The truth about the children... I saw you. You were so moved."

"It is, isn't it?" Sarah replied, trying to manage a nod, but the effort broke her composure. The shame was thick, and the simple lie she had told moments ago—that everything was fine—was now impossible to repeat. Mark's direct observation of her grief had broken her.

"Sarah, Maria, and I are worried about how much Alex is pushing you. Are you sure everything is okay? With your job... and your housing?" Mark pressed, his tone gentle but insistent.

Sarah stopped dead beside the passenger door, the cold metal frame a physical anchor. Her shoulders shook once, and she couldn't speak. She couldn't say "no," but she definitely couldn't say "fine" again. The lie had reached its limit. The shame felt less painful than the lie itself.

"It's not fine," she whispered, the words ragged. "I... I lied. There's so much I haven't told you about my housing and Lily."

CHAPTER 44

THE TEST OF ALLEGIANCE

Sarah's full confession, whispered into the cool Tuesday night air beside the Millers' car, was a dam breaking. Leah was sleeping in her car seat. Sarah collapsed against the vehicle, the relief of the truth and the crushing weight of shame hitting her simultaneously.

"It was an accident," she choked out, her face buried in Maria's shoulder as Maria instantly pulled her into a fierce, comforting hug. "Lily was turning six. She was in her car seat, and a drunk driver hit us. It was quick, but... after she was gone, everyone told me she was 'in a better place,' but all I could imagine was her spirit—her conscious spirit—wandering alone, or worse, knowing the pain she left behind. I was terrified she was suffering in some invisible way because I couldn't save her from the impact."

She pulled back, wiping the fresh tears that blurred the streetlights. "That verse... Pastor Anderson's words... Isaiah 57:2 (KJV). When he said the righteous 'shall rest in their beds' and are 'taken away from the evil to come,' it was like the Holy Spirit shouted, 'She is safe!' It was the first time in years I didn't feel the crushing weight of her spiritual torment."

Mark, who had stood silent for a moment to allow the torrent of grief to pass, placed a steady hand on her arm. "Oh, Sarah," he said, his voice thick with emotion. "You can finally let that fear go. The Bible is God's promise. Your Lily is asleep in Jesus, protected from the evil that comes into this world. She is in perfect rest, waiting for the trumpet. That is God's word, and it is unbreakable."

Maria held Sarah's face in her hands. "That guilt, that shame—it's from the world's false doctrines. We banish it now. Lily is safe. You are safe. You are found."

The immediate spiritual crisis concerning Lily was resolved, but the acute, physical crisis of the eviction remained. When Mark asked, gently but firmly, what she meant by her housing, Sarah pulled the crumpled eviction notice from her pocket.

"Friday," she whispered. "Several days from now. The total outstanding rent is due. That's why I've been working so hard and why Alex has me trapped in the drive-thru. And... that's why I almost took a job at the rival shop that would force me to work on the Sabbath for a $500 bonus. It was the ultimate test of my fledgling faith."

Mark took notice and scanned the sum. His jaw tightened, but his eyes were filled with resolve. "Sarah, you are not alone anymore. You are family," he stated. "We are going to pay the entire outstanding balance tomorrow morning. It will no longer be on your mind. That is settled."

Sarah immediately recoiled, the pride and the years of self-reliance rushing back. "No! Mark, I can't let you do that. I can't take your money. I can find another solution. I just needed you to know the truth."

"Listen to me, Sarah," Mark interrupted, resting the notice on the roof of the car. "This church isn't a club for saints; it's a hospital for sinners, and a family for the redeemed. God put us here for this very moment. In Galatians 6:2 (KJV), the Bible commands us: 'Bear ye one another's burdens, and so fulfil the law of Christ.' This isn't charity; it's discipleship. You accepted the Word, and immediately, the enemy tried to crush your foundation. We are closing that door. You must allow us to fulfill the law of Christ in your life."

The Millers' insistence wasn't an offer; it was a firm, loving act of discipleship. Seeing the absolute certainty and the lack of judgment in their eyes, Sarah could only nod, tears starting again, this time tears of gratitude that burned just as fiercely as the ones of grief. "Thank you," she managed. "Thank you."

The Wednesday Gauntlet

Sarah woke up Wednesday morning with a lighter heart and a quiet, inner strength that wasn't reliant on her bank account. Mark had already transferred the money to the landlord and left Sarah a confirmation receipt before she left. The looming Friday deadline had vanished, and Lily was safe.

She arrived at The Daily Grind. Alex, sensing the subtle shift—the lack of guilt in Sarah's eyes—escalated the aggression immediately.

"Sarah," Alex snapped, blocking the time clock. "You're off the clock. You need to wipe down those display cases first. And I need you covering the drive-thru window *all* day. You're slow on the floor, but you're adequate with a headset. You'll be clocked in when you're standing at your station, not a second sooner. You're lucky I didn't write you up for yesterday's minor error in the caramel ratio."

The hostility was designed to erode Sarah's confidence. Sarah simply met Alex's gaze, the years of cowering before Robert and her own guilt giving way to a strange, almost serene firmness. "I understand," she replied, her voice calm and level. She moved swiftly to wipe the cases, clocking in precisely at the start of her shift, her movements efficient and devoid of resentment. She knew that today, Philippians 4:13 (KJV) was her apron, allowing her to endure Alex's oppressive management.

By the time Mark, Maria, and Leah picked her up, Sarah was physically exhausted, but this time, the exhaustion was a clean feeling. "I can't believe how much peace I have, even when he's right there," she told Mark in the car. "My mind is clear. I still don't know where I'll get next month's rent, but I know I won't be working on Saturday. I choose the Sabbath."

"Then you've passed the test for today," Mark smiled. "Now, let's go learn about the final test for the world."

The Mark of the Beast

The screen at the church glowed with Pastor Anderson's title card: "The Mark of the Beast: The Final Act of Allegiance."

The Pastor began the sermon by pointing out that the world's greatest fear—an economic or physical mark—obscured the simple, scriptural truth that prophecy must be interpreted symbolically.

"The Mark of the Beast is not a microchip," Pastor Anderson stated, pacing the stage. "The Book of Revelation is a book of symbols, and symbols must be interpreted by Scripture. If you understand God's Seal, you will understand the Devil's Mark."

He turned to the Old Testament, the foundation of prophetic truth.

"God's Seal, the sign of His authority, is the Sabbath. Look at Ezekiel 20:20 (KJV): 'And hallow my sabbaths; and they shall be a sign between me and you, that ye may know that I am the LORD your God.' A sign, a seal, a mark—it identifies the one you worship. Every legal seal must contain three elements to be binding:

1. The Name of the Lawgiver: The LORD your God.

2.   The Title of the Lawgiver: Creator of the Heavens and Earth (found explicitly in the 4th Commandment: 'For in six days the LORD made heaven and earth...').

3.   The Territory of the Lawgiver: Heaven and Earth."

"The Sabbath is God's Seal of Creation, placed within the heart of His Law! When you honor the Sabbath, you are signing your allegiance to Him as your Creator and Sustainer. You are recognizing His territory."

The Pastor then pivoted to the Beast power of Revelation 13, emphasizing that the Beast demands worship and introduces a counterfeit mark of authority.

"The Beast Power—identified scripturally as the political and religious entity that thought to change times and laws (Daniel 7:25, KJV)—demanded its own sign of authority. This Beast doesn't want you to worship Satan; it wants you to worship the System, placing the authority of man above the authority of God. And what is that sign? The counterfeit day of rest: Sunday worship."

He then brought up the warning from Revelation 14. "The final warning is given in Revelation 14:9-12 (KJV), the third angel's message. It warns against receiving the Mark of the Beast in your forehead or in your hand. The forehead symbolizes your mind, your decisions, and your convictions. The hand symbolizes your actions, your labor, your economic support. The Mark is not a visible tattoo; it is the enforced, public decision to follow a human institution over a Divine command."

He put a stark quote on the screen: The Sunday Law is a Catholic institution, and its claims to observance can be defended only on Catholic principles... From beginning to end of Scripture, there is not a single passage that warrants the substitution of the first day of the week for the seventh. (The Catholic Press, Sydney, Australia, Aug. 25, 1900.)

"The Mark of the Beast is simply the enforcement of a counterfeit day of rest," Pastor Anderson declared. "It is forced worship, a human law, enforced by civil authority, that conflicts directly with God's Sabbath command. The decision to accept the Mark is the decision to reject the Sabbath Seal and place your allegiance with the human power."

Sarah felt the cold clarity intensify, the truth landing like a struck gong. Her situation with Alex and the rival coffee shop was a miniature, personalized enactment of the final test. The Mark of the Beast was the forced compromise of conscience—the demand to sacrifice allegiance for economic survival.

The eviction notice was the prophetic pressure system. The $500 bonus was the temptation to accept the Mark in her hand—to sell her labor and her conviction to the system.

She realized the choice was never about $500 or job security; it was always about whose authority she would recognize—God's, who commanded rest and promised provision, or man's, who demanded labor and offered a temporary, conditional fix.

The Pastor concluded by holding up an imaginary sign. "The Sabbath is a sign on the hand (your *works*) and on the forehead (your *mind*). The Mark is the same: the decision is made in your mind, and then acted out in your labor."

As the lights came up, Sarah felt a new kind of peace: the peace that comes with total conviction. She looked at Maria and Mark, her eyes bright and resolute.

"I'm going to resign tomorrow morning," Sarah said, the words clean and firm. "Before Alex can fire me, I'm quitting. I won't take the money, and I won't sacrifice my faith!"

CHAPTER 45

RIGHTEOUSNESS BY FAITH

The pre-dawn chill of the city pressed in against the coffee shop's glass facade, but inside, The Daily Grind was already a furnace of human anxiety. The air, usually a welcome blend of roasted coffee and cinnamon, today tasted of stale ambition and fear. Sarah walked past the rushing line of baristas, none of whom she bothered to greet. She didn't belong here anymore.

She held the folded, quarter-sheet of paper in her hand—her resignation. It felt impossibly light, yet heavy enough to sink her entire future. For weeks, fear of eviction, fear of failure, and fear of the bottom line had been her masters. This morning, she was submitting to a different master: peace.

Alex was in the back office, the light over her inventory clipboard illuminating the permanent scowl on her face. She looked up, her eyes immediately assessing her unaproned state.

"Sarah, you're early," she snapped, already irritated. "Clock in, wipe down the display cases, and cover the drive-thru. We're short-staffed. Move."

Sarah walked to his desk, the fluorescent hum overhead suddenly loud in the silence. She did not raise her voice. She did not apologize. She simply placed the folded note on the laminate surface.

"Alex, I won't be clocking in." Her voice was steady, a clear, solid note that cut through the office noise. "I am submitting my resignation, effective today. My final shift will be Friday at 3 PM, ensuring a clean hand-off. You can accept my notice or terminate my employment immediately. Either way, I will not be working this Saturday."

Alex froze. The clipboard slipped from her hand and hit the floor with a hollow plastic clap. She picked up the note, uncrumpling it slowly, his eyes scanning the two professional sentences. Her reaction was not surprise; it was raw, impotent fury that her utility had been challenged.

"You're throwing away your only reliable income for this?" she hissed, throwing the note back at her. It fluttered onto her shoe. "Some cult's day off? Sarah, look at yourself. You're paycheck to paycheck. This little stunt won't impress your new friends when the rent is due. They won't pay your electric bill next month, I guarantee it!"

Sarah met her gaze, her expression now one of complete clarity, not panic. She lowered her voice, the conviction ringing louder than her fury. "Call it what you want, Alex," she added, her voice dropping the last remnants of politeness. "It's my faith, and I'm keeping the commitment."

The cruelty was intended to wound, to trigger the familiar panic that had ruled her life. But Sarah's mind remained focused on the Millers, on the peace of that first Sabbath.

"They already handled my financial need, Alex," she said, meeting her venomous stare. "They fulfilled the obligation you said no one else would meet. My decision is final. You can put my last check in the mail."

Her face contorted. She rose slowly, using her height to loom over the desk, but she did not take a step back. "Get out. Now. You're fired. Don't set foot in here again, Sarah. You are nothing but a liability."

Sarah felt the last psychological chains break. There was no terror, only quiet triumph. She had stood in the economic crosshairs of the world's system and chosen to follow the teachings of the Bible. She simply nodded, turned, and walked out, leaving the apron she had worn for weeks folded neatly in the breakroom bin.

Stepping into the sunlight, she took a deep, shuddering breath. The air smelled of freedom. She was jobless, but she had never felt richer.

Later that afternoon, Sarah described the confrontation in detail, concluding with Alex's final, bitter dismissal. Mark and Maria exchanged a look of profound, sacred joy.

"She just acted out the prophecy on a local scale," Mark observed, a smile playing on his lips as they drove toward the church. "The Mark of the Beast is about economic coercion forcing a choice of conscience. You tried to negotiate time, and he countered with a job or no job at all. He put the mark in front of your face, and you stood firm. Sarah, you are living proof that this truth works in the real world."

"I have nothing for next month," Sarah admitted, yet her tone lacked any anxiety. "But I have peace. I have that day to rest. That's worth more than the whole coffee shop."

"That is the essence of Righteousness by Faith," Maria added. "Works says, 'I must labor and sacrifice my conscience to survive.' Faith says, 'I rest in God's provision, even if I cannot see the path.' You are not just learning the lesson; you are living the gospel."

The Call to the Covenant

The church was packed for one of the final nights of the seminar. Pastor Anderson stood beneath the screen, which displayed the evening's core topic: Righteousness by Faith.

He opened by stating that the final messages of Revelation—the Seal and the Mark—all converge on a single, critical decision point: Who do you trust for your righteousness and survival?

"The Devil's ultimate lie is that you must earn your salvation, that you must constantly strive, labor, and conform to be accepted," the Pastor declared. "This anxiety leads to the crushing fear that your survival depends entirely on your relentless striving. But Christ demands only one work from us, and it is the highest act of allegiance: trust."

He then broke down the doctrine of Righteousness by Faith:

1.   Credited Righteousness: Christ's perfect life is placed on our account. We stop trying to erase our past failures; they are forgiven. Salvation is a free gift (Romans 6:23).

2.   Imparted Righteousness: His character is planted in our hearts. This is the power to live a new life, the very strength Sarah had found earlier that day to walk away from her oppressive job.

"How do you demonstrate you have accepted this perfect gift?" Pastor Anderson's voice rose to a crescendo. "You rest!"

He declared that the Sabbath is the weekly object lesson of Righteousness by Faith. "You stop your labor, you stop striving for your provision, and you declare to the entire universe, 'My entire salvation and my entire livelihood depend on my Creator, not on my own effort.' You sign the contract of faith with your cessation of worldly work. That is the Seal of God."

He then solidified the foundation of trust, asserting that the righteous would endure the final persecution, reinforcing that true faith is tested by tribulation. He finished the sermon with an intense, focused gaze on the congregation.

"The decision to choose the Sabbath is the decision to accept Righteousness by Faith. You quit trying to save yourself. You quit trying to provide for yourself. You rest in Jesus." He paused, allowing his eyes to connect with those in the crowd. "Someone in this room made that choice today, and I know many of you have made that commitment in your hearts this week."

He paused again, his gaze sweeping the room.

"The journey of faith is incomplete without the final, public act of commitment—the signature on the contract. That act is baptism, the public declaration that you are dying to your old life and rising to walk with Christ. I urge you tonight to make that commitment in your heart, and to prepare for that final step."

Sarah looked at Maria, her eyes shining with unshed tears. The call was clear, ringing with confirmation. Baptism. The word landed in her mind with the weight of a stone, a final, public declaration that felt overwhelming. She was saved and provided for, yes, but was she truly ready to die to her old life in front of everyone? She knew she had just taken the first monumental step of faith, but the ultimate commitment of the baptismal waters felt like an entirely new mountain to climb. She closed her eyes, letting the immense choice settle in her spirit.

CHAPTER 46

FROM PANIC TO PEACE

Sarah woke before dawn on Friday. The pre-dawn chill was internal, reflecting the reality of unemployment. She had walked away from the schedule that demanded her Saturday, her day of rest, trusting the provision the Millers had already secured for the immediate future. But now, staring into the abyss of her bank account, the practical fear settled in: how would she secure next month's income? The Millers had handled the emergency, but she couldn't rely on them for her entire livelihood. The challenge wasn't paying the rent today, but proving that a life of faith could be *sustainable*.

The only way forward was to ask for help. After a quick shower, she walked next door. She found Mark, Maria, and Leah having breakfast in their kitchen, and they immediately pulled out a chair for her.

"I just need to borrow a workspace for a few hours," Sarah confessed, her voice tight with anxiety. "I don't have a laptop or a phone to submit these applications."

She sat down at the Millers' kitchen table. Maria quickly handed her a laptop. The screen glowed with the standard job board interfaces. She was staring at a thousand options, yet every one felt like a minefield. The fear was a quiet, suffocating pressure: *What if Alex was right? What if there simply isn't a place for someone who honors the Sabbath?*

Sarah was staring blankly at a corporate compliance listing that required "on-call weekend support" when Maria leaned over, watching her scroll.

"Stop applying for their jobs, Sarah," Maria said, her expression gentle but firm. "You just spent your character trying to get out of the darkness. You don't put your integrity back in jeopardy trying to find your way back to the same structure."

Mark, sipping his coffee, took the laptop and turned it toward himself. "We need to understand the nature of the provision. God doesn't just give you a paycheck; He gives you purpose that aligns with your peace. You're an auditor, Sarah. You're meticulous, precise, and you just proved your allegiance to ethical truth at the expense of your livelihood."

He retrieved a small, laminated card from the counter. It listed local non-profits and mission-aligned businesses known for their community commitment.

"We don't chase the world's gold," Mark explained, tapping the list. "We find the institutions whose work is so necessary that they keep a firm schedule. Places where the mission dictates the schedule, not the profit margin. Your skill is needed somewhere that values integrity over overtime."

He circled one name with a pen: Clean Streams, Inc. They were a small, highly respected non-profit coordinating aid for clean water infrastructure overseas, and Mark had a minor connection to a board member. Their website had a single opening posted: Financial Compliance Coordinator.

The intensity of the next few hours was excruciating. Sarah focused every ounce of her energy into customizing the application for this single, perfect-fit job. She clicked "Send" at 1:30 PM, her heart hammering.

"The Lord will honor your effort," Maria affirmed, looking up at the clock. "Now, we wait. If He intends for this door to open, it will open before the Sabbath begins."

The three of them spent the next two hours in tense silence, clearing up the kitchen. Sarah felt a profound internal struggle between the prayer she was uttering and the anxiety clawing at her stomach.

At 3:40 PM, the landline phone, which was only used for business calls, rang on the Millers' kitchen hook. Maria answered it, listened, and her eyes widened. She quickly handed the receiver to Sarah.

Sarah snatched it up, her voice a little shaky. "Hello?"

"Sarah? This is Eleanor from Clean Streams. I just received your materials. I also spoke with the board member Mark Miller, who recommended you to me. Your résumé is impeccable, but frankly, your cover letter and the timing of your resignation tell us everything we need to know."

Sarah held her breath, expecting a question about her weekend availability.

"We are a mission-driven organization. We need someone we can trust completely. Someone who values principle over pay is precisely what we look for. We've fast-tracked this process. The job is yours, effective Monday. The salary is sufficient, and the schedule is strictly Monday through Friday, 8:00 a.m.

to 5:00 p.m. There are no exceptions, no weekends, and no overtime. We value the rest of our staff takes."

A wave of dizzying relief washed over Sarah. She leaned against the counter, tears welling up as Mark and Maria immediately surrounded her. "Thank you. I accept. Thank you so much."

The phone call ended. The kitchen erupted in quiet, joyful celebration. The long-term fear was gone; the most profound test of faith had been passed. God had provided a new source of income that perfectly aligned with her newfound faith, solving the long-term sustainability issue in the span of one working day.

"That, Sarah," Mark declared, clapping his hands together, "is the difference between relying on yourself or relying on God."

Maria wiped a tear from her eye. "Now, we transition. The work is done. Let's make the house ready for the Sabbath, and then you can join us for the seminar tonight."

Sarah returned to her small apartment a little while later, her steps light and easy. The setting sun was beginning to cast long, golden shadows across her living room, painting the walls in hues of orange and deep red. The entire world felt different now—lighter, safer, affirmed.

She felt the absolute, perfect peace settle over her soul. She was free from the corporate grind, free from the crushing anxiety, and free to trust. The narrow gate had led to life, and that life began tonight.

Just as the last sliver of the sun dipped below the horizon, marking the start of the Sabbath. As the soft flame glowed, she heard a light knock.

Maria stood there with Mark and their daughter, Leah, who clutched Mark's Bible in her small hands. The hallway was filled with the comforting aroma of Maria's lavender detergent. "We're heading to the church for the seminar now. You've had a marathon day—you don't have to come, but we thought you might want to."

Sarah smiled, pulling on a light jacket. "I wouldn't miss it. I think I finally understand what 'provision' really means. I need to hear what Pastor Anderson has to say."

The Seminar: The Purpose of the Last Generation

The drive to the Evangelistic Seminar was quiet, the car filled with a peaceful, expectant energy. Sarah sat in the large sanctuary between Mark and Leah, observing the crowd. There was a mix of serious Bible students, curious newcomers like herself, and established church members. The atmosphere felt less like a church service and more like a university lecture hall on the verge of discovery.

Pastor Anderson, looking tired but energized, came to the podium. He announced the topic, "The Seven Ignored Messages of Jesus," but first addressed an audience question.

"I want to talk about a question that comes up whenever we discuss the final prophecies: the Last Generation," Pastor Anderson began, his voice gaining momentum. "Sometimes people fixate on the numbers or the signs, but they miss the core point of the entire demonstration. The very last generation of God's people on Earth—the 144,000, however you define them—they are not a special class of super-saints. They are simply the final, irrefutable evidence in the great cosmic conflict."

Sarah felt a sharp jolt in her chest. She leaned forward, listening intently.

"What are they demonstrating? They are demonstrating that, by the power of the Holy Spirit, human beings can perfectly reflect the character of God. They are the living answer to Satan's accusation that God's law is impossible to keep, that under economic pressure, under social pressure, under the pressures of daily life, you must compromise."

His words struck Sarah with the force of revelation. She looked down at her hands, recalling the panic of the job search just hours before, and the subsequent, swift, perfect provision. She had been tested on that very point— the compromise between livelihood and conscience—and God had validated her choice immediately.

"But the Last Generation stands firm," the Pastor continued, his voice ringing with conviction. "They show that it is possible to choose righteousness over the biggest paycheck, to choose peace over relentless striving, and to choose the Sabbath rest even when the world is demanding you work hardest. They demonstrate character perfected. And if you are making those decisions today—to trust God with your livelihood—you are practicing to be that generation. You are providing the evidence."

Tears streamed down Sarah's face as she realized her personal struggle was not just a difficult life choice; it was a prophetic act. She wasn't simply struggling to pay rent; she was participating in a cosmic vindication of God's character. Mark gently placed a hand on her arm, acknowledging her emotion.

"May you enter this Sabbath rest tonight with the confidence that your character is the most important prophecy you can fulfill," Pastor Anderson concluded, his voice resonating through the large hall.

He paused, letting the silence settle, then walked to the front edge of the podium. "Friends, this brings us to the close of our week's series," he announced, his tone shifting to a warm, yet urgent, plea. "We've seen the evidence; we've studied the warnings; we've looked at the beautiful invitation. But truth is only useful when it leads to commitment."

"Maybe God has revealed a truth to you this week—maybe He demonstrated His power in your life just today, solving a problem that seemed impossible, or maybe He simply granted you a perfect, inexplicable peace. If you've seen His hand at work, the time to respond is not tomorrow. It's now."

His gaze swept over the congregation. "Baptism is the declaration that you are done with the old life, done with the fear, and ready to stand publicly under the banner of Christ's protection. It's the covenant where you say: 'Lord, I believe, and I surrender.' If you are ready to make that commitment, if you are ready to step away from the life you had and embrace His full provision, please come forward and speak to one of our prayer partners tonight. Don't wait."

Sarah gripped the edge of the pew, her knuckles white. The other night, the appeal had been a distant invitation, a nice thought. Tonight, it felt like a direct personal summons. The job at Clean Streams, the sudden, perfect provision on a deadline, was not a coincidence; it was a miraculous sign, a down payment on this very commitment. *He paid my rent. He replaced my income in four hours. What other evidence do I need?* The forces at work were indeed bigger than a corporate HR department—they were a divine reality, and she was being drawn in. She wasn't quite ready to stand, but for the first time, she felt the narrow gate had opened wide enough that she could see the final, necessary step of surrender. The struggle with her livelihood was over, but the war for her soul had just entered its final, decisive phase.

CHAPTER 47

THE BURIAL OF THE OLD SELF

Sarah awoke on Sabbath morning, and the absence of anxiety was a physical sensation—a weight lifted from her chest. Her previous life had been defined by the grinding physical exhaustion of double shifts, the smell of motel disinfectant, and the constant, cold terror of being financially adrift. Now, there was only a profound stillness. For a long moment, she simply listened to her own breath and the muted city sounds outside. She thought about her resignation and the immediate, staggering provision of the job at Clean Streams, Inc. It wasn't just a coincidence; it was a divine exclamation mark. *You chose principle, and I chose to sustain you.*

Rising slowly, she let the quiet become a form of worship, an act of trust. She stepped next door and found the Miller home quiet and fragrant with fresh coffee. Leah was coloring quietly, and Mark and Maria sat at the kitchen table, their faces peaceful.

"Sabbath morning is when you realize you are not the center of the universe," Mark said, pouring Sarah a cup of coffee. "The world can survive without your labor, and in fact, you survive better when you let the Creator take the wheel. It's the ultimate act of trust and surrender."

Over homemade sourdough pancakes and fruit, they discussed the day ahead: Sabbath School, the main service, a fellowship potluck, and an afternoon of true rest. Sarah felt herself sinking into the rhythm, realizing this wasn't just a day off; it was a weekly reset, a deliberate, sacred boundary between God's economy and man's.

The Church was a hub of energy. Sarah found herself smiling easily, greeting strangers with a warmth she hadn't known she possessed. The service began with music that soared—rich harmonies that spoke of ancient promises and modern hope.

When Pastor Anderson finally approached the pulpit, the anticipation was palpable. Sarah straightened in her seat. He scanned the audience, a warm, sincere energy radiating from him, but Sarah felt as if every point was crafted specifically for the journey she had just walked.

"The greatest barrier to faith is not skepticism, it's fear," Pastor Anderson began, his voice dropping to a conversational hush. "Fear of the future, fear of failure, fear of what you might lose. For some of you, choosing a new path means sacrificing comfort, changing relationships, and stepping away from the known for the uncertain promise of a new life. And when God calls you to a new life, there is one non-negotiable step to formalize that commitment. It is the public ceremony of your surrender, your initiation, your spiritual contract."

The Captivating Appeal: The Great Exchange

Pastor Anderson set his notes down and leaned toward the congregation, his eyes sweeping across the faces.

I. The Vow: What is Baptism?

"Baptism is, first and foremost, a vow of allegiance to the God of Heaven and Earth," he declared. "We do it because Jesus Christ Himself, who was perfect, insisted on being baptized by John the Baptist in the Jordan River. He didn't *need* forgiveness, but He needed to set the example for His disciples, for you and me.

With his Bible open, he read: "And Jesus, when he was baptized, went up straightway out of the water: and, lo, the heavens were opened unto him, and he saw the Spirit of God descending like a dove, and lighting upon him" (Matthew 3:16, KJV).

"But let us ask the fundamental question: What is this sacred rite? Jesus gave the answer plainly to Nicodemus, a man searching for spiritual truth. He told him that to enter the Kingdom, you need more than just good intentions. You need a rebirth, a public sign of a private reality. Jesus said, 'Verily, verily, I say unto thee, Except a man be born of water and of the Spirit, he cannot enter into the kingdom of God' (John 3:5, KJV). Baptism is the birth of water. It is the divine requirement for citizenship in Christ's kingdom. It is time to stop whispering your commitment in prayer and proclaim it to the world, just as Christ commanded us to bring new believers into the fold through this very rite: 'Go ye therefore, and teach all nations, baptizing them in the name of the

Father, and of the Son, and of the Holy Ghost' (Matthew 28:19, KJV). It is an act of simple, yet profound, obedience."

II. The Burial: Why is Baptism Performed?

Pastor Anderson's voice rose, building dramatic tension. "But the beauty is in the drama! The word baptizo means immersion, to be submerged. It is a burial. When you step into that water, you are intentionally going down to drown the old you."

He paused, letting the silence hang heavy. "Why do we perform this public ceremony? Because it is the funeral for the person you used to be. You are burying the person who was chained to fear. You are burying the life driven by the endless hustle, the one who compromised their rest, their principles, or their integrity just to make the rent. You are burying the life of physical weariness and spiritual compromise!"

Sarah felt her heart pound. *Burying the life of physical weariness.* The job at the motel, the constant fear of being broke—that was the *old life.* That life had died the moment she chose God's Sabbath rest over her fear of survival.

"Listen to the Apostle Paul, who defines the entire purpose: 'Therefore we are buried with him by baptism into death: that like as Christ was raised up from the dead by the glory of the Father, even so we also should walk in newness of life' (Romans 6:4, KJV). The water is not just a rinse; it is a tomb."

"Some of you have carried shame, you have carried guilt, and you have carried regret for the things you did in the past. Satan will try to bring it up and accuse you! But when you come up a new creature, that whole past is in the past already. That shame, that guilt, that regret—it was covered by the blood of Jesus! If God is willing to use the blood of Jesus to just wash all that away, then you need to be able to do it too. You must die in order to truly live. This ceremony is performed to visibly link your choice—your conversion—to the death, burial, and resurrection of Jesus Christ Himself."

III. The Resurrection: Clothed in Glory

"And then, the glorious moment! When you come up out of that water, you are born again! You are declaring that your debt is paid, your old life is dead, and you have been resurrected to walk in a new freedom."

Pastor Anderson's tone was now triumphant. "You are given a new identity, a new citizenship! Paul says, 'For as many of you as have been baptized into Christ have put on Christ' (Galatians 3:27, KJV). You step out of the water not as a cleaned-up sinner, but as a brand-new, royally clothed citizen of the Kingdom, filled with the promise of the Holy Spirit for guidance: 'Then Peter said unto them, Repent, and be baptized every one of you in the name of

Jesus Christ for the remission of sins, and ye shall receive the gift of the Holy Ghost'" (Acts 2:38, KJV).

Pastor Anderson stepped away from the pulpit, meeting the eyes of the congregation. He smiled broadly. "The question I have for all of you who have made that choice—the choice to put God first, the choice to accept His provision—is this: Are you ready to make your private conviction a public covenant? If you have already laid down your old life at the foot of the cross, why hesitate to confirm that death and resurrection in the water? We are holding a baptism next Sabbath. Is today the day you stand up and say, 'I'm ready for the burial, and I'm ready for the new life'?"

"But friends, let me tell you something more pressing. We are not just preparing for next week; we are preparing for eternity. The time of Jesus' second coming is coming very, very soon. Scripture is clear: 'But of that day and hour knoweth no man, no, not the angels of heaven, but my Father only' (Matthew 24:36, KJV). We don't know the precise moment, but the signs of the times are all around us—on the news, in our world, and in our hearts. The hour is late, and our King is at the door. Let's not wait another moment to secure our citizenship. Will your reading this book take that step?"

Sarah's Choice

Sarah's breath hitched. The Pastor's words, though addressed to all, landed with the weight of prophecy in her heart. She realized the burial had already happened: she had buried her fear, her old job, and her financial anxiety when she made the Sabbath commitment. The new job at Clean Streams was her *resurrection* before the baptism. It was time to make the sign match the spiritual reality. The decision was no longer a question of *if*, but *when*. Her hands were trembling. *Yes. The old Sarah is dead. I want to be buried with Him.*

Then, the piercing thought arrived, one she'd shoved down for months: *What about Lily?* Her sweet, bright, six-year-old daughter was gone in an instant in the crash. Lily had never been baptized.

The conviction to be baptized herself was overwhelming, but the pain and fear for Lily were a sudden, heavy anchor. Sarah waited near the back as the service concluded and Pastor Anderson, moving with an easy, pastoral grace, began greeting people. He was listening intently, offering a quick laugh here and a prayer there.

When Pastor Anderson finally reached her, his athletic frame stopped, and his eyes—the same eyes that had met hers so sincerely from the pulpit—softened.

"Sarah!" he said warmly, pulling her into a gentle, friendly hug. "It is so good to see you."

The warmth of the hug, the sheer kindness, broke her. Her voice was a cracked whisper, the grief raw and sudden.

"Pastor, I… I know I need to be baptized. I want to. But I have to ask you something," she confessed, tears welling up. "My daughter, Lily, passed away. She was six years old when she was in a car accident. She wasn't… she wasn't baptized. What about her? What will happen to my little girl?"

Pastor Anderson held her hands, his expression deeply sympathetic but utterly peaceful. He looked right into her eyes. "Sarah, you never have to worry about your little Lily. The requirements of baptism are for adults who are old enough to make a conscious choice, to die to their old, fearful life, just as you are choosing to do now. Lily, like all children who die before the age of accountability, is covered by the perfect sacrifice of Jesus. Her salvation never depended on a ritual you performed for her, only on what Christ did for us all."

He paused, squeezing her hands gently. "Jesus was baptized for her, too. He was baptized to fulfill all righteousness, which means covering all of us, from the oldest saint to the youngest child. He did it so we wouldn't have to worry about the ones we love."

He quoted softly: "Suffer it to be so now: for thus it becometh us to fulfil all righteousness" (Matthew 3:15, KJV).

"Lily is safe, Sarah," he finished. "Now, it is time for you to claim that safety for yourself."

The fear that had haunted her since the crash finally dissipated, replaced by an overwhelming, soaring sense of peace. A huge, life-changing weight was lifted from her soul, and a tear of pure joy slipped down her cheek.

"Thank you, Pastor," she choked out, her voice now filled with a wondrous certainty. "Thank you. I have to do this. I have to be ready. I need to be baptized because I want to see her again in the Second Coming. I want to be ready when Jesus returns and calls her name."

Pastor Anderson's smile was radiant. "Then let's get you ready, Sarah."

She walked toward Maria and Mark, who were waiting nearby. Her eyes were bright, and she barely needed to speak.

"I need to be baptized," she whispered to Maria. "Next Sabbath. I want to make that covenant."

Maria's smile was radiant. "That is the most wonderful news, Sarah. We will help you with everything."

The joyful mood carried through to the communal potluck meal. It was loud, chaotic, and wonderful—a true family gathering. The food was rich, abundant, and freely shared. Sarah enjoyed talking to the members, realizing this was the loving community the Millers had promised.

The afternoon was reserved for rest. Sarah spent a few tranquil hours reading, journaling about her decision, and letting the peace of the Sabbath soak into her bones. The anxiety was truly gone, replaced by a profound sense of purpose.

As the sun began to dip, painting the sky in fiery hues that signaled the end of the Sabbath, Mark and Maria came over.

"It's our anniversary, and we haven't been out just the two of us in ages," Maria said, adjusting her jacket.

Mark added, "Since you've become Leah's favorite new person, we wanted to ask if you'd be willing to watch her for a couple of hours. We'll be back before nine."

Sarah felt a surge of warmth. This wasn't just a favor; it was an act of familial trust.

"Absolutely," Sarah replied immediately. "It would be my pleasure. Tell Leah I'm ready for a highly competitive card game. You two go enjoy your date!"

As the Millers hurried off, Sarah walked toward Leah's room. She was no longer simply a transient neighbor, but a trusted member of this little community, and soon, she would be making the ultimate, public pledge of her new faith. The next Sabbath would be the start of everything.

CHAPTER 48

ANCHORED BY GRACE

The profound peace of the Sabbath Saturday settled deep into Sarah's bones. It was a clarity and rest she hadn't known she possessed, a full day spent without the gnawing anxiety of her past or the pressure of her future. The world outside felt muted, allowing her mind to truly breathe and accept the momentous changes happening in her life.

When Sunday dawned, it was no longer a frantic day of recovery and dread, but one of intentional preparation for the week ahead. Fueled by the energy of the previous day's rest, she felt the immense joy of her decision to be baptized, knowing that her life had finally turned a corner, and it was time to put that peace into action.

She was in her small apartment, scrubbing the corners and organizing the chaotic contents of her drawers, when Maria knocked, carrying two mugs of herbal tea.

"I had to bring this over," Maria said, setting the mugs down on Sarah's neatly cleaned kitchen counter. "You're glowing. Seriously, you look ten years younger than you did last week. It's the Sabbath glow, mixed with the sheer relief of commitment."

Sarah smiled, a genuine, easy expression that felt unfamiliar. "It's the peace, Maria. The silence is deafening. Before, Sunday was just dread. Now, it's preparation. I'm preparing to re-enter the world with dignity this time. No more hiding."

Maria leaned against the counter. "What does that preparation look like today? Besides the deep cleaning, which, by the way, is a spiritual practice in itself."

"It looks like finally throwing out the last of the old life," Sarah replied, pointing to a small, final trash bag containing her discarded motel uniform and energy drink wrappers. "And it looks like this." She proudly displayed her ironed blouse and trousers, laid out for the morning. "Getting ready for an honest, one-shift, five-day-a-week job. A job that won't ask me to compromise the rest I found yesterday. And I'm starting a daily routine."

"A routine?"

"Yes. A routine that protects the peace," Sarah affirmed. "I need something solid to anchor my mornings, or I'll slip back into that frantic cycle of just reacting to the day. I want to start with something that reminds me who I am now."

Maria hugged her tightly. "That's beautiful, Sarah. It's not just clothes, is it? It's a uniform for your new calling. Remember that feeling when you walk through those doors tomorrow. You deserve this."

Monday: Stability and New Foundations

Monday morning dawned crisp and clear. Sarah woke up at 5:30 a.m., two hours before she needed to leave. She made herself a cup of black coffee and settled into the single armchair by the window. She opened her study Bible, landing on the book of Psalms.

She read the first few verses of Psalm 62 slowly: *Truly my soul silently waits for God; From Him comes my salvation. He only is my rock and my salvation; He is my defense; I shall not be greatly moved.*

The words resonated far deeper than she expected. For the several years, her life had been defined by instability. The phrase "I shall not be greatly moved" struck her with the force of revelation. She closed the Bible, the realization burning bright: Her stability isn't based on how good she was, but how steady He is. He was her Rock, so she couldn't be moved. The job was simply the ground He was letting her stand on.

As she finished preparing her lunch, Maria knocked, having seen the light under the door. "Good morning, Sarah. I saw your light on so early—you look ready to conquer the world."

Sarah immediately launched into her morning revelation, her voice filled with excitement. "Maria, this job, this routine... It's not just money. It's the physical expression of being spiritually planted. My stability isn't based on how good I am, but how steady He is."

Maria smiled, adjusting the collar of Sarah's newly ironed blouse. "Exactly! You're learning the rhythm of grace. Your daily work is now part of your worship, Sarah. It's no longer just survival. Go get that dignity, girl. And don't forget your lunch!"

Maria insisted on driving Sarah to the Clean Streams, Inc. office on her first day. "Consider it a ceremonial transit," Maria joked as they pulled up. "You don't need to stress about bus schedules today." Her supervisor, Mr. Tanaka, greeted her. "Welcome to your first official day, Sarah. We value results, not busyness."

The work—inputting technician reports, tracking inventory, and preparing client invoices—was challenging but engaging. Sarah quickly learned the layout of the filing system, absorbing the logic behind the data entry.

That evening, Sarah was tired but felt a thrilling sense of anticipation. Maria and Mark picked her up, bundling into the car with Leah, who was already half-asleep in her car seat. They drove to the church for the week's final series of talks with Pastor Anderson. The auditorium was packed, creating a warm, vibrant atmosphere.

"It's the final week, Sarah," Maria whispered as they found their seats. Mark settled Leah with a quiet coloring book and some snacks in the adjacent seat. "He's covering the core doctrines tonight. It's going to be powerful."

Pastor Anderson walked onto the stage. His sermon was titled, "The Anchor in the Storm." He spoke about how choosing faith was an act of choosing stable ground when the world was spinning out of control.

"Maybe you've been running," the Pastor declared, his voice echoing with conviction. "Maybe you've been chasing a paycheck, chasing peace, chasing stability in people or places. However, the Bible tells us that the only foundation that is not greatly shaken is God Himself. Don't just stand on a promise; stand on the Promiser!"

Sarah closed her eyes, clutching the worn pages of her Bible. The message felt tailored for her—a direct confirmation of her morning realization. She was planting her feet, literally and spiritually.

Tuesday: Process Integrity

Sarah quickly picked up the proprietary software. Her concentration was high. On Tuesday, she had her first extended interaction with a colleague, Ethan, who handled logistics.

"You're new, right?" Ethan asked. "Welcome aboard. I'm Ethan... Just wanted to flag that sometimes the field guys forget to initial the 'Equipment Check' box. If that happens, simply add a note to the system; don't try to guess it. Mr. Tanaka is all about process integrity."

"Thanks for the tip, Ethan," Sarah said. "In my previous job, we were often encouraged to just 'make it work,' even if it meant fudging details."

Ethan shrugged. "Not here. Integrity saves us headaches in the long run. And it keeps the water clean, literally and figuratively. We try to keep things drama-free around here."

That evening, Sarah, Maria, Mark, and Leah returned to the church. Maria softly reminded Leah to whisper as Pastor Anderson spoke on the nature of forgiveness and restoration. He focused on the complete cleansing offered by grace.

"You see, the world wants you to carry a receipt for every mistake you've ever made," the Pastor preached. "It wants you to believe you are defined by the debt you owe, the shame you earned. But Christ doesn't just forgive the debt; He erases the record of it. You are not a cleaner trying to scrub off a stain; you are a new vessel, created for new use."

The message hit Sarah profoundly, resonating with Ethan's morning comment about integrity and cleansing. Her work required meticulous data integrity, but God offered total life integrity—a clean slate. She realized that sending the restitution letter wasn't just about clearing a financial debt; it was about accepting the emotional truth that *she* was cleared.

"Are you okay?" Maria asked softly as the final hymn began.

Sarah nodded, wiping a tear. "He's right. I keep seeing myself as the old motel worker or the coffee waitress who was always covering up. But I'm not. I'm starting to believe I'm the new Clean Streams clerk, dedicated to upholding integrity. This time, I'm not faking it."

Wednesday: Restitution Planning and Final Shame

Throughout the day, the thought of restitution—the $472.00 she had taken without permission from her father's accounts when she ran away—moved from the back of her mind to the forefront. This debt had always haunted her, but now that she had found God, she was compelled by a powerful desire to make peace. This specific amount, small but tainted by theft, felt like the last chain holding her to her past shame. She knew she couldn't wait two weeks for her Clean Streams paycheck. Instead, she resolved to use the money she had specifically set aside: the final, unspent paycheck from her last job at The Daily Grind. During her lunch break, she typed up the final version of the restitution letter and included a money order for $472.00, drawn from her last, honestly earned paycheck at The Daily Grind. She placed it in an envelope to mail the very next morning.

That evening, before leaving for the seminar, Sarah sat at Maria's kitchen table.

"I wrote the letter, but I need you to read it before I seal it," Sarah admitted, her voice trembling slightly. She slid the handwritten note across the table. "I feel like this is the hardest part. It's the acknowledgment of the worst thing I did when I left Havenwood—that money I took from my father."

Maria read the letter slowly, her eyes lingering on the passage about Lily. She gently pushed the letter back.

"Sarah, this is beautiful. It is honest, and it is brave," Maria said, tears glazing her eyes. "You're not just sending \$472.00; you are sending a declaration of independence from the sin of theft and shame. You're telling your father that the same power that brought you the Clean Streams job is the power that forgives debt and raises the dead."

"I just pray he reads the hope, not the accusation," Sarah whispered.

At the seminar, while Mark walked a restless Leah up and down the back aisle, Pastor Anderson's message focused on the weight of burdens. He asked the audience to visualize the biggest weight they were carrying and to leave it behind.

"Maybe it's a regret from ten years ago, a debt from last month, or a relationship you ruined," he said. "Whatever it is, you can't carry it into your new life. You were called to freedom, not luggage! Drop it here, tonight!"

Sarah realized that the letter she wrote—the final act of reconciliation—was her way of physically letting go of the burden. The financial debt was almost cleared, but more importantly, the spiritual weight of her shame was lifted tonight, long before the check was sent.

Thursday: Creating a Sanctuary and Assurance

By Thursday, Sarah was efficiently handling the workload. She felt mentally sharp and grounded, a direct result of her devotional routine and the peace that came from her consistent, honest work.

Maria insisted on going with her to a discount home goods store after work.

"You've earned a beautiful space to study and rest," Maria declared. "I know you want to pay back your Dad first, but listen: A sanctuary is as important as a salary, especially for a new believer. A safe place to land every day—that's not a luxury, it's a necessity for your new life."

Sarah picked out a deep forest green for the window treatments. "It feels permanent," she explained. "The past year, I've felt exposed. This green… it feels like a wall. A boundary. This space is mine, and it's protected."

They bought a mattress, soft cotton sheets, a comforting gray-blue duvet, and the brass floor lamp that would anchor her reading corner.

That evening, Sarah carried a profound sense of having built boundaries, both physical and spiritual. The air in the auditorium felt electric, and even Leah seemed to sense the finality, staying quiet as Pastor Anderson spoke on the theme of certainty.

Pastor Anderson read from Hebrews 11, focusing on faith being the 'substance of things hoped for, the evidence of things not seen.'

"You may not have the bank statement yet, you may not have the perfect job, you may not have all the answers," he challenged them. "But you have the promise. And the promise is more solid than any circumstance! Don't just hope for a new life; walk in the evidence of it right now! Your baptism isn't a future event; it's a declaration of who you already are!"

Sarah looked at Maria, and a silent, mutual understanding passed between them. Sarah felt an immense wave of assurance. She realized the sanctuary she had created with Maria's help—the green drapes, the reading lamp, the framed photo of Lily—was the physical evidence of the new life she was already walking in.

The resurrection of her routine was complete, and she was prepared to step into the water on the coming Sabbath, knowing that her past was forgiven and her future was secure.

CHAPTER 49

THE FREEDOM OF FORGIVENESS

Friday dawned with the metallic scent of promise. Sarah woke before her alarm, the sunlight filtering softly through the new forest green drapes, painting the room in a calm, protected hue. There was no anxiety, no quick spike of adrenaline demanding she solve an immediate, crushing problem. The silence was the real miracle.

She had already completed the final, terrifying act hours earlier: the restitution letter containing the money order drawn from her last, honestly earned wages was in the postal system, heading to Havenwood. The chain was broken.

Now, she borrowed Maria's laptop to check her bank account online. The plastic keys were warm from Maria's recent use, and her own fingers trembled slightly as she logged in. The screen flashed the confirmation she had earned: The direct deposit from Clean Streams, Inc. was there: $1,418.52, the first paycheck she could call entirely her own—untainted by debt or compromise.

The number hit her with the force of a revelation. It wasn't just a number; it was validation. It was the physical, undeniable evidence of her steady footing and her integrity. The money she used to pay her debt came from her past shame; this money, clean and plentiful, belonged wholly to her future. It was the material proof of the spiritual peace she had fought for all week.

She sat on the edge of her bed, watching the balance glow. This was what stability felt like. It felt boring. It felt safe. And after years of frantic running and chaos, boredom was the most beautiful feeling in the world. She dressed meticulously, ready to face her job not out of desperation, but out of disciplined strength.

She grabbed her work bag and headed out, where Maria, Mark, and Leah were waiting in the car, ready to take her to work before heading to the old church to set up.

"Hi, Sarah! Mommy says today is your big finish day!" Leah cheered from the back seat, holding out a bottle of cold water.

Sarah laughed, buckling up. "It's surreal. I feel like I just closed a major chapter."

As Mark pulled up to the Clean Streams office park, Maria turned to her. "This isn't just work today, Sarah. This is the first day you walk in completely free. That check you got this morning? It's truly yours. Go own it."

Sarah stepped out of the car, feeling their collective support as a physical force. She walked into the office and felt the familiar hum of the fluorescent lights and the clicking of keyboards, but today, the environment was neutral. The anxiety that used to follow her like a physical shadow—the fear that any misstep, any unexpected bill, could send her spiraling back into ruin—was absent. The chaos was internal, and it had been silenced.

She attacked her data analysis and reports with a calm, deliberate focus she hadn't possessed even during her most successful weeks. She was efficient, not frantic. Every spreadsheet she balanced, every account she verified, felt clean. It was no longer a frantic race for a paycheck to stave off disaster; it was the simple, steady mechanism of her rebuilt life.

When her manager, Mr. Tanaka, walked past her desk, she met his eye and offered a genuine, relaxed smile. Today, she just felt competent. The work was honest, the pay was honest, and the worker was finally honest, too. The hours simply passed, counting down not toward financial judgment, but toward the holy rest of the Sabbath. She packed up her things exactly on time, feeling satisfied.

That evening, the old church buzzed with a mixture of excitement and solemnity as the final meeting of Pastor Anderson's seminar series drew near. Maria noticed the difference in Sarah immediately. "You look like you just finished a marathon and won," Maria observed, as they settled into their seats.

"I did," Sarah replied quietly, the simple statement holding the weight of her entire journey. "The letter is in the mail. It's out of my hands now, Maria. Whether he reads it or not, whether he forgives me or not… I did the right thing. I'm clean."

Maria squeezed her hand, her eyes shining with quiet pride. "You are clean, my friend. And that is a powerful truth."

Pastor Anderson walked onto the stage for his closing address, titled "The Great Exchange: Explaining the Unexplainable." He emphasized that the stability the audience sought wasn't earned by their hard work, but was a gift received by grace, and that their job was to simply live the change, publicly and honestly.

"If you are ready to be buried and rise in resurrection power," he concluded, just as the last rays of the sun dipped below the city skyline, "I ask you one last time: Stand up and claim the stability that you know is now yours!"

Sarah didn't hesitate. She stood immediately, her legs firm, her spine straight.

The drive home with Maria and Mark was quiet, filled with a shared, contemplative peace that felt thicker than the air itself. The fading city lights slipped past the car windows, red and white tracers of a rushing world, but Sarah felt disconnected from the constant rush, anchored firmly in the stillness of the Sabbath.

Maria finally broke the silence, her voice soft. "Mark and I were talking. We've never seen you this… settled."

Mark, focused on the road, chimed in, "It's like the weight just physically came off your shoulders. You're sitting taller. That's what repentance does. You stop carrying what He already took."

Sarah smiled, looking out at the passing lights. "It's surreal. I feel like I finally put down a seventy-pound backpack I've been wearing for years. And it wasn't just the debt; it was the lie. That's what weighed me down."

"The lie is the heaviest burden," Maria agreed, squeezing Sarah's arm. "But tomorrow morning, we are burying it forever."

"You have your white clothes ready for the morning, right?" Maria asked softly.

"Yes. I pressed them this afternoon. They're hanging up," Sarah confirmed. The simple act of preparing the white clothing—a modest, freshly pressed skirt and blouse—felt like laying out a shroud and a wedding dress at the same time: a death to the past and an initiation into a sacred future.

Back in her sanctuary of an apartment, the deep forest green drapes sealed the room against the outside world, creating a silence that was complete and reassuring. Sarah felt enveloped, protected. She moved slowly, savoring the ritual of preparation.

She sat under the brass lamp, which cast a warm, comforting glow on the worn wood of her desk. This small apartment, bought with honest money and furnished with intention, was the first real home she had ever made. She ran her hand across the smooth, polished wood, feeling the solidness beneath her palm. *Stable.*

She picked up Lily's framed photo, a photo she held on to throughout her journey. The little girl's joyful smile met her eyes, a silent, powerful reminder of the reason she had found this path. Sarah held the frame pressed against her heart. *The running is over,* she vowed internally. *The debt is paid. From now on, everything I do will be done from a place of honesty. When I stand in that water, I'm claiming the promise for both of us—the promise that I will see you at the Second Coming.* It was a quiet declaration of hope; a commitment whispered to her soul.

She laid the photo down gently and looked toward the neatly hung white clothes. Her life had achieved a fragile, perfect equilibrium: her material life (the stable job, the protected home, the settled debt) was in order, and her spiritual life (the faith, the community, the baptismal commitment) was resolute.

She slipped into bed. The anxieties that used to claw at her mind—the phantom guilt, the fear of discovery—were silent. This was the Sabbath—the day God rested after creation, and the day Sarah would rest after the painful, difficult reconstruction of her life. She closed her eyes, utterly at peace, ready for the final, cleansing step of her resurrection.

CHAPTER 50

THE WEIGHTLESS ASCENT

The church sanctuary was magnificent in the morning light. Sunlight streamed through tall, stained-glass windows, casting vibrant pools of sapphire and ruby onto the polished hardwood floor. The air carried a faint scent of beeswax and lilies, and remained hushed and cool. Behind the altar, the baptistry was a large, tiled pool, glowing under recessed lighting; the surface of the water was perfectly still, reflecting the vaulted ceiling above.

Sarah sat in the front row, a borrowed white gown covering her simple white clothes, her heart beating a slow, steady rhythm. She was surrounded by six other candidates, a beautiful collection of ages and life stories, including a silver-haired woman leaning on a cane, and seven-year-old Leah, Mark and Maria's daughter, who was sitting cross-legged on the floor near Sarah's feet.

Leah softly played with the hem of Sarah's long white gown. She looked up, her expression earnest. "Are you going swimming, Sarah?" she whispered.

Sarah glanced down at the little girl, a gentle smile touching her lips. "Sort of, sweetie. It's a special kind of swimming that washes away old things."

"I like washing old things," Leah declared, then returned to meticulously straightening a wrinkle in the fabric.

Maria sat beside Sarah, radiating quiet strength. Mark was on Maria's other side, his hand resting reassuringly on Sarah's shoulder. Sarah knew she was walking toward the water clean of action, if not memory.

She opened her eyes as Pastor Anderson approached the podium.

Pastor Anderson scanned the crowd. His voice was warm and strong, filling the large space.

"Friends, family, new members," he began. "Before we witness this turning point—this commitment to shedding the weight of the past and embracing the glorious promise of new life—we must address a question that haunts every honest heart: Why does the righteous suffer while the unrighteous prosper? It is the oldest question in faith. We look around, and we see the dishonest, the corrupt, the cold-hearted, enjoying lives of ease, while those who strive for justice and integrity—those who confess their debt and pay the price, even to their own detriment—face trial after trial."

He opened his Bible, pointing to the pages. "Psalms tell us that the prosperity of the wicked is like the grass that springs up in the morning, vivid and green, only to be withered and cut down by the sun before noon. It is fleeting. It is an illusion of stability. The wicked have only this life for their reward."

Sarah's heart clenched. She had chased that vibrant, temporary grass for years—the quick deals, the easy money, the illusion of control. She had been the wicked, unknowingly building her foundation on shifting sand, only for the midday sun of exposure to wither everything.

"But for those who have surrendered their old selves, those who are walking toward this water today, the suffering you endure serves a higher purpose. As Job said, "when he hath tried me, I shall come forth as gold" (Job 23:10, KJV). Suffering is not always punishment; sometimes it is the fire that refines us, burning away the dross and leaving the gold.

The very trials that brought you to your knees—the instability, the fear, the isolation, the sheer desperation to keep the lies intact—these things were not meant to destroy you, but to prepare you."

Sarah felt a surge of unexpected peace. That was it: preparation. The long, lonely nights, the years of quiet restitution, the sheer terror of facing her creditors and admitting the extent of the ruin—that was the crucible. It had stripped away the desperate, corner-cutting person she was and left behind only the fundamental desire for truth. She finally understood the purpose of the pain.

He paused, letting the silence hang heavy. "The world measures success by the size of the house or the balance of the bank account. God measures success by the steadfastness of the soul. So when you face that long road ahead, that marathon of quiet, honest work, remember this: the unrighteous are chasing a mirage. The righteous are building an anchor. Your reward is not temporary; your peace is not fleeting. Your treasure is eternal, and your anchor is in the presence of God."

The word anchor settled deep within her. She wasn't seeking wealth anymore. She was seeking the stability he described, a peace that couldn't be revoked by a subpoena or destroyed by a balance sheet. The baptism wasn't the end of the difficult road; it was the moment she secured her anchor for the journey ahead.

The Pastor paused, closing his Bible with a soft thud that echoed in the quiet air and offered a final prayer. He walked off the podium and stood beside the baptistry, facing the candidates.

"The sermon is finished," he announced, his voice now lower, imbued with deep solemnity. "The lesson is learned. Now, friends, let us witness the commitment. If you are prepared to bury the old life and rise into the new, please come forward."

Sarah's heart leaped as she stood with a group; the seven candidates, clad in white, began the long, slow walk from the front pews to the raised, tiled platform surrounding the pool.

The crowd watched in reverent silence. As they approached the pool, the air grew noticeably cooler, carrying the slight, clean scent of chlorine from the water. Mark watched from the pew next to Leah, her small hands clasped in her lap, watching wide-eyed. Maria was helping with the baptism.

Pastor Anderson, dressed in a simple, linen robe, scanned the crowd, his gaze finally resting on the candidates. His voice was warm and strong, filling the large space without need for volume.

"We gather this morning not to witness a magic trick, but to celebrate a burial," he began, his voice resonating with deep intention. "Each of these seven individuals has done the hard, often agonizing work of repentance and change. They have decided to stop running, stop hiding, and stop striving. They have chosen to plant their feet on ground that cannot shift."

He paused, looking directly at Sarah, though the congregation wouldn't know why. "The world tells us that if we make a mistake, we must run or lie to survive. We believe in the power of stability. We believe in the power of integrity. For some of you, that means letting go of a habit. For some, it means forgiving a lifetime of hurt. And for one of you, it has meant confronting a devastating financial past, paying the full price of a profound debt, and choosing absolute, radical honesty. Or losing a loved one."

Sarah felt a rush of heat to her face, not of shame, but of recognition. This ceremony wasn't just a religious rite; it was the final affirmation of her new financial and moral constitution. Her past definition—Sarah, the debtor, the fugitive—was about to be drowned.

The ceremony began with the elderly woman, then the teenager. Each immersion was accompanied by applause, cheers, and heartfelt cries of "Amen." With every person who went under and came up, the air in the sanctuary grew heavier with anticipation, marking the relentless, inevitable approach of her own turn.

The Final Confession

Finally, it was her turn.

Sarah walked down the three slippery steps and waded into the pool. The water was waist-high, warmer than the air, a physical embrace. She faced Pastor Anderson, the entire sanctuary now watching, a silent, powerful jury of her peers who had become her family.

"Sarah," the Pastor said, his voice dropping to a powerful, intimate tone. "You stand here today not just because you faced a debt, but because you survived a wilderness. You walked through the shadow of deep instability, the crushing grief of a daughter's loss, and the devastating choice at the edge of despair. And every soul here—and beyond—has witnessed your story, walked in your footsteps, and seen the brutal, beautiful path you took to arrive. The work is done. This water marks the death of the old self—the shattered relationships, the guilt, the fear of exposure—and testifies to the unstoppable grace of God. You are here to finalize the transition from a life managed by ruin to a life anchored by resurrection."

He took her arm, his grip solid, and held her gaze. "The ruin of the past is buried, Sarah. The shadow of your grief is broken by the light of the Cross. Do you declare that you die to the woman of fear, and rise today as a Daughter of God, anchored by the faith that you will see your own daughter again at the Resurrection?"

A sound escaped Sarah that was half a gasp, half a sob. The weight of the world, of her crime, and of her unbearable loss crashed down on her, only to be lifted by the sheer magnitude of the promise. Tears streamed down her face, mixing with the water from the pool. "I do," she choked out, her voice raw but utterly certain, a vow spoken to the crowd filling the sanctuary, to her friends who had championed her, to the unseen witnesses who had followed her story, and most profoundly, to herself.

"Then, upon your confession and the witness of this community, I baptize you in the name of the Father, and of the Son, and of the Holy Ghost."

He leaned her back, and the world was replaced by water.

The water closed over her head.

The sound was immediate and absolute: silence. All the noise of the crowded sanctuary vanished. In the muffled darkness, the past did not flash but dissolved. It wasn't just the flashing red numbers or the empty bank account; it was the constant, exhausting surveillance of her own life—the feeling of running, the perpetual tightening in her chest, the anxiety of the next knock on the door. It was the drowning of all the lies she had told, all the compromises she had made to survive. *Drowned, choked, gone.* For one eternal moment, she felt the absence of pressure, the utter relief of having nothing left to hide.

Then, the Pastor's hand was there, firm and insistent, lifting her toward the light.

She broke the surface, gasping a huge, clean, necessary breath of air. The shock of the cold air on her wet skin was invigorating. The light that poured down from the windows was so bright it felt physical. Everything looked impossibly sharp and utterly new. The applause was not just polite; it was a wave of roaring, joyous sound—a resurrection chorus that seemed to carry all the burdens she had just shed.

She was heavy with water, the gown clinging to her body, but light with freedom. She was no longer Sarah, the architect of her own ruin, but a soul purged. The baptismal water did not just wash away the fear; it washed away the sin itself, swallowed by the cleansing promise of the Lamb's sacrifice. Now, she stood covered in the damp white cotton—her first, physical approximation of the robe of righteousness. She was Sarah, the steward, the one who rebuilt. The two pillars of her life were now permanently aligned: financial accountability anchored by moral and spiritual integrity.

Pastor Anderson helped her climb the last step out of the pool. Maria was there, wrapping the thick, dry, warm towel around her, shielding her from the air, pulling her close. The towel felt like the mantle of the community, a final, physical act of protection.

"You are reborn," Maria whispered, her voice thick with emotion, fierce and absolute. "Now live it, Sarah. Live free from sin."

Sarah leaned her forehead against Maria's shoulder, taking a moment to feel the steady beat of her friend's heart. "My old self is buried," Sarah murmured, her voice clearer than it had been in years. "The debt is settled, the grave is empty."

Sarah stepped away, gripping the towel around herself. She looked out at the seven newly baptized standing together on the platform, glowing in their damp white robes.

The panic was gone. The frantic energy that had fueled her for years was finally spent, replaced not by explosive happiness but by a quiet, profound steadfastness. There was no need for haste, no shadow demanding she look over her shoulder. The path ahead may still hold challenges, but they will be met with measured and honest steps. She was anchored.

The new life had begun, and it felt like peace.

After changing into her dry clothes, Sarah followed Mark and Maria to the fellowship hall. The room buzzed with voices and laughter, sunlight pouring through the windows and catching on steam rising from casseroles and bowls of fruit. The mingled aromas of fresh bread, sweet Jell-O, and roasted vegetables made the air mouthwatering.

They found a seat at a long table, where the young woman with vibrant red hair, Chloe, was saving them a spot. Six-year-old Leah was already there, meticulously inspecting the contents of a three-bean salad, her fork poised with surgical precision. Next to Chloe was the older gentleman, Mr. Henderson, with his smoked brisket, the aroma of pepper and hickory curling through the air. The table was a patchwork of mismatched plates and steaming dishes, children's drawings taped to the wall behind them. The hum of conversation and the clatter of serving spoons made the hall feel alive, welcoming, and safe.

"Sarah, you must be the star of the morning," Chloe said, beaming. "I made the bean salad, but don't eat it unless you like cilantro. I won't be offended."

Sarah grinned. "After what I just did, I think I can survive cilantro. But I'm starting with brisket."

Mr. Henderson carved a thick slice and winked. "We trade recipes here as much as we trade gossip. Take as much as you want."

Leah pointed at a bowl of colorful, sugary Jell-O. "Can I have the blue square first? It's bouncy."

Sarah chuckled and put a piece on the little girl's plate. "Go for it, Leah. You earned it, seated so still during the sermon."

Maria leaned in, whispering, "Just don't ask Chloe about her lemon bars unless you're ready for the full recipe and a kitchen sermon."

Chloe raised her fork. "The secret is prayer and an unholy amount of sugar!"

Laughter rippled around the table, the warmth contagious.

Mark, leaning forward, scooped a spoonful of Maria's famous cheesy potato casserole. "She's traded in the desperate sprint for the honest marathon, Chloe. That's the key now."

Chloe chewed thoughtfully. "The marathon's the best part, though. You stop worrying about outrunning the past and start looking forward. Nobody here cares about the past. They just care that you showed up today."

"That's the difference," Sarah murmured, glancing at Maria. "In the old life, every interaction was about *managing* people's perception of me. Here, it's just... showing up."

Leah interrupted, her mouth full of blue Jell-O. "The blue square is the best color! It makes you jumpy!"

Sarah laughed, a full, unburdened sound she hadn't realized she missed. Surrounded by the warmth of good food and honest faces, she took her first bite of the brisket. It tasted like freedom.

The new life had begun, anchored by integrity and sustained by community.

CHAPTER 51

THE FINAL ACT OF LOVE

The familiar warmth of Mark and Maria's vehicle was a stark contrast to the vast, cool emptiness of the sanctuary. Potluck had concluded, the final prayers said, and now they were heading back to the house. Sarah sat in the passenger seat, wrapped not in a ceremonial gown but in a quiet, deep exhaustion. Her emotions had spent themselves, and all that was left was a serene, steady calm.

In the back seat, Leah was already half-asleep, nestled in her car seat. She was recounting the events of the day in a sleepy, fragmented monologue. "The Pastor was so loud… and Sarah made a big splash! My blue Jell-O was bouncy..." Her voice trailed off into a low, contented hum.

Mark drove slowly, his movements deliberate. The only sounds were Leah's drowsy murmurs and the low burble of the engine.

"You're awfully quiet," Maria said softly, reaching forward to squeeze Sarah's arm.

Sarah leaned her head back against the rest, looking out the window at the familiar neighborhood trees blurring past. "It's the anchor," she replied, her voice husky. "It finally dropped. For twenty years, I felt like I was running a frantic sprint, always looking over my shoulder. Now... It's just the walk."

Mark glanced over, his eyes warm and approving. "That's the difference between trying to save yourself and accepting grace. Now you just keep walking the path of integrity. No fireworks needed."

"No fireworks," Sarah agreed, a small smile touching her lips. The world outside, despite its bright, ordinary colors, felt fundamentally different. The white gown was gone, the water had dried, but the steadfastness of the soul remained.

Saturday night felt like the first true evening of her new life. Maria had insisted on making it a proper celebration. They had dressed in comfortable but nice clothes, leaving the austerity of the week behind for a moment of communal joy. Mark had booked a table at The Hearth, a local bistro renowned for its warm ambiance, comforting cuisine, and discretion in playing music.

The four of them sat in a cozy booth. The air smelled of wood smoke and garlic. Sarah felt entirely, wonderfully present, not scanning the room for threats or calculating how to impress anyone, but simply enjoying the moment.

Leah, perched on a booster seat, was tasked with being the official celebration planner. "We are celebrating because Sarah is brand new!" she declared, stirring the water in her glass with a straw. "And brand new people get extra ice cream!"

Maria chuckled, ordering a glass of wine for herself and Mark. "That's the theory, sweetie. Sarah, try the short ribs. They are divine."

The conversation flowed effortlessly. They talked about Leah's upcoming school play, Mark's latest headache with a city zoning issue, and Maria's plans for a summer garden. The subjects were ordinary, grounded, and absolutely perfect. Sarah realized she hadn't had a truly normal conversation in years—one that wasn't laden with professional jargon, financial anxiety, or subtle maneuvering.

As the meal progressed, Sarah watched the easy, loving dynamic between Mark and Maria—the shared glance, the hand on the knee, the way they negotiated with Leah over how many vegetables constituted a sufficient tax for the promised ice cream. She felt a profound wave of belonging, a warmth that had nothing to do with the bistro's ambient glow and everything to do with the people around the table.

Later, as the desserts arrived—a towering chocolate lava cake for the adults and a rainbow-sprinkled sundae for Leah—Leah offered a spontaneous toast.

"To Sarah!" she held up her water glass, splashing a little, her eyes bright and earnest. "To be all clean and not scared anymore!" The toast was met with a chorus of laughter, the sound ringing clear above the clink of glasses. For Sarah, it felt like the world's simplest, sweetest blessing, a benediction wrapped in the innocence of a child's hope.

Sarah laughed, touching her wine glass to Leah's. The words, simple as they were, were perfectly accurate. For the first time since her old life had shattered, she was not scared. She felt nourished, deeply and completely. The meal was more than just food; it was a physical manifestation of the anchor Pastor Anderson had described: a foundation of grace, community, and unconditional love. The quiet stability of this new pace was the greatest reward she could have ever imagined.

"Thank you," Sarah whispered, tears welling slightly, though her smile remained bright. "For the anchor, for the home, and for the bouncy blue Jell-O."

The Handhold

The second drive home was even more tranquil than the first. The car was saturated with the contentment of a good evening. Maria sat in the front passenger seat, while Sarah and Leah occupied the back row.

The streetlights cast long, cinematic shadows through the suburban landscape. Leah, now fully asleep from the sugar and the late hour, had instinctively reached out a small, warm hand across the seat. She wasn't reaching for her mother or father, but for Sarah, who was buckled in right beside her.

Sarah gently took the tiny hand in her own. Leah's fingers were soft, warm, and utterly trusting. It was a gesture of simple, absolute belonging—the quietest acknowledgment of her new family. Sarah held it loosely, tracing the lines of Leah's knuckles with her thumb.

She looked forward at Mark and Maria, whose silhouettes were perfectly aligned in the front seats. She opened her mouth to speak, but no words were needed. Everything she wanted to say—*thank you, I'm here, I'm staying*—was contained in the pressure of her fingers around Leah's. The sprint was over. This was the steady, measured pace of a woman who was finally home.

They were only a few blocks from the house, nearing the final turn onto the quiet street, when the world shattered.

The first sensation was the sound—a screaming, tearing whine of an engine pushed beyond its limits, followed by a deafening horn blast that seemed to vibrate the metal of their car before any physical contact was made. Mark shouted, jerking the wheel. In the rearview mirror, Sarah saw a dizzying flash of high-beam lights—an oncoming vehicle, completely in the wrong lane, moving at catastrophic speed.

Time seemed to shatter.

The blinding, overdriven light from the wrong side of the road triggered a sensation of absolute, frozen deja vu. The high beams were not just metal and glass; they were the exact same impossible, blinding wall of white light that had borne down on her decades ago.

But this time, Sarah was not paralyzed. As the car spun out of control, she saw Leah beside her—no longer just a passive witness to disaster, but the only adult close enough to act. The memories of being helpless in the front seat, unable to reach Lily, surged forward, but instead of freezing her, they propelled her into action.

She twisted out of her seatbelt and threw herself over Leah, shielding the girl with her body. She pressed Leah down, away from the window and crumpling metal, using every ounce of strength and will to become a living barrier. The scream—no longer just a memory, but Leah's high, terrified cry—galvanized her.

I was too far then. But now, I am here. This time, I will not fail.

The sound of the impact arrived as a violent, metallic roar. The other car struck the rear passenger side of their car—Sarah's side—with the force of a wrecking ball. The car's frame immediately began to crumple inward, a lethal, jagged intrusion of twisted steel and exploding glass, aimed precisely at the space where Leah slept.

The world dissolved into the chaotic symphony of destruction. They were airborne, rolling end over end down the embankment. Each rotation was a new assault: the sound of shattering glass, the sickening crunch of metal yielding, the desperate, muffled cries of Mark and Maria from the front.

Then came the final, agonizing slam as the ruined car landed, passenger-side down, crushing the metal further against the resistance of the earth. The energy of the collision, the violent, crushing pressure, all settled directly onto Sarah's shielded form. She felt the terrible force, but she remained conscious long enough to feel Leah breathing beneath her, the child's smaller body spared from the worst of the impact.

As the dust settled and silence reclaimed the wreckage, Sarah felt an encompassing, profound peace. The pain faded, replaced by the deep certainty that she had finally done what she could not do for Lily: she had protected a child in the moment of crisis. This final, selfless act was not only her redemption but the proof that she had broken the cycle of helplessness and guilt that haunted her.

The world became muted—a low, distant ringing, like the last vibration of a struck bell. The light faded, not into darkness, but into a soft, comforting grey. There was no more breath, no more movement—only the weight of ruined metal above her and the gentle, even weight of the child beneath her. The sprint was over; the anchor she had fought so long to find finally held her fast and drew her into rest.

In the dim silence of the wrecked car, Sarah's face—pressed against the seat, shielding the unconscious child—showed no fear, no regret. Instead, a faint, radiant smile touched her lips. She had kept the one promise that truly mattered; the anchor she'd clung to through every storm had held until the end.

Outside, the night air—once alive with anticipation—was now utterly still. As the world slowly stirred—sirens in the distance, porch lights flickering on—a hush settled over everything. In that suspended silence, the weight of what had happened began to settle, not in a rush, but with a dawning, irreversible gravity.

CHAPTER 52

PEACE AT THE END OF THE ROAD

The silence did not rush in; it crept in slowly, muffling the roar of the impact, dampening the scrape of twisted metal, and swallowing the echoes of shouts. It was a silence deeper than the absence of sound—it was the absence of life.

Mark, hanging sideways against his restraints, was the first to stir. His head was ringing with a sound like shattering stone, but his instincts immediately overrode the pain. He reached across the dashboard, his fingers scrambling for Maria.

"Maria? Maria, are you hurt?"

Maria's voice was a weak, terrified whisper, laced with dust and shock. "I... I think my leg. Leah! Sarah! The back!"

The Miller's car lay canted steeply on its side, the roof crushed into the embankment. Mark fumbled for his safety knife and sliced through his belt, dropping clumsily onto the window glass that now formed the floor. He ignored the throbbing in his ribs and turned to the rear seat.

The destruction there was absolute. The entire rear passenger door and pillar were a compressed ruin, the metal folded inward like paper. He could see Sarah's shape, a dark, motionless mass draped across the space where Leah's car seat had been.

Panic, cold and absolute, gripped him. "Sarah! No!"

He reached into the narrow, jagged gap. Leah's small body, incredibly, was intact beneath Sarah's weight, shielded from the intrusion. She was deeply unconscious but breathing, her tiny hand still curled. Sarah, in her final act, had protected Leah from the worst of the crash, her body absorbing the force and saving the child's life.

Mark pulled Leah out first, his movements agonizingly slow, and handed her to Maria, who was struggling to undo her own belt. Leah stirred, coughing and beginning to cry—alive, shaken, but safe.

He then turned to Sarah. The metal was too tight, too unforgiving. She had become one with the wreckage, her body an unbreakable shield pressed against the fatal geometry of the crush.

As the first distant, high-pitched wail of a siren began to rise over the suburb, Mark collapsed against the seat fabric, his throat raw. He could feel the cool, wet concrete of the road against his cheek, but his eyes were fixed on the shape of Sarah. The anchor had indeed dropped, securing the innocent, but the cost had been the vessel itself.

In the dead center of the suburban night, the silence of final rest was complete, broken only by the approaching, desperate sounds of the world rushing in. The sprint was over, and the walker had found her destination.

CHAPTER 53

BEYOND THE GLASS CATHEDRAL

The year is 2147. The air in the clinical observation room was circulated through quantum-level nano-filters, with a faint odor of charged tritium and ozone. The air seemed to carry a strange, metallic-clean, antiseptic smell—sharp and artificial, as if nothing organic had ever lived there. The walls of seamless obsidian composite absorbed and reflected the holographic monitors, which displayed Rose's cognitive map and biometric data in luminous, complex green projections. A massive thermal window looked out onto the shimmering, eternally reforming megalopolis of Neo-Alexandria. This dense, imposing structure, the central node of the global Optimized World, was in constant flux and served as the ultimate template of algorithmic control, currently choked with a thick, violet cyber-smog.

In the center of this technological apex lay a seven-year-old girl named Rose. She was connected to the world's most advanced technology via a silver filigree neural implant tracing her temporal lobe.

Four figures were grouped around her bed, their tension palpable.

Dr. Lena Varga, the attending physician, spoke with a tone of frustrated precision. "I've reviewed the final diagnostics, Aris. Her cardiac function is 98% optimal, her metabolic rate is textbook, and there is no pathogenic load. Yet, she's fading. She is exhibiting a catastrophic *will* failure—the consciousness is actively withdrawing from the somatic connection."

Dr. Aris Thorne, the Research Scientist and designer of the Aethel implant, adjusted his gold-rimmed optical scanner, his focus entirely on the floating data streams. "The hardware is stable, Lena. But the consciousness is rejecting reality. The Aethel Calibration was a success; we stabilized her collapsing cognitive map by providing a low-stimulus life narrative—the 'Sarah' consciousness—for nearly six hours. That was the trial phase. We verified that the transfer link is secure."

He paused, glancing at the chronometer in the corner: 00:01:17. The countdown timer for the body's final viable state.

"But now, we must initiate Phase II: the irreversible Aethel Eternity Transfer. We must bypass the somatic rejection entirely and upload her cognitive identity into the matrix. This is the promise of the 90-year subjective life. The one-way transfer. We are out of time for diagnostics."

Nurse Chen, calm but efficient, adjusted the blanket. "Dr. Thorne, her core temperature is dropping another tenth of a degree. We need a decision on the Upload Protocol."

Chaplain Aaron Hawthorne stood slightly apart, his plain black tunic a quiet contrast to the holographic technology surrounding him. He spoke with a measured, deep gravity.

"You speak of 'will failure,' doctor," Aaron said, meeting Thorne's eyes. "A will is not just a function of biology. Rose is grappling with the ultimate transition, and your technology is preventing her from finding peace. She needs assurance, not a distraction, before you trap her mind in a closed loop."

Dr. Varga sighed. "Theology can't reverse deceleration, Aaron. The church teaches acceptance of death; we are attempting to make a full life possible, free from physical decay. This is the ultimate humanitarian act."

Thorne tapped a final command onto a floating interface, confirming the parameters. The screen flashed: PROTOCOL READY: AETHEL EDICT IMMINENT.

"All systems green," Thorne declared, his voice rising, fueled by clinical urgency and philosophical zeal. "The Grand Architect's edict hinges on this trial's success. Once Rose's successful and permanent transfer is logged, Aethel integration becomes a global, compulsory protocol. We are awaiting the ignition signal now."

He stared at the countdown display: 00:00:05.

"This is the quantum leap, doctor," Thorne murmured, as if reciting a doctrine. "The Aethel Eternity Matrix is ready to deliver ninety years of subjective, realized life—all desires fulfilled—in less than six hours of real-time. The neural implant creates a complete subjective life for her consciousness. The sequence for commencing that final, irreversible life is ready to upload."

Just as Thorne initiated the final upload protocol—a soft, nearly inaudible chime filling the room, signifying the one-way data transfer had begun—the process abruptly paused as Rose's eyes fluttered open. The sudden movement startled everyone in the room; the doctor, nurse, scientist, and chaplain all froze, their attention snapping to the little girl on the bed.

They were startlingly bright, instantly focusing. She wasn't looking at the glowing projections, the clinical monitors, or the frantic research scientist. She was looking directly at the Chaplain.

The little girl knew the answer: she had lived it. The thought, pure and clear, cut through the technological hum of the upload. The life she had just subjectively experienced—the life of Sarah, who had died securing a child's safety—had already confirmed the certainty she now sought.

She ignored the faint, warm pulse emanating from the implant on her temple. She ignored the noise of the technology that promised her eternity.

Her voice, weak but clear, filled the sudden, absolute silence left by the activated protocol.

"Aaron?"

"Yes, Rose. I'm right here," the Chaplain whispered, stepping closer, reaching for her hand.

She gripped his fingers. "I had a... a funny dream. All water and light. Tell me, before the dream starts again—the *real* one. If I go to sleep now, will Jesus save me in His second coming?"

The research scientist, the doctor, and the nurse—masters of the quantifiable universe—all froze. The highly specific, faith-driven question was an anomaly that their science had no variable for. Dr. Thorne's complex, life-giving device hummed silently, now actively beginning the permanent upload, waiting for the answer to a question no machine could ever provide.

The Final Edict

On the main monitor, the three primary biometric lines—the cardiac rhythm, the metabolic rate, and the neural activity map—did not spike, crash, or flatline. Instead, they performed a simultaneous, perfect, and terrifying descent. A cascade of green data turned amber, then red, shrinking uniformly until all three vanished at the zero marker. Rose's life functions had ceased.

Dr. Varga gasped, rushing forward to confirm the biological death.

But Rose hadn't released Aaron's hand yet. A flicker of movement traced across her face, not the pain of a failing system, but a deep, profound satisfaction. A tiny, certain smile bloomed on her lips, visible even in the dim light of the obsidian room.

Her eyes, which had once held the intense light of the final question, now reflected only a peaceful, knowing distance. As her consciousness definitively left the body, a single, soft word, the answer to the question she had just asked, escaped her:

"Yes."

It was not a gasp of relief or a final breath; it was a firm declaration.

The four masters of science and faith—the scientist who demanded control, the doctor who sought stability, the nurse who tracked the metrics, and the chaplain who offered comfort—were frozen. The transfer, for all its precision, had failed. Her physical life was gone. Yet, the patient, in her final nanosecond of subjective reality, had received an answer to the greatest mystery, an answer that eluded all of them, and had carried it, with a smile, out of the sterile glass cathedral. The Aethel Edict lay in ruins, defeated by a seven-year-old's certainty.

- The End.

"For if we believe that Jesus died and rose again, even so them also which sleep in Jesus will God bring with him."

—1 Thessalonians 4:14 (KJV)

ACKNOWLEDGEMENTS

Opening & Inspiration
This novel, *The Salvation Schema*, is a testament to the powerful contrast between conditional structures and unconditional grace. Its completion was made possible only through the inspiration of God and the unwavering support of my family.

The Divine Source
To my **God**, from whom the inspiration, vision, and enduring truth of this story originated. Thank you for the grace to tell this difficult story of finding light in the shadow.

The Builders of Insight (Contributors)
To my **Kuya & Pastor Ed Anderson**: The narrative of *The Salvation Schema* is built on the theological distinction between rigid legalism and the unconditional nature of true grace. This essential framework for the protagonist's journey was derived entirely from the wealth of insight found in your ministry. Thank you for making your teachings readily available on the www.futureofhope.com website and YouTube channel, which provided the spiritual knowledge necessary to illuminate the truth at the heart of this novel. Your perspective was indispensable.

The Final Word
And to my **Ohana**: You are the unshakeable foundation. Thank you for proving that the greatest love is always found outside of any rigid schema, and that every true story flows from unconditional acceptance.

ABOUT THE AUTHOR

M.B. Anderson is the author of *The Salvation Schema*, a powerful novel of spiritual suspense and psychological freedom. This book connects to their critically acclaimed debut series, *The Architects of Grace Series*, showing Anderson's continued dedication to exploring complex moral and philosophical landscapes.

A native of California, Anderson draws on the vast, complex landscapes of their youth—from the sun-drenched coast to the majestic mountains—to build intricate and compelling fictional worlds.

Anderson brings nearly two decades of high-level discipline and global experience to their writing, having served with distinction in the United States Military. This extensive service instilled a deep understanding of structure, sacrifice, and the profound contrasts between order and freedom—themes that pulse throughout the narrative of *The Salvation Schema*.

When not exploring philosophical concepts through fiction, M.B. Anderson can be found embracing the elemental world: conquering mountain peaks on a snowboard or traversing high-desert trails with their beloved dogs. Anderson currently resides in Arizona and is working on their next novel.

You can connect with M.B. Anderson by writing directly to the author at mb.anderson.writes@gmail.com.